ISOBELLE CARMODY

WAVESONG

BLOOMSBURY

LONDON BERLIN NEW YORK SYDNEY

Bloomsbury Publishing, London, Berlin, New York and Sydney

First published in Great Britain in June 2011 by Bloomsbury Publishing Plc
36 Soho Square, London W1D 3QY

This is a slightly modified version of the first half of *The Stone Key*, originally
published by Penguin Books Australia Ltd, Camberwell.
Published by arrangement with Penguin Group (Australia) a division of
Pearson Australia Group Pty Ltd

A CIP catalogue record of this book is available from the British Library

ISBN 978 1 4088 0694 4

FSC
www.fsc.org
MIX
Paper from
responsible sources
FSC® C018072

Printed in Great Britain by Clays Ltd, St Ives Plc, Clays, Bungay, Suffolk

1 3 5 7 9 10 8 6 4 2

www.bloomsbury.com

WAVESONG

Isobelle Carmody began the first of her highly acclaimed Obernewtyn Chronicles while she was still at high school, working on it while completing a Bachelor of Arts degree and then a journalism cadetship. The series established her at the forefront of fantasy writing in Australia.

She is now the award-winning author of several novels and many short stories for children and adults.

Isobelle divides her time between her home on the Great Ocean Road in Australia and her travels abroad with her partner and daughter.

THE OBERNEWTYN CHRONICLES

Obernewtyn

The Farseekers

Ashling

The Keeping Place

Wavesong

The Stone Key

The Sending

The Red Queen

All coming from Bloomsbury in 2011 and 2012

*. . . we travel the path of waves,
which is full of contradictory currents
and mysterious diversions . . .*

*for my brother Ken,
who climbs mountains when you
least expect*

✦ Character List ✦

Alad: Beastspeaking guildmaster

Analivia: daughter of Radost

Angina: Empath guilden and enhancer; twin brother of Miky

Aras: Farseeker ward

Ariel (aka H'rayka, the Destroyer): sadistic enemy of Obernewtyn; distorted Talent, abilities unknown; allied with the Herder Faction and Salamander

Atthis (aka oldOne): Agyllian or Guanette bird; survivor of the Great White

Avra: leader of the Beastguild; mountain mare; bondmate to Gahltha

Bergold: son of Radost; former Councilman

Brydda Llewellyn (aka the Black Dog): rebel leader

Cassy Duprey: Beforetimer, later known as Kasanda

Ceirwan: Farseeker guilden

Daffyd: former Druid armsman; farseeker; brother to Jow; beloved of Gilaine; unguilded ally of Obernewtyn

Dameon: blind Empath guildmaster

Dardelan: rebel leader of Sutrium

Darga: Jik's canine companion, lost in a firestorm

Darius: Twentyfamilies gypsy; beasthealer

Domick: AWOL Coercer ward; former bondmate of Kella

Dragon: powerful Empath guilder with coercive Talent; projects illusions

Druid (Henry Druid): renegade Herder Faction priest and enemy of the Council; charismatic leader of a secret community that was destroyed in a firestorm; father of Gilaine

Elspeth Gordie (aka Innle, the Seeker): Farseeker guildmistress; powerful farseeker, beastspeaker, and coercer, with limited futuretelling and psychokinetic Talent

Enoch: a coachman; ally of Obernewtyn

Fian: Teknoguild ward

Gahltha (aka Daywatcher): Beast guilden; bondmate to Avra; a formidable black horse sworn to protect Elspeth

Garth: Teknoguildmaster

Gavyn: Beast empath; beasts call him adantar

Gevan: Coercer guildmaster

Gilaine: mute daughter of the Druid; farseeker bound to Lidgebaby; beloved of Daffyd; slave in the Red Queen's land

Grufyyd: bondmate to Katlyn, father of Brydda

Hannah Seraphim: director of the Beforetime Reichler Clinic

Harwood: powerful coercer

Helvar: Norselander and shipmaster of the *Storm-dancer*

Jacob Obernewtyn: Beforetimer; wealthy patron of Hannah Seraphim

Javo: Obernewtyn's head cook

Jes: Elspeth's older brother; Talented Misfit killed by soldierguards

Jik: former Herder novice; Empath guilder with far-seeking Talent; died in a firestorm

Jow: former follower of the Druid; brother to Daffyd; beastspeaker

Kally: coercer and empath

Kasanda: mystical leader of the Sadorians; left signs for the Seeker to help in her quest

Katlyn: herb lorist living at Obernewtyn; bondmate to Grufyyd, mother of Brydda

Kella: Healer guilden with slight empath Talent; former bondmate of Domick

Kevrik: highlander and armsman to Vos

Khuria: beastspeaker; father of Zarak

Lark: Norselander from Herder Isle; son of shipmaster Helvar

Linnet: coercer-knight

Lo: mare at Obernewtyn

Louis Larkin: unTalented highlander; inhabitant of Obernewtyn; honorary Beastspeaking guilder

Malik: rebel leader of Guanette

Maruman (aka Moonwatcher, Yelloweyes): one-eyed cat prone to fits of futuretelling; Elspeth's oldest friend

Maryon: Futuretell guildmistress

Matthew: Farseeker ward with deep probe abilities; slave in the Red Queen's land

Merret: powerful coercer with beastspeaking Talent

Miky: Empath guilden; twin sister of Angina; gifted musician

Miryum: AWOL leader of coercer-knights

Moss: son of Radost; former Councilman of Darthnor

Noviny: former Councilman of Saithwold and grandfather to Wenda

Radost: former ruler of Sutrium and the Council with Jitra and Mord; father of Analivia, Moss, and Bergold

Rasial: white dog with powerful coercive abilities; second to Avra in Obernewtyn Beastguild

Reuvan: rebel seaman from Aborium; Brydda's right-hand man

Roland: Healer guildmaster

Rushton: Master of Obernewtyn; latent Talent

Salamander: secretive, ruthless leader of the slave trade

Sallah: rebel mare; companion to Brydda

Seely: unTalented caretaker of Gavyn; stranded on west coast

Swallow: Twentyfamilies D'rekta, or leader

Vos: rebel leader of Saithwold

Wenda: Noviny's granddaughter

Zade: stallion; member of the Beastguild

Zarak: Farseeker ward with beastspeaking Talent

PART I

✦

SONG OF FREEDOM

◆ 1 ◆

It ought to have felt momentous, going through the pass and seeing the highlands spread out in the pink-gold morning light, because, for the first time, I was riding down to a Land that was free and where I did not need to hide who or what I was.

Yet it was impossible to feel complacent or even secure, because soon, for the first time, Landfolk would vote for their leaders, who might undo all that the rebels had achieved since overthrowing the Council. And where would that leave Misfits like me? The hatred and prejudice against us, which the Council and Herder Faction had encouraged, had not ended with their reign. The wrong leader could easily fan the flames of resentment and unease into a fire that might yet consume us. But as the rebel leader Dardelan had so often said, there could be no true freedom if people were not able to choose their own leaders.

I let my eyes rove along the neat line of trees that bordered Bergold's orchards on the left side of the road, trying to take comfort in their order. But my eyes were drawn inexorably to the other side of the road, where the ground dropped away steeply and suddenly into the dense, complex wilderness of the White Valley. I could see clear across the green treetops to Tor, Gelfort,

3

and Emeralfel—the mountains that separated highland from lowland—and to the Blacklands that bordered the White Valley. It looked untouched and impenetrable, but I knew how many secrets lay hidden there.

It was the way of things, I thought morosely, and it was better not to forget it.

I lifted my face to the sky and closed my eyes, trying to focus on the sun's warmth and on spring's sweet green smell, but too many worries crowded in—the looming elections, of course, and the forthcoming trial of the rebel Malik, as well as whatever was going on in Saithwold. But most of all, I was troubled by Maryon's insistence that Dragon accompany us to Sutrium. Dragon's presence meant that I must constantly face her fear of me. This was painful, because she had loved me once; however, my invasion of her mind, which had been the only way to save her, had destroyed her trust in me. It had been a shock to discover that, upon waking from her coma, Dragon had forgotten our friendship, forgotten my rescue of her from the Beforetime ruins where she had dwelt as a lonely urchin. I had believed Kella and the other healers when they said Dragon would remember in time, but she had not done so. She viewed me only as one who brought pain, and so great was her fear of me that we had been unable to manage a single conversation since she had awakened. Dragon had been willing to make this journey only because both the healer Kella and the old herbalist Katlyn were going.

In truth, I had proposed the expedition as much to get away from Dragon as to fulfill my promise to return the Twentyfamilies gypsy healer Darius to his people. Then Maryon had announced her support for the expedition, because she foresaw trouble looming on the

4

west coast, and I would be needed to deal with it. Naturally, she had offered no further explanation or details. Almost as an afterthought, she had added that Dragon must go to Sutrium.

I felt a surge of anger and fear at the memory of her foretelling, for it had been just such a journey to Sutrium that had initiated the events that left Dragon in a dangerous coma. A cooler voice reminded me that sometimes good comes from bad. Without the coma and my journey into Dragon's mind, I would not have discovered that Dragon is the daughter of the Red Land's murdered queen. And though her fear and hatred distressed me, I now knew that something locked in Dragon's memories would ultimately help me complete my secret quest to destroy the Beforetime weaponmachines. Perhaps this journey to Sutrium would provide me with this knowledge.

"Why cannot ElspethInnle just accept? Why always thinking/gnawing, trying to change the shaping of things?" Maruman sent the acerbic query to me without shifting his languid position on Kella's lap in the wagon.

"If you are irritated by my thoughts, you could stay out of my mind," I sent back tartly.

The old cat did not condescend to answer, but Kella gave me a sidelong look. She had no farseeking abilities, but her healing empathy meant she could not help but feel the emotions flowing between Maruman and me. She turned away at once, not wanting to pry, but her bleak expression told me that her own thoughts were no more happily disposed than mine. Doubtless she was thinking of Domick. He and Kella had been in love, but the coercer's spying before the rebellion had so tormented and divided him against himself that he

5

had finally rejected her and Obernewtyn before disappearing under mysterious circumstances. Kella blamed herself, and I thought it was as much guilt as the desire to heal that was taking her to Sutrium. But I said nothing. Empathy was the one Talent I lacked entirely, and its want made me awkward with emotions and reluctant to trust my own feelings, let alone anyone else's. Besides, what could I say to comfort her, unless it was true that misery loved company.

"One cannot flee from/avoid difficulties of life, ElspethInnle, but perhaps it is possible/necessary to outrun them for a time," Gahltha sent. I felt a rush of affection for the horse's passionate nature and laid my hand on his sleek black neck. The flesh quivered with impatience.

"The wagons are not made for speed," I sent regretfully.

"I/Gahltha am! We will gallop away and then return," he responded eagerly.

With a laugh, I told Kella that we would scout ahead. Gahltha neighed to Welt and Belya, who drew the wagon, then cantered to the lead wagon where the young farseeker Zarak sat on the foremost bench with Louis Larkin. Zade and Lo whinnied a welcome to Gahltha as I explained I would ride ahead for a time. Dragon was in the back of the wagon with the plump old herbalist Katlyn and one of the two injured soldier-guards we were transporting to Sutrium. The other lay on the floor of the second wagon.

"It is a perfect day fer a ride," Zarak said wistfully.

As though his words were a signal, Gahltha sprang away. If I had not learned from hard experience that he loved to leap into a gallop like this, I would have tumbled backward over his rump. I tangled one hand in his mane and caught the thick black whip of my plait with the other. Joy steamed off his body as heat and a kind of vibration that filled me with exhilaration. How many times had we ridden like this in the high mountains, sharing the rush and the wild freedom of our speed?

My muscles soon protested, reminding me how seldom I had ridden of late. My duties as guildmistress at Obernewtyn left little time for self-indulgence. Fleetingly, the weight of that role pressed on me, but then the sheer physical demands of the ride emptied me of thought. I let myself merge with Gahltha until I was no more than an extension of the powerful black horse racing along the road.

It was a reckless pace, but the way was clear well ahead, and walkers rarely traveled the lonely stretch between the turnoff to Bergold's orchards and the pass into the mountains. Aside from the fact that poisons dangerous to the naked flesh streaked the ground and walls of the pass, the rumor that plague had destroyed Obernewtyn had been enough to discourage the curious. Of course, the rebel leaders now knew that Obernewtyn was intact and home to our Misfit community, and I had no doubt that knowledge of our refuge was spreading into the wider community. Even so, I doubted we would have many casual visitors.

Rounding a slight bend in the road, Gahltha stopped and reared suddenly, almost unseating me. I lurched violently onto his neck and saw that a whole section of the ridge had broken away to crumble down into the White Valley, taking a chunk of the road with it. What remained was narrow and badly eroded on one side, and though it would still serve a walker or a careful rider, the wagons could not possibly pass along it. The landslide must have been recent, since the messenger from Sutrium had not mentioned it when he visited Obernewtyn a mere sevenday ago.

"Damn," I muttered. In drier weather, we might simply have run the wheels along the edge of the roadway, but this soon after the thaw, the ground was soggy and the wagons would sink to their axles. I slipped to the ground and sent Gahltha back to warn the others.

After the black horse had galloped off, I began to cast about for boughs and flat stones, laying a border to increase the width of the road on its inner edge. The passage between Guanette and the mountain pass leading to Obernewtyn had been eroding ever since I had first traveled it years back as a sentenced Misfit. Since we had taken over Obernewtyn, the Teknoguild had spoken many times of the need to repair it, but fearing unwanted attention in the valley, they had done nothing. For this reason, travel into the White Valley had always been limited to small expeditions on foot or horseback. It was only in recent times that discreet ramps for wagons had been created from scree.

It was hot muddy work, but I found myself enjoying the simplicity of the makeshift repairs. I tried to imagine a life that required of me no more than this and then realized that such an existence could seem desirable only to one who did not have to do it all the time. In truth, I enjoyed being mistress of a guild at Obernewtyn, despite all the meetings and negotiations and the sheer amount of talk required. My role would change now, though, for Misfits no longer needed to be rescued.

When the wagons arrived, Louis, Kella, and Zarak

alighted at once to sigh and shake their heads, before unhitching the horses. Dragon climbed down, too, casting a look of violent blue-eyed dislike at me. As Maruman leapt down beside her and pressed against her legs, I wondered somewhat bitterly why she felt no antipathy for the old cat, since I had been able to invade her mind only with his help.

Katlyn and Darius remained in the wagons to watch over the soldierguards, but Garth, the Teknoguildmaster, descended and, upon seeing the broken road, began to mutter about this shoring-up technique and that stress.

It took two hours to widen the road enough for the wagons to pass. Katlyn suggested we eat midmeal before continuing, but I did not want to stop until we had reached the White Valley. The habit of caution was strong, and given what the Sutrium messenger had said about robber bands terrorizing remote holdings, I deemed it wiser not to break that habit just yet. Admittedly, the messenger had been referring to the upper lowlands, but it was possible that robbers might roam higher.

When we set off, Dragon sat beside Louis Larkin, with Maruman perched contentedly and rather smugly on her lap. Zarak now rode Zade, for despite being a mare, Lo was large and strong, and she had no difficulty in pulling a wagon alone. Leaving Zarak and Zade to accompany the lead wagon, I dropped behind to speak to Kella, but she had climbed into the back to help Darius tend to the injured soldierguard whose bandages had been dislodged.

My feelings toward the soldierguards were ambivalent. Being in our care all through the wintertime had forced them to see us as different from the monstrous freaks that the Council had labeled us, but these men had killed people and horses I knew and cared for. Rushton, ever focused on the present, had said the most important thing was that they had agreed to tell the new Council of Chieftains exactly what had happened in the White Valley, when Malik had betrayed us. Rushton had also suggested that since I required two wagons, I should use them to return the soldierguards to Sutrium. They were not entirely recovered, but with both Kella and Darius traveling with us, the guards would be well cared for, and by traveling now, they would have time to recover from the journey before the trial.

Garth spoke, interrupting my thoughts to suggest that, given the delay, we should spend the night at the Teknoguild encampment in the White Valley. "You will never reach Rangorn before night now, and Maryon did not urge particular haste, did she?"

"Maryon would never be so hasty as to urge haste," I said dryly. "She said only that I am needed to deal with danger on the west coast."

"I do not see how, since the ships that the rebels were building to reach the west coast have been destroyed. Dardelan's message said there is no chance of landing a force on the west coast for at least another half year."

"Not a force, perhaps," I said, "but I am sure that Dardelan's request for a plast suit means he will try to send a spy across the Suggredoon." We were transporting two fragile plast suits, which the Teknoguild had made during the wintertime; one was for Dardelan and the other was for Swallow, the leader of the Twentyfamilies gypsies, as a gift of thanks. Swallow had requested it as a reward for thwarting Malik's murderous intentions.

Garth regarded me narrowly. "You are thinking of offering yourself as their spy?"

I hesitated, but unlike the other guildmasters, Garth regularly flouted the unspoken convention that leaders of guilds ought to keep themselves out of dangerous situations. "It would explain why Maryon sent me to Sutrium," I finally said.

The Teknoguildmaster grinned. "Very noble of you to ensure the veracity of the Futuretell guildmistress's prophecy." Then he grew serious. "I daresay the others would protest, but it does make sense. After all, you are powerful enough to coerce the guards on the other bank, so you wouldn't be killed upon climbing from the water. You could also farseek Merret or another trapped Misfit to find out what has been going on there."

Garth continued. "I must say I am curious to learn how the Herders managed to sneak a ship into port, burn the rebels' half-constructed ships, and sneak out again, all unnoticed. And what was the use, since the rebels will simply build more ships anyway?"

"We will know better once we meet Brydda," I said.

"Why don't you ask Brydda to ride to Saithwold with you? I doubt anyone would have the courage to hinder the Black Dog, even Chieftain Vos." Garth stumbled a little over the unfamiliar title. Under the old regime, town leaders had been called Councilmen, but the messenger from Sutrium had informed us that the rebel leaders who had replaced the Councilmen were henceforth to be known as *chieftains*. As their leader, Dardelan was to be known as high chieftain.

"Maryon did not foresee trouble in Saithwold, but it is true that Vos has no love of Misfits. And Khuria's letters to Zarak certainly suggest that something is going on there," I said. "It may be worth stopping at a roadside inn to see if we can glean any gossip about Saithwold."

"We can be sure that Vos is unhappy with Dardelan being made high chieftain," Garth said dryly.

"I wonder how Malik took it," I said.

Garth laughed. "I think it is safe to assume that he loathes it. Not only because he coveted the position himself, but also because he knows that Dardelan will allow us to make formal charges against Malik before the elections."

I frowned. "Do you think Malik knows that the soldierguards intend to testify against him?"

Garth gave me a sardonic look. "I think that Dardelan's sense of fair play would ensure it."

I sighed, realizing he was right. The new high chieftain's first decree after being elected ultimate leader of the rebels had been that, after a year, he and all the rebel chieftains would step down from their positions to allow the Landfolk to freely elect future chieftains. Rushton had thought this sensible as well as honorable, but like most of us, he thought Dardelan ought to have kept power for a longer period to ensure stability within the new regime. Others felt that Dardelan ought not to have given such an undertaking at all until the west coast had been secured. But the young rebel was as determined as he was honorable, and the elections were looming.

"Dardelan is not completely naive," I said. "Otherwise he would not insist upon charging Malik before the elections."

Garth grunted. "I think it is only concern for justice

12

that motivates our young high chieftain. I am sure he would say that justice delayed is justice denied. If he was a little more pragmatic, he might have kept the details of his proposed Beast Charter to himself until he had been elected high chieftain. He is well liked, but the idea that no beasts can be owned, that they must be paid for their labor, has alienated most of Dardelan's supporters and enraged his enemies. It might well cost him the election."

"Surely when it comes time to elect their chieftain, people will remember that it was Dardelan who led the rebels in the virtually bloodless coup that rid the Land of the Council and the Herder Faction," I said.

"Isn't it true that Dardelan wants to establish Obernewtyn as a settlement in its own right *before* the elections?" Garth asked. "If that happens, we will vote for our own chieftain."

I nodded. Rushton had been ambivalent about Dardelan's proposal. Having our own chieftain would give Misfits a voice in running the Land, but it would also require the chieftain of Obernewtyn to travel regularly to Sutrium for Council of Chieftains meetings. It was as obvious to Rushton as to the rest of us that he would be our choice as chieftain, and just as obvious that he did not relish the thought. There had been some discussion of the matter in the last guildmerge. Some said that the proposed new settlement would cause unTalents to resent us even more than they already did. Others worried about transforming what had long been our refuge into a village that anyone could enter. We would have to make a decision before Rushton rode down to Sutrium for the ceremony to formalize the Charter of Laws, which was to take place just before the elections.

Dardelan wanted us to lay charges against Malik straight after the ceremony and before the elections.

"Hard to know what is best," Garth grunted, his thoughts no doubt running along similar lines.

I said, "In any case, to respond to your suggestion, we will stay the night in the White Valley."

"Good," Garth said. "There are a few things I would like to show you, for I know you have an interest in the past that our good leader does not share." His expression changed, and before I could extricate myself from the conversation, he added reproachfully, "I must say that is why I was so disappointed when you voted against opening Jacob Obernewtyn's tomb. Surely you want to know more about the Beforetime Misfits who once dwelt at Obernewtyn? Or how Hannah Seraphim is connected to Rushton?"

I suppressed a sigh. Garth was aware of my interest in the Beforetimer who had established Obernewtyn, but he did not know why I was interested in her, and of course I could not tell him. I said, "I am not convinced that opening Jacob Obernewtyn's tomb will add to the sum of our knowledge about the Beforetime or indeed of anything. I see no evidence to suggest there would be diaries or journals kept there."

"If it is no more than the resting place for a body, why create such a solid structure, and why set it on an obscure path where there are no other graves?" Garth reasoned. "Do you know that it was even marked on Beforetime maps we found of Obernewtyn's grounds? And some believe that with Jacob Obernewtyn's body are not only the records we have been searching for, but Hannah Seraphim's body as well."

"In the same grave?" I demanded skeptically.

"The Beforetimers did sometimes bury bondmates together, an' even whole families, though of course nowt at the same time," Zarak broke in, apologetically. "But if they put more than one person in a grave, there should ha' been two names on it and the birth and death dates of each."

Irritation flickered over the Teknoguildmaster's ruddy face. "If Hannah Seraphim died during or soon after the Great White, as we surmise, I doubt there would have been a stone-carver handy to chisel another name into the gravestone. And if Hannah is not in that grave, then where is she?" This last was directed sharply at me.

Before I could frame an answer, Garth looked back at Zarak. "Besides, the Beforetimers did not always date graves. Jacob Obernewtyn's was undated."

"Maybe dates seemed pointless after the Great White," I murmured, but neither of them heard me.

"Maybe Hannah Seraphim was away from Obernewtyn when the Great White came," Zarak said. "She might have been visitin' the Reichler Clinic Reception Center under Tor. There would ha' been a lot of coming and gannin' betwixt the two places."

"Even if I *had* voted to open the grave, Garth, all the other guildleaders still would have refused you, just as on every other occasion you've raised the matter since the grave was found."

Garth scowled. "True enough. If Maryon would just—"

"She is entitled to her opinion and her visions," I said evenly. Inwardly, I cringed at my hypocrisy, for I had often wished the Futuretell guildmistress would keep her thoughts and visions to herself.

15

Garth was not diverted. "The trouble is that the others are overly swayed by her opinions, because they imagine them to be based on futuretell visions that she chooses not to divulge," he growled. "Without her influence, I am sure I could have convinced the guildmerge to see it my way."

"Maybe she *is* basin' her resistance on things she has foreseen," Zarak suggested.

Fortunately, at this moment, we reached the scree ramp down to the White Valley. Zarak dismounted, pulled aside the woven foliage that obscured it, and scrambled down. The two wagons followed slowly, steadied by Zade and Belya, and checked by ropes belayed around tree trunks, paid out slowly by Gahltha, Lo, and the big piebald, Welt. When the others were all safely down, I drew the foliage screen back in place.

Once on the floor of the valley, I felt less anxious, though I was never able to feel entirely at ease here. Nor was I alone in this. The White Valley was generally regarded as being cursed by numerous tormented Beforetime wraiths. And maybe it was, I thought soberly. I did not know what had stood here in the Beforetime or what had become of it, but the valley attracted trouble like a lodestone attracts steel. The renegade Herder Henry Druid had established a secret encampment here, which had been wiped out by a terrible firestorm. I, too, would have died here, if not for the intervention of the mysterious Agyllian birds who had taught my body to heal itself. And here in the White Valley, Malik had betrayed us.

But cursed or not, the White Valley was undeniably beautiful. The trees were a delicate haze of bright new green around damp charcoal-black trunks and branches, and shoots and buds burst from the rich dark earth on all sides. The ground was soft, so we kept to the stone-studded track laid by the teknoguilders. This soon brought us to an avenue where the branches of trees had been interwoven overhead, creating a green tunnel. I guessed that Garth had commanded this new arrangement to conceal the track, part of which had been visible from the ridge road. If anything, the Teknoguildmaster was more concerned now about Landfolk stumbling onto his guild's research site than before the Council had been overthrown.

Because the wagons were hard to haul over the uneven track, we were all walking now, except Katlyn, Darius, and the two soldierguards. Louis Larkin walked behind them with Dragon, while Garth strode ahead, eager to reach his guild's new settlement at the foot of Tor. His intention was to make a formal claim on the land where it stood, including the cavern leading to the submerged Beforetime city under Tor, which we now knew as Newrome.

"I always think of Jik when I come here," said Zarak, catching up with me. "If I had nowt been farseeking without a guide an' without permission, I would nivver have made contact with him, and we nivver would have brought him out of his cloister in Darthnor. He would nivver have come here to die."

"Do you think he would have fared well among Herders?" I asked. "Something more dreadful may have happened if he had remained in the cloister."

"More dreadful than dying in a firestorm?" Zarak asked in a low voice.

"Jik was terrified of being taken to Herder Isle. He said the priests knew about Misfits and experimented on them. Maybe if he had stayed in the cloister, that would have happened to him."

Zarak was silent for a time, then he said, "Why do ye suppose they took some Misfits an' burned others like they did seditioners?"

"Jik said they were always more interested in children with Misfit powers and that some abilities interested them more than others."

"Maybe they wanted to train them to catch us," Zarak suggested.

"Maybe they used them to help create demon bands," I suggested.

Zarak made no response, and when I glanced at him, he was looking at me. For a moment, I saw myself as he must: a long lean woman with a tight-bound plait and overly serious moss-green eyes. I said gently, "Do not blame yourself for Jik's death, Zar. Many things happened to bring him here, not simply the foolish disobedience of one young farseeker."

"Do ye remember that dog Jik insisted we rescue with him?" Zarak said suddenly, half smiling. "He was th' ugliest creature I ever saw."

"The Herders breed them to look like that," I said. "Darga."

"Yes, that was his name. I had forgotten." Zarak gave me a look of curiosity that I pretended not to notice. It was generally assumed that Darga had perished with Jik in the firestorm, but the Agyllian birds that saved my life claimed he lived. They said he would return when it was time for me to leave Obernewtyn to undertake the final stage of my quest—to destroy the deadly weaponmachines left by the Beforetimers.

I had been waiting so many years for that moment that I sometimes wondered if it would ever come.

Zarak had drawn ahead, no doubt discouraged by my silence, but Kella took his place. I glanced at her, wondering if she would regret leaving Obernewtyn to run the healing center she had established in the old Sutrium Herder cloister during the rebel uprising. She and Dardelan had developed a genuine liking and respect for each other during that time, so it was hardly surprising when he asked her to come and run the center and establish a teaching facility for healers. But Kella's acceptance had startled me.

Roland, the Healer guildmaster, had been enthusiastic about his guilden's new venture, and Rushton, too, praised it as an excellent way of further impressing ordinary Landfolk with the usefulness of Misfit abilities. I seemed to be alone in feeling that Kella's departure marked the end of an era. Of course, it was time for us to live in the Land openly. Wasn't that what we had fought and longed for? Yet my heart ached for the days when Obernewtyn had been our secret refuge, just as it had been for the Beforetime Misfits.

Kella gave me a quizzical look, no doubt sensing something of my feelings.

"I was just thinking of the Beforetimers," I told her quickly.

To my surprise, she bridled fiercely. "We are not like them. We would never do to our world what they did to theirs."

Would we not? I wondered morosely. Or was it only that we did not have the ability to destroy as efficiently as they had?

✦ 2 ✦

I HEARD A shout and looked up to see the slender, brown-haired teknoguilder Fian burst through the trees with loud halloos that scattered birds from nearby bushes. Garth beckoned to him impatiently and they spoke, then the Teknoguildmaster strode on, and Fian came beaming to greet me.

At Obernewtyn, I was accustomed to being honored and held in awe for my powers and for what I had done, but I was unused to being liked. Yet Fian liked me. In part, he knew me better than most, having taken part in several farseeker rescues that I had led; moreover, the year he had spent in Sador with the Empath guildmaster, Dameon, had given him an independence of thought and attitude that allowed him to see everyone as an equal, despite differences in rank and power. I valued his friendship as well as his cleverness and unfailing good humor. The fact that he had also unwittingly adopted several of Dameon's mannerisms only endeared him to me more, for the Empath guildmaster was my closest friend.

"Is Dameon nowt with ye?" Fian asked, as if he had read the name in my thoughts. He nodded a smile to Dragon, who shrank behind Kella.

"Dameon has decided he would rather ride to

Sutrium with Rushton and the coercer-knights next sevenday," I said.

Fian's eyes widened. "Did ye say he would *ride*?"

I nodded. "He has been practicing with Faraf, and he wants to see how well he can manage. She knows he is blind, of course, and that she must be his eyes." I spoke as if it was a minor detail, but in fact I wondered very much why Dameon had become so determined to ride when he had always seemed satisfied with being driven in wagons. I could not believe it had anything to do with the case against the cousin who, in order to inherit his property, had reported Dameon to the Council as a Misfit. There were many such cases now, as people who had been dispossessed of their property sued for its return.

"What will Dameon do if he gets his farm back?" Fian asked curiously. "I canna believe he wants to run it himself."

"He means to establish it as a cooperative farm run jointly by beasts and unTalented humans. He hopes ordinary Landfolk will see that it is possible to work with beasts to our mutual advantage, even without Misfit translators. It is a brilliant idea. I am only sorry that it will not be established in time for the elections."

"Alad thinks Dardelan ought to present the Charter of Laws and his Beast Charter at the same time."

I shook my head. "If he did, both would be rejected. By keeping the two charters separate, no matter what happens in the elections, Dardelan will have at least established a basic set of good and fair laws for the Land. And people who dislike the idea of rights for beasts might still vote for him, since Dardelan is known for listening to the opinions of many different people and might be talked out of it."

"He'll nowt change his mind," Fian said stoutly.

I smiled. "I don't think so either."

More teknoguilders came toward us now, but my attention was caught by the long, low, curving building I could see in the clearing beyond them. Constructed from wood and stone, it faced the section of the Suggredoon River from whence I had once set off on a raft to escape the renegade Herder Henry Druid. I had a fleeting but vivid memory of the gallant, red-haired druid armsman Gilbert. He had been one of the few to survive the firestorm that had killed his master.

"Ye see how the buildin' masks th' openin' to the subterranean city?" Fian pointed out enthusiastically. "Garth designed it that way, because he said we want to distract strangers from noticin' the cave an' wonderin' where it leads."

I nodded, impressed by how much had been achieved in the few weeks since thaw. But as I came closer, I saw that there was no glass in the windows, and when I looked through one of them, I saw that the floor had yet to be laid.

"It's nowt finished," Fian said unnecessarily. "Guildmaster Garth felt it were more important to get the whole thing up so that from a distance it would look finished. In case any Landfolk come into the White Valley. We are about fencin' the land now to keep anyone from comin' too close. We can complete th' inside of the homestead later." This was said so carelessly that I wondered if the Teknoguild would ever finish it. Their researches were generally so compelling to them that anything not utterly vital was put off. It would not surprise me to find that in a year, when wintertime

22

returned, the Teknoguild homestead still lacked a floor and windows.

Fian led me around the back of the building to the tents and shacks that presently housed the resident and visiting teknoguilders in the White Valley.

At first glance, the camp reminded me of a Sadorian desert camp, which was not surprising since the excellent cloth huts the guild used had been gifts from the Sadorian tribal leader, Jakoby. But there was also something of a gypsy encampment about the settlement, for there were boxes and bales piled haphazardly and clothes laid out on the grass to dry. Sadorians possessed little, so they did not produce clutter, whereas for both teknoguilders and gypsies, clutter seemed a natural consequence of busy and active lives. Indeed, as with any gathering of teknoguilders, a quiet but intense sense of purpose and concentration pervaded the scene. Here and there, teknoguilders sat cross-legged on the grass, scratching their heads over notes they were making, or perched on barrels or bales reading or poring over some queer Beforetime object brought out of the subterranean city. The day was warm enough that most wore shirt-sleeves or light shifts, but there was a fire burning in a stone-lined pit in the midst of the rough semicircle of tents. Judging by the smells coming from pots suspended over it, something good was simmering away. It was long past midmeal, but the teknoguilders never bothered with formal mealtimes except on special occasions.

"Are ye hungry?" Fian asked, seeing my gaze. "We expected ye hours ago, but there is still plenty of soup."

"Starving," I said, my mouth watering. I had skipped firstmeal, unable to face Rushton sitting stiffly by me and making polite, meaningless conversation with everyone in the dining hall looking on, knowing something was amiss yet being unable to help. The only time we seemed able to behave normally was during guildmerge, when we were guildmistress and Master of Obernewtyn.

Fian hastened to lay his kerchief over a bale for me to sit on, and Garth looked about vaguely as if he wondered where the table and chairs had been put. But the idea did not gain sufficient focus for him to realize that furniture was something else put off until later. Instead, he found a wide barrel, sat on it, and began examining something one of the teknoguilders wanted to show him. Katlyn, Kella, and Dragon came slowly to the fireside with Darius. The gypsy's crooked body, awkward movements, and prematurely gray hair always made me think of Darius as old, but when he laughed at something Katlyn said, it struck me that he was only a few years older than Rushton.

We all ate with good appetite, but afterward, instead of someone producing an instrument and suggesting a song, as would happen around other campfires, Garth heaved himself up and said that he needed to go into the mountain to see something too large to be carried out. He invited anyone interested to accompany him, and most of the teknoguilders stood at once, as did Zarak. Darius and Kella said they had better see to the soldierguards, and Katlyn wanted to look for certain herbs that did not grow in the high mountains. The herbalist intended to try growing them in a cave high above Obernewtyn where the teknoguilders had discovered a hot spring. At Katlyn's request, the cave's top opening had been roofed in thin, nearly transparent plast sheets, for she was sure the warm, moist atmosphere would allow all sorts of unlikely plants to grow there. For her, the gathering of seeds was the expedition's main purpose, apart from seeing her son. When the older woman rose, Dragon went with her, giving me a backward glance that told me her desire was less to gather herbs than to avoid me.

Garth looked at me expectantly, but I shook my head, pretending not to see his disappointment. I had been into the subterranean city many times, and my mood was already too melancholy to endure the complicated mixture of wonder and dismay I always felt at seeing it. Louis Larkin made no response to Garth's invitation, for straight after eating, he had stretched out on his back and now snored loudly.

Once the others had gone, I regarded the old man with fond amusement and thought about the day, many decades past, when he had seen two gypsies come to Obernewtyn to offer carvings to Marisa Seraphim, then Mistress of Obernewtyn.

The carvings, containing secret messages from the seer Kasanda, had become part of the front doors to Obernewtyn. I had long since learned their secrets, but I wanted to be able to see and hear the gypsies who had brought them to Obernewtyn in the hope of learning how they had come by the carvings.

Of course, I could not delve into Louis Larkin's memories without seeking his permission first.

Feeling restless, I farsought Maruman, but I could find no trace of the cantankerous old cat. No doubt he had gone to sleep somewhere. It was almost impossible to probe a sleeping mind unless you knew where the sleeper lay or could make physical contact; even then it was sometimes impossible to enter Maruman's mind. Gahltha had once told me this was because the old cat often went *seliga* when he slept. This was one of the few beast words I did not understand clearly. It meant something like "before" and something like "behind."

I decided to walk to the monument created by the Twentyfamilies gypsies in memory of the Misfits and beasts who had perished in the White Valley because of Malik's betrayal. A lone teknoguilder sat on a log by the fire, engrossed in a book. I did not know her name, but when I touched her arm to tell her my intention, she looked at me in astonishment. I told her where I was going, and she promised to let the others know if they returned before me.

I had not been walking more than fifteen minutes when I sensed that someone was following me. I sent out a mindprobe but found only the minds of numerous burrowers and other little creatures dwelling in the valley. It occurred to me that Dragon might be following me. It would not be the first time she had done so, and she was the only Misfit whose coercive strength would allow her to evade my probe.

I stopped, shaped a probe to her mind, and swept the area again, but it would not locate. Yet my sense of being watched was stronger than ever. I considered turning back but decided against it; if Dragon was following me, she might finally allow me to talk to her. If it was not her, then it must be a large animal with a small brain. This did not frighten me, for all beasts seemed to recognize that I was the Seeker when I beastspoke them. For animals, the Seeker was not the person who was supposed to find and end the threat of the Beforetime weaponmachines but was a legendary figure destined

26

to lead beasts to freedom from humans. I was fairly sure that the mystic Agyllians had concocted this legend to ensure that beasts would protect me, for the ancient birds set my quest to destroy the weaponmachines above the welfare of any individual creatures, human or beast.

Reaching the track leading to the cul-de-sac where Malik had instructed us to lure the pursuing soldier-guards, an eerie sense of the past stole over me, and I forgot about the possibility of being followed. I seemed almost to see the empath twins Angina and Miky; the handsome, ebony-skinned Sadorian warrior Straaka, towering over sturdy Miryum; all arrayed about me, and I glanced up to the tree-lined lip of the cul-de-sac, as I had done during the rebellion, wondering why Malik and his men were taking so long to show them-selves and order the soldierguards we had lured there to lay down their weapons. Then the soldierguards had begun to shoot their arrows.

I shivered, thinking how many more might have died that day if the Twentyfamilies gypsies had not in-tervened. I brought my gaze to rest on the white marker stone that the gypsies had carved. Swallow, who had succeeded his father as D'rekta of the Twentyfamilies, had shown it to me once before, but it seemed less white today. Maybe it was my imagination, for when I came closer, I could see that the stone showed no signs of weathering. I knelt to look at the names carved so beau-tifully and minutely into it, knowing that the Sadorian mystic Kasanda had taught the Twentyfamilies gypsies their famous stone-carving skills. I had no absolute proof that Kasanda and the original D'rekta were one and the same person, nevertheless, there was no doubt in my mind that Cassy Duprey, the young Beforetime artist of whom I sometimes dreamed, had adopted both titles at different points in her long life.

I continued reading the names of the dead, beast and human, chiseled into the marker. The last name was Straaka's, although he alone of the dead was not buried in the valley. The coercer Miryum, whom he had died to shield, had taken his body and vanished, and we had neither seen nor heard of her since. The coercer-knights she had once led were convinced that Miryum had taken Straaka's body to Sador, for Sadorians believed that their bones must rest alongside those of their ancestors lest their spirits wander. That seemed as likely a possibility as anything else, for Miryum had been out of her mind with grief and guilt.

The coercer was not the only guilty survivor of that day. The empath Miky constantly anguished over her twin brother, Angina, for although he had recovered from his wounds, he would never regain his former strength. Once, I had used spirit eyes to look at the lad's aura, and I had seen clearly how the red slashing mark, which echoed the fading scar at his temple, leeched brightness from the rest of his aura, draining it of vitality. The boy's body had been healed, but his spirit had been savagely wounded, and no one knew how to heal such a thing.

I spoke each name on the marker aloud, remembering the owners of the names with a grief that made my eyes sting.

"Do you pray to Lud to mind their souls?" a voice asked.

I gasped and overbalanced trying to turn and stand at the same time. A tall woman with short silken yellow hair and piercing blue eyes stood a little distance away, hands on hips, watching me.

"You are Bergold's sister, Analivia," I said, recognizing her, for she had once saved me from a whipping.

She nodded to the marker. "I heard that many of your people died here. Those are their names scribed on the marker?"

I nodded and said, without really knowing why, "There are the names of animals as well as humans. How did you . . . ?" I stopped, finding it hard to speak of my Misfit abilities openly, even now.

A mercurial smile played about her mouth. "You wonder how your Misfit powers did not detect me? I have always had a knack of being able to remain hidden." Her smile dimmed. "In the house where I grew up, it was wiser to be invisible."

That did not surprise me. Her father had been the brutal and oppressive Councilman Radost, who had once ruled the Council and Sutrium with an iron hand and heart. Not long before the rebellion, he had sent his sons, Bergold and Moss, up to the highlands to establish new Councilfarms, since one man was permitted to hold only so much land. Analivia had lived with Bergold, the eldest of the three. Since the rebellion, Moss and his father had been sentenced to long terms on Councilfarms, but Bergold, a fair and kindhearted young man, had been permitted to continue running his orchards, as a cooperative venture. The orchards and fruit-bottling industry he had established were so successful that they had employed many Darthnor miners who could not work while the road to the smelters and west coast industries remained closed.

"Are you hunting?" I asked politely.

"You might call it hunting, if curiosity can be called a weapon and knowledge prey. I have been watching your people. I have been inside the mountain. The Beforetimers must have loved darkness to build in such a place, but what do your people seek there?"

"Some of us are curious about the Beforetimers and how they lived," I said, realizing that she must have explored the caverns when the teknoguilders were inside them. Given how little awareness the teknoguilders had of anything outside their studies, I was not the least bit surprised, but Garth would be horrified.

"Why are you curious about us?" I asked.

She shrugged. "It interests me that you survived when so many people wanted to kill you. I am interested in survival." She glanced down at the memorial marker. "I suppose you know that Malik is not the sort to give up his hatred because of agreements and treaties. My brother and father were like him. Hatred ran through their veins like fire, devouring all else."

"I heard that they were killed trying to escape from the Councilfarm," I said, uncertain whether to express sympathy, since it was known that Analivia's brother and father had both mistreated her.

But she merely said rather cryptically, "Hatred does not die so easily." She looked around the cul-de-sac. "This is a pretty place to be marked by so much hatred and death."

"Marked?" I wondered if she was referring to the carved monument.

She saw my confusion and said soberly, "I think that terrible happenings mark a place so whoever comes there after feels a kind of echo."

30

I said slowly, "Do you feel the mark of what happened here?"

She did not answer, seeming suddenly distracted.

"Will you come to the encampment with me?" I asked presently.

She shook her head but said that she would walk some of the way back with me. I half expected her to interrogate me, but instead, as we walked, she told me about her life as a girl. Her father had bonded only for a son to inherit his properties and power. It soon became clear that Bergold, his firstborn son, was nothing like his sire, lacking Radost's ruthless ambition and brute will. So Radost turned his attention to his second son, Moss; they were like two vipers in a nest. Only his desire to increase his properties and extend his area of influence had made Radost send Bergold and Moss to establish Councilfarms in the highlands. He had intended, in time, to weld the properties together as one, under his control, but the rebellion had ended his ambitions.

"I am glad of the uprising," she said. "I prayed for many years that the rebels would have the courage to do it."

"Not all Landfolk welcome the change," I said mildly.

She shrugged. "People fear that if the old ways come back, they will be punished for failing to oppose the usurpers. They have to learn not to be afraid. When the Council ruled, fear clogged the air like mist above a moor. You could not breathe without drawing it in."

Abruptly she stopped, and I saw the wagons. Analivia said goodbye and in the twinkling of an eye, she was gone. I tried to probe her but to no avail. I made my way toward the Teknoguild camp, wondering if the yellow-haired woman had learned to conceal her presence because of her childhood or whether she had a trace of Misfit ability. I was passing the second wagon when I noticed one of the soldierguards sitting up and gazing out. I stopped reluctantly to ask if he needed anything.

"I was just thinking that it had been a peaceful wintertime." He laughed humorlessly. "The truth is, I am uneasy about going back to the city. Everything will be changed, and I don't suppose it will be easy for an ex-soldierguard to find employment."

"I am sure that High Chieftain Dardelan will find a place for you," I said coolly.

"You don't like me, do you?" the soldierguard said. "I do not blame you for it, but you don't realize how it was back then for us. How your kind was made to seem . . ." His voice trailed off, and though I waited politely, he appeared to have forgotten what he meant to say. I bid him good day.

"I am not a forgiving sort of person," I muttered as I walked on.

"That is because you are strong," said a familiar voice.

I started violently and then saw the beasthealer, Darius, sitting before me, under a tree. "I'm sorry," I said.

"Sorry about what?" he inquired gently. "About me, because I am so insignificant that you almost walked past me? About that man back there, who must daily grow in awareness of what he did in this valley? Or are you sorry about yourself for having such a nature? But, no, people who are strong forgive themselves least of all."

Darius smiled gently and with a graceful gesture invited me to sit. I lowered myself to the knobbled knee of a tree, shocked to notice that from a certain angle, Darius bore a strong resemblance to Swallow. It was hardly remarkable; Twentyfamilies gypsies seldom bonded to outsiders. Indeed, bonding among them required the approval of the old women who kept track of genealogies so the match would not be too close. I felt a stab of pity for Darius, to have such a face set above a dreadfully misshapen body. Then I wondered at my thought. Should I wish him a face as distorted as his body?

His gentle smile widened as if he heard my thoughts, and I felt the blood heat my cheeks. Twentyfamilies gypsies could see spirit auras with their normal eyes, and who knew what mine told him?

I rose, offering to send food, but Darius heaved himself awkwardly to his feet, saying he would come with me. Back at the camp, Katlyn and Kella were chopping mushrooms and garlic, and the healer looked up and smiled at our approach. She said that Dragon had found several huge rings of mushrooms, and they had decided to make a proper meal. I asked where Dragon was, and Kella told me that she had taken some grain to the horses. Darius examined the herbs Katlyn had gathered. I wanted to tell Kella about Analivia, but Darius held up a small scarlet flower with a crow of delight.

I left them to gloat over their herbs and sat on an upturned barrel beside Louis Larkin. Awake now, the old man was prodding moodily at the fire in a desultory way. Maruman lay curled asleep in his lap.

"He seems to do nothing but sleep lately," I said.

Louis shrugged. "Carryin' a deal of years is a terrible wearisome business."

I did not doubt it, but in Maruman's case, I did not know if it was just age. Until recently, the cat had been a great wanderer; his adventuring had earned him many scars and cost him an eye. But during the wintertime just past, he had not once gone wandering, choosing instead to sleep. I had been glad, but now I worried that the old cat might have abandoned his physical adventures to travel on the dreamtrails, which could be far more dangerous. In his dream journeying, Maruman did not have old bones and weary flesh, but any wound or hurt taken would be echoed by a real wound that would afflict his spirit, and this would affect him physically.

On impulse, I said, "I have been thinking of those Twentyfamilies gypsies who came to Obernewtyn when you were young."

Louis gave me a knowing look. "So that's th' way of it, then. That Swallow."

I stared at him in bewilderment for a minute, then realized what he was implying. Opening my mouth to give him the sharp edge of my tongue, I had a sudden clear vision of Swallow, leaning forward to kiss me after rescuing me.

I wondered if Swallow even remembered that kiss. So much had happened since. He had become D'rekta of the Twentyfamilies gypsies, with all the responsibilities of leading his people and fulfilling the mysterious ancient promises that lay at the heart of their community. Our realization that these promises connected to my secret quest meant that Swallow knew more about me than any other human. So much so that the Agyllians had made use of him more than once when I had been in danger. The overguardian of the Sadorian Earthtemple had even told me that one of Kasanda blood would accompany me to the desertlands where I would receive Kasanda's final message for the Seeker. I knew that Swallow had spoken of me to the seers among his people, and though he had never told me what they said, these days when we met, he was always very stern and serious. I wondered if I had not preferred the devilish gypsy who looked at me with admiration and kissed me without permission.

Louis was still looking at me expectantly, so I said, "Louis, would you let me enter your memory of the gypsies' visit to Obernewtyn?"

The older man's face creased in a scowl. "Ye'll keep out of me brain, girl, be ye Mistress of all Obernewtyn! Look at what happened to Dragon when ye meddled with her!" His voice had risen and I felt the other three look at me. Louis pushed Maruman unceremoniously to the ground and stalked away stiff-backed.

"Cannot funaga control themselves/emotions?" Maruman sent coldly as he climbed onto my lap. I said nothing, for my throat was tight with unshed tears. Louis's words seemed to highlight a growing feeling of my own inadequacy and displacement. Again, I found myself wondering when my quest would claim me.

"It claims you now," Maruman sent. "It has never stopped claiming you. All that you do, ElspethInnle, serves the old Ones and the quest."

[illegible faint text from previous page bleed-through]

✦ 3 ✦

THE FOLLOWING MORNING, we rose in the thin, gray, predawn light, having said goodbye to the tekno-guilders the night before. We did not bother lighting a fire, for we would eat at one of the inns in the upper lowlands. Both wagons had already rattled off, and I was preparing to follow the others when Garth came shambling out in his nightshirt, a blanket draped around his massive shoulders.

"I have been thinking about this daughter of Radost. This Analivia . . . ," he began.

"We have spoken more than enough on that subject," I interrupted him firmly, for he had speculated at length about the young woman after I told him of our meeting. "She might be Radost's daughter and Moss's sister, but she is also the sister of Bergold, who mistreats no human or beast. For Lud's sake, it is common knowledge that her father loathed her! She is no danger to Misfits, and she might very well be one of us."

A look of real agony passed over the teknoguilder's wide face. "But if she continues spying . . ."

"Garth, why are you so worried about people finding out about the sunken city?" I demanded, exasperated. "Do you really think they will rush here to see it or try to prevent your guild researching the past? Most likely, normal Landfolk will merely shudder at your interest and name it ghoulish. The Council has gone. We are free people in a free Land."

He stared at me, speechless, and I grew silent, for my words had the weight of a futureteller pronouncement and I felt slightly abashed.

"What you say is true, Elspeth," Garth said at last. "But this freedom is new and precarious. The world can turn back in an instant, and all our care and work would be lost if it should be decided that Beforetime sites are taboo. At the least, it is better to continue as we have begun, in secrecy, until Dardelan is elected. For all we know, Malik has found new favor during the wintertime. Instead of being made to answer our charges, he might be elected high chieftain! Or the Herders on Herder Isle might be building a secret weapon. Or the Council on the west coast might be on the verge of a successful counterattack. I must protect what we have learned."

I nodded wearily and closed my coat's fastenings, reaching down to pick up Maruman. As I draped him about my shoulders, he sank in his claws to make himself secure and comfortable. Garth still looked as if something further might be said or decided, so I nodded and turned away decisively. I glanced back once to see him still standing there, peering after me.

"Funaga . . . ," Maruman began.

"I know emotions annoy you," I beastspoke the old cat tersely, "but, unfortunately, they are as much a part of us as our bones. We can't set them aside to please you, even if we wished it."

Not even to please ourselves, I thought privately.

"They are untidy/disturbing," Maruman responded

with a fastidious mental shudder that was rather like having someone sneeze inside your head.

"Well, there is nothing to be done about them."

He fell silent, but his indignation was loud. I bit back a desire to tell him that his own emotional emanations were fairly disturbing, but of course he caught the thought and sent a huff of irritation rippling through my mind. I endured it doggedly, concentrating on finding the best footing, until his stiffness softened and he slept, his breath sawing in and out by my ear.

Only then did I reach up and stroke the battered head with a tenderness and pity I would never have dared express when he was awake. Louis had been right in saying the cat was old, though I hated to think it. Maybe it was true that his sleeping of late was no more than a sign of age. I did not know how old Maruman was, but he had not been a kitten when I first overheard his thoughts at the Kinraide orphanage, and I wondered, as I had done countless times since, where he had been born and how he had come to Kinraide. Most likely, he had survived a farmer's attempt to drown an unwanted litter, but that beginning, however traumatic, would not explain his mind's strange distortions. It was possible, of course, that he had simply been born as he was, just as I had been born Misfit. Perhaps I would ask Atthis about his origin when next she communicated with me. After all, the Agyllian mystic ruthlessly used the old cat's distorted mind as a conduit, because those distortions meant he could not be spied upon.

Such memories summoned the pale face of my nemesis Ariel.

When I had first met him, at Obernewtyn, he had been a beautiful, sadistic boy. When we took over, he

38

had fled and somehow wormed his way into the confidence of both Henry Druid and the Council. Later he had joined the Herders, and rumor said he was now high in their ranks. He had lost none of his beauty in the intervening years; the last time I had seen Ariel, he had been a tall, slender man with a cascade of silky, nearly white hair surrounding that astonishing face. He hated Obernewtyn and had harmed us, directly and indirectly, whenever possible. But his antipathy to me was more specific and malevolent; in fact, I believed that Ariel was the Destroyer, destined to resurrect the Beforetime weaponmachines if I failed to disarm them. Atthis had never named him the Destroyer, but Ariel had hunted me on the dreamtrails just as Atthis had warned me the Destroyer would. If I had needed any more proof, Maruman called Ariel *H'rayka*, which means "one who brings destruction" in beastspeak.

The last time I had seen Ariel, he had been aboard a Herder ship laden with Landfolk who were to be sold as slaves in distant lands. One of those slaves had been the farseeker Matthew, and the memory of my final moments with him still anguished me, though Maryon had foreseen his survival. From time to time, those of us who had known Matthew experienced fragmentary true dreams that showed him living in a port city in a hot desert land. Gradually, we had come to believe that Matthew was in the Red Queen's land, which many believed to be a myth. Brydda's seaman friend Reuvan had assured us that it was very real but was so unimaginably distant that few had ever traveled there. True dreams of Matthew showed a brutish horde that had enslaved its people occupying the Red Land. Matthew and others taken from the Land also served the slavemasters, working at extending the city or in the mine pits outside the city.

In my dreams, Matthew had become a grown man with broad shoulders, muscled from breaking stone and working in the mines. I had seen him striving to convince the enslaved people to rise up and overthrow their oppressors. To Matthew's great frustration, they refused because of a prophecy foretelling that the people would overcome the slavemasters only when their queen returned. Their queen, however, had been slain. One day, Matthew had seen a wall frieze depicting the Red Queen and noticed her uncanny resemblance to Dragon. Matthew had realized then that the filthy urchin we had rescued from the Beforetime ruins on the west coast was the Red Queen's lost daughter. Which meant *a* Red Queen *could* return. But the last time Matthew had seen her, Dragon had lain deep in a coma.

In my most recent dream of him, I had seen Matthew trying to persuade people that they had misread the prophecy, that they had to overthrow their oppressors *before* the Red Queen could be restored to them. It had not been hard to guess that Matthew wanted to free the Red Land and bring Dragon to her kingdom in hopes that this would wake her. He did not know that she had awakened and that the shock of remembering her mother's betrayal and murder had erased from her memory everything except her time alone in the ruins. Like Matthew, I dreamed of restoring Dragon to her land, but we could not reach the Red Land without ships capable of making the journey, not to mention maps and charts to show the way.

Over time, I had taken to reviewing the beautiful intricate dream maps the futuretellers compiled from dream journals that each guild kept, looking for dreams about Matthew. From these I learned that the farseeker had ceased trying to convince the people of the Red Land to rise and had begun thinking of returning to the Land. He had the support of other Landfolk who had been taken as slaves, but they were insistent that any plan to steal a ship must be foolproof, because if caught, they would be sentenced to work in a mine within a chasm where a monster dwelt, a fearsome creature called an Entina. I did not know what it was, but Garth speculated that it must be one of the rare creatures spawned on the Blacklands, which had adapted to the tainted earth. Why else would it not venture from its chasm in search of victims?

Several of Matthew's companions had been caught stealing weapons and had been assigned to the deadly mine. Those taken by the beast uttered screams of such intense terror and pain that grown men had fainted hearing them.

I wished, as I had done many times before, that I could communicate with Matthew to tell him he need only bide his time, for as soon as possible, we would come to him with Dragon.

The misty dawn had given way to a soft cool morning when we reached the main road and hauled the wagons back up the scree slope. It was a pleasant ride, and we saw nobody for several hours.

"I had a queer dream last night," Zarak said as we rode along. "I was in the mountains near the hot springs, an' I saw Miryum and Straaka walkin' together. I suppose it was bein' in the White Valley that put them in my mind."

I frowned, remembering that there had been other recordings of dreams about Miryum and the Sadorian tribesman Straaka. It was impossible that they were true dreams, since Straaka had died to protect Miryum, but there must be some reason why people were dreaming of them. When we returned to Obernewtyn, I would ask Maryon.

I was about to say as much when I noticed several wagons coming along a small road that joined the main road just ahead. Given that the wagons were heavily laden with furniture and that there were children and women as well as men on them, I guessed the travelers had come from Darthnor. We had heard reports that some miners had rejected Bergold's offer of work, preferring to pack their families' possessions and leave the region. Despite the rebellion, the miners retained their old loathing of Misfits and blamed us as much as the rebels for the loss of the smelters and metal works in the west that had meant the closure of the mines.

I knew it would be obvious that we were Misfits, given the direction from which we were coming, and my heart began to hammer as we approached the smaller road. I forced myself to nod to the wagoners, and to my relief, we received courteous but unsmiling nods in return. We were far down the road and out of sight before I relaxed, and I smiled ruefully at the memory of the stirring speech I had given Garth in the predawn light about being free people in a free land.

It was late in the day before we passed the blunt black face of Emeralfel, but a purplish haze obscured our view of the whole lowlands spread out beyond. I told myself the day would clear, but as we continued, heavy gray clouds massed overhead. It was foolish and superstitious, but I felt the darkening day to be an ill omen. On impulse, as we approached the hamlet where we had decided to stop for supplies and information, I suggested that Katlyn and Kella continue on in their wagon and wait for us on the road to Rangorn. After they had gone, I tied Gahltha to the wagon and sat on the front bench with Zarak, drawing a simple shawl over my hair.

The hamlet was only one of many nameless clusters of buildings and stalls grown up willy-nilly by the roadside to serve travelers who could not be bothered leaving the main way to replenish their supplies or get a meal in one of the villages or small towns. I had stopped at this one before the uprising, but I had no fear of being recognized. Those who worked in such places were often wanderers themselves, earning a few coins before traveling on. When visiting such villages before the rebellion, I had invariably gone disguised as a gypsy. As we approached the inn that was the hamlet's centerpiece, I noticed several new trading stalls and a number of cottages, and there was now a sign of a horseshoe painted on a board, denoting a blacksmith. Was this growth a sign of prosperity brought about by the changes in the Land? I climbed down and bade Lo pull the wagon around behind the inn, just in case any wagons came along and decided to take a closer look.

Zarak was unhitching the horses when he sent to ask if he ought to make some pretense of hobbling or restraining them. I sent a terse no, suggesting to the horses that they merely graze discreetly among the trees surrounding the hamlet. In the meantime, Zarak ought to fill the feed bins and replenish the water barrel.

The inn was the same rudimentary building I

remembered, constructed of timber and stone, its front standing open to the road. I approached the wide serving bench and sat upon one of the stools set before it.

"What will ye, young mistress?" asked the gray-haired woman behind the counter in a friendly but businesslike way.

"I would like apple cider if you have it. I remember it was very good the last time I came this way." I tossed out the information to suggest I was a regular traveler, and I knew that my lowland accent would tell her and anyone else listening that I might not necessarily have begun my journey in the highlands, though my wagon had come from that direction.

"Will ye have it warmed? It's turned chilly."

"I will," I said equably, knowing that warming the cider would take time in which she might be prevailed upon to gossip.

"Where are ye bound?" she asked as she set a pot of cider to heat over a small fire.

"Saithwold," I answered. "My brother is a woodworker and we have a hire there."

"Saithwold?" she repeated. Then she leaned closer and asked skeptically, "Who offered the hire?"

"The ex-Councilman of Saithwold, Noviny." I spoke loudly, turning slightly to see how the other customers reacted to my words. Most were busy with their own conversations and meals, but at a nearby table, an older man with muddy boots, sitting with a young woman, was clearly listening, as were two tough-looking men by the wall. I could not tell from any of their faces what they felt.

"How long ago did he offer yer brother work?" the woman asked, her voice pitched low now.

I shrugged and dropped my own voice, intrigued by her almost furtive manner. "Before last wintertime, Master Noviny sent word that he had work that needed doing on his homestead, but we could not leave the job my brother was engaged upon. Now we go to Saithwold to see if there is still work and also as a courtesy. It is no matter either way, as there is another hire waiting for my brother in Sutrium."

The woman made a noncommittal gesture, her eyes flickering past me as she poured my mug of warmed cider. I sipped at it, wondering aloud where my brother had got to and resisting the temptation to probe the woman in case she was a sensitive. I knew that Zarak was filling the water barrels from a well behind the inn, but I did not summon him. Glancing casually about the room, I saw that the man and the woman who had seemed to be listening to us were now conversing in low voices, but the two hard-looking men by the wall were still watching me.

"If you have them, I would like fresh bread, honey, and butter," I said. "My brother will want something a bit more substantial. Eggs maybe?"

"I can offer cured bacon as well as eggs," the woman said. "Though it will cost yer. It's the last of an old store, and meat will not be so easy to get if this animal charter is made law."

"Do you think that is like to happen?" I asked, having shaken my head to the bacon.

"I cannot see folk gladly doing without their meat," she answered, giving me no hint of her own opinion.

"The hunting of beasts who prey on humans is allowed within the charter, is it not?" I asked, watching

45

her closely. "The way I heard it, a man might have bacon if he is prepared to face down the boar for it."

"Do ye ken this fingerspeech?" a voice behind me asked curtly. I turned to see the man with the mud-crusted boots, whom I had decided was a farmer. Beside him, the young woman sat with eyes demurely cast down.

"I know a little of it," I admitted warily. "A jack showed it to me and my brother."

"Is it true speech?" the man asked truculently. "Is it nowt some play of speaking? A trick?"

"To what end?" I asked. "My brother and I were skeptical, too, but the ability to communicate even a little with beasts has proven very useful. It is handy to be able to ask the horse or dog accompanying a man if he is trustworthy."

From the corner of my eye, I saw the two men at the other table exchange a purposeful glance as they rose, donning coats and throwing some coins down before they strode out.

"Mark my words, it is a trick," the farmer muttered stubbornly, and turned his back on me.

"You best not speak of fingertalk an' the Beast Charter if you're going to Saithwold," said the woman behind the counter, still in a low voice. Her manner was less guarded now, which seemed to confirm that she had been wary of the two men who had left.

"Is Master Noviny opposed to the Beast Charter, then?" I asked, knowing it was not so.

"Sirrah Noviny isn't chieftain of Saithwold," the woman said crisply as she went to pick up the men's coins.

I sat back, trying to connect what she had implied with what Zarak's father, the beastspeaker Khuria, had written to his son about Saithwold. Before the rebellion, Khuria had gone down to Saithwold to help establish a chain of farseekers between Darthnor and Sutrium, enabling communication among the Misfits. It had quickly become clear that although Noviny was a Councilman, he was also an honest man much admired by those in his region. After the uprising, Khuria had told the old man the truth about himself, and Noviny had invited him to remain in his household. Khuria had been glad to stay, for he found Obernewtyn's bitter winters harder and harder to endure. Judging from Khuria's letters to Zarak after the end of the rebellion, a genuine friendship had grown between the two men. The letters had made it clear that Noviny was almost certain to be reelected chieftain of the region as soon as the people of Saithwold were allowed to make their own choice. Vos, the rebel who currently served as chieftain, knew this and resented it bitterly, but attempts to force local farmers to agree to vote for him had only increased his unpopularity.

Once the pass had been closed with snow, there had been no more letters until thaw. But as soon as the pass had opened and messages arrived, Zarak had shown me the pile of letters from his father, asking grimly if I would read them and tell him what I thought.

They had been arranged from oldest to most recent. The first, sent at the start of wintertime, had reported Vos's growing anger at the Beast Charter and Noviny's willingness to embrace it. There had been several confrontations between Noviny and the new chieftain in which Vos had ranted and Noviny had remained calm and dignified, saying that he was a private farmer and was concerned only with his own affairs. The letter was written with Khuria's characteristic bluntness, but there was a marked change in the tone of the letters that followed. The scribing became strangely formal, and instead of offering incisive evaluations of Saithwold's situation, Khuria offered all manner of irrelevant and even trivial details of daily life. There was no more mention of Vos, nor of beastspeaking and agreements with beasts. The last letter, sent only a sevenday or so before the thaw, seemed maudlin and spoke of infirmity and the wings of time. This missive was so altogether unlike Khuria that either he had not written it, or he was striving to make it seem false.

"He wishes to communicate but he cannot write freely," I had suggested to Zarak.

"That is just what I thought," he had responded worriedly. "On his deathbed, my father would nivver whine like this."

The serving woman set down a platter of fragrant fresh-baked bread, interrupting my reverie. As she arranged crocks of honey, jam, and butter, she said softly, "If there is trouble in Saithwold, ye can be sure Chieftain Vos is behind it." She spoke his title with a sneer. "He is determined the people of Saithwold will elect him chieftain again whether they like it or no."

"He can't make anyone vote for him," I told her. "Each person's name will be marked off as they make their choice for chieftain. That choice will be scribed in secret, then folded, and put into a box that will remain locked until it reaches Sutrium."

"I ken that as well as the next person who can read a notice, but who do ye think will guard the box of votes and bear them to Sutrium?" the woman snapped. "The armsmen of each chieftain, that's who."

Zarak entered, hailing me jovially and commanding the woman behind the counter to bring him a brace of eggs, a mountain of fried bread, and a slab of sharp yellow cheese. The same again was to be wrapped up for our companion who lay ill in the wagon.

A faint unease passed over the woman's face at the mention of illness, but I knew this was only an unconscious remembering of the plague that had swept the Land some years previous, killing many and scarring more. The woman offered Zarak a cider, which he accepted, and as she set about preparing the rest of his order, I told him aloud that there might be strife in Saithwold over the coming elections and suggested we reconsider going there. At the same time, I farsent a command to Zarak to disagree in an arrogant brotherly way.

"It is naught to do with us," Zarak said airily, carefully emulating lowland speech to match our accents. "We are not to vote for the chieftain of Saithwold." He stretched languorously and said that he would rather eat outside and soak up a bit of sunlight. Ordering me to bring him the eggs when they came, he ambled out, humming to himself. I had to repress a smile at how well he played his part.

The woman shook her head at me, provoked just as I had hoped. "He is a comely lad, your brother, but a dear fool," she said tartly. "Ye'll be lucky if he gets no more than a sound beating when ye try getting past the blockade."

"Blockade?" I thought I must have misheard her.

"There is a blockade set up on the road to Saithwold. It is supposed to keep out brigands, but if you ask me, it is the brigands mannin' it," she said, breaking eggs forcefully into a pan. "They provoke trouble with anyone who wants to go to Saithwold and use that as an excuse to stop them entering the town."

"They stop people going to Saithwold?" I asked with mild skepticism.

"Exactly that," she said sharply. "And the blockade doesn't only keep people out. It keeps in them as wants to leave. You try scribin' a letter to Sirrah Noviny to tell him yer coming to take up his offer, and ye'll get back a polite missive from him saying he has no work for yer brother." The woman glanced about, then leaned closer. "I've a sister who went to live in Saithwold wi' her bondmate years back. We have visited back and forth over the years, but at the beginnin' of this wintertime just past, I sent her an invitation an' got back a missive full of small news. My sister nivver even mentioned my suggestion that she come an' visit. I wrote again an' asked her more bluntly. Again she wrote a lot of queer prattle about recipes an' descriptions of th' weather and all manner of news about people I didn't know, but still no answer. I have scribed two more letters since, and it were th' same both times when she scribed back. There is something amiss; I know it well, but I can't go there to see her because of yon blockade." The woman's eyes suddenly brimmed with tears. "There is so much trouble about. Robbers creeping along the road at night in gangs, burnin' an' destroyin' homes, an' kitchen gardens, an' planted fields of good people. . . . Many's the time I wish fer the Council back. I hated their corruption, but at least I could see my sister."

Her voice had risen and I glanced around, but the other patrons appeared indifferent to our conversation. The woman visibly mastered herself. "My advice to ye and that handsome ninnyhammer of a brother waitin' for his eggs is to ferget about Saithwold. If ye've a promise of work in Sutrium, go there and take it up." Her eyes searched my face; then she said quickly, "But if ye do go to Saithwold, mayhap ye'd consent to . . . to take a missive from me to my sister? She's a rare fine cook and ye'll nowt be sorry. . . ." She stopped in confusion, her eyes again filling with tears, which she dashed away angrily.

I said softly, "Scribe your missive and tell me her name. My brother may look a fool, but he is resourceful. If your sister will scribe a message to you, I will bring it out and give it to a jack I know who comes this way regularly. You have been kind to give a stranger so much information, and I am sorry for your trouble."

The woman nodded and vanished for a time. When she returned, it was with red eyes, a laden plate for Zarak, a package of food wrapped in cloth, and a small folded paper that she surreptitiously pressed into my palm. "I'd like not ter charge ye for your meal, but my master is over at that table," she said apologetically.

I paid her, carried the plate out to Zarak, and sat with him while he ate, telling him what had transpired as he wolfed down the food.

"My father made no mention of any blockade, but perhaps he kenned the letter would nowt be allowed to leave Saithwold if he did. Can Vos really expect to force the people of Saithwold to vote for him? He can nowt keep the town closed away forever, and as soon as anyone can leave, they will complain to the Council of Chieftains in Sutrium."

"Perhaps he hopes that whoever is voted head of the Council of Chieftains will refuse to hear any complaints against him," I said.

"There is something else odd," Zarak went on.

51

"Dardelan mun have heard about the blockade from people turned away. Why hasnae he sent up a force of armsmen to investigate?"

He was right, and I could think of no reason for Dardelan's failure to deal with the blockade unless his grip on power was a good deal more fragile than we had been led to believe. Zarak continued. "As for the election, as soon as we tell Dardelan what Vos intends, he mun send some of his armsmen to make sure the votes are nowt tampered with." Zarak warmed to his idea and began to elaborate on how Dardelan might disguise his true intentions under a festive façade.

Suddenly eager to reach Rangorn, I bade Zarak prepare the wagon to leave. I took the plate inside, and some impulse made me ask the woman if the rebel chieftain Malik ever came by.

This time fear flashed in her eyes, but anger, too. She glanced around before saying, "His men have camps set up all along this coast to keep watch for any Herder ships that try to land, but they spend most of their time at inns buying ale and gaming with the local layabouts. Those two who left earlier drink with them regularly, and there is always trouble when they come." She hesitated and then said, "Anyone foolish enough to speak against Chieftain Malik or in favor of his enemies or rivals in their hearing is like to find their house burned down around their ears. By robbers and brigands, of course," she sneered. Then she added uneasily, "I hope I haven't made a mistake and you aren't one of Malik's spies."

"You can be sure that Malik is the last person I would serve," I said.

✦ 4 ✦

As we set off again, I told Darius what we had learned, suggesting he might not want to come into Saithwold with us. But to my surprise, he insisted.

"There may be danger," Zarak pointed out hesitantly.

The crippled healer smiled peaceably and said, "It was ever dangerous to be a Twentyfamilies gypsy, and there is a thing in Saithwold I wish to see."

At these words, I struggled to keep my composure.

Khuria had once told me of a magnificent statue of a man in Noviny's garden, and his description had made me wonder if it had been carved by Cassy Duprey, when she had been D'rekta to the Twentyfamilies. Swallow had told me enough of the ancient promises that bound the Twentyfamilies to make me aware that their first leader had charged his people with the maintenance and protection of the carvings she had created to communicate with the Seeker. If I was right, the statue in Noviny's garden might very well be a message to me. Darius's interest certainly suggested it.

So far, I had found only one of the signs mentioned in the clues carved on the original Obernewtyn doors: an enormous glass statue with my face in the sunken city under Tor. I had dived to see the statue, convinced that I would find concealed in it one of the keys mentioned on the Obernewtyn doors. But instead of a key, I had found only an inscription and the artist's name: Cassy Duprey. Soon after, water had filled the protective airlock, shattering the statue, and I had been devastated, convinced that I had failed my quest at the first test, because I had not found the key.

But later, the teknoguilder Reul had mentioned that Beforetimers communicated with their computer-machines by pressing on scribed letters built into the machines, spelling out sentences. This, he had explained in his dry crisp way, had been called "keying in a command." Seeing my rigid attention, he elaborated, saying that a key word or phrase might also be required before a computermachine would accept a command or offer any information.

This had made me realize that the phrase carved into the glass statue's base—*Through the transparency of now, the future*—might be just such a "key."

That had led me to wonder if the other keys referred to on the Obernewtyn doors might not be physical keys either. Indeed, one bade me "seek the words in the house where my son was born." Whatever those words were, I was sure that they, too, would prove to be a key to the mechanisms of the Beforetime weaponmachines I must find and destroy.

Discovering the glass statue had also made me realize that Cassy Duprey's decision to leave messages and clues for me had been made much sooner than I had supposed—not when she had been living in the Land as D'rekta of the Twentyfamilies, as I had thought, but *before* the Great White, when she had carved the glass statue.

54

Of course, it was possible that the glass statue and the words upon it were no more than a significant gift to a new friend and perhaps the seed from which the eventual plan to send messages to the Seeker had grown. But the Agyllian mystics had insisted I return in haste to the highlands to find "the last sign" before it was lost, and finding the glass statue seemed to fit their warning too well for it to mean anything else. Only later had it occurred to me that the Agyllians might have summoned me to the highlands to save Dragon, whose deepening coma threatened the keeping place of another sign referred to on the doors—something locked in her suppressed memories.

I visualized the words to the second and most obscure of the clues as Fian had translated them from gadi:

[That which] will [open/access/reach] the darkest door lies where the [?] [waits/sleeps]. Strange is the keeping place of this dreadful [step/sign/thing], and all who knew it are dead save one who does not know what she knows. Seek her past. Only through her may you go where you have never been and must someday go. Danger. Beware. Dragon.

I was sure that Dragon was "the one who does not know what she knows" and that Cassy or Hannah had foreseen Dragon and all that had brought her to me, impossible though that seemed; however, Fian's translation had so many alternative possibilities and blank spaces and ambiguities that sometimes I was afraid I had misread all the signs. During the early part of the winter, I had even flown the dreamtrails again with

Maruman to try to take a clearer rubbing of the doors' carvings, for they had been destroyed in reality, but our first visit had affected the dreamtrails, so we had been unable to find them again. Or that is what Maruman had said, though perhaps he had simply been unable to focus his mind well enough to lead me to them.

We had not long taken the turnoff to Rangorn when Zarak spotted the other wagon waiting by the wayside. We stopped briefly to share what had happened at the inn.

As we rode on, the others began to speculate about Saithwold and Vos. Finally, Katlyn said comfortably, "I expect Brydda will explain everything." The others nodded so readily that I wondered if we were not putting too much faith in the big rebel. He had been a true friend to us and to beasts, as well as to his rebel comrades, but Brydda and Dardelan were no longer trying to overthrow a vicious and oppressive authority. *They* were the authority now, and they must control the Land and protect its people while living up to the ideals they had expounded during the years of oppression.

At length, we passed the rutted, little-used back trail leading to Kinraide. I glanced along it and thought of my early years in the Kinraide orphanage and my brother Jes. How long ago that day in the orphanage seemed when he had embraced me and promised he would come for me at Obernewtyn as soon as he had his Normalcy Certificate. How certain he had been that he was in control of his life. And I, borne away in a carriage bound for Obernewtyn, had felt utterly powerless. One day, when there was time, I would go back to

Kinraide and see if I could lay flowers upon my brother's grave.

The road passed the dense, eerie Weirwood, within which lay the deep narrow chasm known as Silent Vale. As a girl, I had been marched here from the Kinraide orphanage with other orphans to gather deposits of poisonous whitestick. We had been given gloves and special bags, for merely brushing against the stuff could cause vomiting, blisters, and the loss of teeth and hair. Of course, in those days, there had been an overabundance of orphans to be disposed of, I remembered bitterly.

On the other side of the road was the stream, which was all that remained of the Upper Suggredoon after it flowed through the mountains and drained through Glenelg Mor. It was forded just before a cold, dark, poisonous river from the Blacklands joined it, transforming it into a wide, fast-moving, and now tainted river known as the Lower Suggredoon. As the wagons lumbered across the ford, I looked downriver and saw the white patches of the Sadorian tents used by the men of the rebel Zamadi, who had been given the task of guarding the banks of the Suggredoon to prevent an invasion of west coast soldierguards.

It was growing dark by the time we headed north on a smaller road to bypass Rangorn and cut across sloping green fields. The path turned to follow the lower edge of the dense forest that ran all the way from Rangorn's perimeter back to the foot of the Aran Craggie range. Here, where the river flowed out after its tumultuous journey through the mountains, Grufyyd had found Domick, Kella, and me washed up on the riverbank following our dramatic escape on a raft from the Druid's encampment.

The road brought us at length to the narrow track leading to the land where Katlyn and Grufyyd had once lived with their son. I wondered how Katlyn felt, knowing that she must soon look upon the charred ruins of her home. As a child, I had dwelt in this region, too, with my brother and parents, but I had no desire to see the ruins of my old home. It could only remind me of the dreadful death my parents had suffered at the hands of the Council.

We reached the clearing where Katlyn and Grufyyd's house had once stood, and I gaped in disbelief, for *there stood the house*, exactly as I remembered it, perfectly whole and utterly unmarked. I turned to find Kella looking no less astonished. At the rear of the wagon, Katlyn sat staring, pale and stunned.

We climbed down silently from horses and wagons, and before anyone could recover enough to speak, the front door of the little homestead opened, and out stepped Brydda Llewellyn, huge as ever, the brown beard and great shaggy mop of his hair shining in the light from his lantern. Hanging it on a hook beside the door, he strode forward, scooped up his gaping mother, and kissed her soundly, asking how she liked his surprise.

"I know you never wanted to come back here after I destroyed the old place to prevent the soldierguards from doing so, but I have a fondness for this hill and this view, so I have been rebuilding the cottage, little by little, since the rebellion. I think there is not a finer house in all the world, and though I know you and Da are happy at Obernewtyn, I thought you might like to spend the wintertimes down here."

Katlyn answered him, but she was laughing and

crying at the same time, so not a single word was understandable. He lifted her again and swung her around with a laugh. I noticed Dragon gazing at Brydda, a shy, bemused smile upon her face, but when she caught me looking at her, her face shuttered.

Brydda noticed this, but even as I began some vague explanation, I found myself swept into a bear hug that crushed the breath out of me. I had not expected the embrace or how much it would warm me. These days, no one touched me, not in friendship or in love, I realized and was horrified to discover tears blurring my eyes. *It is your own fault for being so prickly and remote,* I told myself savagely.

Fortunately, Gahltha chose that moment to approach, and Brydda released me to greet him and the other horses warmly in the fingerspeech he had invented. I did not know it well, having no need of it, but my beastspeaking ability allowed me to understand that Brydda was telling Gahltha that Sallah grazed in the fields beyond the forest. She was a large fiery mare who would accept no human as her master; she allowed Brydda to ride her only because she regarded him as a friend and an ally.

Once the horses had left, we told him the news from Obernewtyn in between ferrying items from the wagons into the house for Katlyn. There was not much news, but the big rebel listened with grave courtesy. Once the fetching and carrying was done, Katlyn and Kella shooed out all of us except Dragon so they could prepare a feast fit to celebrate a home's resurrection. We would have to eat it outside as a picnic, Brydda said apologetically, for he had not yet arranged to have furniture sent up, and he began to set out a rough trestle table and upturned log seats, hoping it would not rain.

I asked Zarak and Louis to walk down to Rangorn during the meal preparations to see if they could learn anything more about the blockade in Saithwold. Darius went to tend the soldierguards, then took a short walk to ease his cramped muscles. That left Brydda and me.

"Maryon insisted that we bring Dragon," I said without preamble.

Brydda frowned. "I gather that she has not remembered you?"

I shook my head. "Roland told me that she will. Maybe that is why Maryon sent us on this trip together." I changed the subject and told him about Khuria's letters and what I had heard at the inn. Brydda was not surprised by any of it.

"For the last moon or so, we have had numerous reports from people turned away or beaten up at this blockade," he said. "We have also had complaints from people who received letters like Khuria's. Dardelan sent a messenger to question the blockaders, but Chieftain Vos claimed that he is protecting the people of the Saithwold region from brigands and ruffians. I wanted to ride to Saithwold with a troop of armsmen and shake him until his teeth rattled, but Dardelan would not allow it. He says that we must not be seen as oppressors who can solve problems only with force."

"Surely Dardelan will not sit back and let the people of Saithwold be forced to vote for Vos against their will," I said indignantly.

"He will act only if someone from the region lays a formal charge against Vos before the Council of Chieftains. You see, it is too well known that Vos allies himself with Malik and that Dardelan and Malik are at odds. If Dardelan acts against him of his own volition, people will say that he is not impartial, and he can't risk that, given that he will be one of those to judge your charge against Malik."

"But how is anyone in Saithwold to lay a charge if they are not allowed to leave or scribe a letter without fear of it being destroyed?" I demanded. "And what of Malik? I have heard that he is behind the so-called robber burnings."

"I have heard the same. But, Elspeth, think," Brydda said. "In a very short time, Obernewtyn will lay a serious formal charge against him. I have no doubt that, with the soldierguards' testimony, the Council of Chieftains will agree that there is a charge to answer. In which case, Malik must remain in Sutrium. That will severely limit his mischief. It will also make anyone think twice about voting for him as a chieftain. And when he is found guilty after the elections, as I have no doubt he will be, he will have to serve a long sentence on a community farm."

"And what about Vos?"

"Straight after the elections, you can be sure that Dardelan will find some pretext to enter Saithwold and deal with him."

"Are you so sure that Dardelan will be elected high chieftain, Brydda? I understand there is some concern about his proposed Beast Charter."

The big man rolled his eyes. "I did suggest he wait until after the elections to reveal the Beast Charter, but you know Dardelan. He said it would be dishonest to hide his intentions. However, he means to make it very clear that the charter will not be formalized until all

Landfolk have had the chance to offer their opinions and ask questions. Given how gently he went about publicizing the Charter of Laws, allowing people to argue for changes in it, I doubt anyone will feel he is like to force anything on them."

Brydda's certainty and calmness began to allay my fears. I said, "You might mention this to him. On the way here, Zarak had an idea about how Dardelan might ensure that Vos does not cheat in the election. He suggests that as many chieftains as are willing march into Saithwold on voting day. Dardelan can claim they have come to celebrate the first elections. For that reason, there should be tumblers and musicians and other sorts of entertainers, and if possible, the chieftains should bring their families to lend the day a festive air. Needless to say, the chieftains would bring a substantial honor guard of armsmen. Vos will not dare to complain, nor will he dare to bully anyone or tamper with votes if other chieftains are looking on. Maybe Dardelan could even open the sealed box of votes and count them on the spot so Vos can't later claim they were tampered with."

Brydda's eyes glinted with amusement and admiration. "During the rebellion, I thought that Zarak had the makings of a fine strategist, and now I am sure of it." He sobered. "If you will take my advice, we should go directly to Sutrium tomorrow and leave Saithwold alone for the time being."

I shook my head. "I promised Zarak."

Brydda sighed. "It may not be a bad thing. You can spread the word in Saithwold that Dardelan knows what is happening, so people there won't do anything rash. If you don't object to riding back along the main road, I could ride with you as far as the blockade. I doubt that whoever is manning the barrier will refuse you entry, knowing that I will witness it. But you will have to coerce yourself out again if they are really preventing people from leaving."

"I will do it if we need to, but why must we go to Saithwold by the main road? It would be quicker to go via Kinraide and Berrioc."

"It would," Brydda agreed, "but I need to speak with a rebel who lives just after the Sawlney turnoff before I go back to Sutrium. It would not take long, and we can just go on from there to Saithwold."

I opened my mouth to agree with the change of route when a cold premonition of danger flowed through me. At the same moment, Kella, Katlyn, and Dragon emerged from the house laden with platters of food. Brydda leapt up to help them set the plates on the trestle and to fetch more lanterns. By the time this was done to Katlyn's satisfaction, the premonition had faded.

Louis and Zarak returned red-cheeked from their walk as we were sitting down to eat, and Zarak explained that there had been little talk in Rangorn about the blockade outside Saithwold. The gossip was all of Zamadi's men and the soldierguards stationed on the opposite bank of the Lower Suggredoon.

Listening to his description of the camps, I realized that if both riverbanks were heavily guarded even this high upstream, it would be impossible to enter or emerge from the Suggredoon, even in a plast suit, unless there was a diversion. But it would have to be something very clever, since the Councilmen and soldierguards would expect just such a trick.

As we ate, the moon rose and a chill wind began blowing at our backs. But the fire gave off waves of delicious warmth, and we shifted to sit around it as we finished the meal with slices of plum tart. Only then did I think to ask Brydda about the ship burning. I told him what Garth had said, and he nodded.

"It would be impossible for a ship to come into port, decant enough men to set fire to the ships being built, and then vanish, all without anyone noticing anything; therefore, we know that the raiders did not come by ship."

I stared at him. "You mean someone from the Land destroyed them?"

He nodded grimly.

"But who would do such a thing? And why?" Kella cried.

Brydda shook his head. "As to why, most of the Council of Chieftains believe the ships were destroyed to prevent us from landing a fighting force on the west coast. But since the shipbuilding began again as soon as the debris was cleared, nothing was accomplished but a delay. Dardelan thinks *that* might have been the reason for the burnings."

"A delay?" I echoed. "To what end?"

Brydda shrugged. "Maybe to give the Council more time to prepare their defenses, or maybe to allow time for some other plan to unfold. Maryon's futuretelling about trouble on the west coast all but confirms it, and there is no doubt that our enemies are plotting to regain this part of the Land."

"But who burned the ships?" Kella repeated her earlier question. "The Councilmen and all soldierguards who did not die or escape over the Suggredoon are in prison or working on Councilfarms, and all of the Herders left."

"They are to be called *community farms* now," Brydda explained. "It may be that some Herders or soldierguards did not leave, either by accident or design, and are now bent on working against us so that their masters can return. Or maybe the saboteurs are people who have lost power or property since the rebellion and want things back the way they were."

"The sabotage couldn't have anything to do with Malik, could it?" I asked.

Brydda met my eyes. "It occurred to me, but how would it serve Malik to have the ships burned? More likely he would want them completed sooner, knowing that Dardelan will insist upon taking part in any west coast landing, where he might be killed or injured or simply fail."

The others began talking more generally of the elections, and I told Zarak what Brydda had said about Saithwold. As expected, he was still determined to go there, but he agreed that it was worth the extra time to go back via the Sawlney turnoff if it meant that Brydda would escort us to the blockade.

"Brocade will likely be reelected chieftain of Sawlney," Brydda said, answering a question from Zarak a little later. "He has spent a good bit of time currying favor with powerful farm holders in his region. In truth, his election would not necessarily be bad. Brocade openly opposes the Beast Charter, but he dislikes violence and is moderate in other areas."

"Who do ye predict will be made chieftain of Darthnor?" Louis asked, no doubt thinking of his friend Enoch, the old coachman who dwelt on a small property in Darthnor with Rushton's defective half brother, Stephen Seraphim.

"Lydi may win, but the locals are divided between him and one of their own, Webben. He is a mine overseer who wants the road to the west reopened. He is constantly making representations to the Council of Chieftains, demanding that they negotiate with the west coast, despite the fact that we have no means of communicating with them, nor the slightest indication that they desire it. Do you know the man?"

"I do," Louis grunted. "He dislikes Misfits but mayhap more out of Darthnor tradition than any real conviction."

"Is there no possibility of Bergold being elected?" I asked.

Brydda shook his head. "He is thought to be too . . . eccentric. In any case, he has not put his name forward."

I said nothing, for it suddenly seemed to me that, for the beasts and Misfits, it did not matter who won each town's election, so long as Dardelan was returned as high chieftain, for his honesty and ideals would influence the rest.

At last, Darius rose slowly with a groan, saying he needed to sleep. Watching him hobble away, I saw that he moved a good deal more stiffly than before. I mentioned it to Kella, who explained that his joints were becoming inflamed from the wagon's jostling. She rose, saying that she would see if he would allow her to drain off some of his pain. After she had gone, Katlyn told us that the healer had twice on this journey performed the service for the gypsy healer, though he had protested each time.

"Maybe he feels a man ought to bear his own pain," Brydda said.

"Or he is afraid of becoming dependent on the relief she offers," I countered.

"It might not be pride or fear of dependency that makes him refuse her help," Katlyn said, regarding both of us with slight exasperation. Before I could ask what she meant, she rose, kissed her son, and bade us all good night. She held out her hand to Dragon, who went with her, yawning like a cat. She neglected to look back at me with especial dislike, and I felt unexpectedly cheered. Perhaps this trip would at least lessen her dislike of me, even if it did not restore her memory. Maybe I had made a mistake in trying to make her remember our friendship and all along ought to have been trying to form a new one.

Brydda rose to get more wood for the fire, and Louis and Zarak packed up the meal and carried away the dishes to wash them in a bucket of water drawn from the well. I stayed where I was, for Maruman had crept into my lap during the meal and had fallen asleep. I did not want to disturb him, because he had been unusually subdued all day, either sleeping or simply gazing at the passing world from Kella's lap or my shoulder, offering few of his usual acerbic asides. And he had not even once glared at the moon, now glowing overhead. I looked up at it, as yellow and ripe as a wheel of cheese, and thought again of the premonition I had experienced earlier that night.

✦ 5 ✦

"I HAVE SOME Sadorian choca," Brydda said, jolting me from my reverie as he dropped an armful of wood beside the fire. "Would you like a mug before you go to bed?"

"Is the sky wide?" I asked dryly.

Brydda threw back his head and laughed. He knew as well as I that the delicious, sweet brown powder was both scarce and violently expensive now that Sadorian ships no longer docked at Sutrium. The Sadorian tribal leaders had ruled that neither of the two precious remaining greatships would make port at the Land until Salamander ceased preying on ships that sailed into Sutrium. Their policy of nonaggression meant that they would not engage Salamander's notorious *Black Ship* in battle unless he attacked Sador, and as far as I knew, he had never even landed there. This meant that choca and other Sadorian luxuries had to be transported by the difficult coastal route or carried by smaller vessels daring or greedy enough to brave the hidden shoals close to shore, where Salamander's larger vessel could not venture.

Brewing the choca carefully, Brydda explained that it had been a gift to him from Bruna, Jakoby's headstrong daughter.

"Has she returned to the Land on horseback, then?" I asked with some surprise.

Brydda shot me an enigmatic look. "She never left. After the destruction of the *Zephyr*, when Jakoby departed by land, Bruna stayed. She has been an honored guest in Dardelan's house ever since. Bruna's mother sent the choca."

Brydda handed me the fragrant brown liquid and asked if I had brought the plast suit Dardelan requested. I nodded, explaining that it was laid flat in a special compartment constructed within the wagon's base and that, although the specially treated plast was impervious to taint over a certain period, the fabric was nonetheless very fragile. I asked openly if Dardelan meant to use it to smuggle a spy across the Suggredoon.

Brydda looked at me like Garth had. "Dardelan had thought of asking you or another coercer to swim across the river and spy for us. We had even begun planning the diversion of all diversions, but then we learned that all soldierguards guarding the other bank wear demon bands."

I stared at him in disbelief. Not long before the rebellion, the Herder priests had created demon bands to prevent Misfits from coercing or farseeking their wearers, but only upper-rank priests and a few Councilmen and soldierguard captains had ever worn them. "You can't mean that *everyone* guarding the other bank has a demon band?" I asked, thinking I must have misunderstood.

"All," Brydda repeated flatly. "You can see them when you look with a spyglass, once you know what you are looking for. Obviously, the Herders are producing and supplying them. We only knew it after Reuvan found a Port Oran man washed up on a bit of sandy shore near the mouth of the river. Some drunken soldierguards had thrown him into the sea after he had objected to their manhandling his daughter. He had drunk too much tainted water to be saved, but he told us quite a bit, about the demon bands, for instance, and that the Herders have formed an alliance with the west coast Councilmen. Of course, we guessed as much. He also said that Salamander is working openly for the Faction, or with it. He runs three smaller ships that patrol our coastline now, as well as the *Black Ship* that regularly sails between Norseland and Herder Isle and across the strait to the west coast. Salamander openly buys any prisoners in the Councilmen's cells, so he must have made some accommodation with them as well."

"Did the man say anything about the rebels?"

"Only that there are no rebels left in Port Oran or any other towns close to the Suggredoon. He did say rebels are rumored to be causing havoc higher up the coast, in Aborium and Murmroth. But things are bad over there. Food is scarce in the cities, because most of their grain and vegetables came from this side of the Suggredoon, as well as ore for their smelters. There are small farm holdings all down the coast as well as in the hills about Murmroth, but their produce is limited by the land's barrenness. The man said most people survive only by fishing, but even that is being affected by the poisons the Council spilled along the remote and unguarded portions of the coastline before our ships were burned."

"It sounds awful," I said, aghast.

"The man cursed us for the disaster our victory brought to the west coast, and then he begged us to invade and save his daughter," Brydda said grimly.

I did not need to ask if the man had already died. It was in his face. "So if even a Misfit cannot slip across the Suggredoon now, why did you ask about the plast suit?"

"Because Dardelan intends it to be worn by a spy who will swim ashore on the west coast just past the river mouth. The area is unguarded, because a rocky shelf extends a long way into the water, just under the surface, making it too shallow even for a ship boat, and no one swims there because the water is tainted."

"Whoever wears the suit will have to be very careful not to tear it on the rocks—and they will have to be a strong swimmer, because the sea around the river mouth is very wild."

"Reuvan all but has fins," Brydda said, smiling.

"Reuvan!"

"He volunteered."

"Why didn't Dardelan's messenger mention any of this?" I asked.

"Dardelan wants it kept quiet, given that the ship burnings mean we have secret enemies. Only he and I and Reuvan know about the man washed ashore, and now you. That is partly why I suggested this meeting: to tell you in person what has been happening and to make sure you brought the plast suit. Reuvan will leave as soon as he has it."

"Once ashore, what will he do?" I asked.

"Conceal the suit and make his way to Port Oran, where he will see if anything of the rebel network remains there. If there is no one, he will move from town to town up the coast. Once he makes contact with the west coast rebels, he will let them know what is happening in the Land. But his main task will be to learn what the Council is planning. Because there is no doubt in Dardelan's mind, or mine, that something is afoot, else why the demon bands? Of course, Reuvan will try to reach your people as well. That is another reason I wanted to speak with you. We need to know how to reach anyone not in communication with the rebels."

"How will Reuvan share what he learns with Dardelan?" I asked. "Will he signal over the river?"

"That would be dangerous, because he would have to get close enough to be seen from our side of the river. The best place for that would be the old ferry landing, where the banks draw closest to one another, but the soldierguards have a barricade there to keep everyone well back. And the remainder of the river is patrolled and makeshift watchtowers have been erected. The plan is that Reuvan will carry the suit back to the coast, put it on, and let the current carry him back to Sutrium. We will be watching for him, of course."

"What if the suit is damaged on his way there or if he is washed out too far? Even ships don't go out into the middle currents."

"And who told you that?" Brydda asked, straight-faced.

I sighed. "Reuvan."

"Just so. If the suit is damaged, he will find some way to signal us," Brydda said. But he looked suddenly weary, and I knew that, for all his apparent confidence, he was worried about the young seaman.

I thought again of the premonition that had assailed me earlier. "I begin to fear that we were too quick in letting people know of our refuge."

Brydda shook his head. "If you had kept your refuge secret, it would have made Landfolk even more mistrustful and suspicious of you. Take heart, for all is not ill in this new time. The Council is gone from this part of the Land, and with them, the soldierguards and Herders and their whole machinery of corruption. Good new laws are about to be established, and soon people will elect their own leaders. Of course, some still fear your kind, but many more do not, having seen clearly your loyalty during the rebellion. Do not be impatient, for the changes have begun and will continue." He lapsed into silence for a moment, then said, "When people first began to speak of the rebellion, I imagined that once the Council was gone, the Land would become a sort of paradise. But of course, it is not that simple. It will be many years before we have real stability, and no doubt there will be almost as many steps back as forward."

"You could just walk away from it all," I pointed out, once more hearing the fatigue in his voice. "No one would ever say you had not done enough."

"I would say it," Brydda said with gentle finality. "Enough is not measured by what you give but by what is needed." He reached out and took my hand in his. "Something is wrong between you and Rushton, isn't it?"

I cursed his knack of knowing what he could not know, but still the words burst out of me, low and raw. "Rushton has changed since he was imprisoned in the cloister in Sutrium. He does not remember what happened, but something is broken in him. I cannot look inside his mind to see if it can be mended, for he will not permit it. He does not want my Talent, and he does not want me. There is nothing to be done."

I looked down at Maruman, who slept on obliviously. I was glad, for my grief would have irked him.

73

"Elspeth." Brydda said my name gently, and when I looked up, I saw pity in his eyes. "Come. It is time you were asleep." He reached down, scooped Maruman into his arms, and pulled me to my feet. He led me to the bedroll Zarak had spread beneath a wagon, and I lay down, feeling suddenly utterly exhausted. Brydda placed Maruman gently beside me, and the old cat rolled close with a soft snore. He had not even awakened, and I wondered if he slept or traveled the dream-trails.

"Sleep," Brydda commanded gently, and left me. I closed my eyes, and sleep rolled over me like a soft, heavy blanket, obliterating consciousness with a gentle finality.

I dived through the cloudy swirl of memories and dreams that clamored at me in the upper levels of my mind, shielding myself until I was deep enough for them to fade into a thick brown silence. I continued to descend until I heard the siren song of the mindstream that runs at the deepest level of all minds and that contains the thoughts and memories of all minds that have ever existed. The urge to join the stream and give up my individual existence was as potent as ever, but I held myself until the pull of the mindstream was in exact balance with the pull to rise to consciousness.

I had come deep to avoid dreaming, but even as I looked down into the shimmering beauty of the mindstream, a bubble of matter detached itself and rose toward me, as shapeless and shining as air rising to the surface of the water.

The bubble engulfed me.

I saw Cassy Duprey sitting in a Beforetime flier. I

could not tell if it was the same flying machine I had seen her in before, but she looked different, subtly older. Perhaps it was just the plain dark clothes she wore, instead of the bright colors she usually favored; or maybe it was the fact that her wild mass of dark crinkling hair was restrained in a complex coil against her neck. A very beautiful, haughty-looking older woman with the same choca-toned skin as Cassy sat opposite her. A certain likeness about the facial bones suggested they were related. Could this be her mother? I wondered. She did not act like a mother, for Cassy wept, and the woman made no move to comfort her.

"What did you expect, Cassandra?" she finally asked, her tone irritated. "He was a spy."

"He might not be dead," Cassy said in a voice thick with tears and despair.

"Don't be foolish," the woman responded crisply. "Samu vanished while spying on officials in the Chinon Empire. If he is not dead, then he will wish he were."

Cassy groaned and leaned over as if she had a stomachache, her forehead pressed to her knees.

"Don't you think it is time to end this orgy of grief?" the woman said, glancing at her watch. "Samu knew the price he would pay if he was caught. He thought it was worth it. If you loved him, you might honor his choice." Her lips twisted into an ugly shape as she said the word *love*, but Cassy, head on her lap, did not see it.

"Must people always pay the worst price for doing what is right in your world, Mother?" she whispered.

The older woman glanced out the window at the sky for a long minute, her expression remote, as if she were thinking about something completely different.

Finally, she returned her gaze to her daughter. "I did not say he was doing the right thing, Cassandra. Only that he thought he was. People always think what they are doing is right. Look at your father and his Sentinel project. He and the government think it is right to put the world's fate into the hands of machines. He thinks it is responsible and mature to relinquish control of the weapons we have created. We may all pay for his doing what he thinks is right." There was a queer expression on her face, and the queerness had spread into her voice.

Cassy lifted her head and gave her mother a long, bitter look. "If you think Father is wrong, Mother, why don't you tell him so? Why don't you tell the whole world? You have the power to do that, and it would not even cost your life."

"Wouldn't it, Cassy?" her mother asked: "You think the government would allow me to criticize its pet project? You are such a child."

"What are you talking about?" Cassy demanded.

"I am talking about the real world, Cassy, where we all live. Not the world of heroic and foolish boys and girls. I chose to leave your father, because he had become a man I did not like, a man who believed in things I could not believe in. He let the world and his own fears turn him into a puppet. I can't stop what he does any more than I can stop what the government does. The best I can do is stay away from him and his world and keep you away from it. I don't want to hear any more about you going back to that place. I don't want you there again. Not ever."

"But, Mother, he has invited me, and I need . . . I mean, I want to go. It will be the last time."

Cassy's mother gave her a hard, coldly intelligent look. "Why would you want to go there again, when you resisted going there so violently in the first place, despite my having no choice but to send you?"

"I . . . I just . . . I was doing some painting there. Yes, I hated it, but I want to finish the work I began."

Her mother regarded her for a moment and then smiled. "You are lying. But I will make you a bargain. You tell me why you suddenly want to switch to the university at Newrome, and I will allow you to visit your father this one last time. But I want the truth, and I will know if you lie."

Cassy's face changed, and a peculiar expression filled her wide, almond-shaped eyes. "Do you really want to know, Mother? Because if you do, I'll show you."

Her mother frowned. "Cassandra, I have had just about enough of these childish—"

Cassy cut her off. "Remember that big splashy series of advertisements sent out by the Reichler Clinic a while back, Mother? The ones asking for anyone who thought they might have paranormal abilities to come and be tested? Well, I went—"

"But that was a hoax. There was a scandal over falsified research results. Surely you were not foolish enough—"

"Yes, there was a scandal, but it was about the man who was running it—William Reichler. He supposedly wrote a book, only he hadn't come up with the testing methods the clinic used or written the book. It was another scientist, who died. Reichler stole his work and put his own name to it. He was after money, and he got it by conning rich people into making donations, convincing them that everyone had paranormal abilities, which could be awakened with the right techniques, just as the book said. Then he was exposed and there was the scandal. But not everyone he hired was crooked. A lot of the researchers who worked for the Reichler Clinic really believed in what they were doing. So when William Reichler died, they kept the clinic running. . . ."

"The clinic was destroyed," Cassy's mother said. "Reichler burned it to cover his tracks, only he was killed before he could get away."

"William Reichler was killed. And the building that had housed the clinic at Inva was destroyed, but the Reichler Clinic is an organization, not a place. It relocated to Newrome. It is still operating."

Her mother's lips curled in disgust. "And I suppose whoever is running this place persuaded you when you visited Newrome last month that you have paranormal abilities. Cassy, will you never grow up?"

Cassy smiled. It was as cold as her mother's. I felt her mind reach out. She had fashioned a mindprobe so clumsy that it must have hurt her mother badly as it entered her mind and spoke her name. I heard the older woman gasp with pain and clutch at her head.

"Is that proof enough for you, Mother?" Cassy asked aloud. "Or are your own senses as untrustworthy as you keep telling me mine are?"

Her mother's mouth hung open. Her eyes bulged in disbelief. "You . . . what did you . . . ?"

The memory dissolved, and the mindstream sang its song to me, alluring, infinitely sweet, promising release from pain, sorrow, and desire. I dared not stay there any longer. Wrenching myself upward, I was too weary to armor myself against the strands of thought floating past. One brushed me, and all at once, I was inside the old dream of walking along a dark tunnel, hearing the drip of water into water. Ahead was the dull yellow flash, flash, flash of light, like a signal.

"Stop," said a woman's voice, beautiful and strangely loud. "Do not enter or you will die."

The shock of hearing a voice in a place where I had never before heard one woke me. I opened my eyes and found myself blinking into daylight, the dreams slipping away like dawn mist. I thought of the vision I had experienced of Cassy, weeping at her lover's death, and then of her mind forming a clumsy but powerful probe to invade her mother's mind. Clearly, Hannah Seraphim had taught her to use her Talent. Cassandra, her mother had called her. Not far from Kasanda . . .

"Get up, ElspethInnle," Maruman sent peevishly. "I am hungry."

We were on the road again by midmorning, having bade Katlyn farewell. She was to remain in Rangorn, herb gathering until Grufyyd brought down a wagon in a few days to collect her. When we left, the herbalist was tying what she, Kella, and Dragon had collected into bunches to hang up and dry.

The rest of us parted just over the ford. Kella, Dragon, and Louis Larkin set off in one wagon for Sutrium via Kinraide and Berrioc with both soldier-guards. Zarak, Darius, and I took the other wagon and went with Brydda back the way we had come, first to the Sawlney turnoff and thence to Saithwold. I had tried to convince Darius to go with the others, partly because I worried about his inflamed joints and partly to see if he might give his true reason for wanting to go to Saithwold. But he simply smiled serenely and said he would stay with us.

I rode Gahltha to begin with, but once Brydda had made his brief call at the farmstead on the Sawlney turnoff, he suggested I dull Gahltha's coat, tie him to the back of the wagon, and ride inside. "A young woman of your description riding a magnificent black stallion would be as good as a message to Vos that Elspeth Gordie is visiting Saithwold," Brydda said.

I was not sure I was as well known as Brydda seemed to think, but I did as he suggested, drawing my shawl over my head and lifting Maruman into my lap as I joined Zarak on the bench seat. Darius lay in the back. I wished again that I had managed to convince him not to come, but perhaps all Twentyfamilies gypsies regarded it as their sacred duty to check on their D'rekta's carvings whenever they had the chance.

When at last we reached the turnoff, I was surprised that there was no sign of armsmen or blockade on the smaller road, but Brydda said the blockade was not immediately visible from the main road. Sure enough, around the first bend, we came upon it: a solid barrier of planks nailed together and running from dense underbrush on one side of the road to the other. The surly looking fellow slouching before the barricade gave an unmanly squeak of fright as Sallah pranced to a stop. Brydda roared laughing, but before the red-faced man could unleash a tirade of abuse, the big rebel called out a greeting, naming him Tam Otey.

The man squinted shortsightedly at Brydda, and then his face changed. "Brydda Llewellyn, are you riding to Saithwold?" He sounded truculent, but there was alarm in his eyes.

"Will you try to stop me if I am, Tam?" Brydda asked in a mocking voice that made the other man's expression twist with anger.

"Chieftain Vos will not like that you sent no word of your visit."

"I have no wish to visit your precious chieftain, man. There are a lot more than him living in Saithwold province, though maybe he has forgotten it." Brydda's voice had a hard edge, and the other man scowled, but before he could respond, a man standing behind the barrier spoke in a cold, authoritative voice.

"No need to get shirty, Llewellyn. Tam here only asked if you intend to enter Saithwold region."

"Stovey Edensal," Brydda said flatly. "It is strange to see you here minding Vos's front door. Were you not once Malik's man?"

"Answer," the man said in a stony voice. "Do you wish to enter this region?"

"I intended to escort these good people, whom I met upon the road, to Saithwold. The lass is anxious about the rumors of brigands. But seeing how well you have the road guarded, I can leave them and return to Sutrium," Brydda said.

"We have orders to find out what they want before we let them through," Stovey Edensal said stiffly, after a slight hesitation.

Brydda nodded to Zarak. "Tell the man your names and business, lad."

"I am Zar and these are my two friends, Ella and Darius. We mean to visit my father, who works for one of the farm holders in Saithwold region," Zarak said, suppressing his highland accent.

"Is your father expecting you?" the armsman demanded.

"He is not," Zarak answered equably. "I had a missive from him some while back, and he sounded a bit low in spirits. I decided to call on my way to Sutrium to cheer him up."

"There!" Brydda said with cheerful impatience. "Neither the boy nor his companions are robbers, so you may set the barrier aside with a clear conscience."

Stovey looked from the wagon to Brydda and made a gesture with his hand. Three tough-looking armsmen emerged from each side of the bushes where they had been concealed, and my heart began to race, but all six merely set about moving the barrier to let the wagon pass. After Lo and Zade had pulled the wagon through the gap, the barrier was replaced and Zarak turned to shout thanks to Brydda for his kindness.

"You owe me a mug of good ale for my troubles," Brydda bellowed. "Look for me at the Inn of the Red Deer when you arrive on the morrow."

"We might stay a night or two with my father," Zarak called, "but I promise you'll have your ale within a fourday."

"I look forward to it," Brydda roared.

Their prepared speeches completed, I beastspoke the horses to urge them on. My last sight of the blockade was of Brydda astride Sallah, talking down to Tam Otey. He had reckoned that no one would come after us while he was watching, and it seemed he was right.

The moment we were out of sight of the blockade, the horses broke into a gallop. Maruman complained bitterly at the ride's roughness, but I ignored him. I had never been to Noviny's homestead, but I knew that his property ran along the outer edge of the Saithwold region. The entrance should not be far along the road, and with luck, we could reach it before we were pursued. At last we saw a gateway with Noviny's sigil and name painted on a metal shingle swinging from a post beside it. The gate stood open, but it was so narrow that it took a good deal of maneuvering to get the wagon through. The track beyond it was only a little wider and badly rutted, which surprised me, for Noviny had struck me as a meticulous man.

"Noviny gave my da a cottage not far from the front gate," Zarak said, looking around, but it was Darius who spotted the thatched roof that rose above the trees a little way from the entrance. A clearing at the start of the path leading to the cottage enabled the horses to draw the wagon off the track, where it would not be visible to anyone glancing into the property from the main road. I suggested we unhitch the horses and shove the wagon under a huge spreading tree with weeping branches to hide it from the sight of anyone coming along the track as well.

Zarak had to help Darius down, and when I saw his strained expression, I asked if he would not rather stay in the wagon and rest.

"It will be better for me to walk about a little," he answered, but his rigid smile alarmed me. However, there was nothing to be done immediately, and at least he could lie down in a proper bed in Khuria's cottage. Noviny might even employ a healer. With the horses' help, we shoved the carriage out of sight. I arranged branches to conceal the protruding part of the wagon while Zarak hurried off to see if his father was asleep, as neither of us had been able to farseek him. Darius lowered himself to a log with a stifled groan as I sent a general probe in the direction of Noviny's homestead. It was blocked by areas of buzzing rejection that betokened tainted earth. I remembered that the Saithwold Herders had laid caches of tainted material during the rebellion to confound the ability of Misfits to communicate with one another.

We heard footsteps and turned to see Zarak alone, a worried expression on his face. "He's nowt there, an' it looks as if nobody has lived there for some time." Anxiety strengthened his highland accent.

"He probably just shifted to the main house during the wintertime," I said soothingly. "There's too much tainted stuff about to farseek him, though." I looked at the gypsy. "Can you walk, Darius? We had better leave the wagon where it is, given the state of the track."

Gahltha offered to carry him, but when I conveyed the offer, Darius thanked him and said he would rather walk. We set off, moving slowly and leaving the horses to graze near the wagon so they could warn us if we were pursued. They would follow us up to the homestead later. Maruman lay across my shoulders in offended silence, his claws sunk in painfully deep. I kept trying to farseek the homestead, but areas of tainted resistance continued to block me. I wondered if Noviny realized how much poisoned material was strewn about his land. It ought to be cleaned up before it began to seep in and poison the groundwater. But perhaps Noviny knew about the tainted matter without having any idea how to remove it.

After a time, the sound of dogs barking filled the air.

Four great hounds with faces as ugly as Jik's friend Darga came racing down the steep, rutted road, gnashing their teeth menacingly. I beastspoke them and they stopped at once. They came to me, the lead dog whining and baring his neck in such a show of inferiority that Zarak gave me a curious look. Unlike Talented communications between humans, beastspeaking was audible to anyone with the Talent; other beastspeakers had often seen animals behave reverently or heard them address me as Innle, which was the beast word for Seeker. I had found it wiser to offer no explanation, for people were usually too shy or awed to question me. But Zarak was neither.

"Try farseeking your father again," I said quickly.

Distracted successfully, his face took on the distant focused look all farseekers acquire when they send out their minds, but after a moment, he shook his head in defeat. We walked to the top of a long slope, and there stood a graceful, low, stone homestead and a cluster of well-kept outbuildings. The front door burst open, and Khuria stepped out carrying a cudgel and frowning suspiciously. Zarak gave a relieved shout and ran to embrace his father.

Khuria was a taciturn man, but after holding his son tightly for a long moment, he looked at the three of us in open consternation. "I dinna expect ye to come here!" he said.

"The letters you sent Zarak were designed to summon us, were they not?" I said, puzzled by his reaction.

"Aye! But I dinna imagine anyone would manage to get past th' blockade. I thought the letters would bring Zarak there, an' once he'd been turned back, he'd ride to Sutrium and tell Dardelan. I fear I have brought all of ye into deadly danger." His eyes settled on Darius, whom he had never met, and Zarak introduced the beasthealer to his father. The older man greeted the gypsy with warmth; then he sobered abruptly. "I only wish I were nowt meetin' ye under such circumstances."

"Don't worry, Father," Zarak broke in eagerly. "We know what Vos is tryin' to do, and High Chieftain Dardelan knows it as well. We saw Brydda Llewellyn last night in Rangorn. He rode with us to the barricade, the only reason they let us through without a fuss. He told us Dardelan will deal with Vos after the election."

The old beastspeaker ran gnarled hands through his thinning hair. "I wish that we had only Vos's ambitions to contend with. Well, I will say nae more, fer this is Noviny's story to tell. Come inside an' ye will hear it soon enow."

I wanted to insist on some immediate answers, but I noticed that Darius was looking grayer than ever, so I held my tongue. We had barely stepped inside the door of the homestead when he fainted dead away. Zarak managed to catch him, and the young woman coming along the passage toward us commanded we carry him to a small bedchamber. Once Darius was stretched out on a bed, she examined him with a swift efficiency that marked her as a healer. Then she said, "He is very hot. I will prepare something to lower his fever." She drew a sheet over Darius's twisted form and ushered the rest of us through a well-appointed kitchen, where the staff gaped at us, and into a large round room containing a fire pit sunk deep into its center. She introduced herself abstractedly as Noviny's granddaughter, Wenda, and bade us wait while Khuria fetched her grandfather.

"I must go back and tend to your friend," she added, and left.

Somewhat dazed by the speed at which things were happening, I set Maruman down and eased off my muddy boots before lowering myself onto one of the worn embroidered cushions set around the fire pit. Maruman was already kneading one enthusiastically when Zarak joined me.

"What do ye think is the matter with Darius?" he asked.

"I don't know, but I wish I knew why Khuria looked so appalled to see us."

We heard footsteps, and the door opened to reveal Khuria and the older man I remembered as Councilman Noviny. Although the man was straight-backed and had a very direct gaze, his hair had turned snowy white, and there was a frailty about him that I had not noticed during the trials. But he smiled warmly as Khuria brought a carved chair with a very upright back and set it close to the fire. Noviny turned his eyes to the leaping flames for so long that I wondered if he had forgotten us.

Finally, I said gently, "It seems there is more trouble here than Vos wanting to win an election."

Noviny sighed and looked at me. "If Vos were wise or even sensible, he would know perfectly well that Chieftain Dardelan and the other rebels will never allow him to usurp the leadership of Saithwold. But he is vain and foolish, which has made him the perfect pawn for a true villain whose own ambition is darker than anything Vos could imagine."

My heart sank. "What villain?" I asked. But even as I said it, I thought of Brydda saying, *"Stovey Edensal . . . Were you not once Malik's man?"*

✦ 6 ✦

"Before I say anything more, I must ask how you got past the barricade," Noviny said.

I let Zarak explain, and Noviny nodded. "I thought it must have been something like that, since you could not have used your Misfit powers."

"What is going on here?" I asked. "Why was one of Malik's men guarding that barricade?"

Noviny gave me an approving look. "Stovey Edensal, I imagine. And he is manning the barricade, because he is mind sensitive to the Talents exhibited by your people. Unlike the other men there, he will not wear a demon band, for his task is to identify any Misfit attempting to use Talents to enter the region. It is sheer luck that you did not attempt to enter his mind."

"Demon bands!" I said, unable to believe I was hearing about them again so soon after Brydda had mentioned them. On the other hand, Malik and Vos had managed to get their hands on demon bands even before the rebellion. Indeed, a demon band had prevented us from realizing that Malik meant to betray us. No doubt more had been found in the abandoned Saithwold Herder cloister.

"Ye mun have noticed," Khuria now said, "that ye were unable to farseek us here."

"It is no secret that the Herders here and elsewhere in the Land made a practice of laying tainted matter and studding the tops of the cloister walls with poisoned fragments, knowing it would inhibit Misfit Talents," I said.

"That was done before the rebellion," Khuria said grimly. "But Vos's men continue doin' it. They have poisoned the region's entire perimeter as well as many fences within."

"But to what end?" I asked. "Surely not so that Vos can be reelected chieftain."

"No, although that is certainly what Vos believes," Noviny said. "Let me tell my tale from the beginning. It will be quicker and more orderly."

I stifled a feeling of impatience and nodded.

He continued. "When Vos's men began to call at homesteads in and about Saithwold before wintertime, demanding that folk pledge their votes to him in the coming elections, I thought him a fool. Once Dardelan learned what was happening, the Council of Chieftains would deal with Vos. But Vos's oppressions increased. People's letters left Saithwold only if they were not critical of the chieftain or the situation here. Vos issued a decree forbidding citizens to travel without permission because of the danger of being waylaid by brigands. Then the blockade was set up, supposedly to prevent robbers or unsavory folk from entering our region. Little by little, we realized that no one secured permission to travel and that the blockade was as much to keep us in as others out.

"It was obvious to me that the other rebel leaders would soon realize what Vos was trying to do, but I could not see Dardelan moving against him until after the election. Therefore, I advised neighbors and friends who sought my advice simply to wait. All would be put right in time.

"But having assured everyone that all would be well, I became troubled, for the dogs told Khuria of men creeping about my property. Khuria kept watch, and he saw Vos's men laying tainted caches and overheard them saying it was being done on Malik's advice. That made me very uneasy. Vos is foolish enough to suppose he could get away with forcing himself upon this region as its chieftain, but Malik would know his efforts were doomed to failure. So what was Malik up to?

"Then I heard a rumor that a second blockade had been set up on the other side of Saithwold—that is, on the road leading from the town to the cliffs. The new barricade was meant to prevent robbers creeping into the town from that direction, but I began to wonder if its true purpose might be to prevent anyone venturing near Malik's main coastal camp. Then I decided that this might be the purpose of both barricades."

"Are you trying to say that Malik does or does not want Vos to become chieftain of Saithwold?" I asked, trying to contain my impatience.

"I am saying that Vos's chieftainship and all that he has done to ensure it is irrelevant to Malik except as a distraction," Noviny answered.

There was a soft knock at the door, and Wenda and a servant entered, carrying trays laden with mugs, jugs of ale, bread and cheese, and pie. Noviny remained silent as his granddaughter and a red-faced lad laid a small table. When they had finished, Wenda assured me in her gentle voice that Darius was sleeping.

"Do you know what is wrong with him?" I asked.

She nodded. "His fever is the result of severe joint inflammation. But I am preparing some poultices that will ease him, and he will be more comfortable by to-morrow."

"I trust Wenda," Noviny said when the door closed behind his granddaughter. "But she does not know what I am about to tell you. Nor have I dared to impart it to any of my friends or neighbors or even to trusted retainers."

"Tell us," I said simply.

Noviny nodded. "As a young man, I went on long rambles about the wild parts of Saithwold, and though I am no longer young, I know this region like the back of my own hand. I announced my intention to take a ramble toward a lake I know, not far from the Sawlney border. I set off at a deliberate old man's pace, making sure any number of farmworkers and neighbors noticed me, until I reached a dense copse through which a stream flows. Within the copse, the stream cuts into a deep gorge. It appears utterly inaccessible, but I knew from my boyhood adventures that one could enter it and follow the stream to the other end of the gorge, where it emerges in thick wood not far from the coast.

"I am no longer the agile boy I once was, and it cost some effort to clamber into the gorge, but once inside, it was not hard to follow the stream. Some hours later, I came out of it and was immediately assailed by the scent of the waves. I knew well where I was, but I did not know the exact location of Malik's camp. I very nearly walked into the midst of a group of Malik's armsmen. Indeed, I would have if the wind had not brought a man's voice to me. I froze, and it was just as well, for had I taken another step, I would have tumbled into a deep hollow where Malik's men had made their camp.

"I retreated hastily and made my way carefully around the hollow until I could see into it. I was disappointed to find it was not the main camp but an outpost obviously set up to keep watch over the steps leading down to the beach below. There are three such ways up from the beach, which here is a mere strip of sand so narrow as to be invisible from above unless you are close to the cliff's edge.

"I knew I had not the strength left to find my way to Malik's proper camp, but I reasoned that if I could get close enough to these men, they might speak freely enough of their master's affairs to confirm my suspicions. I walked up the coast until I could no longer see the camp, and I crawled along the edge of the cliff using the sea grass as cover until I was near the camp. I could go no further without crossing the stone steps that go down to the beach, but when I lay still, I could hear the conversation quite well.

"I do not know what made me look down. Maybe I wanted to be sure I was not too close before I settled myself properly to listen, but what I saw gave me so great a shock that I nearly cried out."

"What did ye see?" Zarak whispered.

"A ship," Noviny said grimly. "Anchored so close to the beach that it must have been in danger of running aground. Men were rowing a ship boat toward the beach, and a group of Herders got out when it was dragged up. Malik and some of his armsmen came across the sand to meet them. They must have been waiting at the base of the cliff, out of my sight. Several of the priests heaved wooden crates from the boat and set them on the sand,

and then Malik and the priests held a long conversation. It was clear that this was not their first meeting, and eventually Malik's men took up the crates and the Herders hustled some of the people who had come with Malik into the ship boat. I had not noticed before, but now I saw that they were not only men but women and children. And they were roped together."

"Slaves?" Zarak hissed in disbelief.

Noviny nodded. "I believe that the poor wretches were farmers and their families and servants, taken by Malik's men in the guise of brigands before their land and homesteads were burned to make it seem they had been killed. I have no doubt they were given to Salamander. It was dreadful to lie there and know I could not help them. At last the ship boat was rowed away while Malik and his men carried the crates toward the steps. Fortunately, they were heavy, and Malik and his men were concentrating so hard on them that they angled straight across to the camp without even glancing in my direction.

"I dared not move as the afternoon wore on, and after Malik rode off with a couple of his captains, night fell and the armsmen lit a fire and cooked their supper. Still I lay there, hungry, thirsty, cramped. I was too stiff now to crawl backward, and I knew I must wait until it was dark enough to stand without being seen. The wind blew in from the sea, so I could hear little conversation, but I had heard enough talk between Malik and his men during that long afternoon to know that he had made a pact with the Herders to allow and aid a secret invasion."

"An invasion!" I echoed incredulously.

Noviny looked grim. "Finally, it began to rain, which put out the cooking fires and drove the armsmen into their tents, giving me my opportunity. I got up and hobbled away, praying no one would look out and see me.

"It was a difficult trip back here. By the time I arrived home, I was fevered. For days I was ill, and Wenda and the servants feared that I had stumbled into a tainted trap on my ramble. It was fortunate they thought so, for this was the tale that traveled into town, which Vos would have heard and passed on to Malik."

A faint smile crossed his crumpled features. "I daresay our chieftain hoped I would perish and was much disappointed when I did not. I have taken care since to seem permanently weakened by what happened, to assuage his jealousy. In truth, the adventure did take something from me that I have not managed to regain."

He sighed. "Since that time, my sole concern has been how to get word of the invasion to the Council of Chieftains." He shook his head. "I could not leave Saithwold, nor send a message clear enough to be useful. Sevendays passed and then winter was upon us.

"In desperation, I confided in Khuria, thinking he could communicate with one of his beast friends and ask them to carry a message to Obernewtyn. But none of the beasts could safely cross the poisoned perimeter. At last he suggested scribing letters to his son that would not mention our plight at all but would be so uncharacteristic that his boy would seek him out."

Noviny looked at Zarak. "We expected you to be turned back at the blockade. Khuria believed you would then return to Obernewtyn and seek the aid of your master, who would ride out with coercer-knights only to find they were unable to penetrate the region with their abilities. Again they would be turned back at the barricade, but they would have discovered that the armsmen guarding it wore demon bands. This would prompt the Master of Obernewtyn to ride to Sutrium and demand that Dardelan investigate what was happening in Saithwold. It was an unwieldy plan, but we could devise no other."

"The last thing we expected was that you would manage to get through the blockade with a sick man an' the guildmistress of the farseekers, and you would be trapped here, too," Khuria said gruffly.

"We came knowing something was wrong and accepting the risk," I said firmly, and I explained my encounter with the tavern woman. Noviny took the note she had scribed, smoothed it out, and read the name and address upon it. Then he nodded.

"Lacent Ander," he said. "I know her, and her husband, Rale. I will see this note is taken to her, but I fear that you will be unable to make good your promise to bring a letter out for her sister. Like Khuria, I must apologize for having dragged you into danger."

"You are right in guessing that Dardelan will do nothing before the election," I said, "but if he adopts Zarak's suggestions about how to deal with Vos, he and a group of other chieftains and their armsmen and women will arrive in Saithwold without warning on the day of the voting, ostensibly to celebrate. There will be too many to forbid entry, and the minute Dardelan rides in, I will farseek him to let him know what Malik is about."

"I'm afraid that will be too late," Noviny said grimly. "You see, the invasion is to happen before the election. Malik spoke of the timing with great amusement."

I mastered a surge of panic, realizing this was what had lain behind the premonition I had experienced in Rangorn. "All right. Then we have to do something ourselves to stop the invasion. You said there are steps down to a small beach? Are they narrow steps such as outside Arandelft, which will not allow two men to walk abreast?"

Noviny nodded. "Narrower and steeper, but there are three sets of steps along the Saithwold coastline, and I don't know which the invaders will use."

"Then we will keep watch over all of them. Surely every man and woman in the region will help, especially if you ask it."

"Guildmistress, you do not realize how things are in Saithwold province these days," Noviny said. "We live under constant surveillance by Vos's men. Even movement from one farm to another is regarded suspiciously unless it is a regular event. If a person visits another unexpectedly, he is like to be brought before Vos for questioning. And Vos reports everything to Malik, who has camps of his men right along the stretch of coastline from the road to Sador down to the end of Saithwold province, because his men are supposed to be guarding it. Even if we could muster a force without it being discovered, how are farm holders, however brave and strong, to deal with the likes of Malik's men? For that is who they would have to fight before they could even begin to think of defending the beach steps."

I scowled at the fire. "I am a fool. I had forgotten about Malik's part in this."

"He is not a man who can be overlooked," Noviny said wearily. "You can be sure that Stovey Edensal will soon be riding to report that three people in a wagon escorted here by Brydda Llewellyn managed to enter the province."

"One thing I dinna understand," Zarak said. "What

sort of invasion can priests mount? They are nowt warriors, after all. Will they command Malik's force, or will
they bring soldierguards from the west coast?"

"There was no talk of Councilmen or the west coast
in what I heard," Noviny said. "As far as I can understand, this is a Herder invasion. But those sent will certainly be warrior priests."

"Warrior priests . . . ," I echoed, some memory nag-
ging at me.

Noviny nodded. "You say that priests are not warriors, lad, but there have always been priests trained to
fight. There was a name they called themselves, but I
do not recall it. A number of them inevitably accompanied the higher cadre priests as honor guards when
they came to the cloister here. Having seen them practice, I do not doubt their skill.

"And while it is true that initially these warrior
priests were just a small force within the priesthood,
even before the rebellion, that was starting to change.
The head priest of Saithwold—a Nine and a proud,
cold man—often spoke disparagingly of the Faction's
soldierguards. More than once he implied that his masters were growing weary of spending their coin on the
temporary loyalties of soldierguards. Once, he said that
a soldierguard was a cur whereas a warrior priest was
intelligent, courageous, and loyal unto death to the
Faction's principles and ideals. When I admired their
discipline after seeing the warrior priests exercise, the
Nine told me that they trained on Norseland under the
most stringent conditions," he said.

"Warrior priests . . . ," I muttered again, and then I
remembered. Domick had mentioned warrior priests
several times in the last garbled messages before his

disappearance, and I was sure that he had even mentioned a vast training camp, though he had not said it was on Norseland. I could see that Faction leaders would much prefer fanatical warrior priests, who did not have to be bought, to soldiers for hire, and it made sense that, having fled the Land, they would do all they could to increase their numbers against future need. An army of their own kind would free them from having to rely on or accommodate anyone outside the Faction. And, of course, they would have at their disposal all the young novices and acolytes from the abandoned cloisters in the Land.

"Do you think the west coast Councilmen know anything about this invasion?" I asked.

"I have thought much about this. I think the Herders did not warn the Councilmen this side of the Suggredoon about the rebellion, because they wanted them to be defeated. And I think they warned the Councilmen on the west coast, not because they favored them but to ensure that we did not take over the whole Land. They were practicing a strategy called *divide and conquer.* They knew they had not strength enough to confront the east and west coast Council and its legion of soldierguards, so they allowed the rebels to defeat them in this part of the Land. The rebellion thus had the effect of producing two lesser powers, each in control of one part of the Land, with the added advantage that each saw the other as the primary enemy. That has left the Herders free to develop a force and play their own secret game."

"But how does Malik fit into this?" Zarak asked.

Noviny shrugged. "I have no doubt he has been offered wealth and the sort of power he yearns for in the

Land, after the Faction reclaims it. Remember, he failed to be voted high chieftain, and he is now about to face a trial here for his betrayal of your people."

A chill slipped down my spine at the realization that, in coming to Saithwold, I had put myself within the reach of Malik, who hated me. I was about to ask how many knew that Khuria was a Misfit, when Zarak asked, "But how did the Herders get to Malik in the first place?"

" 'Tis my guess he signaled the ships and offered to betray the rebels, lad," Khuria said. "He was in the perfect position to do it without anyone kenning it. But it might also be that someone here got to him and made him an offer, fer it is well kenned that he loathes Misfits an' Dardelan's championing of ye. Then there is th' Beast Charter."

"Are you sure that the west coast is not involved in the invasion?" I asked, thinking of Maryon's prediction of trouble in the west.

"I do not doubt it," Noviny answered. "The Councilmen see the Herders as allies, and the Faction would encourage that. Not only can the Herders control Council activities to some extent but they can also make sure no pact or truce is made between the west coast Councilmen and the rebels here. But rest assured that when they are ready, the Faction will dispense with both the Council and the rebels and take control of all the Land themselves."

Zarak leapt to his feet. "I am sorry to interrupt, but, Guildmistress, ye said we would have to wait until the election before anyone would come here. Yet what of the Master of Obernewtyn? Surely the moment he arrives in Sutrium for the ceremony to celebrate the new Charter of Laws, finds ye absent, an' hears what Brydda says, he will ride here with the coercer-knights. And I dinna think they will be turned away, for even if they cannot use their Talents against men wearing demon bands, they are skilled fighters. It will be nothing fer them to overcome those louts guarding the barricade."

In that moment, Zarak reminded me of Matthew, who had been much given to notions of romantic rescues. But I knew that the last thing Rushton would do when he discovered my absence would be to ride to Saithwold. He would accept Dardelan's decision that matters be left as they were until the elections and be relieved that I was not in Sutrium. Grief and desolation clawed at me, but I stifled them and said aloud that we dared not wait and hope to be rescued. Too much was at stake. Then I stopped, realizing that I had no more idea than Noviny how to stop the invasion. After an uncomfortable silence, Noviny sighed and suggested we eat.

I took little food, my appetite gone, but Zarak had heaped his plate high, and between mouthfuls he said, "I can nowt believe Malik has made this bargain after he fought to free the Land."

Noviny said wearily, "I think he fought, as many do, not to rid the Land of oppression but to create a situation in which he could gain power. Instead, he is to be tried for betraying your people. So not only does he stand to gain the power he wants from the Faction, but he will also take revenge on the rest of us."

"It will not come to that," I said through gritted teeth. "We will get a message to Sutrium."

"How?" Zarak asked eagerly.

"I am not sure yet," I admitted. I looked at Noviny and asked, "Is it common knowledge here that Khuria is a beastspeaker?"

Noviny shrugged. "It was clear from the beginning that Vos would torment any Misfit in this region, so we never spoke of it openly; however, there are many who probably harbor suspicions."

"Okay," I said. "Now, who normally shops for your household?"

"Wenda and one of the servant girls take a small cart into town once every sevenday," the older man answered, looking perplexed.

"If you will permit it, then, tomorrow Wenda will take me to town to see what patent medicines are available for my crippled companion. Better to act as if we are innocents who got into the region by chance."

"You will be harassed by Vos's armsmen, if they do not insist on taking you to him. And they will all wear demon bands, so you will not be able to prevent it," Noviny warned.

"I *want* them to take me to him, because I assume that is where Vos's men live as well. If I can reach a single armsman, I can impose a coercive command to remove his band whenever a certain control word is spoken. That means I can get to him later and coerce him to help us spread the word to Dardelan and the others. I will also do my best to stop anyone regarding us as a threat, by playing the innocent fool. Just one thing: Is Malik like to be there?"

Noviny shook his head decisively. "Malik rarely enters the town, and I doubt very much he will be at Vos's property. His plans require him to stay very much in the background at this stage. But you can be sure he will demand a full report from Vos."

"Will Vos not recognize you?" Zarak asked.

"I think the chance is slim, because Vos is the sort of

man who does not look at anyone properly, especially not those he believes are his inferiors. But just in case," I added, "I will change my appearance."

I retired early that night, more to think than anything else, for I was wide awake. I kept turning over and rejecting plans, occasionally getting up to gaze out the window at the dark wood behind the homestead and wonder what had become of Maruman. He had stalked off in a rage when I told him that he could not accompany me to town, refusing to listen when I explained that if I carried him on my shoulder, I might as well put up a sign announcing myself as a Misfit. Gahltha had told me not to worry, saying he would go and find the old cat, but neither had returned, and now I worried about both of them.

My mind shifted to Zarak's touching certainty that the Master of Obernewtyn would ride to my rescue. Absurd and impossible as it was, I wished it were so. But Rushton would not come. It was not that he hated me or wished me harm; it was only that he no longer loved me or wanted to be near me.

Why, I wondered bleakly, was it so much more hurtful to love him hopelessly now than before I had known that he cared for me? I cursed myself and turned over, forcing my mind back to the problem of sending a message from Saithwold about the invasion. It was deep in the night before I finally slept.

I dreamed I was walking along a wharf toward a knot of people. There were men and women and boys, all roped together. *Slaves*, I thought, recognizing the wharf, though it was not the one in Sutrium.

What am I doing here? I wondered. Then one of the slaves turned and I recognized his face. It was Matthew, but he was a boy again. It was a memory dream.

"Elspeth!" Matthew farsent urgently. "Ride on past, fer Obernewtyn's sake!"

I beastspoke Gahltha, asking him to slow down and pretend lameness, and then I slipped to the cobbles, pretending to examine his hooves. On one level, I knew that I was dreaming of my last moments with Matthew, but another part of me was in that moment, desperately measuring the distance to Matthew, trying to see the lock on his shackles and calculate how long it would take to unlock it, mount Gahltha with him, and gallop away. The nearest soldierguards were close—one carried a short sword, and two held bows in their hands; all of them were wary and alert. Perhaps I could coerce them into fumbling or even into not seeing me move.

"It's no good," Matthew sent, resolution and despair in his mindvoice. "Ye mun let 'em take me."

"Matthew, they're taking you away on a ship!"

"I ken it," Matthew sent calmly. "An' ye'll let them because we are outnumbered. I'm nowt afraid. . . . I love ye, Elspeth. I'm sorry about Dragon. . . ."

His mental voice faded as he walked over the gangplank, over the water.

"Matthew!" I sent in anguish. The cry, coming from the self who had lived through that awful parting and the self who now dreamed of it, was so strong that it catapulted me out of the memory dream. I had the sensation of falling through darkness, and suddenly I was on a steep stony road following a line of men with picks and other digging implements hoisted over their shoulders. The man directly in front of me turned, and

I gasped, for I saw that it was Matthew, but now he was a grown man. I had dreamed of him like this before, but the dream had never felt so real. At the same time, I was very conscious that I was not present in the dream, save as a watcher, for though his eyes seemed to search mine, I knew he could not see me. A man ahead called out to ask him what the matter was.

"It's nowt," he answered, turning away from me. "I thought I heard someone shout my name."

A hand grapsed my shoulder, shaking me gently.

"Matthew?" I mumbled.

"Guildmistress, I am sorry to disturb ye." It was Zarak, looking pale and excited. He whispered, "I have an idea I mun tell ye."

I sat up and shook my head, my mind still full of the dream, which had begun as a memory and then turned into something else when I cried out Matthew's name.

"What time is it?" I rasped, gathering my wits.

"Just before dawn." The farseeker leaned forward in his eagerness. "I have been thinking that Malik's betrayal could be made to serve us. If we let the Herders land an' disembark their force, rather than trying to stop them, we could commandeer their ships. Just think of it! With a ship, we could gan to the west coast immediately, rather than waiting months and months for the new ships to be finished!"

I blinked at him, trying to take in his suggestion.

"There is no way the west coast Councilmen could be prepared for an attack so soon," he continued. "And if they are not involved in plans for this invasion, they might not even ken it is happening. Seeing Herder ships approach, they will assume they came from

Herder Isle. We could land in their midst before they realized it."

My mind raced ahead, seeing further possibilities. If we took possession of the Herder ships and captured the west coast, I could then petition Dardelan to send a ship to the Red Queen's land, restore Dragon to her kingdom, and free her people, free Matthew, and find whatever it was that Cassy had left there for me.

"It is a good thought," I said. "The only problem is that we would have to allow ourselves to be invaded to get the ships. We would need a force ready and waiting to capture the invaders, which means getting word out to the other chieftains."

"We *have* to find a way," Zarak said.

"If we are fortunate, I will learn something today that will help us. Now go away and let me get dressed. I will see you in the kitchen."

After he had departed, I sluiced myself with cold water, dried, and dressed, wrinkling my nose at the stale smell of my shirt. Despite the hour, everyone was up and eating firstmeal when I entered the kitchen.

We spoke of Vos and his ambitions, and of Darius's health. Then I announced that I wanted to go and see what kind of patent medicines the town had. Wenda nodded, saying that her grandfather had mentioned my desire to go into town and that she would take me. Then she asked apologetically if I would like to borrow a skirt and shirt of hers. I accepted with alacrity, knowing that her demure style would make me look quite different if I dressed my hair to suit. Besides, her offer told me I probably smelled worse than I realized. We could stop at the wagon on our way back from town so I could collect a change of clothes.

After firstmeal, Wenda brought an armful of dresses, shirts, and jackets to my room, and eventually I emerged wearing a narrow gray skirt, a yellow shirt, and pale green jacket, my long hair braided and pinned into a bun at my neck. Before we departed, I visited Darius, who was eating from a tray and looking a good deal less frail than upon our arrival. I waved away his apologies for his collapse and briefly related what Noviny had told us. He agreed we must get word of the invasion to Sutrium at all costs, though to my disappointment, he had no more idea than I how this might be done.

Despite my impatience, it was midafternoon before Wenda and I were traveling along the main road to the township in a little, open two-seater cart pulled by Gahltha. He had refused to let me go to the town alone. Touched by his devotion, Wenda had suggested that he pull the cart.

It was a gray day with low dark clouds, and feeling a spit of moisture, I glanced at the sky apprehensively, aware that rain would render me unable to coerce anyone without physical contact. Wenda was a peaceful companion, for she spoke little, but instead of making plans, I began to worry about Malik. Noviny had assured me that the rebel chieftain seldom entered the town, but in my experience, those things you most passionately wish not to occur have a way of happening.

As we approached the town, I could see stores lining either side of what was effectively one long, empty street. In other times, the wares from those stores had spilled onto these same verandas on long trestle tables, and other sellers had sold food and drink to a cheerful throng of people from tables in front of the verandas. Now, both street and veranda were so empty that the town looked deserted. But there were people about. I noticed one man standing against a wall and another leaning over a balcony, armsmen wearing Vos's colors. We passed yet another one fletching arrows and whetting the edge of his short sword. Another lounged on a step smoking, a cudgel laid across his knees. All of them watched us pass without smiling, and my skin rose into gooseflesh, for each time I tried to probe one, I encountered the buzzing resistance that told me they wore demon bands.

Although I could see smoke dribbling from more than one chimney, there was no sign of life in the houses built between the stores, save the occasional movement behind a curtain. At last we reached the cluster of stores and businesses at a crossroads that was the heart of the town. Wenda eased back on the reins, and Gahltha drew up obediently to the hitching post. She climbed down gracefully from the carriage and gathered up her shawl and basket. I followed, feeling awkward in the skirt's unfamiliar narrowness. I wished that I was wearing my own comfortable clothes, but it was just as well to present a picture of feminine helplessness for the watching armsmen to report back to their masters. Certainly, no description they would give could evoke in anyone's mind the name of Elspeth Gordie.

We had just entered the store when it began to rain. My heart sank, but then I realized it did not make any difference, for I could not probe any of the armsmen. The store was the good solid sort at the center of any small town. Shelves all about the walls were piled with various goods, but there were also many empty shelves. No doubt it was difficult to amass stock when everything coming in and out of the region had to be brought by people approved by Vos. Several tables in the shop's center were heaped with bolts of cloth, ribbons, and ropes; bottles of buttons and other fittings; cards of needles; and several shining sets of scissors. Presumably, this pretty display had been set up to divert attention from the half-empty shelves.

"Good day, Mistress Arilla," Wenda said to the woman behind the counter.

"Good day, Wenda," the woman responded crisply. "I am afraid our supplies have not come in from Sutrium yet."

"I only want flour and salt, Arilla, though my friend here wishes to see your patent medicines." Her tone was reserved, and I had the sense that both of them were playing a part. Then I realized that the woman's restraint arose from my presence.

"What is your ailment, lady?" she asked.

"I am not ill," I said, adopting a fussy and overly cultured lowland accent. "It is my friend who has need of medicines. He is crippled and his joints have become badly inflamed on our journey. It is very tiresome, for we had meant to go on almost at once to Sutrium." I sighed. "It is quite likely we will have to remain in Saithwold for a sevenday or more, unless you have some elixir that can help."

The woman flicked a glance at Wenda, no doubt wondering why she did not offer her own herbal lore. This spurred me to add, "Wenda has offered various herbs, but I am not a great believer in herbal lore, if you will forgive me for saying so, my dear," I prattled. Wenda's face showed no emotion, so the woman indicated a case of brown bottles. Labels about the neck of each bottle had the benefits of its contents scribed on them, and I went over and pretended to read them.

"What will you have, Mistress Wenda?" asked the shop woman again in a cool, flat voice.

"Just a small measure of salt and some flour, if you please, Mistress Arilla," Wenda said.

"We have only rough-ground flour, I am afraid. Will that do?"

"It will have to do," Wenda sighed. She addressed me then. "Have you found anything that might ease your friend's sickness?"

"I am not sure if these medicines will do," I said in a querulous voice.

"What he needs most is rest," Wenda said, pretending impatience. "I can mix a tisane that will do him more good than those patent medicines."

I gave her a bothered look and joined her at the counter. The storewoman put the flour down by the smaller parcel of salt, and Wenda paid her out of a thin purse. We crossed to the door and opened it to find that it was now pouring. I pulled up my coat collar and walked out onto the veranda, only to have an armsman step into my path. He was a big powerful-looking man with thinning brown hair gone to pepper and salt and shrewd blue eyes in a face that I might have liked, had he not worn Vos's colors.

"Ye mun be one of them the Black Dog escorted to the barricade yesterday," he said. "Are ye aware that ye neglected to mention whose property ye were visiting?"

"Why should I have mentioned it?" I snapped before remembering I was supposed to be frivolous and silly.

The man frowned, but I thought there was amusement in his eyes. "Th' men at the barricade were supposed to ask ye. But nivver mind that now. I see by yer companion where ye're stayin'." He gave a mocking bow, rain spilling from the brim of his hat. "I am Kevrik, armsman to Chieftain Vos who governs this settlement, charged with learning the names of the newcomers to Saithwold."

"I am Ella," I lied haughtily. "And now if you will be so good as to stand aside, we wish to leave."

The armsman stepped aside, and Wenda came out onto the veranda beside me, closing the door behind her. She gave the armsman a brief cool look before going to the carriage and thrusting her basket into the sheltered space beneath the seat. Then she climbed up and swiftly unraveled a sheet of waxed cotton over her head to serve as a makeshift cover. She beckoned to me, but the man caught my arm. "I assume they also neglected to mention at the barricade that it is the custom for all who enter Saithwold province to pay their respects to its chieftain?" He spoke loudly to be heard over the rain.

"If the manners of those louts at the blockade are anything to judge by, I can understand why your chieftain must order himself up guests," I said tartly. Before he could respond, I added, "But custom you said. Did you mean that a visit to your chieftain is a courtesy or a law?"

"Dinna ye think a courtesy ought to be observed as strictly as if it were a law?" Kevrik asked mildly.

"Courtesies are best preserved in free air, I think," I snapped. "However, you may tell your chieftain that I will wait upon him tomorrow or the next day. There can be no rush, since we are delayed by my friend's illness."

I tried to pull my arm free of his grip, but he kept a firm hold of me, saying, "Ye mun wait upon Chieftain Vos now, my lady."

110

"I cannot force Wenda to journey with me in this rain, and I need to take some medicine back to my friend," I protested.

The highlander nodded. "Then it is simple. Wenda will return to Noviny's homestead with the medicine for yer companion, an' I will take you to pay your respects to the chieftain."

I scowled, looking down to hide my elation at the thought of being taken exactly where I wanted to go. Ironically, Wenda insisted that if I must face Vos, she would accompany me. The rain having abated, I coerced her into agreeing to leave without me, and then I had Gahltha to contend with for he refused to obey Wenda when she tried to leave. I laid my hand on his warm wet neck under the pretext of calming him, hoping I could buy myself enough time to convince Gahltha not to make a scene.

"I warned you this would happen," I sent him.

"You said you would be taken to see this chieftain. You did not say you would go alone," he sent.

"I must go with this man willingly, or he will force me," I sent.

"I will not allow him to harm you," Gahltha sent wrathfully, shifting angrily so that the small cart creaked and tilted.

"Be still, my dear," I bade him. "It is not only him. There are many other armsmen in these streets, with knives and arrows and clubs. If you fight, you and the girl will be hurt, and still they will take me. Let me go with him now, and I promise that I will soon return."

I could feel his anger fade into resignation. He said dryly, "Maruman/yelloweyes will be furious, for he made me promise not to leave you."

"I fear that is true," I sent, suddenly conscious that the armsman had returned and was watching me. I pretended to adjust the bridle. "Now, let me go and I will come as soon as I can."

Kevrik hurried me along the muddy street to a covered wagon and gestured for me to climb up to the seat. Then he climbed up beside me. "I've nivver seen that horse before. It's yours, en't it?"

I hesitated, and, irritatingly, he took this as an admission. "I thought so. Yer one of them beastspeakers, aren't ye? Like the old Misfit that serves Noviny." His eyes widened. "That's who th' boy who came with ye is kin to! An' I suppose he is a beastspeaker, too."

My heart sank at the realization that Noviny had been wrong in thinking that Khuria's Talent might be a secret. The only consolation was that Kevrik had only just connected me to Khuria, so neither Vos nor Malik would know yet that Zarak and I were Misfits. That meant I had a little time to maneuver. Being identified as a beastspeaker would make Vos less likely to realize who I really was.

"Two of use are beastspeakers. Our crippled friend is not a Misfit," I said at last. "And none of us owns the horse. He is my friend, and I had to beastspeak him because he was refusing to leave me with you."

"He dinna want to leave ye," Kevrik marveled, shaking his head in wonder. He took up the reins purposefully. I squinted at his horse's neck and, to my astonishment, saw the glimmer of a demon band. Kevrik made the sort of chucking noise used by men who have no other means of reaching the mind of a horse, and the copper horse set off at a sedate canter.

112

⋆ 7 ⋆

"THIS HORSE IS wearing a demon band," I said, suddenly glad there was no need to pretend I was not a beastspeaker. We had left the town behind, and a wall of thick forest ran along either side of us, broken by the occasional gate leading to a road that must wind its way to a farmstead.

Kevrik shot me a look. "I suppose ye tried to communicate with her."

I struggled against outrage and lost. "It is barbaric that you put a demon band on a beast without asking if it agrees to accept the danger."

"Danger? What are ye blatherin' about, lass?" the armsman asked.

I stared at him, wondering if it was possible that he and all the other armsmen wearing demon bands did not know that tainted matter gave the devices their power and that it would eventually penetrate the metal tubing and poison the wearer's bones and blood. Then it occurred to me that Garth had only warned us about the dangers of the demon bands in guildmerge just before wintertime; how would those here have learned of it?

I drew in a sharp breath, suddenly realizing that the heavy crates Noviny had seen the Herders deliver to Malik had probably been filled with demon bands.

"Tell me what ye meant by sayin' demon bands are dangerous," Kevrik prompted.

"They cause wasting sickness," I said, careful not to reveal that I knew he and the other armsmen wore demon bands, for how should a beastspeaker know that?

"That's a lie," Kevrik said sharply, his hand going unwittingly to his collar. "You see for yourself that the mare is not sick."

I shrugged. "Demon bands are no more than metal tubes encasing matter taken from the Blacklands. The taint will not hurt immediately, just as it does not kill a man immediately to walk on tainted Blacklands. The sickness comes later when the bones crumble and the flesh wastes from them. The demon bands take longer, because the taint is much weaker and has to seep through the metal casing."

I glanced away into the dense wood at the roadside, and said, "But surely your chieftain has told you of the danger?" I pretended not to notice the armsman's blank face and added, "Unless . . . Can it be that Chieftain Vos does not know the demon bands contain tainted matter?"

Still the armsman said nothing, and I went on as if musing to myself. "I guess he found a supply of them in the abandoned cloister and thought to use them to prevent Misfits from manipulating his mind. But surely the Herders did not leave demon bands for horses?"

From the corner of my eye, I saw Kevrik's brow crease, and I wondered where he and the other men imagined the horses' demon bands had come from. And what had Malik told Vos to explain the appearance of demon bands big enough for horses? Kevrik shifted uncomfortably on the seat beside me, and I guessed with satisfaction that he itched to wrench the demon band from his neck, but he had probably been ordered to wear it at all times.

The road we had been traveling along was the same one that turned from the main road to Sutrium, but now we came to a place where the road forked. One way led to the coast and the other turned down toward Sutrium. Kevrik took the latter, and I said, "Wenda mentioned that there is a second blockade this side of the town. I suppose it is on the other road?" Kevrik said nothing, so I went on as if he had answered. "Why do you need a barricade this side of town? How many brigands will dare to come along the coast with Malik's watch camps set up all along it to make sure the Herder ships don't come in to land?"

I watched the armsman closely from the corner of my eye, because although I could not reach his mind to read it, I still had eyes to see a start or a look of guilt that would tell me Kevrik knew about Malik's bargain. But he only said distractedly, "The brigands are insidious, and it is just as like that they would take a secretive route."

He might believe that, I thought, or maybe he knew that Malik's men were the brigands and had decided to hold his tongue. Or perhaps he simply thought the second barricade was making sure that none of the region's inhabitants could leave to report Vos to the Council of Chieftains. But could he really be so foolish as to imagine that Vos would get away with oppressing the people he was supposed to represent and lead?

My mind turned to Vos. If he had been any other rebel leader, I might have tried telling him the truth about Malik's treachery and the pending invasion, but

Vos would undoubtedly go straight to Malik to report what he had been told.

"How . . . how long does it take for a demon band to cause harm . . . to a horse," Kevrik asked, somewhat jerkily, and I realized he had hardly been listening to anything I had said since I had mentioned the taint inside the demon bands.

I had to work to keep triumph from my voice when I answered. "I am not sure, but given that a horse is flesh and blood, as we are, it would take the same time as for a man. That is several months. Of course, that would depend on whether it had been worn constantly or not. A horse cannot take the band off at will, as a man can." I did not quite succeed in hiding a renewed jab of anger.

Kevrik said, "Vala is my horse and I care for her, no matter that you beastspeakers think yer the only ones to have any love fer beasts."

"We love them as friends and fellow beings. You love this mare as a possession," I said coldly. Before he could say anything, I added, "But if you love her in any way, you will remove the band as often as possible."

There was a long silence, and then he said, "Is it true some of you Misfits can enter a person's mind even if they are nowt near?"

"Some Misfits can. It is called *farseeking*, but usually farseekers only communicate with other Misfits who have that ability. To farseek someone with no Talent is more difficult," I added. In fact, it required both farseeking and coercive abilities to manage it, but I did not say so, because the perception among many un-Talents was that a Misfit could have only one ability, and it was always better to be underestimated by enemies. "But why do you care?" I asked. "We Misfits have given our word to the Council of Chieftains not to use our powers on any person, save those who are enemies and wish harm to us."

The wagon slowed as we drew near a wide gate with ornate carved posts, and I knew we had reached Vos's homestead when the mare turned into it so willingly.

"What if ye suspected harm was intended but could nowt be sure? Would a Misfit wait to see or penetrate a man's mind to find out if he was an enemy?" Kevrik asked once the wagon was through the gate.

"In such a circumstance, that Talent would be as a weapon. You might take out that knife in your sheath, if you thought a robber was stalking you. But you would not use it on him until you were certain he was a villain."

He nodded and said nothing more until we came in sight of another gate. This one led to a cobbled courtyard surrounded by fenced enclosures and various barns and outbuildings. Set back from these, in the midst of a smooth lawn, was a large rambling farmhouse with wide stone steps leading to a veranda and an ornate front door between two fluted stone columns. Kevrik stopped the carriage on the cobbles, then bade me wait while he announced my arrival to his master. It was again raining, but lightly, as he ran to the house, so I climbed down from the carriage and went to the mare. Despite being in contact, the band would not let me reach her mind, and I gazed into her long face and gentle eyes, wondering if she could tell I was the Seeker or whether that knowledge would only come to her when our minds touched. I murmured soft nonsense to her, and she put her ears forward in a friendly alert fashion that suggested Kevrik had probably spoken the truth when he said he cared for her.

I examined her face and neck and listened to her heart, but there was no sign of the wasting sickness. The hair on her coat was not even rubbed under the demon band, which suggested that she had not worn it long. The catch was a simple hook, and only the fact that the mare was yet unhurt kept me from it—that and the certainty that Kevrik would remove the horse's band and his own as soon as he could.

The front door opened, and a group of armsmen spilled from the homestead into the rainswept yard.

"What were you doing to the horse, Misfit?" demanded one of the armsmen brusquely.

"I wanted to see if she showed any sign of wasting sickness," I said truthfully. This was greeted with blank silence, which told me that although Kevrik had obviously reported that I was a beastspeaker, he had not mentioned what I had said about the demon bands. I said, "It is caused by demon bands if they are worn too long."

The anger in one or two faces gave way to apprehensive expressions, but most burst into rough laughter or jeered in disbelief. "Do not think to trick us into taking our bands off, Misfit," said one man in a mocking voice. "We are not the fools you take us for."

I widened my eyes innocently. "You are wearing them, too?" Before any of them could speak, I asked, "Where is your chieftain? I have come to pay my respects to him." I turned and marched across the yard to the door and through it. The armsmen, clearly sent to force me hence, crowded hurriedly after me, muttering and treading on one another's toes.

The front door led unexpectedly straight into an enormous front parlor. Here, rather absurdly, Vos sat upon an ornate chair on a raised dais. He wore a demon band that had been polished and set with jewels, his collar laid back so that it could be clearly seen. I wondered waspishly how he would feel when he realized what a pretty death it was. His narrow-jawed face made him look more ratlike than ever, despite his fine red-dyed robes and oiled hair. He observed me with such exaggerated disdain that I knew he hardly saw me at all for admiring his own posturing.

"What is your business in this region, Misfit?" he demanded in his thin bullying voice.

I made an exaggerated bow that anyone less arrogant would have perceived as a mockery, and said, "Good day, Chieftain Vos. My name is Ella. I am a Misfit but I prefer you to call me beastspeaker." Vos reddened with anger, but before he could think what to say, I went on smoothly. "As to what I am doing here, that is nothing more than an accident." I gave a light laugh. "You see, I was traveling to Sutrium when my friend Zarak expressed a desire to see his father, the beastspeaker Khuria who serves Sirrah Noviny. Saithwold was not much out of our way, but I feared encountering brigands. We were arguing the matter when the rebel Brydda Llewellyn heard us and offered to escort us to Saithwold. As it turned out, there was no need for him to bring us all the way because of the blockade you have set up near the main road. We meant to remain in Saithwold only a night, but, unfortunately, one of our party is now ill. Sirrah Noviny's granddaughter has some skill in healing and seems to think it will take at least a sevenday and maybe two before he will be able to travel. It is a pity, but what can be done?"

Vos scowled and a bold idea flashed into my mind. "I had not thought to come here today, but now that I

119

am here, I wonder if there is any possibility of my sending a missive to Brydda Llewellyn with your next messenger to Sutrium. We were to meet him in a twoday or so, and I would let him know that we cannot now come to Sutrium so soon."

Vos gave me a cold smile. "I am sure that Sirrah Noviny had much to say to you and your friends about matters here that you are eager to report to the Black Dog."

I shrugged. "I do not know what you mean. In truth, I have had little chance to talk with Sirrah Noviny, for we arrived only yesterday, and my friend's sickness has preoccupied all of us since then. Khuria and his master do complain somewhat about the barricade, to be sure, but I cannot see why when it is for their own protection. They ought to be glad of it, but in my experience, men do hate to be locked up as much as cats, even when it is for their own good. All the same, it seems to me they exaggerate its effect on their lives, for Zarak's father said people cannot pass the blockade. But that is nonsense, for how else should Zarak and Darius and I have come to Saithwold?"

"What did he say to that?" Vos asked.

"More of the same. But it is the nature of old men to grumble, and I daresay they did not mean me to take it seriously." I looked around as if distracted and said vaguely, "Well, I will see for myself how Saithwold is in these next sevendays, will I not?"

"You will see what I permit," Vos snapped.

I pretended to have mistaken the threat in his words for an offer.

"You are most kind, Chieftain!" I gushed. "It would be very agreeable if you would allow your armsman to take me about in his wagon. Ours is unwieldy and Noviny has only a small uncovered cart, and there has been so much rain!"

Vos was clearly confounded by my inability to realize that I was under threat, and I reminded myself to be careful not to overdo it. All that I said would be reported to Malik, who was far from a fool. It was enough that I had sown seeds of trouble concerning the demon bands. As the chieftain sat glowering at me, I gathered my wits and sent a probe roaming through the house, but I could not find a single mind to enter.

Vos suddenly twisted his features into a gruesome parody of a smile. He had realized that it would be to his advantage to let me write an innocuous letter to Brydda, for he now announced that a rider bound for Sutrium would come first thing in the morning to collect my missive. My heart leapt in triumph, but I arranged my face in a mild expression of gratitude and bobbed a curtsy. "I thank you, Chieftain Vos. You are a man of courtesy, though I had heard it said you have no love for Misfits. I hope the armsman who brought me here can convey me back to Sirrah Noviny's homestead, for my friends will be anxious."

Vos nodded curtly toward Kevrik, who stood amidst other armsmen to one side of the dais, his expression preoccupied.

Outside, I discovered that the rain had again stopped. As I climbed into the wagon, I cast out another general farseeking probe. Once again, I could not locate a single unbanded mind. Either the armsmen and servants wore bands constantly, or they had donned them upon my arrival. I turned my thoughts to the letter I would scribe to Brydda. On the surface, it would praise Vos's courtesy, and for good measure, I would scribe disparagingly of Noviny's overreaction to the barricade, pointing out our own ease of entry as proof that he was wrong. But as soon as Brydda saw the pricks I would make in the page, he would recognize the language Dameon used to scribe messages, and soon after that, they would know about the invasion. I could hardly wait to get back to Noviny's farm.

Kevrik suddenly asked, "Did ye speak true about the demon bands?"

"I did," I answered. I thought he would ask other questions, having broken the silence, but he lapsed back into frowning reverie. By the time we reached the town, it was beginning to rain again. My initial feeling of triumph faded into fear that Malik would guess that I meant to use the missive to send a hidden message. I told myself it did not matter if he assumed this, since he could not possibly know that we knew about the invasion. He would envisage any secret communication as being solely about Vos's activities, which could only serve him.

Just so long as he did not guess who I truly was.

By the time the carriage approached Noviny's gateway, it was raining harder than ever, and thunder rumbled ominously in the distance. It was only dusk, but the stormy sky made it seem much later. To my surprise, instead of urging the mare through the gate, Kevrik pulled the wagon to a halt, explaining that the track was too narrow and ill kept for it. "I am afraid ye mun walk up to yon household," he said with unexpected courtesy, and to my surprise he handed me a blanket, bidding me drape it over my head for some meager shelter from the rain.

Turning to trudge up the muddy track to Noviny's homestead, I wondered why a man as courteous as Kevrik seemed to be would choose to serve Vos. By my judgment, the armsman was not a natural bully, nor did he appear to be a man who hungered for power over others. Perhaps there had been no other way of making a living save to bear arms, and he had offered himself to Vos with no knowledge of what the man was like.

I was shivering with cold, for the clothes Wenda had given me had been soaked through more than once that day. Doubly regretting the rain because it prevented me summoning Gahltha to fetch me, I stumbled suddenly and fell to my knees, muddying and ripping the sodden skirt. I felt like cursing Noviny for the state of the track, but he had explained that it was kept narrow and uneven to inhibit Vos's armsmen from coming in wagons.

It occurred to me that I must be near Khuria's cottage and the concealed wagon. Indeed, I had intended to stop there but had forgotten. By the time I groped my way to the wagon, unlaced the canvas, and slipped inside, the storm was directly overhead, and rain was hammering down. I tied the canvas shut, deciding I might just as well wait out the storm. It was dank and chilly inside, but I lit a lantern and a small fire in the cooking brazier. Teeth chattering, I drew water from a barrel and set it to warm for soup. Then I peeled off my sodden borrowed finery and toweled myself briskly, thinking I would have to replace the skirt when I had the chance. I felt more myself dressed in my own comfortable trousers and shirt as I crumbled herbs and dried mushrooms into the soup. While it cooked, I tried squeezing some of the moisture from my boots, then set them as near to the brazier as I could, for I had no other footwear save a pair of thin sandals.

As the wagon slowly filled with warmth and the wholesome fragrance of the soup, I was glad I had not gone straight up to the homestead bubbling with triumph, for I realized now that I could not simply rely on a missive with a secret warning to stop the invasion. There was too much danger of that plan going awry. And now that I had ceased to fret at it, a different idea for dealing with the invasion had begun to form in my mind. I pondered it, wondering if I dared put it into practice, for it would be very dangerous. I had no doubt that were I to present it at guildmerge, it would be rejected as far too risky. But I was not at Obernewtyn with strong allies about me. I was trapped in a hostile province with dangerous enemies on all sides.

I drank the soup, alternately refining the plan and wishing there was some way to let the others know I was safe, but it was too wet and wild outside. The wagon gradually grew so warm that I began to drift to sleep, but I woke at once when the rain stopped. I tried farseeking the house, but the tainted patches of earth still blocked my probe. I was about to reach for my boots when it occurred to me to try farseeking Gahltha, since he might be grazing nearby. To my delight, the probe found him at once. He was not far away, but the contact was tenuous. Relief that I was safe filled his mind, but fearing that our connection would be broken, I wasted no time in asking him to go to the house to let Zarak and the others know where I was.

"I/Gahltha will come and carry you there," he offered, but I refused, saying I was warm and dry and might as well wait where I was until daylight. Reluctantly, Gahltha obeyed, warning me that I had better be prepared to face Maruman's wrath. The probe began to dissolve. I sent a swift farewell, extinguished the little fire in the brazier, and lay down. Able to relax at last, I fell immediately into a deep sleep.

I dreamed of Matthew standing on a red rocky bluff gazing hungrily out over a dawn-bronzed sea. As on the previous occasion, I was aware that I was simply a disembodied watcher in the vision dream, which again had a remarkable clarity. I did not need to hear Matthew's thoughts to guess he was thinking of the Land, for there was an unmistakable yearning in his face. Then he turned, and I saw a long puckered scar down one lean brown cheek that I had not noticed before. Matthew smiled as Gilaine came to join him, and once again I was glad they had found one another; the mute empath-farseeker had met him when he and I had been taken captive by her father, the fanatical renegade Herder Henry Druid. I did not know how they had encountered one another in the Red Land, but it was no great surprise, since Misfits were naturally drawn to each other.

For a time, they merely gazed companionably out to sea, until Matthew sighed and said, "Ye ought not to be seen talking to me, just in case there is trouble over this." He touched the puckered scar.

Gilaine did not speak. Indeed, she could not, for she was mute, but when Matthew sighed and shook his head, I realized that they were farseeking.

"I am careful," Matthew now said. " 'Tis just that I nivver expected to be attacked by another slave. I kenned the people here dinna want to fight the slavers, because the Red Queen is supposed to come an' set the whole thing in motion, accordin' to their prophecy. But I always thought they refused me because they believed it would be impossible to win without her. I dinna realize they'd think of me as a threat fer trying to make them act before the prophecy had come true. Pity Naro did nowt realize I have abandoned my plan of rousin' the people against their oppressors." He shook his head to whatever Gilaine said. "I canna tell them about Dragon, because they will nowt ken that she is truly the daughter of their queen without seein' her. An' even if they did believe me, how should I tell them about her bein' in a coma?"

Another pregnant silence, and Matthew frowned. "I wish I *could* believe she has woken, Gil. But that's too much like the happy ending in an empath storysong. When I were a lad in th' Land, I saw life as a grand story full of heroes an' villains an' sleepin' princesses that mun be wakened with a kiss. I nivver guessed it might be a sad story that ends in misunderstandin' an' tragedy." A silence. "I have nivver lost heart. I just ken that mebbe I have been wrong tryin' to force a battle. Mebbe the prophecy is true, an' Dragon mun come here before this Land can be free. I mun gan back to th' Land. I am sure I can convince Elspeth an' th' others to let me bring Dragon here, once they understand that it may be th' only thing that will wake her."

Gilaine laid a hand on his arm, and he flushed, then paled. "I dinna expect her to love me. I scorned her affection when she was a lass, so how could she love me now? An' she will be a queen. It'll be enow fer me if she can be restored to her people an' will let me serve her." There was a caressing quality to his voice that made me think of the blaze of wonder I had seen on his face

126

when Dragon had tried courageously to save two children from a Herder just before she had fallen into her coma. He had been enchanted by her heroism, but something in his voice and face now suggested that boyish infatuation had ripened into something deeper and more real.

They were staring out to sea again, and Matthew said in a different voice, "I dream of them sometimes— Elspeth, Dameon, an' Rushton. Th' others. They all seem older. . . ."

Gilaine looked eagerly at him, and he smiled at her. "Well, of course ye do, for if anything could reach across all that distance, it must be the love between Daffyd an' you." His smile faded and again he looked out to sea. "I just wish I kenned what is happening in th' Land. The slavemasters talk of it but mostly in their own language to one another, as ye ken. The slaves from th' Land talk, but it's hard to glean much more than that the rebels have driven out both Council and Faction on one side of the Suggredoon, while the Council and Herders have the west coast, an' from what you saw of Daffyd . . ." He broke off as a man whose face was vaguely familiar joined them. It was not until he spoke that I recognized Jow, Daffyd's elder brother. Both brothers had once served Henry Druid, before realizing they were Misfits.

"You'd do well to keep your mouth shut hereafter, lad," Jow said. "It'll be the Entina pit for you if you're caught fighting." Gilaine must have made some protest, for the man touched her cheek gently. "Speaking of it won't make it happen, child."

"He is right anyway," Matthew said grimly. "It is only lucky that no one saw Naro attack me, so I could claim I had fallen. The masters were suspicious, of course, but as an overseer, I get more work out of a crew than any other, so it would be a terrible waste to feed me to th' Entina."

Jow laughed. "You conceited young whelp. But it's true you have a gift for moving men about a job that would be hard for the masters to replace. Still, you'd best lie low for a while."

I woke with the complete certainty that I had not merely true-dreamed of Matthew; I had seen him and the others *in the present*. The only way to have done so over such distance was on the dreamtrails, which meant I must have drifted onto them in my sleep. I had too little knowledge of the mysterious and dangerous dreamtrails to know how this could have happened, but to feel sure I was right, I had only to think of my previous dream of Matthew, in which he had seemed to hear me call out his name. The thought that I had made contact with Matthew in the Red Land was thrilling and revolutionary, but it went with another thought I had sometimes had: that true dreams were merely dreams experienced while the mind drifted close to the dreamtrails. I decided to endure the discomfort she always made me feel and discuss it with Maryon when we were back at Obernewtyn. If I was right, perhaps I could ask Maruman to guide me to Matthew on the dreamtrails.

But what had woken me? By the darkness, it was still night, though perhaps not far from dawn. I got up, shivering with cold, and peered through a small gap in the laced canvas. The chink of sky visible through the overhanging branches was the dense starless indigo of predawn, and the air was so damp that it must have rained again while I slept. I decided to walk back at once, rather than waiting for Gahltha to arrive. I would be able to tell the others of the letter I would scribe for Vos and outline my plan over firstmeal. I began marshaling the arguments I would need as I groped for my boots. I was about to pull them on when I heard a branch snap loudly.

I froze and sent out a probe. It would not locate, but when it brushed several areas of buzzing resistance, the hair on my neck prickled, for that could only mean men with demon bands. I was able to distinguish four separate areas of resistance close by and two farther away in the direction of Khuria's cottage.

Another branch snapped, and then I heard a man hiss softly that the wagon must be close. I felt sick. Their knowledge of the wagon's whereabouts meant they had been up to Noviny's homestead to question the others. Worse, the stealthy approach meant that they knew I was inside it, for Zarak would never willingly give me away.

Hearing another footfall very close, I reached down and carefully unfastened the disguised hatch in the wagon floor that was the lid of the compartment where Swallow's plast suit lay. Lifting it open slowly to prevent the hinges creaking, I climbed carefully into the cavity. Hauling my boots and wet clothes in with me, I lay down flat and lowered the hatch. Once it was in place, I felt for the pin that would allow me to secure it from beneath.

I relaxed my muscles, trying to calm my breathing so that I could hear, for the coffin-like compartment had been built solidly to ensure that it would not give out a telltale hollow sound if it was knocked. Minutes passed until I heard a hiss of triumph and a furtive rustle as the canvas was thrust aside. The wagon rocked as first one, then a second and a third man climbed in, their boots loud on the wooden boards over my head. I heard one curse, and through a crack to one side of the compartment's lid, I saw a light flare.

"Empty," snarled a voice. "The boy lied."

"I dinna think so," said a man in a rough highland accent. "She has been here, all right. And from the smell of it, she cooked."

"Where is she, then?"

"She got away. Vos won't like it," said another man.

"Malik will like it even less," responded the highlander. He bellowed an order for a thorough search of the area surrounding the wagon. There was the sound of a locker opening overhead, then rummaging and banging and our belongings shattering. Finally, someone hammered at the floor. I trembled as the point of a knife showed between the boards, but Grufyyd had done his work well, and the knife would penetrate no deeper because of crisscrossed metal strands laid in a grid under the wood. After a moment, the knife was withdrawn.

As the search continued, I learned from their talk that a troop of armsmen had ridden to Noviny's homestead during the night, and Khuria had been tortured to make Zarak say where I was. It was horrible to think that this had been happening while I slept. But why had Vos sent his men after me? Or were they Malik's men, dispatched when he heard about the meeting with Vos? And where were the others now? They might still be in the homestead, but it seemed more likely they would have been taken to Vos's property where, as chieftain, he would have cells.

But what about Maruman and the horses? Gahltha must have been taken prisoner, or he would have come to warn me, so I tried to beastspeak Maruman. The probe would not locate. I told myself it was inhibited by the tainted ground between us, but at the same time I had a dreadful vision of the armsmen slaughtering all the beasts to ensure that none could help me.

The wagon rocked, and I realized that the armsmen were climbing out of it. I pressed my ear to the wood to listen. The other searchers had returned with news that there were no tracks or any other sign of me. The rain had been too heavy.

One of the armsmen said they must take the wagon back to Vos's and suggested using their own horses to draw it. Another pointed out that it would be impossible since the wagon had no proper harness.

"Let's burn it, then," said another.

Hearing this, I turned onto my belly and closed my fingers around the pin that held the bottom of the hidden compartment in place. Grufyyd had created the second opening in case a person concealed there needed to slip away. But finally the highlander, who appeared to be the group leader, said that the wagon had better be taken back to Vos's in case Malik wanted to look it over.

There was much groaning as they dragged it out from under the tree and pushed it onto the track, where they tried to hitch two horses to it. By the time the wagon set off at the uncomfortable jerky pace that comes of mismatched horses, my senses told me that dawn had come and gone. I tried to beastspeak the horses, but both wore demon bands whose strength was such that it produced a queer discomforting numbness in my mind.

"What is this?"

Hearing Malik's cold unmistakable voice made my scalp crawl.

"This is th' wagon that th' mutants used, Chieftain," answered the highlander who had elected to ride along with the carriage after commanding the others to continue searching for me. As he explained where they had found the wagon, it became clear that Malik had neither sent the men nor instructed Vos to do so. It was also clear that Malik knew I had vanished but did not know who I was.

"I should have been informed before anyone made a move against Noviny and these mutants," Malik said, his voice sharp with displeasure.

"Chieftain Vos commanded that the servants were to be sent home, an' Noviny an' his granddaughter be taken prisoner, along with the mutants an' the horses. One of the mutants turned out to be a gypsy, but the armsmen took him as well, just in case. All other beasts were killed, as well as two maidservants an' a man who refused to leave."

I bit back a cry, thinking of the servants I had seen and the dogs that had greeted me upon our arrival. And Maruman!

"You said the mutants were questioned?" Malik prompted.

"They were nowt questioned until they were brought back to Vos's homestead. That is when we realized th' female mutant, who had presented herself to Chieftain Vos, was not among them. At first the mutants tried to tell us that one of the women killed was the missing woman, but after we tickled the mutant

132

lad's da, he told us she had sent a horse to tell him that she was waiting out the storm in the wagon."

"Probably the other mutants used their freakish powers to warn her as they were being taken away."

"They couldn't have, Chieftain," the highlander said. "The armsmen put demon bands on the lot of them at Noviny's place. But mebbe the female mutant saw them pass. . . ."

Malik grunted. "What did the mutant boy say they were doing here?"

"Only what th' female told Chieftain Vos yesterday: that they were headed for Sutrium an' had merely stopped here on th' way fer the lad to see his da. But it's clear they came because of something the old man scribed in a letter. Chieftain Vos had th' captives thrown into the cells an' gave orders for us to find the woman. That is when I sent a rider to ye, Chieftain."

There was a silence; then Malik said, "Very well. Take the wagon to Vos and make sure the prisoners are not questioned again. I will deal with them myself when I come. Tell him to concentrate his men and his efforts on finding that female mutant. With luck, she has stumbled into one of the perimeter traps and is dead. If so, I want to see her body."

I heard the sound of horses galloping away, then the slushy clop of hooves and the jingle of harness as the wagon lumbered on. I laid my face on a fold of the plast suit, insisting to myself that Maruman had not been slain and wondering if I really had the courage to put my plan into action.

✦ 8 ✦

I MUST HAVE fallen asleep for I woke to the sound of horses' hooves clattering over cobbles and realized that we had reached Vos's holding. I tried to picture the layout of the yard I had seen the day before. When the wagon turned left and came to a halt, I reckoned we had stopped in front of the barn that stood nearest the grass surrounding the main house in a sea of green. As the horses were freed from their makeshift bindings, I sent out a probe for Gahltha and then tried to reach Lo and Zade, to no avail. A large area of buzzing rejection came from what I guessed to be the direction of the corral. Perhaps Gahltha and the others were in the midst of the banded horses, and the collective disruption of their demon bands prevented me from reaching them. I farsought Zarak and Khuria with no more success, before remembering the highlander had spoken of their being demon banded.

After the two horses that had drawn the carriage were led away, I rolled on my back and was reaching for the pin that held the overhead hatch when I heard the voice of the armsmen who had brought the wagon in with the highlander.

"I do not see why we should be worried about making sure Chieftain Vos does what Malik commands," he said in a low, truculent voice. "He is not our chieftain."

Another voice told him authoritatively not to be a fool. "Do you think Chieftain Malik camps in Saithwold province these long winter months because he is concerned about protecting our coastline? He could just as well leave that to his men. I believe he intends to offer his name to the Council of Chieftains as candidate for Saithwold."

"But Chieftain Vos—"

"Will do nothing because he will be under charges for setting up the blockade and trying to force the people here to vote for him. Why else would Malik encourage him to do such things? But the main point is that Chieftain Malik is like to take on those of us who have proven useful to him."

"All right, but how are we supposed to make sure Vos obeys Malik's command not to question the prisoners again?"

The other man answered in a sneering voice, "Vos can be steered as easily as a sheep. Didn't you hear the highlander say in Vos's hearing that it is Malik's practice to keep prisoners in isolation and solitude to weaken their wills? If he follows his usual pattern, Chieftain Vos will simply appropriate the idea as his own."

The banging sound of a door came from the direction of the main house, ending the conversation. I heard the sound of many boots approaching and then Vos's voice, sneering at the wagon's smallness and its "grotesque and freakish ornamentation." To my horror, one of the armsmen again suggested burning the wagon, adding that the prisoners be made to watch. But Vos said loftily that he had decided the prisoners

135

would stay where they were for the time being. A bit of isolation would stew their terror and make them more amenable when they were again questioned.

Vos derided the wagon for a little longer, then ordered it to be dragged out of his sight. There was a good deal of pushing and shoving before I heard the muffled sound of receding boots, and I prayed that the wagon had been pushed into the shed. It would be much easier to sneak out under cover.

After listening for a long time to be sure there was no one close by, I turned onto my belly, pushed aside the plast suit as carefully as I could, and pulled the pin at the bottom of the concealed section to release the lower hatch. I hung my head out, startled to find myself looking down at thick green grass. The wagon was not in the barn after all but on the grass beside it. With a sinking heart, I visualized all the windows in the long side of the homestead that would face me as I crept out.

I opened the hatch farther, hung my head right down, and looked around, but it was not until I gathered my courage and climbed out that I discovered that the wagon had been pushed under a weeping tree growing beside the shed. Better still, the barn door was flung open so wide that it blocked part of the wagon from view. I closed the hatch and crept along the side of the barn into the dense trees surrounding the homestead, giving thanks for the barn door's protection. All I had to do was stay hidden until dark, then slip inside to find the others. I refused to let myself dwell on how I would rescue them when all of the armsmen wore demon bands. I told myself that I should first find the horses. They might be able to tell me where the prisoners had been taken, and Gahltha would know what had happened to Maruman.

I moved through the trees behind the barn and around to where I had seen the corral, only to discover a large empty yard I would need to cross before I could reach it. I could not see any armsmen about, nor could I check for smaller buzzing areas of disturbance because it had begun to rain again.

My heart leapt into my mouth when, among the horses, I spotted a coal-black head I would have known anywhere. *Gahtha*. I beastspoke him and was close enough that I ought to have reached him even in the light rain, but he did not respond. The buzzing repulsion and the glint of metal about his neck gave it away. He had been banded! Gahltha could not reach me any more than I could him, yet his sense of smell was acute. He lifted his head and wheeled suddenly, causing an eddy in the slow swirl of horses. Then he was at the edge of the yard, his nose quivering.

I crouched and slipped through the fence posts into the empty yard. I ran across it, bent low, for I had spotted a group of armsmen sitting on the front porch of the homestead, talking and cleaning their weapons. Assuring myself that they could not possibly see me with all the moving horses between us, I had almost reached Gahltha when, to my astonishment, he laid back his ears and bared his teeth at me!

I stopped incredulously. What was the matter? I moved toward him, but this time he reared up slightly and gave a low, urgent whinny, stopping me again. I recognized the whinny he had given as a warning and looked around, but I could see no one. Baffled, I took another step. Gahltha snorted and shook his head.

"Gahltha?" I whispered, and reached out to him. But this time he snapped at my fingers and backed away, making the horses nearest him shift and prance. Was he in pain? The possibility that he had been harmed filled my mind with such a red blaze of anger that I struggled to compose myself. I was signaling laboriously for him to come when I heard a soft voice behind me.

"So, I was right."

I spun, heart hammering, to find the armsman Kevrik standing by a door I had not noticed in the side of the nearest outbuilding. With the delicacy of a true dagger handler, he held a short throwing dagger, point first. This was what Gahltha had been trying so hard to convey.

"I ken well how to use this, lass, in case yer thinkin' of makin' a run for it," Kevrik said in the same soft voice.

"How did you know I would come here?" I demanded, instinctively keeping my voice low.

"I was nowt sure, but having seen ye with yon black horse yesterday, I dinna think ye'd leave without him." I must have glanced at his throat, for he touched the demon band. "I believe ye about these being dangerous, but I can't have ye making me cut my own throat now, can I?" I must have reacted because his smile widened. "Unlike many of my comrades, I ken that Misfits can have more than one Talent. Nowt that anyone is like to listen to me, since I returned ye as I was bidden and am now suspected of letting myself be ensorcelled by ye. Capturing ye would be th' only way to restore my reputation."

"Why didn't you stake out the cell where my human friends are held?" I asked. "Are they so inaccessible that I would have no chance of reaching them, or don't you think we Misfits care about human friends?"

His teeth flashed white. "There are many armsmen in the house, and a guard is posted to stand outside the cell holding yer friends, which is in the basement. That, I suppose, is th' information ye were trying to trick out of me." My anger must have shown, for his grin faded and he tossed the knife purposefully up and caught it by the handle without ever taking his eyes from me. "I have to admire ye, lass, still plottin' to turn this moment to yer advantage when ye ought to be in despair. I'd nivver expected Misfits to show such courage and determination, nor to be loyal or clever. The stories told to us would have ye as vicious and cowardly near-beasts."

I opened my mouth and then closed it, suddenly struck by the fact that he had not made any attempt to call for help. Perhaps he intended to take me straight to Malik, since he was in disfavor with Vos. "Maybe you should be as clever," I said fiercely. "Of all people, Malik does not deserve anyone's loyalty."

Kevrik lifted his eyebrows, once again throwing the knife and catching it. I took a small step toward him anyway, growing reckless in my urgency. "You say you believe me about the demon bands? I will tell you something else that you ought to believe. Malik is a traitor—and not just to Misfits. Even now, he betrays you and Vos and all the rebels."

The amusement in the armsman's eyes was gone. "What are ye blatherin' about?" he demanded.

"Haven't you wondered why he supports Vos's pointless plots, which any fool can tell will not gain more than the most temporary chieftainship of Saithwold? Perhaps you imagine, as some others here do, that Malik supports Vos's folly the better to usurp his claim on Saithwold. If that is what you think, you are wrong. Malik desires vastly more than being chieftain of Saithwold. He is using Vos and Saithwold and all of you as a distraction to stop anyone from learning what he is really doing, until it is too late."

"Too late for what?"

"To stop him," I said, heartened by the fact that the armsman had not defended Malik. I took a deep breath. "Malik has made a pact with the Herders. Noviny saw him meeting with them down on the beach. He agreed to let a force of Herder warriors land, and he has used Vos's activities as a way of isolating Saithwold so none of the other chieftains will get wind of it. The tainted traps laid all about the province's perimeter and the demon bands that you and the horses wear are simply to make sure no Misfit scries in this region and learns what Malik is up to. If not for them, I could have farsought someone to warn Dardelan and the Council of Chieftains about the invasion. As it is, I am trapped here, my friends are prisoners, and soon hundreds of Herder warriors will invade. I do not know what has been promised Malik for his treachery, but you can be sure that all who aided the rebellion will be slain or given to Salamander as slaves to be sold over the seas."

"How did Noviny just happen to witness a secret meeting between Malik and the Herders?" Kevrik asked.

"Noviny suspected him of being behind the burnings up the coast, so he went looking for proof. Since learning of the invasion plan, he has done nothing but try to get word to Dardelan. That is why he had Khuria scribe those letters to Zarak. He thought the lad would be turned away and would make enough of a fuss that Dardelan would have to send in some armsmen. He never imagined that Brydda would ease us through the blockade."

For a long moment, Kevrik looked at me, knife

poised; then he lowered it. "Most of us have believed that Malik meant to take over Saithwold. Some felt it would be a better billet to serve him, while others, me among them, dinna much like the idea of being Malik's man but saw little else for it. Yet if all ye say is true . . ." He paused for a moment. "It is said that Malik betrayed many of yer people to their deaths."

"No one has better cause than me to know it, for I was one of those who survived his treachery," I said fiercely. "He knows me and hates me specifically, though not by the name I gave Vos, for he strove against me in the Battlegames in Sador. We Misfits lost the Battlegames and, therefore, the chance to join the rebellion as equal allies, but Malik's ruthless tactics caused him to forfeit the respect of his fellows. That is why he is not high chieftain. He blames Misfits for that, and if you take me to him, have no doubt that you will win his favor." I stopped, breathless, praying that I had not misjudged the armsman's essential nature.

The highlander gave me a long look, then in one smooth movement, reached up, undid the demon band, and removed it. "The favor of a treacherous leader is a precarious thing," he said. "Me mam used to tell me dreadful tales of monstrous Misfits who would come and eat me if I dinna heed her. I am no longer that wee lad, an' meetin' ye yesterday has troubled me, lass; I tell ye straight. Ye admitted to being a Misfit, but I dinna find ye evil-natured or freakish. Indeed, yer bonny and braw and clever, and in coming here, ye have proven yerself a true friend. I think we can be al-lies, unless ye now use yer powers to make me slit my own throat and prove me wrong."

I drew a deep shaky breath and managed a soft

141

laugh, hardly able to believe that I had managed to convince him. "I will not slit your throat nor even read your mind, for with these words, you have made us allies, and because of them, I will tell you the plan I have to thwart Malik. Indeed, with your help, it just might have a chance of succeeding."

"What can I do?" he asked simply.

My gratitude was so great that I had to blink away a hot rush of tears. Only then did I realize how deeply I had feared being unable to save the others. I mastered myself and said, "First, we must get my friends out of their cell."

"I fear that is impossible," Kevrik said regretfully. "I could gan to the cell easy enow. It is the first in a long corridor of basement cells an' can be reached by descending a flight of steps. I might manage to trick the guard outside their door into letting me take the prisoners by telling him Vos has changed his mind an' wants to question them again, but the key to the cell hangs around the chieftain's neck, an' all men ken it. There's no way to get it from him, save knockin' him on the head. An' since he has ten armsmen with him at any moment, I dinna think we will manage that very easily."

I pondered his words. "Could you persuade the guard watching the cells to remove his demon band for a moment?"

"Probably," Kevrik said. "But that would nowt solve th' problem of opening the door."

"What about the other guards? Could you persuade them to remove their collars?"

He shrugged, frowning. "I could say th' catches on some demon bands are faulty an' Vos wants me to check them. But if suddenly everyone lacks demon bands, it would soon be noticed an' the alarm given," Kevrik said.

"The bands only have to be off for a few moments. I can put a command into the mind of each armsman that will endure for some time even after the band is restored," I said.

Kevrik blinked. "What command?"

I told him, then asked, "Is the door of the cell made of bars, or is it solid?"

"Solid," Kevrik said apologetically, not realizing that this was what I had hoped. He went on, "But what of th' lock."

"I can open the lock."

Kevrik's eyes shifted, and he said hastily that I had better uncollar my friend. I turned to see Gahltha glaring down at me, his nostrils flared wide with indignation. With an exclamation of remorse, I turned and unclasped the demon band, wincing at the mental tirade that the black horse immediately poured into my mind. I stopped him by telling him my plan.

"No! There is too much risk to you/ElspethInnle," Gahltha sent at once.

"This is the only way to stop Malik, and if we succeed, Dardelan and the rebels will be able to defeat the Herders and then go and free the west coast, so that I can pursue my quest. And if my plan fails, all will be lost anyway, for the Herders will reclaim the Land and Misfits will be put to the flame or made slaves."

"What of your quest if you are hurt or killed, ElspethInnle?"

I sighed. "I don't know, Gahltha. So many times in my life, I have put my quest first, but often, even when I did not think it, I discovered that I was serving it.

143

Perhaps Maruman is right in saying that all I do serves my quest." I swallowed a hard lump of fear in my throat. "Tell me . . . what happened to him? I heard that the animals were killed save for the horses."

"Not Maruman," Gahltha sent. "He warned me they were coming, but they were upon us before I could beastspeak Zarak or Khuria. The dogs and a goat were slain, and five milk cows with their calves. None of them saw Maruman, but he was watching. The last message he sent was that he would find you and warn you of what had happened."

I felt a rush of relief. "He must still be out there somewhere," I said aloud.

"Lass, it is too dangerous to stay here like this," Kevrik said urgently, glancing across at the homestead.

I nodded and looked into Gahltha's eyes. "Do you think the horses here will be able to find their way to Malik's camp without riders?"

"I will lead them where you have said, ElspethInnle," Gahltha sent. "But your plan could fail."

"If it does, then you must do your best to reach Brydda or someone from Obernewtyn who can warn the others about the invasion. You will have to jump the barricade."

He looked at me.

He did not say that the armsmen guarding it would not hesitate to use their weapons on him. He did not say the chance of his getting by alive was so slender as to be almost nonexistent. I lay my face against his silky black neck and felt his pulse against my cheek. "Tell Zade and Lo and the other horses that I can't uncollar them yet, because an armsman might notice. But if we succeed, they will be free of the foul things forever."

144

✦ ✦ ✦

Kevrik wanted to wait until full dark to move, but I was filled with a sense of urgency almost as strong as a premonition. Fortunately, miserable weather kept the armsmen inside, except for those who had some duty. Kevrik came and went, gradually describing the layout of the house and making the few preparations we needed, as I worked out what to do. I told him that we would use the rear entrance to the house, which was toward the back of the long wall facing the barn. I would go along the tree line until I was opposite the entrance, and when it was safe, he would signal so I could cross the grass to enter. The greatest danger would come when I was out in the open, for anyone glancing from a window would see me. Kevrik advised me to push my hair beneath the collar of the armsman's cloak he had brought, saying I would be taken for an armsman if I acted like one.

When I was in place in the trees, with a good view of the rear door, I saw armsmen stacking firewood against the wall beside it. Kevrik went to speak to them and then went back in the direction of the barn, only to emerge fifteen minutes later in the trees beside me, panting.

"Dinna worry. They will go in when they have finished, because it is nearly time for nightmeal, an' most men who have no duty will gan to the dining hall, which is toward the front of the house."

"Tell me about the demon bands for the horses," I said as we settled to wait. "I am certain the Herders created them and gave them to Malik, but why?"

"I dinna ken why, but a sevenday back, Malik rode up and gave Vos a crate of them. He said that since Noviny harbored a beastspeaker, we mun protect ourselves from the possibility that our horses might be manipulated to give messages or even to harm us. A lot of us wondered where Malik had got the bands, but none of us dared question him. One of the men asked Vos, an' he called the man a fool. He said, of course, that they had been found in the cloister. But we searched that cloister—" He broke off and nodded to the door. The men stacking wood had gone in. I ran my eyes along the side of the building and saw that several windows that had shown light were now dark.

Kevrik went back through the trees toward the barn. A few minutes later, I saw him cross the cobbled yard to the front of the homestead and disappear inside. My heart raced with apprehension until he reappeared at the back door. He glanced about once, then beckoned. I took a deep breath, rose, and stepped out purposefully. I had retrieved my boots from the wagon, but at the back door I hastily pulled them off so I could move silently in my socks.

I followed Kevrik as he moved deeper into the house. The passages were empty, but I stayed a little way behind him, knowing that at any minute someone might step out. The rooms we passed were both unoccupied and unfurnished, but this was no surprise, for Kevrik had told me that the house had been built to accommodate the number of servants and armsmen Vos imagined he would eventually amass.

Suddenly Kevrik splayed his fingers downward in the warning signal we had agreed upon. I flattened myself against the wall and froze. I had wanted Kevrik to leave off his collar so I could reach his mind, but he said that would look suspicious if noticed, as was bound to happen when he raised the subject of demon bands.

Kevrik looked at me. "Are ye sure?" he mouthed.

I nodded, then listened anxiously as he turned a bend in the passage ahead and spoke a greeting. We had agreed that he would greet each man he met by name so I would know how many there were. One, then. I crept closer to the corner and heard Kevrik explain that Vos had ordered him to check all demon band catches, for some had proven faulty. When I heard the snick of the fastening mechanism, I shaped a delicate coercive probe and carefully entered the armsman's mind. It took only a moment to fashion a simple block that would prevent his noticing me as I passed or noticing the others when we returned. I waited impatiently as Kevrik examined the demon band at length, obviously imagining I needed more time. At last he told the other armsman his band seemed fine, and I heard the snick of its being fastened on again.

I padded around the corner. The armsman stood looking at the wall, as I had commanded, and he did not turn as I ghosted past him, leaving an astounded-looking Kevrik in my wake.

"I canna believe it worked," Kevrik whispered when he caught up with me. A faint unease in his expression told me he was wondering if I could tamper with his mind as easily. Then he flushed, and I guessed he was wondering if I was reading his mind now. I made no comment, because although his fears were scribed clear upon his face for anyone to read, if I tried to allay them, he would regard my awareness as proof that I had invaded his mind.

"How long does it last?" he asked when we had gone around another bend in the passage.

"About half an hour, as long as nothing happens that opposes the suggestions I have put into his mind."

"Like an alarm being given?"

"That still might not cause the block to crumble, but if we were in the process of creeping past at the moment an alarm went . . ."

"I see." Kevrik sucked in a breath of air and blew it out. "I suppose—" He stopped because we heard voices and footsteps around the next bend in the passage. Kevrik strode quickly ahead, and I heard him greet two men and explain in an authoritative voice that Chieftain Vos wanted all demon band clasps examined as some had proven faulty. There was a little silence, and then I heard the men remove their bands. One of them made a bawdy comment about Kevrik's skill with his hands, and as Kevrik responded in kind, I slipped into the minds of first one and then the other. When I glided around the corner past where they stood with Kevrik, momentarily blank-eyed, they turned to the wall.

He joined me a few moments later, his face pale. "I am nowt sure I can take too much of this, lass. I keep expecting someone to see ye an' shout an alarm."

Despite his anxiety, we managed to negotiate the passages without difficulty, leaving three more armsmen coerced behind us. The worst moment was when we encountered a group of five men. When Kevrik spoke their names, I began to sweat. It was not the number of men that troubled me, but the fact that five were enough to produce an amorphous group mind that had also to be coerced. Knowing the notorious instability of group minds, I instructed each man to hand his demon band to Kevrik and then to forget that he had done so. Having the armsmen unbanded meant that I could check on their blocks and refresh them if they began to crumble. There was the risk that the absence of the bands might be noticed, but I had no choice. I kept control of their minds and made them all turn to the wall as I passed so that no matter what happened, they would not remember my face. When Kevrik joined me a few moments later, he held out the bands with a questioning look. When I explained, he thrust them atop a high shelf we passed.

At last we reached the steps leading to the basement cells. Kevrik descended and I followed, grimacing when the stone became slimy underfoot. But I was less concerned about my socks than the knowledge that there was only one way in and out of the cells; if an alarm was given now, we would be trapped. My blood churned with a mixture of nervousness and excitement that I welcomed, knowing it would sharpen my responses.

Kevrik touched his finger to his lips as he reached the bottom of the steps, and I stopped and listened. I heard him greet the armsman guarding the cells and was relieved that there was only a single man. Kevrik offered his tale, but the armsman refused to remove his demon band.

"Not with them freaks so close!" he expostulated. "Maybe this is just what they've been waiting for."

"Dinna be a fool," Kevrik said jovially. But the guard insisted he would wait until Chieftain Vos himself came to give the order. There was a bit more arguing, followed by a great thump and silence.

"Ella!" Kevrik hissed. I went down and saw a tall armsman crumpled on the ground at Kevrik's feet.

"He would nowt be reasonable, so I had to knock him on the head and take off his band," Kevrik said, his accent thickened by agitation. "Can ye make it so that he won't remember what happened when he wakes?"

"I will have to wake him to coerce him, which will require physical contact." I wrinkled my nose as I laid my hand on the armsman's thick and none-too-clean forearm. I inserted a coercive probe into his sleeping mind and made him wake. When his eyes flew open, Kevrik started back with a gasp of alarm, but the guard only lay glassy-eyed and placid, his gaze fixed on the pitted rock wall of the basement passage as I had coerced him. I was able to make it stronger than the others because I was touching him. Finally, I restored his demon band. When I rose and stepped back behind Kevrik, the armsman yawned, rose to his feet with a guilty expression, and then walked away from us to the far end of the row of cells, rubbing his jaw absently.

I turned my attention to the cell door, which was just as solid as the armsman had said. I did not bother trying to farseek Zarak or Khuria or the others, knowing that they all wore demon bands. I put my fingers on the lock, closed my eyes, and focused hard to transform mental energy into a physical force. I felt out the shapes inside the lock carefully, struggling to understand how they worked. It was more complex than I had expected, and Kevrik shifted impatiently beside me.

"A person's thoughts weigh nothing," I gasped at him. "To move matter with your mind is the hardest thing. Opening this lock is like trying to move a wagon with a spoon."

At last, I heard the tumblers click and sagged back in relief, trembling with fatigue. I had closed my eyes for a moment, which was when Kevrik turned the lever and opened the door. Before I could stop him, he had stepped into the cell, and my heart sank as I heard a sickly thud.

150

✦ 9 ✦

ZARAK STOOD OVER Kevrik's unconscious form triumphantly, but when he looked up and saw me in the doorway, his face sagged in disbelief.

"I am glad you took to heart farseeker rescue instructions to keep yourself ready to escape at any moment, no matter how hopeless the situation," I told Zarak, trying for irony. "Unfortunately, poor Kevrik will have a terrible headache that he does not deserve."

"He is one of Vos's armsmen," Zarak protested.

"He was," I said, taking in Khuria, Noviny, and a pale but determined-looking Wenda sitting together in one corner. Darius was awake, too, but he lay with his head in Wenda's lap. They all looked alert, though Khuria had a bloodied face.

Zarak looked down at Kevrik in dismay. "I am sorry, Guildmistress. . . ."

I shook my head impatiently. "Never mind that now. Take the others up the steps and make your way toward the back of the house and out the back door. The guards you will encounter ought not to take any notice of you, because I have coerced near a dozen of them. But be ready to strike if anyone reacts, for it might be someone I did not meet coming in. You will have to do it physically, because they will be wearing demon bands, and we do not now have Kevrik to convince them to remove the bands. Take his dagger and his cloak. That ought to give anyone you encounter pause enough for you to deal with them. But make no noise, else we will have the whole house down on us. Once outside, go straight across to the trees and make your way to the barn. You will find our wagon this side of it, pushed under a tree. Lo and Zade are waiting behind the barn. Hitch them up to the carriage, get in, and wait for me."

They all stayed where they were, gaping, and I felt like stamping my foot to wake them. At last Zarak went to help his father and then Noviny to their feet. I bit my lip, seeing how badly the old beastspeaker limped, knowing he had been tortured so Zarak could allow me more time to escape. But he gave me a crooked grin that told me his spirit was as strong as ever. Noviny had not been as badly hurt, but he looked years older as he bent to help Wenda with Darius. The gypsy showed no marks of violence, but his face was blood-less under his dark skin.

"Can you manage?" I asked, knowing that if they could not, we were all doomed.

"We must," Noviny said, and Darius managed to nod. As they passed by me, I saw that the gypsy's face shone with sweat, and his breath sawed harshly in and out. But there was nothing I could do for him.

"What about you, Guildmistress?" Zarak asked.

"I must wake Kevrik and relock the cell door so it seems you are still inside. Go and help the others. I don't know how long the blocks on the armsmen will last. One of them was on a group mind."

Zarak looked alarmed, spun on his heel, and went. I dropped to my knees beside Kevrik's limp form and laid a hand on his cheek. Unconscious, he looked younger. I reached a coercive probe into his mind to bring him to consciousness and then thought better of it.

Several minutes later, I hurried past armsman after armsman, each of whom obligingly looked the other way. Kevrik had been right in saying there was much less movement during mealtimes, and in any case, most activity and attention in the homestead was focused toward the front of the building and the entrance to the property. I got outside without mishap and arrived at the wagon just as Zarak was helping Darius into it. I was about to summon the strength to unlock Zarak's demon band when Gahltha farsent me urgently. I ran lightly along the back of the outbuildings and through the empty yard after a hasty scan to be sure there were no armsmen near. Gahltha was waiting at the side of the corral, and he gave a soft whinny of greeting before telling me that three funaga had ridden in while I was gone, leaving their mounts tied to the other side of the corral. The horses were demon banded, but he had learned that they had come from Malik's camp.

"I have told them who you are and what you want the horses here to do, and they are ready to help," he said. "They have offered to throw their riders and trample them, if you wish it." Gahltha's eyes were fierce, as if the idea pleased him. I climbed into the corral and moved through the horses to the side closest to the homestead. I could easily reach the three tethered outside, and I undid the demon band of the first I reached, a big dappled-gray beast with intelligent eyes. Fortunately, none of the horse bands had locks, for Malik and his ilk only ever feared that beastspeakers would coerce the minds of their mounts. It never occurred to them that beastspeakers were not animal coercers and that horses might collude to attack of their own free will. Freed of the demon band, the gray horse greeted me as Innle and told me that his name was Dovyn. I asked him to explain to his comrades that I would not undo their bands because one missing could be an accident, but not three. Then I explained what I needed them to do when they returned to Malik's camp.

Gahltha was questioning Dovyn's companions about the number of men and horses in the camp. I could not hear their answers because of their demon bands, so I left him to it and returned to the wagon in time to see three men wearing Malik's colors striding across the yard. I prayed that Dovyn's missing band would go unnoticed. The three riders mounted up and would have galloped away at once had Vos not come hurrying from the homestead to command them to stop. They obeyed, but none of the three dismounted. I was afraid that Vos might notice Dovyn's bare neck, but the horse kept his head down so his mane fell forward. Vos began to speak, his voice querulous and indignant, as he bade the armsmen tell their chieftain that he was sorely needed. One of Malik's men answered coldly that his chieftain had heard that message already. Malik's answer was what they had come to deliver, namely that Chieftain Vos must concentrate his efforts on finding the Misfit his men had managed to lose.

To my horror, Vos pointed frantically toward the barn and asked if they wanted to see the wagon where the Misfit had hidden. Fortunately, the barn door partly blocked the view of the wagon from the yard, and it was now dark, so no one noticed that there were horses tethered to it. Dovyn's rider said his master had already seen it and that it was not a wagon he wanted but the missing woman. Then the three wheeled their horses and rode off. Vos stared after them for a scowling moment before storming back into the house.

Afraid that he might be headed for the cells to interrogate the others about me, I called Zarak. He came to the open canvas, and I reached through and laid a hand on the demon-band lock. Gritting my teeth, I focused my mind, but the band's taint was so strong that it would not let me concentrate energy into force. Frightened that the empty cell would be discovered even before they had escaped, I reached deep down into myself where my black killing power lay coiled in the depths. The last time I had awakened it, I had nearly lost control, but this time I drew on it without waking it. I heard the lock in the demon band click.

My mind felt numb from contact with the taint, and my head spun from the effort of opening a second lock so soon after the first, but I was elated to discover that it was possible to harness that black and terrifying power within my mind without being overmastered by it.

Zarak wrenched the band off his neck with a look of profound revulsion, and seeing that he meant to hurl it from the wagon, I bade him keep it. Wenda came forward expectantly, lifting her hair from her throat.

I shook my head regretfully. "I have no more strength now. I am sorry," I croaked. Swiftly, I wove a coercive net to take in the fatigue clouding my brain, and farsought Zarak. "I am going to create a diversion to draw Vos's household to the back of the homestead so you can escape. Get Darius as comfortable as you can, because Lo and Zade will gallop as soon as they are out of sight of the homestead."

"But where will we gan?" Zarak responded. "Th' main road is barricaded, an' there will be armsmen all over th' roads lookin' fer you."

"Most of them have been sent to Noviny's property or to the barricade. And you will not be going that way."

"The coast road is barricaded as well. . . ."

"You will not be going that way either." I sent him the mental picture I had given Lo, when we had let her out of the corral, of a track leading off the main road just before it forked. Kevrik had suggested it.

"The abandoned cloister?" Zarak sent in disbelief. "But there is only one road in an' out."

"The armsmen will be looking for Misfit fugitives who want to escape Saithwold. They are not going to look in an empty cloister on a dead-end road," I sent with a tartness that made the young farseeker wince. "If you encounter anyone on your way there, Lo or Zade must beastspeak their horses to throw them. You won't be able to do it because of the demon bands. Bind them and take them with you. Put them in one of the old cloister cells. Ask the horses to follow you."

"What about you?" Zarak asked.

"I have other matters to attend to," I said in stern guildmistress tones to discourage him from asking any more questions. Then I bade him and the others farewell and leapt down from the wagon.

I made my way back along the tree line until I had reached the same place where I had hidden earlier, opposite the rear door. Forming a coercive probe, I sought the minds of the five armsmen I had left unbanded. To my delight, four of them were together playing cards in a room near the end of the homestead. Their minds told me that they were on duty, guarding Vos's armory. I smiled.

A moment later, one of the men leapt up crying out that he smelled smoke. The others "smelled" smoke, too, and one managed to "see" flames without any coercion at all. To my surprise, instead of trying to rescue the weapons in the armory, the four men fled down the hall and outside, bellowing in terror. Puzzled, I dipped into one of their minds again to find that piled in one corner were eight small wooden kegs filled with a black powder, which the armsmen believed would explode and destroy the house.

It seemed highly unlikely, but in moments there was a wild clangor of bells, and people began spilling out of the building from all directions, giving credence to the armsmen's belief that the whole house was in danger of being destroyed. I waited until they had all run down toward the rear of the homestead and then farsent Lo and Zarak. I found one of the men without bands and made him "see" a host of armed strangers creeping through the woods toward the back of the house, and a senior armsman ordered the others to investigate while he tried to find out where the fire was. He ran back into the homestead, and I knew I did not have much time.

I farsought Zarak again and was delighted to find that the wagon had already left the cobbled yard and was swiftly nearing the entrance to the property. By my reckoning, it was not more than half an hour to the road leading to the cloister, and with luck, they might make it all the way there without being seen.

"We will deal with anyone we meet," Zarak sent determinedly.

I withdrew from him only to find that the search for the fire and intruders was beginning to flag. Doubts were flowering, and any minute it would dawn on someone that they had been tricked. I reached into the minds of the unbanded men and managed three more sightings of people creeping about the house, prolonging the search for another half hour. Then someone discovered that one of the armsmen guarding the armory had no demon band. In a short time, all five unbanded armsmen were found and brought before their chieftain.

"The Misfit is here and trying to release her companions," Vos screamed at his men. "Find her!"

I ran back through the trees to the barn and across the cobbled yard toward the corral. I heard a shout and ran faster, but my wet socks slipped on the damp cobbles, and I went down hard. I was surrounded in seconds, and it was all I could manage, as I lay there, winded and dazed, to command Gahltha to do nothing, for I knew he could see me from the corral. If he tried anything, he would be killed. All the armsmen glaring down at me held knives or bows with arrows already nocked. I lay very still.

"Get up," snarled a senior armsman as he arrived with a lantern and took in the scene before him.

"I'm not sure I can. I think I have sprained my leg," I gasped.

Another armsman reached down, obviously intent on dragging me to my feet, but the senior armsman told him sharply not to be a fool. Was I not the Misfit witch who had forced their comrades into removing their demon bands and serving me? Who knew what I would do to someone who touched me?

The armsman snatched his hand back and gave me a look of frightened loathing.

"I will need a . . . stick if you want me to stand," I said, levering myself awkwardly into a sitting position as more armsmen emerged from the house.

Before any of them could decide whether there would be any risk in giving me a stick, Vos came hurrying along the side of the homestead with more of his men. I noticed Kevrik among them, a purple swelling over the eye where Zarak had struck him. But from the smug triumph on Vos's face, he had no idea yet that his prisoners were gone. I tried to reach Kevrik's mind, but the demon band he now wore made it impossible. He looked down at me coldly.

"So," Vos sneered, his eyes glittering with triumph in the lantern light. "You thought you could use your filthy powers to rescue your friends, but see how you have failed. Here is the man you used to help you trick others into removing their bands." He was pointing to Kevrik.

"Let me kill th' witchling who made me betray ye, Chieftain," he begged hoarsely.

Vos laughed. "You shall have her, but first, Chieftain Malik will wish to question her."

"Then let us ride now and take her to him!" Kevrik snarled.

A look composed equally of arrogance and unease crossed the chieftain's narrow features. "It is dark now, and Chieftain Malik commanded that none should come to his camp without first sending a message."

"Sirrah, surely that could not mean you?" Kevrik demanded. "Are ye not the equal of Chieftain Malik, since ye are both chieftains, an' ye are within yer own region? Let us take the freak to him, for will he nowt be eager to ken that she is taken prisoner? Let Chieftain Malik witness how yer men captured the Misfit when his own armsmen failed."

"You speak well, Kevrik," Vos approved, his cheeks flushed. He turned to the other armsmen. "I have decided that we will ride immediately to the camp of Chieftain Malik and deliver this creature to him."

Several of the other armsmen, one of them the highlander whose voice I recognized from the wagon, sought to dissuade Vos, but the more they talked of Malik's commands, the more stubborn Vos became.

"Am I Malik's armsman to be commanded hither or thither? Besides, I wish to see Malik, and since he cannot be bothered to come here, then I will go to him, and in triumph, bringing him what he most desires."

Still some of his captains argued until Vos flew into a rage and ordered them to make ready to ride.

Malik was the same solidly muscled, gray-eyed, gray-haired man he had been the last time I saw him, but he wore his arrogance with a vicious new edge that must have been honed by the secret bargain he had made with the Herders. He listened impassively to Vos's description of my capture—by his telling, a brilliant coup in which Vos himself was a central figure. Without the congratulations and accolades from Malik that Vos clearly expected, the story at last foundered to an uncertain end.

"Did I not inform you that I wished you to send word that you had caught the Misfit? Did I not command that a messenger be sent if you intended to come here?" Malik inquired coldly. The light from lanterns hung about the encampment gave his face a sinister ruddy glow.

Vos's bluster about being Malik's equal shriveled, and he said, "You did, however . . . ah . . . it is a dangerous Misfit that my men caught. Not just a beast-speaker but a powerful coercer."

Malik all but curled his lip in derision. "Your men caught her after they first let her escape and after you acted against my express orders to do nothing about Noviny or his visitors until I gave you leave." Vos tried to speak, but Malik ignored him. "But I am sure Chieftain Dardelan will be most understanding when you expalin to him why you took Noviny and his granddaughter and their guests prisoner and interrogated them."

Vos paled. "But . . . if the freaks had used their powers to escape, they would have reported me to the Council of Chieftains."

Malik gave a bark of laughter. "Do you really imagine that the Council of Chieftains will be forever ignorant of what you have been doing here?"

"You said I would have your full support if it came out," Vos stammered.

"So you would have, had you not decided to take prisoners against my orders. And now you march into my camp, though I warned you against it."

"I am sorry, Chieftain Malik," Vos gabbled, unraveling with fear. "I hope that you will not take this . . . eagerness of mine amiss. I will take this creature and return with my men to my homestead."

"The mutant might as well remain here," Malik said. He turned to look at me. He had glanced at me indifferently when we arrived, and I thought that he had not recognized me under the mud and dirt. But now, seeing

161

the look of gloating hatred in his metal-gray eyes, I knew I had been wrong. He knew exactly who I was.

A cold shiver of terror ran down my spine. I forced myself to seek the mind of the horse Dovyn, whom I had unbanded, but the probe would not locate. His missing band had probably been discovered and replaced.

"Why are you here in Saithwold?" Malik demanded.

My mouth was so dry with fear that I had to work my tongue to produce moisture enough to speak. "We had letters from the beastspeaker Khuria, who serves Master Noviny. The missives did not sound like him, so we—"

Almost casually, Malik drew back his hand and struck me in the mouth. It was an openhanded blow with the back of his knuckles but hard enough to make me stagger sideways.

He asked in an almost bored voice, "What did you know of matters in Saithwold before you came here?"

"Nothing until a woman at an inn mentioned the blockade. She said that Chieftain Vos was trying to force people in Saithwold to elect him."

Vos let out a strangled cry of dismay, but Malik silenced him with a cutting gesture.

"And the Black Dog?"

"Brydda said the high chieftain knew what Vos was trying to do but that Dardelan didn't want to act against him until after the elections. He did not want us to come here, but when I said that Zarak was determined to see his father, he offered to help us get past the barricade."

Malik sneered. "You would have me believe that despite knowing there was trouble in Saithwold, Brydda Llewellyn, a known friend to freaks, escorted here the guildmistress of Obernewtyn and doxy to its master, and left her without protection?"

I heard Vos gasp at hearing my title, but Malik ignored him.

"Brydda didn't think there would be any real danger," I said. "The worst we imagined was having to wait in Saithwold until after the elections, and in the meantime I would be able to stop anyone from doing anything rash, by telling them that Dardelan meant to deal with Vos."

Malik struck me again, this time with a closed fist that glanced off the side of my head and knocked me to the ground.

"Get up," he said coldly.

I struggled to my knees with difficulty, because my wrists were bound. The blow had set off a great explosion of pain in one ear, and I fought a blackness that fluttered about the edges of my vision, wondering what Malik wanted from me. I was answering his questions truthfully, and he could have no idea that we knew of his bargain with the Herders.

"Get up," Malik said once more.

Trembling, I obeyed. When he stepped toward me, I instinctively lifted my bound hands to protect my face, but he sank his closed fist into my stomach. I doubled over, gagging at the force of the blow, and fell to my knees. When I managed to heave in a breath, he ordered me up yet again. I obeyed as slowly as I dared, tensing for another blow. Instead of hitting me, Malik asked what Noviny had told me. When I opened my mouth to answer, he punched me again in the stomach.

I fell badly this time because of my bound hands, banging my head on a rock, and when Malik told me to get up, my limbs would not obey. I stayed curled on the muddy ground, praying that he would not kick my head or face. When he did not move or speak, I looked up to find him staring down at me, his features utterly empty. The moon had risen and seemed to ride on his shoulder. No wonder Maruman hated the moon, I thought dazedly. It was on Malik's side.

Malik turned to Vos, who looked frightened out of his wits. "Do the other prisoners know that you have caught this one?"

"No," Vos said in a thin voice. "They have not been questioned since the first interrogation, just as you ordered."

"Good. Go back to your homestead. Remove Noviny and his granddaughter to their homestead and have them kept there under guard. Do not speak of this Misfit's capture to them. Offer no explanation and make sure your men are equally silent. The other two Misfit freaks and the crippled gypsy are to be questioned again. Edel," he addressed one of his own men, "accompany Chieftain Vos and conduct the interrogation. Begin with the cripple and torture him until he dies, regardless of what he does or does not confess. Make sure the other two witness it, then begin on the boy. That will loosen the old man's lips if they are keeping anything back. Find out why they came, what they have learned here, and what they intended to do. I will expect a report by tomorrow."

Edel nodded, but Vos stammered a protest. "The . . . the Council of Chieftains will want to know what happened to the Misfits, Malik. And if this woman is truly the bondmate of the Master of Obernewtyn . . ."

"This is a freak, not a woman," Malik snarled. "I

will deal with her as all mutants ought to be dealt with. It is nothing to do with you. As far as anyone else will know, you saw her but once when she came to pay her respects to you, and then you had her taken back to Noviny's property."

"But if she talks—"

"You need have no fear of that."

Vos swallowed the meaning of this as if it were a stone. "But the other Misfits . . . Noviny and his grand-daughter will say that they and the cripple remained my captives when they were returned to their home."

"If you are ever accused of anything, you will let it be known that Edel performed the interrogation of the Misfits at my command." Malik's tone was so indifferent that it sounded like boredom.

"But the Council of Chieftains will—"

"I will deal with the Council," Malik said with cold finality. "Now go."

Vos hesitated, perhaps expecting something more formal to pass between them, but Malik made no face-saving speech. Finally, with as much dignity as he could muster, Vos commanded his men to mount up and ride back to his property. They obeyed silently, watched by Malik's men.

Malik was now speaking quietly to one of his men, and I closed my eyes for a moment, battling fear. My tongue found the jagged edge of a chipped tooth, and my lip stung where it had been split. I could also feel the drain of energy as my body tried to repair itself. There was no way to stop the process, for it was not activated by my will, and opening the locks had depleted me, though that fatigue was still coercively netted. I did not dare push the pain I now felt into the same net,

165

because pain trapped in this way doubled and tripled in a very short time.

I was so intent upon my thoughts that I failed to notice Malik's armsman circling behind me. When Malik abruptly ordered me to get up, I obeyed, relieved to find that my limbs would obey. But even as I stood, swaying slightly, I felt the cold metal of a demon band snap around my neck.

✦ 10 ✦

To MY HORROR, I discovered that my powers were trapped inside my mind like a bear caught in a cage. I told myself that this was merely normality, but the thought that this dreadful isolation and passivity of mind could be called normal sickened me. No wonder unTalents loathed us. At the heart of their hated must be bitter envy.

I might have been better able to stifle my horror and fear had I not known that, in banding me, Malik unwittingly left me unable to play my part in the plan I had set in motion. I fought a suffocating wave of panic and tried to focus a probe to work the lock, but the taint emanating from the band was too strong. Desperately I tried to reach the black power at the bottom of my mind, but pain and the healing of my body drained me of the energy I needed to rouse it.

"Ye ken Vos will nowt keep his mouth shut," grunted the man who had fastened the demon band about my neck as he poured a mugful of some dark liquid and handed it to Malik. The chieftain drank it off, then shrugged.

"I have given him makework enough to occupy him for the time being, but the fool's role is almost at an end."

"What about her?" The armsman nodded in my direction.

"The freak is irrelevant," Malik said dismissively.

"Obernewtyn's master might nowt agree if the woman is truly his doxy. He might come riding in looking for her with some of those coercer-knights of his, regardless of what Dardelan wants. It would be inconvenient if their arrival coincides with other matters."

He is talking about the invasion, I thought.

A smile curved Malik's thin lips. "I doubt Rushton Seraphim will be in any haste to get his woman back. After the priests had their fun with him, I am amazed that he could stomach her presence these long months. He might look like a man, but all that makes a man is gone. He is no more than a shell."

Bile rose in my throat, and tears stung my eyes, for what Malik said was true. Had Rushton not said as much to me himself? For Malik to know so much, the Herders with whom he had struck his bargain must have boasted of what they had done when they had Rushton imprisoned in the Sutrium cloister. I ground my teeth in fury, and some of the quaking terror left me.

"If all is so well, Chieftain, why do ye have a troubled look about ye?" ventured the armsman.

A flicker of impatience in the cold face of his master faded into a brooding puzzlement. "It is true," Malik said slowly. "I am troubled. Something nags at my mind." To my dismay, he turned to look at me. "How did that fool Vos manage to capture her, of all mutants? That is what nags at me."

My heart hammered because Malik knew me as only

a former opponent can. Perhaps he was remembering the last occasion on which we had faced one another, when victory had turned to ashes in his mouth. I tensed as he took a step toward me, but he stopped, hearing the sound of horses' hooves drumming. Malik and his men turned to face the road, no doubt imagining that Vos and his troop were riding back. But when the horses came in sight, they were riderless, though many wore saddles and even dangerously dangling reins. Malik and his men stared, perplexed and astonished.

Malik was the first to regain his wits. "Shoot! Shoot them, you fools, for they are coming to save the freak." His men tried to obey, but it was too late. The stampeding horses were upon the camp. Men screamed in terror and pain as they fell under flashing hooves. A few men shot arrows or threw a spear or knife, but not a single horse fell. I realized with elation that the men did not know how to fight horses, for their training had always focused on their human riders. Without warning, more horses leapt from the bushes. They were unsaddled and unbridled, which told me they were the horses that had been left in the corral back at Vos's property. Gahltha had released them as I had requested. Then I saw him, black and powerful in the moonlight, rearing and stamping down hard, his nostrils flaring.

Huts were trampled, lanterns smashed, and brief flames extinguished as the horses rampaged through the camp. Men who had not been trampled fled from the devastation, only to find their own horses, led by Dovyn, herding them back. An armsman who tried to attack the horses was crushed so savagely that others threw down their weapons at once. I had run to one side of the camp the moment the horses appeared. Now I saw Gahltha turning his head this way and that, clearly wondering why I was not beastspeaking him.

I drew breath to call his name, but a hand closed over my mouth, and I was lifted from my feet. My captor turned and ran with me into the trees bordering the camp. I could not fight because of my bound hands, and I could not summon help with my mind because of the demon band, so I tried to bite the hand pressed over my mouth in order to scream. I was suddenly hurled to the ground so hard that I was winded. It was dark away from the campfire and lanterns, but a shaft of light, reaching through the trees, briefly illuminated Malik's face, contorted with urgency as he used his kerchief to gag me. I could still hear the horses and men screaming and shouting when Malik threw me over his shoudler. Then he began to run, dodging trees and crashing over bushes and fallen branches. Gradually, the sounds of the camp faded into the monotonous thud of his boots and the snap of foliage breaking or swishing as it sprang back after we had passed. Malik was breathing hard but regularly, revealing his strength and stamina. My heart sank at the realization that he might go on in this steady way for half an hour. By then we would be far from the camp. Worse, I was sure that none of the horses had seen him take me.

Malik ran without stopping or slowing for what seemed an eternity. When he did finally stop, he was panting, but he clearly still possessed strength. He drank some water from a bottle on his belt, seemed to listen for a time, and then he set off in a slightly different direction, this time walking. I could hear nothing but the creak and rustle of trees and wondered where he was taking me. Not to the coast, as I had expected, to signal his Herder friends. As far as I could tell, we had traveled parallel to the road back to Saithwold town.

A sickening hour of hanging half upside down passed before Malik stopped and hurled me to the ground. Sheer luck kept me from hitting one of the snaking tree roots protruding from the leaf litter, but instinct made me lie very still as if I had been knocked unconscious. I could tell by Malik's breathing that he was weary now; if he felt safe enough to sleep, I might have a chance to escape, for my legs were not bound.

I heard Malik moving and sensed that he was looking into my face. I kept my breathing slow and even, knowing he would not be able to see clearly in the dappled tree shadow. There was a long silence, but I continued to feign unconsciousness. I was just beginning to think I must have been mistaken in thinking he had been looking at me when I felt a knife's cold edge against my face, and the gag fell away.

I gasped and opened my eyes to find Malik's moonlit face so close that I instinctively recoiled. He pressed the knife against my neck and gave me a cruel, knowing smile that exposed my hope of escaping as the foolishness it was. His eyes told me that I would never escape him. Not alive. I felt a shudder of terror as I suddenly understood that Malik had brought me with him not as a hostage, but to finish what he had begun in the camp. Madness glimmered in his eyes along with a pleasurable anticipation that told me he meant to take his time in killing me, exacting as much pain as he could. He wanted me to grovel in terror before him.

He sat back on his heels as if the fear in my eyes had assured him that I understood his intentions. He took the knife from my throat and ran his thumb across the edge of his blade in a caressing gesture, never taking his eyes off me. His nostrils quivered as if he hungered for even the odor of my fear.

"You are a monster and a coward," I said, looking directly into his eyes.

He laughed with real enjoyment. "You think I am that idiot Vos, to be taken in by feigned sleep or provoked to hasty action by an obvious attempt to anger me? No. I mean to take my time killing you, and nothing you do will hasten your dying. I have in mind to deprive you of all your senses first. Hearing, speech, smell, touch." He pressed his knife in turn to my ear, my lips, my nose, my bound hands as he spoke the name of each sense, and then he lifted the tip of his blade and rested it under my eye. "But first, your sight."

"You are wasting time in which you might escape." I tried to sound cold instead of frightened, but, oh, I was frightened. I had never been more afraid.

He said very calmly, "What makes you think I need to escape?" He grinned at the consternation I could not conceal, for his words seemed to imply that there was something I did not know. Was he referring to the invasion, or was there something else? His look of terrifying concentration quenched my attempts to think. He lifted his knife and kissed the flat of it in a deadly salute.

I closed my eyes and let terror roil through me and flow away. I turned my mind from what was to happen and pictured Maruman and Gahltha, Dameon, Dragon, Matthew. And Rushton. The memory of those I loved could not be cut out of me, I told myself fiercely. Even when I died, my vision of them would live on in the mindstream. I wished that I could harness my mind's power and give myself to the mindstream, depriving Malik of the satisfaction of hurting me, but the demon band would not allow it.

I summoned up a mental image of Rushton as he had been when we had parted last. I saw his coldness with compassion rather than disappointment and sorrow. I felt boundless gratitude that he had come into my life to show me how deeply I could love, and it was a little burst of light in that dark moment to realize that being able to love was life's real gift. Without those people and creatures who had made me love them, I would be a lesser being. Even the pain of loving was a gift that had deepened me.

I felt the knife point scratch along my cheek just under my eye like the single claw of a kitten—a testing, teasing touch. I kept my eyes closed and thought of my quest. There was an unexpected peace in surrendering to the knowledge that I could not fulfill it. I had been willing to give up everything, including my life, but now it was time to die. I would try to keep silent when he hurt me. I could do no more.

I heard a thump and resisted the temptation to open my eyes, certain that was what Malik was waiting for. He meant my last sight to be of him. Instead, I pictured Maruman. I saw his battered old head and body and his single bright eye, and I waited.

Then I heard the breathing of two people, though I held my own. One was heavy and regular and the other, fast and uneven. I opened my eyes to see Kevrik leaning over an unconscious Malik. He looked up at me and grinned. "I hit him hard enow to brain a bull, but he's still breathing."

173

"Oh, Kevrik," I gasped. "I have never been so glad to see anyone!"

"Doubtless," the armsman said wryly. He gently pulled me upright and grabbed Malik's knife to cut the ropes about my wrists. I shook my head and asked him to untie them. "We will need the rope for him," I croaked, nodding at the unconscious Malik.

Kevrik laid aside the knife and set about loosening the ropes, talking as he worked. "I've been following ye since he took ye from the camp. I thought he would nivver stop. Then when he did, I heard what he said, an' I was afeard he'd stab ye afore I could get near enow to hit him with the rock. It was cursed ill luck that I dinna have my dagger." He frowned over a stubborn knot. "I have nivver seen anyone look at any creature wi' as much black hate as Malik looked at ye before he struck ye. An' when it took me longer than I expected to fall far enough behind Vos an' th' others so I could turn back to th' camp, I near went mad. I was sickened by what he had done to ye, but more sickened by the fact that others did nowt to stop him. Men I have laughed and drunk ale with and regarded as strong and courageous, all standin' by and watching a man beat a bound maid." He grimaced as if he had bitten into something foul.

"When I finally came within sight of Malik's camp an' saw ye'd nowt been kilt, I was so relieved that I dinna wonder why ye were nowt talking to me inside my head as ye said ye'd do in that dream ye put in my mind when I was unconscious outside the cells. When I did notice an' wonder, I thought maybe ye'd been stunned. I was still ditherin' like a ninnyhammer when the horses Vos an' his men had ridden came gallopin'

174

hell fer leather along the road. It was only because I'd been looking at ye that I saw Malik grab ye. If I'd blinked, I would ha'e missed it. I just plunged after ye."

The ropes loosened and fell away, and the armsman began to massage my wrists gently. I winced at the pain, but that pain was life, and incredulous joy swept through me. I had expected to die. I had prepared myself for it, and yet here I was, still alive. My quest had not relinquished me after all. Kevrik unhooked a water bladder from his belt, and I took it from him gratefully and drank. Then he took a long draft and restored it to his belt.

"What now?" he asked.

The welling delight I had felt a moment before faded as I thought of Gahltha and the horses. "I need to return to Malik's camp. I was so sure I would be there to tell the horses what to do that I told them nothing save that they should stampede the camp and disarm as many men as they could. But even if they succeeded in that, how can horses keep humans prisoner?"

"It's a long walk back," Kevrik said. "The best or worst will have happened by now."

I felt sick at the knowledge that he was right. "Do you think we are closer to the road or the old cloister?" I asked.

"The road," Kevrik said decisively. "But it's still a good long walk. More if ye mean to bring him."

"I'm afraid we've no choice," I said. I plucked at the demon band about my throat. "I wish I could get this off, because then I could farseek Zarak to come and help us." Malik stirred and groaned. "Better tie him up well before he wakes. Then we'll make a litter and drag him between us."

"I can carry him some of the way," Kevrik said as he tied the chieftain's hands.

I fashioned bandage sandals for myself from strips of Malik's shirt. Then I helped Kevrik get the rebel across his shoulders, grateful the armsman was almost as big as the chieftain. Even so, Kevrik staggered slightly under his burden before standing upright. We walked almost a half hour before Kevrik's knees began to buckle. While he rested, I used the time to replenish the tattered bandage sandals. Then we constructed a rough litter. I did not look forward to pulling it, for my stomach hurt, and a fierce jabbing pain in my chest suggested that Malik had cracked one of my lower ribs. But worst was the weariness as my body fought to repair the damage and cope with the netted fatigue I had released. When we rested again after another bout of walking and dragging the litter, I had to fight the overpowering urge to just lie down and sleep.

When we headed off again, the moon had set and the forest darkened, making it harder to see our way. It was growing cold, too. This, as much as a desire to reach the road and find out what had been happening, kept us moving. As always when I was in physical discomfort, I found myself longing for absurd luxuries instead of simple necessities: a freshly made bed or a long soak in one of the hot springs in a mountain valley. I imagined eating a fresh-baked roll with butter melting into it as I sat in the battered chair that stood on my little turret-room balcony, Maruman lying on my lap.

Thinking of Maruman frightened me, because Gahltha had said the old cat intended to seek me out, but he had not done so. Hours had passed between the time the others had been taken from Noviny's place and when the armsmen had returned for me—easily time enough for Maruman to have found his way to me. I feared less that he had been injured than that what happened had sent him into one of his fey wandering states.

I wondered if the blue-black night sky would ever lighten. It was impossible to believe that it had only been the previous evening when I had sat in the wagon on Noviny's property, listening to the rain and brewing soup.

"How long until the sun rises?" I asked.

"Three hours maybe," Kevrik panted, squinting up at the sky. The next time we stopped, I borrowed Malik's knife and nearly cut my throat trying to pick the demon band's lock so we could summon aid. Kevrik tried, too, but after only a minute he shook his head and said he had not the nerve for it. I must be patient and he would get a key for the band.

Malik muttered something in a slurred voice, and Kevrik and I exchanged an alarmed look. He was definitely waking. The highlander fetched a stone and gave the chieftain a solid knock on the head. By the time we went on again, the sky was lightening to a deep indigo. To pass the time and to take my mind off the horses, I asked Kevrik what happened after he had awoken outside the cell in Vos's homestead.

The guard had awakened him, he said. The man remembered being hit by Kevrik, who had pretended to recall nothing and "noticed" that neither was now wearing a demon band. Kevrik remembered all that had happened between us, of course, but he also had a "memory" in which I told him how he had been knocked out and how I had decided to use this accident

177

to make sure Vos did not regard him with suspicion. Kevrik then told the cell guard that the alarm bells they could hear must signal the capture of the Misfit who had tampered with their minds. Ironically, that had been the simple truth, and Kevrik had arrived just in time to do as I had asked: suggest to Vos that I be taken at once to Malik's camp.

"You took a great risk, yet still I do not understand what you meant to achieve."

"How else could I have made sure that I would be in the camp when the horses stampeded? I knew that we needed to overcome Malik and his men and take them prisoner as swiftly as possible so that someone could be sent to Sutrium to warn the Council of Chieftains about the invasion. Of course, I did not bargain on Malik grabbing me, but I daresay he did not bargain on you. How many of your men will stand with us if they know the truth about Malik's plan?"

"A good many of them," Kevrik answered. "Once they are convinced it is not a trick. I would suggest letting Noviny speak to them. He is known as an honorable man."

We walked very slowly now, for we were both weary, and my bandage sandals were wearing thin once more. Kevrik began to talk again, perhaps to distract himself from fatigue. He said that he had tried to saddle Gahltha to ride to Malik's camp, thinking the black horse would want to go along. But Gahltha had backed away so determinedly that the armsman realized he had some other instruction.

"He was to release the other horses from the corral and deal with the armsmen who would try to stop them," I said.

He nodded. "I realized as much when th' black horse an' th' rest came past the tree where I was hidin'. I could tell they kenned I was there an' on their side because your black horse came an' butted his head against me." He laughed softly at the memory. "Then th' other horses came gallopin' along the road an' stampeded through the camp. Your black horse leapt out and the rest followed. No wonder Malik an' his men stood there like dolts through it."

We both fell silent, lacking the breath for anything but dragging. Then, at long last, just as the rising sun stained the sky with a pink and lemon glow, we saw the road.

Not until we had almost reached it did I notice the dead armsman lying in the middle of the road. From the queer horrible angle of his neck, he looked as if he had broken it when thrown from his horse. Sickened, I wondered how many men had died as a result of my commands.

We propped Malik against a sturdy tree, and Kevrik dragged the armsman's body off the road, for it seemed disrespectful to leave it lying there. I was shocked to see him riffle through the man's pockets, but then he held up a small gray key with a shout of triumph, and a moment later the demon band was unlocked.

I resisted the urge to hurl the loathsome thing into the trees and instead set it on the ground, knowing that sooner or later, someone was going to have to clean up the tainted material around Saithwold. Then I gave over thinking in the sheer joy of being able to send my mind spinning out. Having briefly experienced normality, I thought it such a wretched limited state that I wondered how Malik could value it so.

First I sought out Gahltha. He was still at Malik's camp, and his welcome and relief were no less than mine at finding him safe. To my amazement, he said the horses were in control of Malik's camp. The uninjured armsmen were penned up against the cliff edge, guarded by horses. Gahltha had sent Dovyn and a few horses back to Vos's property, for the gray horse had a plan to ensure the humans there did not leave. They were too far away for him to beastspeak, Gahltha explained, but he was confident that Dovyn would manage, despite the fact that the men had weapons and a house to take refuge in. Indeed, he seemed surprised at how worried I had been. It occurred to me with some shame that, in imagining they would need a human captain, I had underestimated the horses almost as much as Malik had.

Predictably, Gahltha wanted to come and get me at once, but I insisted that I was safe and bade him stay to keep a close watch over his human prisoners. "We can't risk any of them signaling the Herders; they might call off the invasion."

"Is that not what you want?"

"It was, but now it seems we ought to let them land so we can take their ships, as Zarak suggested."

During the laborious walk through the trees, I had done some thinking about Zarak's idea of permitting the invasion so we could commandeer the ships. It would be a brilliant coup, allowing us not only a swift and unexpected way to reach the west coast, but also the means of bringing Dragon to the Red Land. To simply turn back the invaders would be a lesser victory, and the Faction warriors would be stronger when they invaded next. My only fear now, other than someone signaling the Herders, was that Malik might have planned to give some final signal to let the Faction know it was safe to land. The only way of learning would be to probe Malik. This would also allow us to learn the exact timing of the invasion. The thought of delving into Malik's mind filled me with revulsion even as Kevrik removed the unconscious man's demon band.

Withdrawing from Gahltha, I tried to farseek Zarak, but I realized he and the others must have set up camp close to the cloister's tainted walls, for the probe would not locate. I sent my mind back to Gahltha, asking him to send a horse to let Zarak and the others know what had happened and to suggest they bring the wagon in the direction of Noviny's property, where they would find Kevrik and me waiting by the roadside.

I farsought Dovyn, who sent that many of the thrown riders had walked back to the homestead by the time he and the other horses had returned. Dovyn said the humans believed that the horses had been forced to throw their riders. Instead of regarding them as enemies, they had begun herding them into the corral. Dovyn had expected this, and he had urged his equine warriors to allow themselves to be corralled, for Gahltha had shown them how to unlatch the gate and escape whenever they wished.

Nothing had happened for some time, and then several funaga-li came to saddle horses and ride off. The horses had thrown them as soon as they were out of sight of the homestead and returned at once, to the evident dismay of the humans, again allowing themselves to be caught. As Dovyn had surmised, the funaga-li were incapable of understanding that the horses acted under their own volition, and all of them had retreated into the house, clearly believing they were under siege by a human army. Soon the doors and windows of the homestead were bristling with armsmen who shot arrows out into the darkness all night long, though no one had approached. I could guess that Vos imagined an army of vicious Misfits surrounding his property and killing every rider he sent out.

Stifling laughter, I asked what had happened to the thrown humans, and Dovyn explained that dogs had been enlisted to keep watch over them. The two species did not normally cooperate in this way, but neither did they normally make war on funaga. The gray horse added that dogs were perfect guards, because their acute sense of smell allowed them to scent the intention of a captive funaga-li to attack or attempt escape. I guessed their human prisoners were far more unnerved at being attacked and guarded by a pack of dogs and horses than they would have been by a group of humans.

There had been no arrows fired since dawn, Dovyn sent, for the funaga-li had been able to see that there were no enemies creeping closer. Vos must be sadly puzzled about what was going on. He would have discovered by now that his prisoners had vanished, and he could have no idea how that had happened.

Dovyn also told me that the men at the blockade had fled at the sight of riderless horses galloping back from Malik's camp.

I felt a touch on my arm and bade Dovyn farewell. When I opened my eyes, Kevrik nodded at Malik.

He looked unconscious, but if he was awake, I wanted to know it. I shaped a probe and had barely entered the black tumult of his mind when I was engulfed by a ghastly vision of torture, where I was the victim and Malik stood over me with bloodied hands. His eyes flew open.

"Get out of my mind," Malik hissed through gritted teeth.

I withdrew, shaken to discover that he was mind-sensitive. It explained much, though not all. I wondered what he would say if I told him of Garth's belief that this sensitivity was itself a minor Talent, which made him a Misfit, too.

"Check his ropes," I told Kevrik calmly, holding Malik's burning gaze. Then I said coldly and purposefully, "I have no wish to enter the cesspit of cruelty and violence that you call a mind, Malik, but I will do so if you speak another word that angers or offends me, or if you try to escape. I will enter it and wipe it clean. Do not doubt that I can do it."

Malik seemed to teeter on the point of exploding; then abruptly all the tension melted out of him and his face grew calm. Watching this transformation, unease snaked through me, and I remembered his avowal that he had no need to plan an escape. To find out if he was referring to something other than the invasion, I would have to probe him. I decided it could wait until I reached Vos's homestead.

"You and your kind—" Malik began.

"Are here to stay," I concluded savagely. "Now keep your mouth shut, for I meant my threat." I turned my back on him. I was trembling slightly, but not out of fear. Malik's relentless hatred had disturbed the black killing power deep inside me. I felt it stir, like someone sleeping, almost waking, and then settling back. It

183

frightened me. The last time I had fully awakened that power, it had proven to have a dark will of its own, and I had a ghastly vision of myself coercing Malik to cut his throat or set himself on fire.

To distract myself, I tried farseeking Zarak again, and this time my probe located immediately. "Where are you?" I asked.

"We are coming to get ye just as Gahltha told me ye wanted. We have just turned onto th' main road," Zarak sent. "I suppose ye could nowt reach us before, because we were camped inside the cloister walls. It was empty as ye thought, though it looks as if something had been planned there, fer there is a great pile of earth an' rock just inside the walls, an' all manner of tools. To tell ye th' truth, I regretted settin' up inside, fer the cloister is a strange creepy place full of ghostly bumps and echoes. We were in the midst of breakin' camp to move outside th' walls fer tonight when Gahltha's messenger galloped up. Is it true ye were Malik's captive?"

I winced. "I will explain everything later," I sent briskly. "Right now, Malik is my prisoner, and Malik's men and Vos and his men are sieged by the horses. They have done brilliantly, but they need some human hands to deal with their prisoners. Ask Noviny to start thinking about who we can ask for help."

"I'd like to know how the horses managed to get away from Vos and his men," Zarak said, and then laughed. "I know! Ye'll explain everything later. There is one other thing, Guildmistress," Zarak said, and the tone of his voice was suddenly subdued. "You should know that Darius is worse."

A chill ran through me. Yet how should we have achieved so much without any casualties? Did not life always demand its sacrifice? I sent to Zarak to ask Wenda about the most experienced healer in the region, determined to send for that person as soon as possible, but then I felt Kevrik's hand on my arm again. I opened my eyes to see him looking with consternation toward Saithwold town. I followed his gaze and almost groaned aloud to see men on horses galloping toward us. They could only be armsmen who had been stationed at the main barricade or who were searching for me, and I cursed myself for lacking the wit to stay off the road and out of sight. Too late now to untie Malik and hide with him, for if we could see the riders, they could certainly see us.

"There is no need for you to be caught," I told Kevrik. "Go into the trees and hide. Wait for my friends in the wagon."

"I will stand with ye," Kevrik said stoutly. "They will be Vos's men, so maybe I can convince them of the treachery Malik planned."

From the corner of my eye, I saw Malik give the armsman a look of burning fury. But I had no time to think of him. I stepped into the road and shaped a beastspeaking call, praying that one of the approaching horses was unbanded. To my surprise, my probe slid into the lead horse's mind as smoothly as a hot knife into butter. Then I realized why. I knew her.

"Esred!" I sent, hardly able to believe my own senses. The horse responded with delight, but as she returned my greeting, incredulous relief splintered into a confusion of longing and despair, for riding upon her back was the Master of Obernewtyn.

Rushton.

PART II

✦

SONG OF THE WAVES

· 11 ·

RUSHTON CLIMBED DOWN from Esred and went to help Dameon off Faraf. The long-legged Empath guild-master ought to have looked absurd on the small pony, but Dameon had a way of conferring dignity on any-thing he did. Rushton hung back to allow Dameon to sense his way to me. I ought to have been glad, as my feelings for the Empath guildmaster were a good deal less complicated than those roused by Rushton. But what I longed to do with a passion that shocked me was to rush over and fling myself into Rushton's arms. Ironically, that was a thing I had never allowed myself to do, even in the days when it might have been wel-comed.

Dameon embraced me, and I gave myself to the kindness and affection that flowed from the empath as naturally as warmth from the sun. Fortunately, affec-tion for me had not caused him to abandon the emo-tional barrier he erected habitually to protect him from the overwhelming force of other people's emotions, be-cause the fierce tangle of emotions I was experiencing would have felled him.

"So, you are a rider now," I said. "How does it feel?"

"Painful, but only in one place," Dameon said dryly in his cultured lowland voice. He held me a little away from him now, and his milky eyes seemed to examine my face. "What have you been up to?"

"I will tell you in a moment," I temporized. "First tell me how in Lud's name all of you come to be here."

"Maryon," Dameon said simply.

Of course. "Would that the Futuretell guildmistress had seen that we were riding into danger in Saithwold *before* we left Obernewtyn," I said tartly.

"She visioned it the day after you left," Dameon said. "Of course, the knights would have ridden out at once to stop you, but Maryon—"

"The Futuretell guildmistress said you must not be stopped." Rushton finished his sentence.

My skin prickled at the sound of his velvety voice, with its grainy hint of highland accent. Girding myself, I looked into his handsome, craggy face, into dark green eyes that had once caressed me as tenderly as his hands had done. Something inside me ached and twisted, but I was careful to offer only my cool guildmistress's expression, knowing he wanted no more than that from me, as I asked calmly, "Why?"

"What happened to your face?" Rushton asked in a strange, flat voice.

I lifted my hand to my cut lip self-consciously, realizing I probably looked dreadful. And what did Rushton feel seeing me like that? Certainly there was no hint of emotion in his expression. "This is nothing," I told him lightly. "I would have been dead if not for Kevrik. He is, or I should say, was, one of Vos's men." I looked at the armsman. "This is the Master of Obernewtyn, Rushton Seraphim."

Several expressions chased themselves across the highlander's face, but he stowed Malik's knife and said

190

solemnly, "Sirrah, I am pleased to meet ye. I have always been taught to regard Misfits as dangerous human-shaped beasts or worse. I am shamed now by my former ignorance. I have nivver seen such courage and determination as this young woman has shown, an' if all Misfits are like her, then 'tis an honor indeed to meet their master, be ye beast or human or some part of both."

"There is none to match the guildmistress of the farseekers," Rushton said, but there was no warmth in his voice.

"You asked what Maryon foresaw to stop us coming after you immediately, Guildmistress," Rushton said. "She said that despite the danger you would face, you would avert a catastrophe. I assume that the prediction had somewhat to do with your prisoner." He glanced at Malik, who gave him a stony look, then added, "Maryon was almost certain you would triumph without our help."

"Almost certain," I echoed, and was startled by how bitter I sounded.

Of course, I understood. If I had been stopped from entering Saithwold, no one would know about the invasion. Or if they had come soon after I had entered Saithwold, Malik would have warned the Herders to postpone their invasion, and it would only have been his word against Noviny's if he were accused. Instead, I had come to Saithwold, and with Kevrik's help and the horses' courage and cleverness, I had triumphed over Malik. Maryon had been right, yet I could not help but remember that dreadful moment when Malik had held his knife to my eye.

"What has been happening here?" Rushton asked with a touch of impatience.

191

I told them almost everything, from Brydda's assistance in getting us through the barricade to my rescue by Kevrik, and I watched Malik pale when I told of the invasion. By the time I had finished my story, his expression was stony again, giving away nothing.

I concluded by telling them Zarak's idea about taking the invaders' ships. "But before we can plan anything, we will need to coerce the details of the invasion out of Malik."

"I will take him to Sutrium this night, so one of the knights can coerce all he knows from him, before the Council of Chieftains," Rushton said. "We must ensure that no one can accuse us of putting words in his mouth."

"Where are Zarak and the others now?" Dameon asked.

"They were hiding in the old cloister, but they ought to be along any time," I said. "We were going to Vos's property—"

"We will ride ahead to secure it," Rushton said decidedly and bade Asra and Hilder ride to Malik's camp to help Gahltha and the other horses herd their prisoners to Vos's property.

Dameon chuckled as the knights rode off. "This seems to have been as much a victory of beasts as of humans."

"Clearly, Maryon was right in saying you had no need of us," Rushton said coolly. There was something in his tone that I did not like, but before I could fasten on it, he turned to Kevrik. "Will you ride with us, armsman? You can speak with your fellow armsmen and explain what Malik has been about." When the armsman nodded, Rushton suggested that Dameon wait with me for the wagon so Kevrik could ride Faraf.

"I will bear the funaga-li as well as you," Esred sent to Rushton, stamping her hoof and farseeking to me and those who could hear her. "But tell him that if he so much as tickles my belly with his heels, I will give him a brand that will mark him forever." I took some pleasure in relaying the threat, but Malik said not a word as he was mounted up on the mare, his hands still tied behind his back.

Kevrik mounted Faraf gingerly, but she bore his weight stoically, commenting to me that she did not suppose they would gallop. Abruptly, as Kally and Linnet remounted, Rushton asked if it was Malik who had beaten me. I had carefully glossed over how I had got into Malik's hands, but even as I opened my mouth to suggest we exchange stories later, Kevrik began eagerly describing how I had been captured by Vos's men and taken to Malik. My heart sank as Rushton led the armsman deftly to relay what had happened at Malik's camp—in particular, the beating interspersed with questions.

"You watched and . . . did nothing?" Linnet asked him scornfully.

"If she had nowt made me promise to do nothing to interfere in what happened in Malik's camp, I could nivver have stayed still," Kevrik told her, flushing slightly. "But th' worst of it was when Malik grabbed her and ran, in the midst of the stampede. It was sheer luck that I saw her taken." He described the headlong run through the trees, and when he repeated Malik's threats just before he had rescued me, there was a profound silence.

"Thank you for saving the life of the guildmistress, for it is clear that she would not have survived her adventure without you," Rushton said. He turned to me and asked in a low, glacial voice, "Am I correct in assuming that you deliberately allowed yourself to be handed over to Malik? Does it matter at all to you that you contravened the agreement of all guildleaders not to put themselves into danger?"

Anger rose in me, as clean and hard as a blade. "It is strange that you should object to my putting myself in danger, given that you and Maryon were prepared to allow me to ride here knowing there was danger waiting for me. At least I chose it with Malik, but neither you nor Maryon gave me the choice. Why did you not come after me and simply tell me what she had seen? Do you think I would have balked at coming here if you had told me that facing danger would enable me to avert a catastrophe? Have I given you such cause to doubt my courage? Was I not conveying Dragon to Sutrium, even though she hates me, because Maryon said I must? And what of *that* foreseeing?"

Rushton had grown very pale. "I asked that of Maryon, and she said that one foreseeing did not negate another, even when they appeared to conflict. You were to take Dragon when you left for Sutrium, and so she has gone to Sutrium. Nothing was said of you arriving with her, Maryon says. And her foreseeing concerning Saithwold was that no one must go after you, else you would not do what you were meant to do. You speak as if I chose this."

Dameon reached out to lay a quelling hand on Rushton's arm. "This is a difficult time, and it is not yet over," he said gently.

Rushton gave a jerky nod and said in an expressionless voice that he was sorry if I thought he had done wrong in obeying Maryon. He bowed to us both, turned on his heel, and mounted Esred behind Malik, saying that he would see us at Vos's homestead. In a moment, he and the others continued along the road.

Watching them ride away, I found myself thinking of the night before I had left Obernewtyn. Rushton had come to my chamber with the letter for Dardelan, which contained Obernewtyn's formal charges against Malik. Taking the missive, I had summoned the courage to ask why he had been avoiding me for most of the wintertime. Rushton had answered in a weary voice, "Do you not understand, Elspeth, you who are so bright? Is it not obvious? There is nothing left in me to feel emotions with."

The quaking in me grew, and I began to tremble so hard that my teeth chattered. I was furious with my weakness, but I could not stop. Dameon gave an inarticulate exclamation and put his arms around me, drawing me close.

"You are in shock, dear one," he said compassionately, leading me to the side of the road. "Let us sit down to wait for the wagon."

As soon as we were seated, he began to emanate a low, soothing flow of emotions. He told me of a walk he had taken through Obernewtyn's orchards with Alad to visit the teknoguilders in their caves. He had sensed that they were being followed by the strange, silent boy Gavyn, whom beasts called *adantar*. Dameon had called his name, and I imagined the boy stepping out and coming to the blind empath, accompanied by the dog Rasial, who had become leader of the Beastguild at Obernewtyn in the absence of the mare Avra.

"He so rarely speaks, and yet I felt his desire to

communicate very strongly," Dameon said softly. "I asked if he wanted to tell me something, and he said that Seely was coming to see him."

"Seely!" I echoed.

Before the rebellion, the unTalented Seely had fled with her young Misfit charge all the way to the mountains from the west coast for fear of what the Council would do to the boy at the behest of his stepmother, Lady Slawyna, who had guessed her stepson was a Misfit and wanted his Councilman father's property to pass to her own son.

I had found the pair and brought them to Obernewtyn, but during the rebellion, Seely had returned to the west coast with the teknoguilder Jak to help set up a refuge in the Beforetime ruins. Like all of the Misfits I had sent there to aid the rebel groups, she had been trapped there when the Suggredoon had been closed. Gavyn had never seemed to miss her, though he had once or twice mentioned dreaming of her. But how could she visit him unless the west coast was won from Council and Faction? Was this a sign that we would capture the invasion ships and use them to reach the west coast?

Forcing myself to calm down, I asked Dameon if, since my departure from Obernewtyn, there had been any new dreams of the Misfits I had sent to the west coast recorded in the dream journals. He said that he had inquired after the strange encounter with Gavyn, and there had been only one recorded dream. In it, the young empath Blyss and the coercer Merret had been waiting outside a city for a messenger from the rebel Gwynedd.

"The city must be Murmroth," I said, but Dameon shook his head, saying the dreamer had scribed that the city was right on the coast. Murmroth was the only coastal town not situated right on the coast.

"If messages are being exchanged between us and the rebels, it may be that Tardis is less opposed to us than she was," I said.

"I think hers was an inherited hatred rather than the fierce and fanatical hatred her father apparently had for Misfits, and it may be that circumstances have so altered in the west that old prejudices have melted away. But it might also be that something has happened to Tardis, because from what was said in the dream, it sounds as if Gwynedd is the leader of the Murmroth rebels now.

"And, no," Dameon went on, anticipating my next question with a smile, "there have been no dreams of Matthew, save for one brief dream I experienced only last night." The empath went on to describe the dream, in which Matthew and another man had been speaking of a ship anchored offshore from the Red Land, which rumor said was delivering a new shipment of slaves. Matthew had been insisting that the ship was the very same that had brought him to the Red Land, in which case it was likely to go back the way it had come once it had emptied its holds. The remainder of the discussion had been about the possibility of boarding the ship and stowing away, which both men had acknowledged as difficult and deadly. Then there had been some incomprehensible talk of something called The Spit, which Dameon said seemed to have put Matthew off the idea of stowing away.

"A true dream?" I asked, knowing it was always harder for Dameon to tell, for his dreams were scent and smell and sometimes taste dreams.

"It felt real, but it was too brief to be sure," the Empath guildmaster said.

Suddenly Dameon stiffened. "I hear a wagon."

I scrambled to my feet and saw the wagon in the distance. I farsought Zarak with relief and found that he already knew about the arrival of Rushton and the others, for Asra and Hilder had stopped to speak with them. But when Lo brought the wagon to a halt, Zarak looked shocked.

"What happened to your face?"

"It looks worse than it is," I said lightly, taking his hand and climbing into the back of the wagon. Darius lay bolstered on all sides by blankets and took up most of the floor space.

"We will send for a healer as soon as we can," I said as Zarak helped steer Dameon to the seat opposite his father, where there was room for his long legs. As the wagon lurched forward again, Khuria introduced Dameon to Noviny and his granddaughter. Dameon held out a hand, and Wenda put her own awkwardly into it. The empath released her hand and asked if she was a healer. She looked startled, nodded, and then flushed, realizing he could not see her.

Noviny asked me what had happened at Malik's camp, for Gahltha's equine messenger had not been much of a tale-teller. I obliged, describing the stampede and concentrating on the courage and brilliance of the horses. When I concluded, Noviny gave a great sigh and said it was a relief that he no longer had to worry himself sick trying to think how to notify the Council of Chieftains about the invasion.

I noticed the glimmer of metal at Darius's throat, and remembering the key Kevrik used to free me from my demon band, I drew it from my pocket and crouched down beside Darius to insert it into the lock. His waxen skin felt clammy and cold against my fingers as I unclipped the band and pulled it gently out from around his neck. Handing the key to Zarak to remove the other demon bands, I pulled the blanket higher around the gypsy's neck.

"Poor man," Wenda said as Zarak removed her band. "His limbs were already inflamed and giving him pain, and then he was so roughly handled by the armsmen. They did not care that he was hurt." She added, "I was able to find some good healing herbs near the cloister to bring the swelling down and ease his fever. But then he fell into this still, cold sleep. I do not know how to treat him, for I do not understand what ails him, unless it is shock. That can sometimes come after an event and have strange and deadly effects, especially on someone who is already ill."

"If it is shock, I can help him," Dameon said, and he asked Wenda to guide his hands to the cripple's chest. This done, he closed his eyes and concentrated. Then he drew back and shook his head. "He is not in shock," the empath said with authority. "There is something causing him so much hurt that he withdraws from life rather than endure it."

Dameon now turned his blind eyes to me. "I cannot cure what ails him, Elspeth, but I can help him rest more serenely until we reach the healing center in Sutrium."

I bade him do what he could, and we all watched in silence as the Empath guildmaster closed his eyes again. There was no sign of his empathising and no great change in Darius, except that, to me, his expression seemed to grow more peaceful. When Dameon opened his eyes again, he looked weary but serene as ever, and Wenda let out a breath she had unconsciously been holding.

"It must be confusing," she said, smiling shyly at Dameon, "to feel what another feels. How can you tell it is not your own feeling?"

Dameon gave a soft laugh. "There are times when it is *very* confusing to be an empath," he agreed.

By the time we came within sight of the gate to Vos's property, we were cramped and hot, but despite my eagerness to get out of the wagon, I bade the horses wait until I farsought Dovyn. He told me that Rushton and the funaga had arrived and had subdued the funaga-li, and he bade me enter without fear.

Presently, Zade and Lo were unhitched from the wagon and released to join the other horses grazing peaceably on the homestead's green lawn. The rest of us stretched our limbs gratefully, save Wenda who said she would remain in the wagon with Darius until he could be carried to a bed. Sover, standing by, heard her and promised to arrange it at once. He was that rarity, a coercer with secondary abilities as an empath.

He went into the house and returned with Rushton and several frightened-looking servants. As Zarak, Sover, and Harwood gently lifted the injured gypsy, Rushton greeted Noviny, who introduced his granddaughter, naming her a healer and explaining that she had been caring for Darius. Rushton bowed to the girl, thanking her so warmly for her care of the crippled gypsy that she blushed prettily. To my shame, I felt an ugly stab of jealousy at this proof that only I left the Master of Obernewtyn cold.

You are a fool, I told myself savagely, and felt Dameon flinch. Contrite, I reined in my emotions and forced myself to calmly ask Rushton what had happened upon their arrival. As he turned to answer me, I saw his reluctance, and it made me realize something that I had not known or maybe had not wanted to acknowledge. It was not that Rushton felt nothing for me. It was the opposite. It was as if he constantly struggled to control a powerful aversion to me. This thought gave me such pain that I nearly gasped, and I was glad for Dameon's sake that he had moved away.

As if from a great distance, I heard Rushton explain that it had been a simple matter to take control, since Vos gave himself up as soon as he saw them ride in with Malik as their prisoner. The rebel leader had been horrified to learn Malik's true intentions and insisted that he had known nothing of this dastardly plot, that everything from the barricades to the attempt to have himself made chieftain had been Malik's idea. He had been tricked and bullied. Rushton said this speech had made Malik turn a look of such blazing fury on the rebel chieftain that Vos had nearly passed out. Vos was now confined to his room, as were those of his men whom Kevrik said could be trusted. The rest were in the cells.

As we all went inside the house, Rushton told Noviny that he and some of the knights would be taking Malik to Sutrium as soon as they had eaten.

"Perhaps you would like to come. I believe it would be far more effective for you to tell the Council of Chieftains what you saw that day from the cliff rather than our reporting it secondhand," Rushton said.

I did not hear Noviny's answer, because Linnet

was telling me that she had prepared a room and a bath for me.

I sank blissfully to my neck in a bathing barrel filled with fragrant hot water. The air was full of steam and made me feel as if I had drifted into a dream, but I made myself wash my cuts and my hair until it floated about me like strands of black silk.

There was a soft knock at the door.

A swift probe revealed that it was Dameon and not Rushton, as my treacherous heart had hoped. "Come in," I called, and after a slight hesitation, he entered, gasping a little at the clouds of steam that enveloped him, and then his face turned toward me unerringly.

"I have been sent to fetch you for the meal," he said, standing in the doorway.

"I am just trying to summon the energy to get out," I said.

Dameon smiled, but there was an awkwardness in his expression. For a moment, it came to me that he was troubled at my being in a bathing barrel, but then I chided myself for being absurd. Even if I had stood naked before the empath, he would not be able to see me. Something else must be bothering him. Ashamed that I had been so full of my own troubles and doings that I had not even thought to ask Dameon how he had been faring, I said, "Stay a little and talk to me, if you can bear the steam. There is a bench along the wall on your left where you can sit."

He made his way to the seat so clumsily that I was startled. Dameon's usual grace made it hard to believe that he did not see. Then I almost laughed as I realized he was in pain! I remembered all too well the awfulness of my early riding days, and I asked, as delicately as I could, how he felt. He took my meaning at once and laughed, seeming suddenly to relax.

"Wenda has given me some salve that I am told will help." His smile faded. "In truth, I am more bothered by imagining you at Malik's mercy than by my own small discomforts. Do you think he meant to kill you?"

"I think when he beat me in front of Vos, he was making a point to him and his men. But the more he hit me, the more he wanted to hit me."

"I cannot bear to be near him," Dameon confessed. "His hatred is like some putrid fountain whose noise and stench I cannot ignore."

I sighed. "I wonder how the other rebels will react to all that has happened here. Especially those who have supported Malik."

"Rushton wants to question him in front of the other chieftains to make sure we cannot be accused of falsifying anything. But it is my feeling that his former allies will discover they always suspected him of being a traitor," Dameon said with rare cynicism. "Ironically, his treachery is more likely to bring peace and stability to the Land than anything anyone else has done, because no matter what the individual chieftains believe or how their desires conflict, none of them wants the Councilmen or the Herder Faction back. Their outrage at Malik's betrayal will force the chieftains to stand united for the first time since the rebellion was won, and they will have to work together to meet this threat, rather than concentrating on their own regions. Rushton hopes that Dardelan will use the threat of invasion as a reason to postpone the elections a moon or so, and that will please the rebels, too. Indeed, it may be put off longer still if Dardelan decides to do as Zarak has suggested and take the ships, for he is certain to want to use them immediately to surprise those on the west coast."

As he spoke, I climbed out of the barrel and began to towel myself. Dameon tilted his head, his sensitive hearing allowing him to track my movements as I padded over to the clothes Linnet had left me.

"Tell me how Maryon's futuretelling came about," I said, taking a towel to my hair again now that I was dressed.

Dameon nodded. "I was in a meeting with Rushton and the coercer-knights when one of the younger futuretellers came running in to say her mistress wanted us urgently. When we arrived at the Futuretell guildhall, Maryon was still drifting in and out of a trance. She told us much that seemed to have no meaning, but what was most important and unambiguous was that danger awaited you in Saithwold. The coercer-knights set up a great baying that you must be rescued. But Maryon bade them be silent, for she needed to think. Then she was quiet again for a long time. At last she said that no one must go after you, because a path awaited you in Saithwold that was yours alone to tread. There was some puzzlement at this, because Zarak at least would be with you, unless something was to happen to them. Rushton asked, but Maryon said she did not see anyone in your party coming to permanent harm. You were the only one in danger, and the probability of your surviving was high.

"Rushton asked what was so dangerous to you in particular, but Maryon just said there was danger there that would eventually threaten everyone in the Land and that your going to Saithwold would avert a catastrophe.

Then she mentioned something about ships, which made no sense until you told us of the invasion and Zarak's idea about capturing the ships."

"So Rushton agreed to let things unfold as they would?" I asked coolly.

Dameon laughed. "He told Maryon in that icy, cutting tone he sometimes has, which is worse than being shouted at, that she ought not to tell us someone was in danger if we were to do nothing about it. Maryon only said rather loftily that we would need to ride to your aid but not yet. She would let us know when it was the right time. And so she did, though it seems that you had managed everything by the time we arrived. Unless our part is to finish what you have begun by taking Malik to Sutrium."

"You saved me from having to coerce Malik," I said fervently. "For that I am more than grateful."

Dameon stood and said gently that he had better go back to the others or they might think he had lost his way. At the door, he turned back to tell me that Gahltha and the prisoners—scathed and unscathed—from Malik's camp had arrived and had been dealt with.

After he had gone, I crossed to the mirror that hung by the door to comb and plait my hair. Wiping the moisture from the glass's surface, I grimaced at the sight of my battered face. Before the bath, many of the bruises and grazes had looked like dirt. But now that I was clean, I saw that the whole of one cheek and my temple were a mass of black and blue swelling around a long angry-looking gash. My lip was also swollen and split in two places, and I had a spectacular black eye.

I sighed and told myself I was lucky no one could see the bruises on my body.

◆ 12 ◆

THE PASSAGE WAS cold after the bathing room's steamy warmth, and I shivered as I padded along it toward the front of the homestead. I farsent Gahltha briefly and learned that he was in the midst of speaking with the other horses, so I withdrew, promising to come and see him later.

I did not know where the kitchen was, but I followed my nose to the big front room where Vos had interviewed me to find the carved chair had vanished and the pompous dais had become a trestle laden with platters. There was no formal seating, and everyone was merely filling plates of food and going to sit about a fire in the enormous hearth. I was startled to see a number of strangers filling their plates. Near me an old woman with a ruddy face spoke intently to a stocky younger man wearing farm clothes and an air of authority, and closer to the fire, two older men and a young woman were talking with Noviny.

There was a brief hiatus as I entered and everyone saw my face. In that momentary silence, I had the strange sensation that they all saw me as I truly was: an outsider who had only seemed to belong.

"Hurry up, Guildmistress," Zarak called, "or the savages will fall on this food I've managed to save for ye." There was a burst of laughter from the coercers about him, and the feeling of remoteness faded as I made my way to the fire. Dameon smiled at me, seeming as ever to sense exactly where I was, and patted the seat beside him. Only then did I notice Maruman sitting on his lap, glaring balefully at me with one yellow eye.

"Maruman!" I cried softly. But when I reached for him, the old cat hissed and turned his head away. I tried to enter his mind, but it was closed to me.

Dameon winced, giving me some indication of the level of Maruman's ire, and said, "Rushton sent Harwood and Yarrow to get him, and they only just returned. I am afraid Maruman did not much enjoy the ride."

I was grateful to Rushton for his thoughtfulness, though I had no doubt he had done it as much for Maruman as for me, for he had always been fond of the old cat. And I ought not to be surprised that Maruman was angry, since Gahltha had warned me that he had regarded my failure to return to the farmstead as a personal affront. An affronted Maruman was a formidable prospect, and I sat down and regarded him with longing. I took the plate Zarak handed me, asking, "Who are the strangers?"

"A couple are Vos's men that your Kevrik says can be trusted, and the others are locals Noviny sent for after Rushton asked him to summon a few of the leading members of this community capable of making serious decisions about Saithwold now that Vos and his followers have been ousted."

"But surely Noviny will—" I began.

"He would take over. Indeed, these locals asked it of him the moment he told them what had been happening. But Noviny has agreed to ride to Sutrium tonight with Rushton," Dameon said.

"If it were only a matter of governin' Saithwold, it could wait until he returns," Zarak put it. "They're takin' Vos with them as well," he added, scowling. "As a *witness*."

"A witness!" I echoed wrathfully. "He meant to cheat in the elections, he allowed your father to be tortured, and he unlawfully imprisoned Noviny and the others of his own free will! And he was going to let one of Malik's men kill Darius and torture you!"

Dameon laid a restraining hand on my arm, nodding pointedly at Maruman sleeping in his lap. But he only said, "A contrite and helpful Vos will be of far more use than a resentful prisoner, since he will not be disagreeing with everything that is said and defending himself. Indeed, he has already voluntarily handed chieftainship of Saithwold to Noviny, saying it has been a burden that he is glad to set down, if you can believe it."

"I can believe he said it," I replied, determined that once the invasion had been dealt with, I would lay charges against Vos to the Council of Chieftains.

Rushton raised his voice to announce that he and Noviny and some of the others would ride to Sutrium with Malik within the hour. "Other than that, I want to remind you of the urgent need to make sure that word of what has happened does not leak out of this province. For that reason, neither barricade will be removed at this time. Some of Vos's men, recommended to us by Kevrik, will man it so nothing here will appear to have changed. A coercer will be at each barrier at all times, dressed as an armsman and ready to probe those wanting to enter the region, in case they serve Malik. Those wearing demon bands are to be taken prisoner and coerced after their bands are removed to see if they are aligned with Malik. Malik's camp will be reconstructed and peopled by coercers clad in his colors. Anyone who comes to the camp for any reason is to be taken prisoner."

He glanced at the little group of townsmen. "Life here should appear unchanged to those outside this room, until we can find out what Malik knows and High Chieftain Dardelan summons a force to deal with the invaders. By my reckoning, that will take no more than a threeday."

He added that after the invasion had been dealt with, those armsmen who had served Malik would be taken to Sutrium to be judged, but for the time being they would remain in cells beneath the homestead.

Then he turned again to the townsfolk. "We are relying upon you locals to monitor your neighbors and make sure you do all you can to prevent any rumor starting about changes here," he told them sternly. "I know that some of you are concerned about being dishonest to friends and even family, but console yourself that this is for a short period and that it is only to protect them and the Land. Soon you will vote for a new leader, and both peace and freedom will return to Saithwold province."

"It will return when Noviny is chieftain," said a woman whom I suddenly recognized as the one who had served Wenda and me in the shop. Those about her laughed and said aye, and Rushton smiled, too, dropping his stern expression for a moment. Then he continued seriously. "I have no doubt who you will choose to lead you when you are free, but for now, remember that it is Noviny who chose *you* to serve Saithwold through the dangerous days that lie ahead. I leave here the head of the coercer-knights, Linnet, to advise you and to aid you, as well as to perform the duties I have mentioned. If you have any trouble or fear during this time, send a messenger to seek out Linnet, and she or another knight will come to your assistance. If you see her and the other knights about with Vos's men or even Malik's men, have no fear. They will be coercing them.

"Finally," Rushton continued, his eyes moving to the fire where I sat between Zarak and Dameon, "Elspeth, guildmistress of the farseekers, who has been instrumental in defeating Malik and freeing Saithwold and is a powerful coercer, and Dameon, who is guildmaster of the empaths at Obernewtyn, will remain in this region to act as joint chieftains until Noviny returns. Know that it was Noviny's suggestion and one of which I heartily approve. They will coordinate the activities of the coercer-knights, and for the time being, it is to them you must look when you need guidance."

I clenched my teeth, outraged that Rushton had not bothered to consult me before deciding that I would remain in Saithwold rather than go on to Sutrium. As if he felt my indignation, Rushton's eyes, green and unreadable, met mine briefly. Then he turned to speak to one of Vos's armsmen. The noise level rose again, but instead of engaging in the conversations about me, I picked at the food on my plate, my appetite gone.

Maruman turned to glower at me and leapt down from Dameon's lap to stalk over to a partially opened window. I half rose to go after him, but Dameon caught my arm to stay me, saying gently, "Let him go, Elspeth. You are too emotional to deal with him right now."

Knowing he was right, I sat back down. Rushton was coming toward the fire with Noviny and Linnet.

The older man was describing the Herder warriors' training exercises, which he had witnessed, and gradually the heat in my anger faded as I listened, for he might have been describing coercer training, with its emphasis on breathing and balance as well as on strength. Noviny added that the warrior priests' favored weapons were a short metal-shod pole and a handheld sickle-shaped blade.

Noviny went on to say that although the warrior priests wore robes and had their heads shaven, there were distinct differences between them and ordinary priests, even in their attire. The tunics of the warrior priests were a much darker gray than the traditional pale gray worn by Herders and were split on one side so they could reach their weapons, which they carried in holsters attached to belts.

Hearing this, Linnet suggested they must see themselves more as warriors than priests.

"I am not sure that is true," Noviny said. "When I heard the warrior priests speak and move about, it seemed that they see their weapons and their ability to fight as a kind of prayer that they dedicate to Lud. For them, fighting is praying."

Again prompted by Rushton, he speculated about the increase in numbers of the warrior priests just before the rebellion and about how many more there would be if the priests had trained as warriors the hundreds of acolytes and novices who had fled with the rest to Herder Isle. The figures he mentioned took my breath away.

Rushton thought for a moment. "Given what you have said, Noviny, I think a coercer would be a match for a warrior priest in an equal battle, and though they may exceed the number of coercers we can muster, the cliff paths are all too narrow for more than one person to ascend at a time. Even so, we would need to capture the warrior priests immediately and silently so as not to warn those coming behind. We cannot allow them to form a massed force."

I was still infuriated with Rushton's decision to keep me in Saithwold, but I could not undermine his authority before the others, so I said in a voice harsh enough to show my anger, "The warrior priests are certain to wear demon bands, so the coercers' Talents will be useless."

Before Rushton could respond, one of the locals called out to say he hoped *they* would not be expected to fight, for what had farm folk to do with battles.

Rushton turned to look at the man, but when he spoke, he spoke to all those gathered. "There is a battle to come, make no mistake about it, and it will be fought in this region. The coercers from Obernewtyn will fight, but understand that this is not a battle between Misfits and Herders. Nor are the rebel conquerors defending a land they have stolen from others. We are all—Misfits, rebels, and ordinary Landfolk—free men and women who must fight to remain so. This will be *our* battle for *our* Land.

"As for the details of our defense, that is not something that can be decided here." His eyes flickered my way without ever meeting my gaze. "That will happen in Sutrium once we have learned the precise details of the invasion from Malik."

Noviny went to speak with the man who had spoken, and Rushton turned back to me. "I am sorry I did not have the chance to warn you about what I would say, but I assumed you would wish to remain until

Darius can be taken safely to his people. That will be at least a sevenday according to the healer who now tends him," he said in a low voice.

His explanation ought to have mollified me, but his cool formality stripped the words of comfort. I was still trying to think how to respond when Zarak said, "I have been thinkin' on how we can gan to the invaders' ships without havin' to fight our way to them. Noviny was tellin' me about these deep caves at the foot of the cliffs, just along from the stone steps, where he saw th' Herders meet with Malik. . . ."

"I have said already that we will not know where along the coast the invasion force will land until Malik has been interrogated," Rushton cut in sternly.

Zarak flushed and looked mortified, but Rushton reached out to grasp his shoulder. "You have a fine mind, lad, and I think if your guildmistress will permit it, you might ride along with us to Sutrium tonight, for we will need such skills in the days ahead." Rushton released him, saying in a louder voice, "It is time for us to leave for Sutrium. Make your preparations."

A babble of talk erupted, but rather than becoming engaged in it, Rushton turned on his heel and strode across the room toward the door.

Zarak looked at me pleadingly, and despite my own emotional turmoil, I could not help but smile. Even if I had wanted to refuse him, I could not have done so anyway with Khuria standing behind his son, beaming with pride. I nodded, and Zarak hugged his father and raced to get his things.

As the room gradually emptied, those locals who had attended the meeting came to bid Dameon and me a rather stiff farewell, but after the empath spoke a few

213

words to them, they were smiling, and I knew he had bathed them in waves of calmness and trust. I wondered, as I had often done before, at the morality of this, for was it not another form of coercion, even if it was benevolent?

"... Garth was completely astonished," Dameon was saying.

"Astonished about what?" I asked, realizing he had been speaking.

He smiled wryly. "I was saying that Rushton summoned Garth back to Obernewtyn the same day you left the White Valley and ordered him to open Jacob Obernewtyn's grave. As you can imagine, the Teknoguildmaster wasted no time. You know how obsessed he is about Hannah Seraphim. Strangely, there were no bones in the grave, nor any sign that a body had even been there. Instead, there was a suit, which Garth says is the Beforetime version of our plast suits, and a notebook with the pages sealed in plast. The writing in the notebook begins as a letter to Hannah Seraphim, though later parts seemed more like a journal, from what I heard."

"*Jacob's* journal?" I guessed, my interest quickening.

Dameon nodded. "He scribes that he is weary of his loneliness and has decided to leave Obernewtyn. He says that he will take with him the key Hannah left behind. Since she never returned, it will never lie with them in the grave they had prepared to hold their bodies."

"Never returned from where?" I asked, baffled.

"He did not say where, but the letter appears to have been written over a period when he was making elaborate preparations to leave. Some of what he scribes makes me sure he intended to go into the Blacklands beyond the mountains above Obernewtyn."

"Poor man mun have been mad," Khuria said.

"If he is speaking of the Blacklands, then the letter was scribed after the Great White," I said. "But what does he mean about being alone? Even if Hannah was not there, there would have been others."

"The letter tells that the others had decided to take refuge from the missiles and something called a *fallout* in what used to be the building that housed the teknoguilders of their time. And you know what happened to it, of course. The upper levels were destroyed and the lower levels crushed, not by weapons but by immense movements in the earth, which were the result of the Great White.

"Jacob scribes that Hannah had warned them that Obernewtyn would be the safest place for them during the holocaust, but when it all began, everyone was frightened that she might have made a mistake. After all, she had never foreseen her own absence. So they voted to go into the lower chambers of the Teknoguild laboratories. Jacob scribed that he would have been with them, but he was in the house trying to reach Hannah on a computermachine. From what he says, he spoke to her, and that was when she promised him that she would return, for she had foreseen that their bones would lie together at the end with the key."

"What is this key he speaks of?" Khuria asked curiously.

Dameon shrugged. "Jacob said only that it had been given to Hannah in trust and that she was supposed to hold it safe for someone else, though I do not know how she could have done that if they were supposed to take it to their grave."

"I wonder where Hannah went," I said.

"It mun have been as my lad has always thought," Khuria offered. "Hannah were in Newrome under Tor when the Great White came, an' she died there."

"But Jacob scribed that he spoke to her, so maybe she escaped the flooding of the city under Tor but had no way of getting through the mountain pass to Obernewtyn," Dameon said. "Remember, the pass would have been a good deal more poisonous right after the Great White."

"Jacob had a plast suit, though. Why dinna he use it and gan to *her*?" Khuria wondered.

Dameon frowned. "He must have had two suits, because he scribed that he was going to wear one and leave one for Hannah in the tomb so she could follow him. But I don't know how he thought she would manage that, since he did not leave any information about where he meant to go."

Khuria said grimly, "I have seen a glimpse of what lies beyond the high mountains, and I tell ye that no one could gan there an' live, even if they wore a plast suit. It is a vast unending desolation that stretches to th' horizon. Jacob'd nowt last more than a sevenday there without food, an' less without water, and if he took off his suit to eat or drink, he'd die eventually of wastin' sickness."

"He would not last long," I said. "The air above tainted earth would also have been poisoned back then, Garth says. He would be dead within hours."

"No," Dameon said. "Jacob scribed that he was taking an air purifier and food and water in special containers that he could use without taking the suit off. He also had some sort of device to eliminate waste."

"Even so, he was alone, and how much food and water could he have carried?" I said.

"Poor man," Khuria murmured. "He mun have been driven mad waitin' in vain all those years for the woman he loved."

"We don't really know if there was anything between Hannah and Jacob, despite what Garth thinks," I pointed out, somewhat startled by the old man's romanticism.

"They mun have loved one another, else why choose to share a grave?" Khuria asked.

"You could not read his words and doubt that he loved her," Dameon said slowly. "Yet maybe *she* did not love him."

"Why did Rushton command the grave be opened?" I asked.

"Maryon said it must be so," Dameon said. "She did not say why."

The others began speculating about why the Futuretell guildmistress would want an old grave opened. I said nothing, for it seemed to me quite likely that Maryon had been manipulated by the Agyllian birds guiding my quest, to ensure that I knew the key that ought to have been in the grave was not where it was meant to be. But if that were true, what was I supposed to do about it? The only thing I was sure of was that the key Jacob had taken with him must be the one referred to in the carving on the Obernewtyn doors.

"... *that key which must be [used/found] [before all else] is [with/given/sent to] she who first dreamed of the searcher—the hope beyond the darkness to come.* ..."

Which meant I had been wrong to think that the words on the glass statue under Tor, created by Cassy Duprey and given to Hannah, were the key referred to by this line. It must be as I had first thought: that the key had been sent to Hannah concealed in or with the glass sculpture. Hannah must have promised Cassy that the key would go with her to her grave, neither of them foreseeing that the Great White could separate Hannah irrevocably from the key or that Jacob would go into the Blacklands, taking it with him.

But I refused to fall into despair—at least not until I had read Jacob's journal, for there might be a clue in it that only I would understand. Or maybe the clue waiting for me in the Earthtemple in Sador was the result of a later futuretelling by Kasanda, which would direct me to the missing key. Perhaps it was good that Rushton had not asked me to come to Sutrium, for it left me free to return directly to Obernewtyn. After all, Dameon could surely manage Saithwold in my absence.

A question occurred to me. "How did Garth react to Maryon's command to open the grave?"

Dameon laughed. "As you can imagine, given her previous opposition to his requests, he was torn between wanting to embrace her and wanting to strangle her."

A gust of cold wind blew around us, stirring the flames in the fire, and I turned with the others to see that the outer door had opened. Zarak stood there, wearing boots and greatcoat, his cheeks pink with exertion and excitement. "Rushton said to tell you we are about to leave," he said.

The wind had the smell of the sea in it, as well as the scent of storms to come. Apt, I thought. The sky was blanketed in cloud that allowed neither moonlight nor star shine to show through. But several of the coercers carried lanterns whose flames danced and fluttered even behind their glass shields.

I breathed in the sweet wild air, realizing that thinking of my quest had cooled the anger I felt toward Rushton. I looked at Malik. His face might have been carved of rock for all the emotion it showed. This thought reminded me that I had yet to see the statue that stood in Noviny's garden. At least the delay in our departure would give me time to find out if it was another sign from Kasanda to the Seeker.

I saw Kevrik preparing to mount up, and realizing that Rushton must have asked him to go to Sutrium as well, I went to bid him farewell. I was interested to see his clumsy attempt at fingerspeech. He flushed and smiled when the horse made no response. "I have already learned a few words in beastspeech, an' young Zarak has promised to teach me more as we ride. He says he owes me a lesson fer th' headache he gave me in the cell."

"I have not thanked you properly for saving my life," I said seriously.

His expression sobered. " 'Tis I who should be thanking ye for allowing me the chance to become a free man. I dinna mean that I am nowt in a cell either. I mean free of foolish prejudices that are as bad as bars. Some of th' men who served Vos feel the same way after meeting Linnet an' the knights, and your Rushton is an impressive sort of man, by anyone's standard."

I gritted my teeth at hearing Rushton referred to as mine, but before I could correct Kevrik, Rushton was calling everyone to mount up. Kevrik obeyed with alacrity as Rushton came over to me. "I wish you a safer journey than thus far, Guildmistress," he said formally.

"Give my good wishes to Dardelan and Reuvan," I managed to say composedly, but as he mounted Esred, I thought again of what had passed between us the night I had ridden out from Obernewtyn.

"You must tell me what is wrong," I had pleaded. "Why do you not touch me or smile at me or look at me?"

He had sighed, and when he did look at me, I had seen only a deadly weariness. If I could have stopped him answering then, I would have. For I suddenly knew, as if I were a futureteller, that if he spoke, his words would destroy something precious. But it was too late.

"Do you not understand, Elspeth, you who are so bright? Is it not obvious? There is nothing left in me to feel emotions with," Rushton said slowly. He glanced toward the turret window, which overlooked the wall encircling Obernewtyn and the jagged mountains surrounding us, their tips blanketed in snow. Then he looked back at me. "We loved, you and I. That is a truth. But not all love lasts forever, and that is also a truth. I do not love you any longer. Since I woke from my . . . time in the cloister, I have felt nothing. It is as if all capacity for feeling has been burned from me. I remember love, but I do not feel it any more than one who has had a limb amputated. At some moments, there is something . . . and I have waited to see if it would grow into true feeling, but it has not, and I know now that I am nothing more than a limbless person who experiences an itch in a leg that is no longer there."

"Rushton, if you would only let me help you remember what happened in the cloister, perhaps your ability to feel would return," I said.

"I do not wish to remember," Rushton answered flatly. "I am sorry, for I know that what I say must give you pain, and yet you need to know the truth so that you can be healed of . . . of what you feel for me." He looked out the window again, his green eyes remote.

The pain of his words cut so deep. But I could see that even the pity he expressed was nothing more than a mimicking of that emotion. He could not truly feel pity any more than he could feel love. Yet he seemed to have lost none of his devotion to Obernewtyn. Or was that just another simulation? How cruel pain made me in that moment. How I wanted to scratch at that calm face to see if he felt even that.

"I . . . see," I managed to say, the words jerking from my mouth. "I am glad you have explained it to me. I had not thought of love as a wound that might need healing. Well, it must be possible, for you have managed it without even a scar. Maybe it is not so difficult as I might have imagined."

The metallic taste of blood woke me to the present, and I realized that I had bitten my lip. Everyone had mounted now, and they were riding out the gate. Malik was at the back between two coercer-knights, and he turned to look back. I expected to see loathing in his eyes, but instead he gave me a look of vicious triumph.

A shiver of premonition came to me as I remembered Malik saying in the woods that he had no need to escape. I had felt sure he meant the invasion, but he knew now that we were aware of the bargain he had struck with the Herders, so why that look of triumph? I shaped a probe to call them back so we could coerce Malik at once and learn what lay behind that look. But the thought of facing Rushton again stopped me sending it. Whatever secret Malik nursed would be wrested from him by a coercer in Sutrium on the morrow.

I stood for a long time after the sound of the horses' hooves faded, only half conscious that the wind had grown stronger. No one spoke to me as they drifted back inside, and I guessed they imagined that I pined for Rushton. No doubt they thought that we had quarreled. Would that it were so simple, for quarrels could be mended. I had felt myself devastated by what Rushton had said that last night at Obernewtyn, but I understood only now that I had not accepted his words. When Rushton had ridden up on Esred earlier that day, I had looked for signs of his love, feeling certain that such love as we had shared could not simply be extinguished like a fire.

But now hope was truly dead.

Whatever the Herders had done to Rushton had changed him irrevocably. Hearing of what Malik had done to me, he had behaved as if an injustice had been done that he would see was put right. Remembering Malik's sly hateful words about Rushton being hollowed out, I wondered if what lay behind his triumphant look of malice was his awareness that Rushton could not love me. After all, he witnessed the coolness between us as Rushton bade me farewell.

I had meant to look for Maruman to mend the rift between us, but my heart and mind were full of turmoil and grief. I stumbled along the side of the house to the back door and went directly to the bedroom I had been shown earlier. Opening a window in case Maruman

222

recovered from his dudgeon and came seeking me in the night, I farsent Gahltha to say good night, only to find that the old cat was with him. Relieved that he was safe, I withdrew and lay on my bed, fully clothed. I fell at once into a dream.

I dreamed vividly of the day my parents had died. I saw the soldierguards burst through the door of our home as my mother prepared nightmeal. One soldierguard grasped my mother about the waist, and Jes flew at him. The soldierguard swatted him away as if he were an insect, and Jes hit the wall with a loud crack and fell down, lying half stunned against it. I ran to my mother and tried to climb into her arms, but another soldierguard tore me away from her and hurled me over to where Jes was beginning to stir. My mother was dragged outside, and then two soldierguards pushed us after her. I heard her calling out to neighbors and friends to help us. But though people's faces appeared at windows, no one tried to stop the soldierguards or the Herders directing them.

We were brought to the central square of Rangorn, where moon fairs and sevenday markets were held. Here a small crowd stood gathered about a man tied to a pole in the midst of a woodpile. I realized as we came nearer that the man was my father. He spoke my mother's name with grief, and she cried out his name and then our names. Anguish crossed my father's features as he saw us, and he cursed the Herders standing by, pale and gray-robed, their heads bald and gleaming in the sunlight. My mother only begged the priests to take us away so we would not see the burning.

The older of the priests answered her in a dry, fussy voice, saying that we were the children of seditioners and must see where our parents' treachery had led so we would not follow in their footsteps. Then one of the soldierguards held us while another daubed our cheeks and foreheads with the stinging dye used to mark the children of seditioners.

"Don't let them do this," my father cried out suddenly in his strong rich voice. "There are more of you standing here than these foul priests and the few brutish soldierguards that serve them. Rise up and bind them and let us begin the rebellion here and now, which this Land needs to cleanse itself."

I looked at the Herders and saw unease cross the face of the younger one, but the older priest only gave a prim, cruel smile and leaned forward to light the kindling with his torch. I saw no more, because Jes pulled me to face him and held me tightly so that I could not see the burning. But I heard it and smelled it.

I felt my brother's trembling, suffocating embrace, and days later, my upper arms still bore the handshaped bruises of Jes's grip. I heard my father groan and curse the Herders and the Faction, and I heard my mother plead over and over with her friends and neighbors to care for us before her voice rose to a scream. When the screams and groans stopped and a terrible smell filled the air, I looked up at Jes and saw tracks of fire running down his cheeks, where tears reflected flame.

I wept then, too—the desolate weeping of a child deprived forever of her life and family.

✦ 13 ✦

I woke before dawn, hollowed out by the vividly detailed memory dream.

I was too wide awake to go back to sleep, for it was near morning. Resisting the temptation to farseek Maruman, I decided to find out what sort of mood the old cat was in without actually beastspeaking him. I lit a lantern, washed my face, and dressed before pulling on my boots and brushing my hair. As I left the room, a few intrepid birds were already giving out notes, tuning themselves for the dawn chorus. Rather than going straight outside, I decided to go find some food. Aside from being hungry myself, food was always a good way to coax Maruman out of a temper. If I could find some fish, the battle would be half won.

It took me a little time to find the kitchen, but it was not deserted, as I had expected at such an early hour. A young boy was seated on a bench before the stove, poking at the fire. He leapt to his feet when he saw me and began to stammer an explanation. His father had sent him to rake up the embers and stoke a fire for firstmeal.

"Good," I said. "I need someone to give me directions to the larder. Do you suppose your father would object if we had a bite to eat before he comes?"

The boy said, "There is some bread we could toast, Da told me not to touch any food . . ."

"I will make you a bargain," I said, hiding a smile. "If you will toast some bread, I will spread jam upon it. And let us light a lamp."

In just a few minutes, we were seated companionably before the fire, eating thick, half-burnt slices of bread smeared with a delicious tart blackberry jam. Gazing into the fire and listening to the boy tell me that his little sister had picked the berries for the jam, I thought of Jes and how tightly he had held me to stop my seeing our parents' awful death. He had done his best for me. The strangeness that had come over him before I had been charged Misfit had been no more his choice than the repression of those memories had been mine. Our minds devised these responses to help us survive. And maybe Dameon was right about Rushton's love being buried beneath what had been done to him by the Herders.

Hope stirred in me, small and frail, but hope nonetheless.

The sound of a door opening interrupted my thoughts, and I turned to see Linnet enter. She said in a grave, urgent voice, "You'd better come, Guildmistress."

I handed my plate to the boy and followed the coercer, my heart beating fast with apprehension. "What is the matter?"

"I'm not sure. One of Malik's armsman offered us information in return for his release. He said the only reason he had continued serving Malik, once he had made his pact with the Faction, was because he would have been killed if he had seemed to waver in his loyalty. He has a woman up in Sawlney who is carrying his child, and he wants to go to her. Naturally, I told him that we would get all the information we needed from his master, but he said that it would not come soon enough to save us from the invasion. I asked what he meant."

"Why didn't you tell him that the quickest way to prove he was telling the truth would be to let you probe him?"

"I did, and he agreed to it. But I made the mistake of putting him back in his cell while we cleared another to conduct the interrogation. Another armsman attacked him, and he is so near to dying now that anyone entering his mind would be at risk of being taken with him."

We had reached the steps leading to the cells, and I ran down them, past the waiting coercers. A big armsman lay on the floor in a pool of blood. I recognized him from Malik's camp. I knelt next to him, noticing that his breathing had an ominous whistling sound.

"Can you hear me?" I asked. His eyes found my face, and I saw that he was able to hear and understand me. I leaned close to his ear and said, "Tell us what you know, and we will find your woman and see that she and the child are cared for."

The man's eyes widened, and I saw the effort it cost him to move his lips. "Klah ... los ... ," he gasped. Rosy blood bubbled from his nostrils.

"It must be the name of his woman," Linnet said.

But I was looking down into the armsman's face and saw his eyes move rapidly left and then right. No.

"Try again," I urged him.

"Clos ... ," he spluttered.

"Close?" I guessed. Again his eyes flicked left and right. A cloudiness in them indicated that we had very little time.

"Please," I said. "Let your child be told that his father fought to keep the Land free."

This time the tendons in his neck stood out as he spoke. "Clois . . . Kloh . . ." He sank back, his lips sheened with blood.

"Dead," I said softly, and reached forward to close his staring eyes.

"Could he have been trying to say *cloister*?" Linnet guessed.

"It may be. You had better coerce the man who attacked him. I think we can say this is serious enough to warrant it."

"I doubt it will do any good. The dead man claimed to be the only one who knew what he was offering to tell us. Indeed, he said Malik would have killed him for what he knew. The other armsman attacked him purely because he meant to collaborate with us."

I looked down at the dead man and remembered Malik's triumphant look as he rode off. "He said that any information obtained from Malik would come too late to save us from the Herder invasion?" Linnet nodded. "That makes no sense, for Malik will have been coerced by tomorrow or the day after, and Dardelan will send a force here immediately to prepare for the invasion."

"It was before wintertime that Noviny overheard Malik, and the timing of the invasion might well have been changed since then," Linnet pointed out.

She was right. "Then if the armsman spoke truly, the invasion would have to take place tomorrow or even today!" I thought again of Malik's look of triumph. "We must organize our own defense immediately."

"But what are we to defend? There are three places where an invasion force could come ashore in Saithwold," Linnet said.

"We must put watchers at each set of steps and instruct them to send word the moment they spot ships approaching," I replied. "That will give us time to move a force to meet them. In the meantime, we need to gather a fighting force."

"We must send word to Rushton and Dardelan," Linnet said.

"So we will, but we need something more than a few choked words from a dying man. I will ride to the cloister and look around."

Linnet nodded decisively. "I will send out some knights to watch for ships at each accesspoint."

"You might also send someone to investigate those caves Noviny mentioned to Zarak as well," I said. "See what sort of force we could conceal in them."

Linnet gave me a searching look. "You still intend trying to take the ships?"

"I think we must try," I said. "With luck, Dardelan and the others will arrive in time to help."

Linnet strode out of the cell, and I heard her instruct a coercer to summon Khuria and all the knights to the kitchen. I glanced down at the dead man one more time before going after her.

As we ascended the steps, Linnet said she would ask Khuria to gather the men and women nominated by Noviny to help guide Saithwold in his absence. "We will need their help to assemble a force big enough to deal with any warrior priests we take as prisoners," she explained. "But we knights must be at the top of the steps to receive these warrior priests."

"Given the sort of numbers we will have, it might be wiser to try trickery at the top of the steps, rather than force," I said. "Why not coerce a group of Malik's men to meet the invaders and lead them into a trap away from the cliffs?"

"The invaders are going to expect to see Malik," Linnet pointed out.

"Then prepare for that. Have the coerced men claim to be taking the invaders to Malik. If we are right in guessing that the cloister is a secret armory, the Herders can be told Malik awaits them there."

"Maybe one of Malik's men will know," Linnet suggested. "I will coerce the leaders among them as soon as I set the others to their tasks. It is a pity your friend Kevrik left."

"Talk to those of Vos's armsmen that Kevrik said were decent people. One of them is bound to know which men Malik might have confided in," I said, but I had no great hope he would have confided in anyone.

By the time we reached the kitchen, some of the co-ercers were beginning to assemble, but I did not linger, for I was eager to find out if we had been right in our guesses about the cloister. Farseeking Gahltha to meet me in front of the house, I fetched my greatcoat and went outside to find he was already waiting. I grasped his mane, threw myself onto his back, and in minutes we were galloping hard along the road. It then occurred to me that the slaves Noviny had seen might have been held in the cloister to be handed over to the Herders. Remembering the pitiable state of the prisoners we had found locked in Sutrium's cloister cells after the invasion, I farsent Linnet to ask her to send Wenda and the carriage after me, just in case there were any poor wretches in the cells.

The sun was near to rising behind the trees as we approached the rutted track to the cloister, and I could see the pale, stone wall that enclosed it quite clearly. It stood as high as the tallest trees in the mist-wreathed forest that hemmed it on three sides, and had a secretive air.

I slipped down from Gahltha's back, hot from the exertion of the gallop, and approached the enormous metal gate sagging off its hinges. I could feel the numbing buzz of the tainted walls, and my heartbeat quickened. Why freshen the taint in the walls, if not to keep something concealed from Misfit Talents?

I was about to go through the gate when I noticed Gahltha hanging back. Guessing that the taint was troubling him, I stroked his soft nose and told him to wait outside since he could not come into the cloister buildings with me anyway. He agreed with relief, and I went through the gateway alone. But I stopped again inside, assailed by a premonition of danger. As usual, it was so vague as to be useless, save as a reminder that I would not be able to reach Gahltha's mind until I came back through the gate. Then I chided myself for being a fool, for of course I could call out to him.

I took a deep breath and looked around. Cobbles ran from the gate to the front of the cloister, but on either side of the cloister building were green swathes of grass. On the south lawn apple trees grew in neat lines parallel to the side of the building. The sun had not yet

231

risen high enough to cast any direct light on them, and it struck me that I had foolishly failed to bring a lantern or candles and a tinderbox. Since it was too dark to enter the building, I decided to look at the tools and piles of earth Zarak had mentioned until Wenda arrived, for there would be lanterns or candles in her wagon.

I walked through the trees toward the back of the cloister, passing under long glassless windows set into the cloister wall at intervals. These gave me the discomforting feeling of being watched, and my unease grew until suddenly I realized what was causing it. Despite the sun having risen, I could hear neither bird nor insect. The profound silence inside the cloister wall reminded me of the deadly Silent Vale.

Reaching the back of the cloister, I saw more fruit trees growing here, and behind them, against the wall, rose several high mounds of earth and the tools that Zarak had mentioned, resting against a small stone shed. Going closer, I saw that the mounds had a hard crust, which meant they had been exposed to the weather for some time. They were the same dark choca hue as the earth showing through the wet grass; but there was enough earth to fill a great pit and no sign of a digging site.

The most likely place to bury something dangerous would be in the cells, which traditionally had earthen floors. If I was right about farm holders being held here before they were given to the Herders, Malik could have used them to dig in secret, for once locked in, they would have required no guards. The armsman killed might have stumbled onto knowledge of what was happening by overhearing a prisoner, for armsmen would have been required to escort them to the coast. Perhaps under the floor of every cell I would find that a crate of weapons had been buried, or barrels of the explosive black powder that had so frightened Vos and his men. If so, the number of crates might indicate the size of the invading force.

The rear door of the cloister was a great oaken slab that was firmly closed and would not budge, so I returned to the front of the cloister, where the door, like the gate, had been wrenched off its hinges and lay splintered and graying on the cobbles. The sun was now high enough that it cast a dull brightness inside the stone-flagged entrance hall, which was covered in a dense litter of leaves and dust. Three doors led out of the hall, and a set of steps went up to the left. Two of the doors led to passages that ran toward the back of the building, and one led to a room on the right, partly visible through a half-opened door.

Half an hour later, I had walked through numerous chambers, around the kitchen, and along all the subterranean passages, but none of the rooms or cells was occupied. Nor had I found any evidence of digging in the cells, the passages, or their walls. As I stepped out into the sunlight, I thought of the tools left leaning against the stone shed.

In minutes, I was standing in front of the shed, holding the heavy metal lock that fastened the door. It was hard to form a probe dense and delicate enough to manipulate the lock workings this close to the tainted wall, but at last I heard the telltale click.

I opened the door and stared, even though I had been expecting something of the sort. There was no floor in the shed, save for a rim of earth around the walls. The rest was a great gaping hole and a ramp of earth descending into darkness. A tunnel!

There was a row of lanterns and a tinderbox on the earth ledge, and I selected one, checked the oil reservoir, and lit the wick, before venturing into darkness. I pictured a chamber at the end of it, full of crates of weapons and barrels of black powder, but ten minutes later, I was still walking, the sloping earth ramp and earthen walls having given way to a natural passage through the region's soft rock that must have once been a subterranean watercourse. Aware that such a passage could go on for miles, I wondered if this was an escape tunnel of the sort the Faction had often built to allow secret movement in and out of cloisters. Judging from the packed-earth floor, much of what had been dug out of the tunnel had been used to fill the bottom of the rift and create a flat base.

Another fifteen minutes and I was regretting that I had not told Gahltha what I intended to do. But having come so far, I could not bring myself to turn back.

Another fifteen minutes passed, or so I judged it, and the tunnel still led downward. I could no longer believe this was merely an escape tunnel, for it would have surfaced long before now. I wondered if Wenda had arrived at the cloister yet. If so, she would come looking for me, but it would take time to find the tunnel entrance. When she did, I hoped that she would wait for me with Gahltha or even return to the homestead to tell Linnet and the others about the tunnel. Very soon I would have to turn back, whether or not I wished it, for the lantern's oil reservoir was nearly empty. If only I had thought to take two lanterns. But who could have guessed at the tunnel's length?

Suddenly, the flame in the lantern was snuffed out, and I was plunged into darkness.

I knew I ought to turn back, but the draft of air that had blown out the flame suggested I might not be far from a shaft leading to the surface. If there were steps, I could get out that way and farseek both Linnet and Gahltha.

I set the lantern to the side and went on cautiously, hands outstretched to keep from running into anything. Then, in the stillness, I heard a voice. I held my breath and listened hard, but I had not been mistaken. Someone was talking, and if there was a speaker, there must be at least one person listening. Was it possible there were Herders here already?

I hesitated but could not resist going on, for I wanted to hear what was being said and get some idea of how many Herders there were. If I was truly fortunate, they would not be banded, and I could learn everything we needed to know from them. I walked very carefully now, anxious that I might alert the speakers to my approach. Even so, I stumbled several times, because the ramped earth that had leveled the tunnel higher up had given way to undulating stone.

Finally, I stopped to remove my boots and tuck them under my arm, knowing that I could move more stealthily without them. I was very aware, too, that the speakers might suddenly decide to come along the tunnel. In that case, I would have no choice but to fly back to the cloister like a fox with hounds on its tail.

The flow of air grew stronger, and there was a

tantalizingly familiar scent in it. The air smelled of the sea!

My mind raced, for though by my reckoning I had been moving constantly in the direction of the coast, I did not think I could have reached the cliffs. Then a thought struck me. At several places along this part of the coast, narrow inlets opened up and the sea flowed in. What if this tunnel opened into one of them? It was an intriguing idea, but even if a shipmaster could maneuver his vessel along such a narrow channel at high tide and manage to disgorge Herder warriors in a tunnel opening, how would the ship turn to leave?

I was so intent on my thoughts that I tripped and fell sideways, stifling a cry and throwing out my hands, but there was nothing to catch ahold of. I landed with a sickening crunch.

✦ 14 ✦

I OPENED MY eyes to pitchy blackness. Both hands were pressed against my body, and when I tried to move, pain lanced through my head. At first I thought I had been captured and tied up, but there were no bindings about my wrists or body. I could not move because there was stone all about me. Swallowing hard, I told myself I must have fallen sideways into a crevice running off from the tunnel, and now I was wedged there. I felt about with my fingers and toes and butted my head gently forward, trying to get an idea of the space into which I had fallen, but to my dismay, the movement caused me to slip farther down into the crack.

Suppressing panic, I lay completely still, willing myself to calmness. I felt extraordinarily weary, which meant that my body had been draining my energy to repair whatever damage I had done in the fall.

Ruthlessly, I quashed fear and imagination and commanded myself to think, for only I could get myself out of the predicament into which I had literally fallen. Using my fingertips and toes, I began very slowly and carefully to ease myself back up the crack. Only because I had fallen sideways into the cleft instead of headfirst did I notice the play of light against the stone as I inched myself upward. I froze and saw that the light was growing stronger, which could only mean that someone was coming along the tunnel with a lantern.

I kept my eyes fixed on the crack, for if it was Wenda, I would have only one chance to call out softly and stop her from blundering into whatever lay at the end of the tunnel. Then I became aware of the thud of feet; not just the feet of one person, but of many people marching in time. Surely that could mean only one thing: *The invasion was under way!*

At least I am not a captive, I told myself, fighting a wave of despair. Once the marchers had passed, I would have to go in the opposite direction to warn the others. But what of Wenda?

The light grew brighter, and now I could feel the vibration of the marchers' boots through the stone. Soon they were passing the opening: an endless line of grim-faced, shaven-headed Herders in dark gray robes moving up the tunnel toward the cloister. Save for the color of their attire, they looked no different from any other Herders, except they were more powerful-looking, and I seemed to feel their relentless purpose. These must be the warrior priests Noviny had described. No wonder Malik had looked at me in triumph. He had known that the invasion force was on the verge of arriving.

I willed the column to end so I could renew my efforts to escape the crack, praying that Wenda would hear the thud of the Herders' feet if she was coming along the tunnel.

By the time the last warrior had passed, my whole body ached with tension, but I did not move until the light had faded completely, and even then I lay for a time listening.

Finally, I gathered my courage and strength and began moving myself carefully back up the crevice. Once I managed to get one arm free, it was easier, though I muttered a curse at the realization that I must have dropped my boots into the crack when I fell.

Back in the tunnel I took a deep breath, considered a moment, and then set off in the same direction as before, for I reasoned that I would sooner or later reach the tunnel's end. The only trouble was that the tunnel was still angling down.

After a time, I heard someone speak again and froze. He sounded quite near, and a faint light showed ahead. These things and the draft suggested I was right about the tunnel ending in steps or a shaft that led to the surface. Elated to think I might be able to escape the tunnel in time to warn the others, for the marchers could not possible have reached the cloister yet, I hastened my steps.

Suddenly, the tunnel curved into a large cavern. I stopped dead, unable to see into the cavern properly because of the angle at which the tunnel entered it. There were chinks of fire or lantern light high up, and I decided to climb the inner wall that separated the end of the tunnel from the cavern to see what was there.

The cavern was enormous, with the same undulating stone floor and walls as the tunnel, and the light came from a small fire built in a pit. From the blackened patches in other places, it looked as if there had been many fires lit. This and the number of bedrolls strewn about made it clear that the invaders had been here for some time. The warrior priests I had seen must have come ashore and hidden here.

The sole occupants now, however, were two inner-circle Herder priests, each sitting on either side of the fire. One was elderly and wore the golden armband of an inner-cadre priest. This made him the likely commander, so why had he remained here when the warrior priests had marched up to the cloister? Unfortunately, both priests were banded, as the marchers had been, so I could not probe them.

A gust of sea-scented air blew through the small hole in the stone wall I clung to, and I could actually hear the muted boom of waves, and I thought again that the tunnel must lead to one of the inlets.

The lesser of the priests began to speak. "Salamander said he wants as little killing or maiming as possible because it is a waste."

"What Salamander wants is irrelevant," said the senior priest coldly. "The One feels that a high number of deaths is desirable, both as a lesson and to cut down the corrupted population, which has accepted the dominion of freaks and Luddamned mutants. Once the Land is stabilized, we will breed a people without such undesirable tendencies as courage, inquisitiveness, and aggression. Far better to have a population born to obedience. The idea is to have a population that knows nothing but slavery and reveres its masters as superior beings that rule by Lud's will."

The two were silent awhile; then the younger spoke again. "What is the relationship between Salamander and Ariel? I have always wondered."

"It is my understanding that they met over the sale of the rabble left after the firestorm that destroyed Henry Druid's secret settlement. During that exchange,

Ariel suggested to Salamander that he might serve himself in serving us."

"Salamander must be wealthy beyond the dreams of ordinary men, and yet he is ever greedy for more slaves to sell. And his greed is matched by the greed of those who rule the Red Land for slaves to work their mines."

"Only after he began to serve the Faction did Salamander acquire real power and wealth. The One says that this is a sign he is doing as Lud requires."

"Even so, it seems strange to me that, despite the new ships he has purchased, he continues to master the *Black Ship*," said the younger priest.

The older man shrugged. "The *Black Ship* is unique, both in its ability to attack other ships at sea and its capacity to carry men. It is because he agreed to take part in this invasion that we were able to bring as many Hedra as we have. His *Black Ship* alone took double the number of the other two ships."

Crouched precariously upon the high stone ledge, I frowned. Surely far more men than I had seen marching along the tunnel would have fit on three ships, especially if one of them was Salamander's *Black Ship*. But if that was so, then where were they?

". . . his price was the rebels and their supporters alive and saleable," the younger priest was pointing out. "Which is why he desires as few deaths as possible."

"He will have slaves aplenty after this day's work, regardless of how many are killed in the invasion," the older priest said indifferently.

The pair was silent for a time, and the younger

241

priest said, "I am told that those who rule the Red Land are heathens who do not believe in Lud. I have wondered sometimes whether it can please Lud that we enable Salamander to send them so many slaves."

"The purifying flame will sear the Red Land someday. Lud will suffer no unbelievers. But Ariel has been to the Red Land, and he assures the One that his influence is strong there. When the time is right and Lud wills it, Ariel will open the way for the Faction."

"What do you suppose motivates him? Ariel, I mean," the younger priest asked, now adding wood to the fire. "There are times when his words make me doubt his faith."

"That had troubled me on occasion, as it has others among our brethren. But though he is high-handed and arrogant, Ariel has served us well. He, after all, proposed allowing the rebels to overtake the Council in this part of the Land in order to lessen the power of the Councilmen. And he suggested that this Malik would be willing to open a way for our invasion. Even these were his ideas and his invention," added the priest, tapping at the demon band about his neck with a grimace. "I wish he would find some way to protect us from the taint, but at least we need wear them only on land."

"Is it true that he also suggested building a force of our own warriors who would be pure in mind and body? Who would fight not for glory or gain, but for Lud?"

"Yes, the creation of the Hedra was his idea, and it so pleased the One that he agreed to let Ariel build his own dwelling on Norseland. It is a pity he won such decisive favor with the One."

The younger priest frowned. "I do not understand."

"Well, Ariel has great influence with the One, and there are times when we have been glad of it. But there are also times when Ariel makes speeches to the One about Lud and retribution and the Herders being chosen to rule the world, which render the One . . . very excitable. And when the One is excitable, there is almost always blood. Sometimes the bloodletting is less than convenient. More than once, good informants have been rent limb from limb because the One required them to be purified immediately."

"I heard that the One wanted every single man, woman, and child in the Land slain," said the younger priest, lowering his voice as if the words shocked even him.

"The One is very pure. How should he not be when he is so dear to Lud and knows his grief at the waywardness of his children? But on this occasion, Lud, in his infinite wisdom, prompted Ariel to offer words to the One that stayed his hand."

"Are you saying that Ariel influenced the One?" asked the younger priest, sounding shocked.

"Of course not," snapped the older. "Naturally, being the chosen first of Lud, the One is incapable of being influenced by lesser beings. Say rather that Ariel is the instrument of Lud, and for this reason, you must take care never to speak against him. Even some of the questions you have asked me might be cause enough for the One to become . . . excitable. Remember what happened to the last priest who questioned Ariel's motives? They say he died screaming, driven mad by Lud for his blasphemy."

"All who displease Lud die screaming and raving," the younger priest said piously.

"It is one thing for slaves and novices to be put to death," the older man said querulously, "and quite another for inner-circle priests to suffer the same rough end. The priest who died was as I am, an inner-circle Nine, for Lud's sake! And his death meant a host of others had to be put to death, because they had sworn loyalty to him. It was an unnecessary violence. . . ."

"It is rumored that the One offered to make Ariel a Nine, and he refused. He told the One that Lud desired him to serve the Faction as an outsider, until such time as the Herders had dominion over the world."

The older priest said nothing, and the younger priest glanced at him, then leaned forward to gaze moodily into the fire. I sat back on my heels. The exchange between the priests was fascinating, but I could not sit up here forever like a roosting pigeon when anything might be transpiring above us.

I readied myself to climb back down, but a movement caught my eye. It had come from the shadowed end of the cavern, and I gaped to see a man emerge from the darkness. He was tall and lean and swatched in a hooded black cloak that made it impossible to tell if he was a warrior priest or an ordinary priest. But when he reached the two by the fire, he pushed the hood back. I saw that, instead of being shaven, his head was entirely covered in a loose black cloth similar to that worn by the nomadic Sadorians when they travel across the blazing white heart of their desert land, only he also wore black bandages about his face, concealing all but fierce yellow eyes.

Salamander.

If I had not been holding my breath, I would surely have gasped aloud, so great was my surprise, for seldom did anyone see the infamous slaver so close, let alone so far from the sea and his *Black Ship*. I wondered what he hid so carefully under all those layers of black, since a simple mask would have disguised his identity well enough. It took only a moment to confirm that he wore a demon band.

"Where is Malik?" Salamander asked. His voice was deep and smooth, but the words were distinct despite being slightly muffled by the cloth over his face.

"He has not come. I think we must assume that something has gone wrong," the older priest said.

"It matters not," said Salamander. "If he has been exposed, Ariel has made sure the rebels will get nothing out of him. When one of the freaks attempts to read Malik's mind, it will collapse, taking the intruder's mind with it."

"And if they torture him physically?" the younger priest inquired.

"He will not be tortured," said the other priest with a sneering laugh. "The boy chieftain does not approve of torturing prisoners."

"Then we proceed with the next stage of the invasion?" Salamander asked.

"Yes," the older priest said. "The Hedra will soon be in place in the cloister."

"We must leave at once," Salamander said decisively.

The priests gathered up their cloaks and slung cloth bags over their shoulders while Salamander took up a resin torch, lit it, and then kicked the fire apart. When the priests announced themselves ready, he turned without hesitation and began to walk back the way he had come.

They disappeared into the shadows at the far end of the cavern, taking the lantern light with them, and I realized that I had been right. There was a way to the surface from this end of the tunnel! Fortunately, there was a faint glow from the embers of the fire, and I climbed down from my ledge and hurried after the three men, picking my way around bedrolls and other obstacles.

Thinking of what I had overheard, I realized that if Rushton and the others had *not* ridden into Saithwold when they had, I would have coerced Malik and died. Was that why Maryon had sent the others after me? Instead, another coercer would die trying to probe him. Surely that would make Dardelan realize something was wrong and send a force of fighters to Saithwold.

I had reached the shadows now and saw another tunnel leading off the chamber. It was dark and had a dank smell that made me gag, but there was light ahead. I went toward it carefully, because I did not want to stumble into Salamander and the priests. Gradually, the drumming of the waves grew louder and the briny reek of the sea stronger.

At the end of the tunnel, I peeped out. What I saw took my breath away.

Before me was a cavern many times larger than the one where the priests had sat, but instead of being floored in stone, there was a vast pool of water that reflected a great opening in the side of the cavern. Daylight flowed through it, and I could see the sea washing against the stony spikes that edged the opening. But I could not see the sky, only a long, sun-streaked stretch of cliff wall, which told me that I was looking into one of the narrows. But the truly astonishing thing—the *impossible* thing—was that three greatships were floating on the cavern lake, one of them as large as the giant Sadorian spicewood vessels. Its black hull told me it was the infamous *Black Ship* mastered by Salamander.

He and the two priests had reached the edge of the lake, where a ship boat had been pulled onto the steeply sloping stone shore. As I watched the three men climb into it, my head rang with the strangeness of what I was seeing, for how had the ships got into the cavern? Obviously the sea would flow into the cavern at high tide, but a ship could not possibly pass through the stone spikes.

But then I saw that this was not quite true. There was one section where there were no stone spikes, but it was barely the width of the *Black Ship*.

The ship boat had almost reached the *Black Ship*, and I was struck again by its similarity to Sadorian ships. But there were many additional constructions on the *Black Ship*'s deck, not to mention the great ugly bulb of wood and metal spikes protruding from the prow, which must be used as a battering ram.

So absorbed was I in my examination of the ship, I did not immediately notice how many people stood on its deck, and when I did, I looked at the other ships and saw that it was the same. At least as many gray-clad warriors stood upon the three ships as I had seen marching up the tunnel. Doubtless the rest were to be set down on the beach where Malik had received the crates from the Herders, or divided among all three beach accesses to the Land in Saithwold province. The Faction had left nothing to chance.

I tried to think what to do. Obviously, the only way

to reach the surface was to climb back up the tunnel, but if I did that, I would walk straight into the hands of the Herder warriors in the cloister.

My eyes fell upon the ship boat, now tethered to the *Black Ship*, and I saw with mounting excitement that the other two greatships also towed ship boats. Those aboard the *Black Ship* were now weighing anchor, and as I watched, long oars came out and the ship began to turn its misshapen prow toward the gap in the stone spikes.

I licked my lips and looked at the two remaining ships. The nearest was not so far away, and its ship boat tugged and bobbed on the waves in my direction. It was not dark, of course, but I doubted anyone would be looking back into the cavern. All attention would be fixed on the *Black Ship*, which edged toward the gap in the spikes.

I thought of the inner-cadre priest in the other cavern, fingering his demon band and saying he was glad they had only to wear the devices when they were on land. If he spoke true, and I could board a ship, then I could take it over by coercing first its shipmaster and ultimately everyone aboard. I could learn all the invasion plans and even use the ship and those aboard to help me stop the other ships from escaping.

Heart pounding, I worked my way around the side of the cavern, keeping low. Then I crawled down to the water's edge behind a rib of stone and put my hand into water that was so icy I shuddered. But I dared not dither, because I would be seen more easily out of the water than in. Gasping at the cold, I entered the sea and struck out for the ship boat. I was delighted to find that the tide flowing toward the cavern's opening was carrying me straight toward the ship. But it was so strong and swift that delight turned to horror as I found myself being swept inexorably *past* the ship boat.

The tide was ferocious. I could not stop myself.

I was dimly aware that the *Black Ship* had left the cavern and that the second ship had turned to approach the gap. It hit me that if I made it past the stone spikes into the narrow, my only chance of survival would be to board one of the ship boats. I glanced back to see the second ship moving rapidly into place. I gave up struggling against the pull of the waves and arrowed forward, steering myself between the stone fangs. For one terrifying moment, I seemed about to smash into a looming pillar, but I shot past it into the inlet's violent waters, which immediately dragged me under.

I kicked hard to reach the surface and managed to suck in a breath of air, but then I was dragged under again. By the time I fought my way back to the surface, I saw the second ship leaving the cavern. Dragged under again, this time I swam hard toward the middle of the inlet. I surfaced in calmer waters, but two ships had already gone down the inlet toward the open sea.

I had just readied myself for the last ship when a wave crashed over me again, pulling me under the water. It was like being eaten by a whirlwind. I tumbled and turned, and water forced its way up my nose and down my throat. My chest began to hurt with the need to breathe. I remembered the shipmaster Powyrs telling me that the sea was unforgiving to those who tried to fight it and forced myself to go limp.

Incredibly, as if it had only been waiting for me to surrender, the sea spat me to the surface. I had time to gasp a breath of air and to see a few streaked purplish clouds in the blue slice of sky before a green shadow reared up and struck me down again. I went under three more times before I managed to reach less savage waters, but my relief was short-lived, for the third ship was emerging from the sea cavern. Even as I watched, I could see that the ship was not approaching the gap at the right angle to pass through. The shipmaster had miscalculated, and I heard a terrible grinding sound as the ship hull was ground against the side of one of the stone spikes. After a long moment, the tide turned the ship enough that it passed through the gap and turned to sail after the others!

Exhausted, I let the tide carry me down the narrow in the ships' wake. Despair filled me, for no matter how I conserved my strength, I could not swim all the way out of the narrow and around to one of the beach accesses.

"Oh, Maruman," I whispered, knowing I would never see the old cat again.

I noticed a large stone pinnacle jutting up from the water in the shadows near the stone wall of the narrow. Without hesitation, I struck out for it, knowing that if I could just get a decent foothold, I could wait there until the tide turned and then swim back to the sea cavern.

Driven by the outgoing tide, I hit the stone pinnacle hard enough to stun myself, but instinct made me cling to the rough, porous rock until my senses returned. I climbed above the waterline. Immediately, the wind cut into my chilled skin like icy blades. I tried hard to ignore the voice telling me that I would freeze to death if I stayed until the tide turned, because what was the alternative?

For a time, I thought of everything I could have done differently. The thought of the Herder warriors waiting in the cloister filled me with fear for my friends, but my mind also jumped to the food they might have left behind and the warm fire I could have kindled from the embers of their cook fires. I shook my head and told myself not to sit there like a fool day-dreaming about food and fires as I slowly froze to death. If there was one stone spike, there would surely be others, or maybe some rocks at the base of the cliffs where I could rest. Somehow I had to make it to one of the beaches. I did not know which of the narrows I was in, but I did not believe I was far from the beach where Noviny had seen Malik and the Herders. Once out of the narrow, I would only have to swim around to it.

I lowered one numbed foot into the water, seeking for a grip on the stone so I could lower myself easily. Then I gasped, jerking my foot up instantly, *for something had pressed momentarily but firmly against the sole of my foot!*

I peered into the shadowed waves, trying to see what had touched me. I had just about convinced my-self that I had merely touched a part of the stone pinna-cle, when to my horror, I saw a long dark shape rise to the surface of the water. My mind leapt immediately to the many-toothed fish that Reuvan had once described, saying that he had seen it attack and tear to pieces a seaman who had fallen overboard. *Shark,* he had named it, and I clenched my teeth to stop whimpering with fear. Reuvan had said that the savage creatures were drawn by blood, and I had a dozen grazes all bleeding into the sea, sending out a deadly summons.

Was there any possibility of reaching the creature's

mind? I wondered. I did not know of any beastspeaker who had ever managed to communicate with a fish. Water inhibited the ability to communicate mentally for some reason we did not understand. To even try to reach a fish's mind, physical contact would be necessary.

I peered down, wishing I could see through the shadows and the shifting reflection of cliff and sky. Finally, in desperation, I lowered my foot and slapped it on the surface of the water because Reuvan had said that vibrations also attracted sharks.

It must have been waiting just deep enough that I could not see it, for the enormous fish erupted from the water right under my foot, pushing up so hard that it dislodged me from the stone spike. As I fell, I opened my mouth, but I did not utter the scream shaping itself in my throat. For in that moment of contact, a bell-like voice sounded in my mind, offering help.

✦ 15 ✦

I MIGHT HAVE drowned if the fish had not nudged me back to the pinnacle, for fright had drained the last of my reserves. As I clung to the rock, I no longer feared that I would be eaten, for even that brief contact had shown me a female mind with no trace of the rapacious hunger or mindless aggression that Reuvan had said characterized sharks. Indeed, as I watched her circle, I saw that she was not a shark at all, but a warm-blooded ship fish of the kind that were said to have occasionally rescued drowning seamen.

She butted my leg and again I heard her bell-like voice in my mind. "This one is Vlar-rei. Name of Ari-roth."

The words were like music. I was so enchanted that it took me a moment to realize that she had responded to a thought, even though we were not in physical contact. That meant that while I needed to be in touch to hear her mindvoice, she could "hear" my thoughts without contact.

"I am ElspethInnle," I thought.

"Morred-a," she sent, brushing against my leg.

I realized she had translated my name into her language. Then I thought of the name she had applied to herself. *Vlar-rei.* It was not her own name but the name

253

of her kind, and I knew that I had heard it before. Yet how could that be when I had never spoken with a ship fish?

Then it came to me. Locked inside Dragon's coma dream, I had seen her mother, the Red Queen, leap from the slave ship that had stolen her and her little daughter from their homeland. She had summoned whales to destroy the ship and her tormentors. Then she had summoned a ship fish to bring Dragon to shore. She had told me that ship fish called themselves *Vlar-rei* and that in human speech this meant "children of the waves." I shivered with wonder because that this really was their name proved what I had guessed from Dragon's coma dream: her mother—the Red Queen—had been a powerful beastspeaker with a rare ability to commune with sea beasts.

A sleek gray head emerged from the water in front of me, and the ship fish turned slightly to fix one round, gray eye on me. Lifting her smooth snout, she uttered a long, complex, musical call. Somehow I knew that the trilling call was a language that did not echo her spoken words but elaborated and explained them—except I had no means of understanding it.

"This one answers the call," she sent, swimming close to make contact so I could "hear" her.

"The call?" I thought.

Her smooth body touched my leg again, and I heard her beautiful voice. "What is needful?"

"Can you help me to reach land?" I was so cold now that it was becoming hard to think clearly.

Ari-roth responded with a coiling trill of notes. Then she brushed me again and said merely, "Morred-a must make a mindpicture of the place she wishes to go."

Gingerly, I passed an arm around her smooth leathery flank and let go of the pinnacle. She took my weight, and I had the queer sensation of her mind swimming through mine. Like Maruman, she ignored my shield as if it did not exist.

I formed a mental image of the beach Noviny had described, hoping it would be enough. The ship fish merely gave another fluting call and bade me take hold of her more securely by the side and back fin, but to avoid her blowhole, for it was sensitive. I adjusted my position as she had instructed, and she moved smoothly away from the rock and along the channel.

Without my noticing it, the sun had set, and this time when I looked up, I saw stars caught between the black jaws of the cliffs. *Can so much time have passed since I rode to the cloister?* I wondered. Gradually, as we passed along the dark narrow, I realized that I was no longer cold.

"This one feeds Morred-a," Ari-roth sang imperturbably.

"Feeding me what?" I echoed, uncomprehending.

A bright picture swelled to fill my mind. It showed my body, as if seen through spirit eyes. It was no more than a dim shadow amidst a fluctuating halo of colored light, but the light was dim and the colors faded. Even the vivid slash of red corresponding to the damage done to my spirit by the life I had once taken was pale and faded. A ship fish shape emanating blue light appeared in the vision, and a tendril of light reached out from the ship fish to me. Gradually, my aura grew brighter and the colors stronger.

"This one feeds ohrana to Morred-a," Ari-roth sent as the vision faded.

"You have my gratitude," I told her, realizing that *ohrana* must be the ship fish word for "spirit energy." I wondered, too, how many ship fish had rescued seamen and helped them in this way without their ever realizing it.

"No," Ari-roth sang, answering my private thought as if it had been directed to her. "This gifting given only by Vlar-rei to Vlar-rei. But Mornir-ma asked that help be given to Morred-a when she called." She lifted her head and gave a rising trill.

"Mornir-ma?" I echoed, confused. Did she mean Dragon, for the beasts called her Mornir?

"Mornir-ma sings to friends who swim long ago, of Morred-a who will swim in the waves to come. Very beautiful is the song/singing. Those who listened sang she song, too, that the waves would remember it. Now all who hear waves, hear the plea-song of Mornir-ma for Morred-a."

I drew a long shaky breath, wondering if I could be understanding her correctly, for she seemed to be saying that she had fed me from her aura, because someone had asked it long ago on my behalf. Mornir-ma. Dragon's mother?

It was fantastic to imagine, but Cassy might have futuretold my need to the first Red Queen, who, like her descendant Dragon's mother, may have possessed the Talent to commune with sea beasts. But even if the first Red Queen had sung to sea creatures to ask help for a woman she had never met, how could Ari-roth have known I needed help now? She had spoken of a call, but I had not called anyone.

"Morred-a called," the ship fish responded calmly.

"What did I call?" I asked, utterly bewildered.

"Mornir-ma sang in the long ago, that Morred-a would call. *Mar-ruhman*. Ari-roth heard and followed the ripples back to Morred-a."

Mar-ruhman, I thought incredulously. *Maruman?* Then I remembered. I had called his name in sorrow and longing when I had thought I would drown. Cassy had foreseen me do so on the verge of drowning. A great chain of legend had been forged through time, to make sure that I would be saved.

"What did Mornir-ma sing of me?" I asked. I was trembling but not from cold.

"That Morred-a would say the sacred word *Mar-ruhman* to the waves when she was in dire need, and all aid must be rendered unto her, even the gift of ohrana, for by her deeds would the song of the waves go on, and without her, the song would be sung no more."

I felt astonished by what she told me, yet my life was caught in a web of prophecies, so how should I be surprised that sea creatures subscribed to the land-beast legend, which made me their Savior? But as always when I encountered the faith of others in those prophecies, I felt a dreamy powerlessness, which the dark water all about me seemed to emphasize. I tried to take in the knowledge that by calling Maruman's name, I had summoned the aid of the ship fish because of a song sung by a woman I had never met but whose daughter I had befriended and whose memory held a secret that I needed in order to complete my quest. My mind reeled at the complexity, and I could not even begin to understand how my cry had reached Ari-roth.

Oblivious or perhaps indifferent to my confusion, the ship fish swam in my mind and the waves so swiftly, yet serenely, that it seemed no time at all before we were passing out of the narrow inlet. For a long time, we swam straight out to sea, for Ari-roth explained that there were shoals all about the mouth of the narrow, where the currents were treacherous even for ship fish.

The open sea was far calmer then it had been inside the restricted inlet, and seeing the vast starry sky stretched over an inky sea where stars floated, I became calmer, too. Ari-roth turned and began to follow the Land's high shadowy coastline. As we cleaved through the water, I was enchanted to see patches of phosphorescence shimmering on the water's smooth surface. The despair and hopelessness I felt earlier evaporated. I was not cold or hungry or tired, and all my aches and pains had faded.

I knew it was the effect of being fed Ari-roth's ohrana, but it seemed that, however long I lived, at the end of my life, this time of fluid serenity would be one I could summon to remind me of the beauty of living. I found tears upon my cheeks.

"Morred-a makes an offering to the waves." Ari-roth spoke the words in my mind with approval.

The moon now rose, a rich yellow-gold, shining like a burnished coin shaved at one edge. I thought of Maruman and imagined how he would glare at it. As it rose higher, its yellow richness fading to silver, I brought my wandering attention to bear on the land. We were passing along the coast of Saithwold province, but I could not see any of the three beaches or the steps cut into the cliff. As if sensing my desire, Ari-roth angled toward land. But the moon had climbed high before we passed the jutting brow of the cliff that hid two narrow beaches. Two ships were anchored close to shore at the first beach, but neither of them was the *Black Ship*. Salamander must have taken the warrior priests aboard his vessel to the third beach, closer to Sutrium, perhaps even directly to Sutrium. I decided to ask Ari-roth to set me ashore on the second beach. I could mount the steps and farseek Gahltha to come and find me. But first I needed to see if the warrior priests aboard the ship had gone ashore, as I suspected.

I asked Ari-roth to bring me closer to the ships, and though I doubted anyone would be looking out to sea, I adjusted my position and sank lower in the water so that my head barely rose above Ari-roth's shining fin. Soon I could make out steps cut into the cliff and several darker patches at the base of it, farther along the beach, which might be the caves Noviny had mentioned.

Turning to the deck of the nearest ship, I saw so little movement that either the entire force was belowdecks, or they had gone ashore. My instincts told me the latter, for the ships had surely arrived well before the moon had risen, and any commander would have taken advantage of the darkness.

I knew that the wisest course would be to ask Ari-roth to set me ashore on the second beach, but I had spotted the ship boat bobbing against the hull of the nearest ship. If I could get aboard, and it remained against the hull of the greatship, I might manage to farseek someone and learn what was happening ashore. It occurred to me that I could do what I had meant to do in the sea cavern: take over the minds of those aboard the ship.

"Does Morred-a wish to go ashore?" Ari-roth asked serenely.

"No," I told her, "just as far as the small vessel, but I

259

must not be seen by those aboard." To be sure she understood, I pictured the ship boat.

Ari-roth sang soothingly that the funaga saw only what they expected to see, but just in case, the sea would conceal our approach. Then she bade me hold my breath. Seeing her intention, I sucked in a lungful of air and tried not to be afraid as she dove under the water. Our speed was so great that I felt as if I had put my head under a waterfall. My ears began to ache as the weight of water above us grew, and I prayed that Ari-roth would realize my lung capacity was not as great as hers. Ari-roth heard and bade me calm myself, lest the song of my fear summon azahk. The image she offered told me she spoke of sharks. I would have felt frightened at their mention, but my need for air was too urgent. To my relief, Ari-roth turned back toward the surface, and we sped upward even more quickly than we had descended. Before I had the chance to gasp in a breath and register the looming bulk of the greatship and the smaller shape of a ship boat, I heard a voice say distinctly, "Did you hear that?"

Without hesitation, Ari-roth twitched me from her back and leapt into the air, rising from the shadow cast by the ship into the moonlight. For a moment, she was gloriously limned in silver, then she dived back into the waves, only to leap up again. Someone cried out in delight, and a man shouted to someone else to come and see. A stern voice commanded them all to shut their mouths lest they wake every fool who slept on the Land. The men fell silent, but still Ari-roth leapt and cavorted so magnificently that I knew their eyes would track her.

I caught hold of the edge of the little ship boat and

was elated, if surprised, to discover that it had been lashed to the metal rungs of a ladder leading up the side of the ship. I soon realized why. A number of boards had been roughly hammered on to patch a splintered gash in the hull. This must be the ship whose shipmaster had miscalculated the gap when leaving the sea cavern. The ship boat had obviously been lowered and lashed to the ladder to offer a stable platform from which repairs could be carried out.

I shivered and realized that I was growing cold without Ari-roth's aura to keep me warm. Hunger and thirst were returning, too, along with the pain of my cuts and bruises and a deadly weariness. Ari-roth had leapt out of sight now, but the stifled cries of admiration and splashes told me she had gone around to the other side of the greatship to give me the best chance of boarding unseen. Unfortunately, I was much weaker than I had thought, and it took several attempts to lever myself up onto the edge of the ship boat. To my dismay, my grip slipped, and I slithered forward to land in the bottom of the boat with a distinct thud. Immediately, I reached for a crumpled canvas lying at one end of the boat and pulled it over myself, wrinkling my nose at the stench of fish. I was not a moment too soon, for almost immediately, I heard the sound of boots and a voice directly above.

". . . heard something?" a man's voice asked.

"One of the boards might have sprung free." The answer came in a voice that sounded far too young for a shipman. Both speakers had the soft-edged accents of Norselanders.

I heard someone else approaching, and the older Norselander said with stiff politeness, "The sighting of a ship fish augurs well, Master Herder."

"Superstitious nonsense, Shipmaster," snapped another man in a sharp, disapproving voice. "There is only the righteous will of Lud for good or ill, and as we are his chosen and serve him, we have no need of omens to know that we will be victorious."

I caught my breath, for surely it was the voice of the old priest I had heard in the cavern. But I had seen him and the other Herder board the *Black Ship*, so Salamander must have come here to let the Herder transfer to this ship. Perhaps he had also set down his force here. I sent out a probe, focusing on the Herder, knowing that if I could reach and control his mind, I would be able to use his authority to prevent the remaining ships from leaving. To my intense disappointment, I encountered the unmistakable buzzing rejection of a demon band. The older Norselander was speaking now, and I tried his mind. It was barred as well, which could only mean that everyone aboard was demon-banded because of their closeness to the Land. On impulse, I tried their younger companion and was astounded to find he was unbanded!

His name was Lark, and as I had guessed from his voice, he was little more than a boy. But not just any boy. He was the son of the Norse shipmaster who commanded the vessel! Delving into his mind, I found that he did not wear a demon band, because he had stowed away to be with his father, so no band had been provided for him.

I turned my attention to the conversation between the two older men, reflected in the mind of the boy, and heard the priest bid the shipmaster come with him to look at a map. The older man gave the boy a quelling look, which the boy took in well enough for me to momentarily see the shipmaster. He was a tall, hand-some Norselander with long, fair, side plaits; direct, very blue eyes; and a weary, troubled air.

Left alone, the boy turned to look down at the ship boat where I lay hidden. To my relief, he was not worried about an intruder so much as the hasty repair coming undone, for the Herders had refused to allow them to stop and repair the hull properly. If only they would let his father do his job! All would have been well if the priests aboard their ship had not insisted on deciding when the ship would leave the sea cavern, for the resulting damage was a good deal more worrying than the priests seemed to realize. *Perhaps they thought their precious Lud would keep a holed boat afloat because of the righteousness of its passengers,* Lark thought sourly.

Underneath the boy's concern about the damaged ship, I found a deeper fear arising from the knowledge that only his father's refusal to allow it had stopped him from being hurled overboard when the Hedra captain had discovered him hiding in the hold. The boy's mind told me that both the Norselanders and the Herder priests called the warrior priests of their order *Hedra,* and I remembered that the priests in the cavern had used the same term. The boy thought of how his father had defied the old Herder priest, saying bluntly that if the boy was killed, he would not master the vessel, and none of the other seamen had the skill for it. The Hedra captain, Kaga, had then proposed that Lark's tongue be cut out as a punishment, but again his father had refused to permit it.

I dropped beneath the boy's conscious thoughts and began to scour his mind for memories of his movements about the ship to familiarize myself with its layout. In doing so, I learned that twelve shipmen and eight priests were on board, and six of these were high-ranking Hedra, with Hedra Kaga most senior. All of the Hedra but Kaga and the other five had gone ashore with the Hedra from the *Orizon* and the *Black Ship* before the latter had returned to Herder Isle to report to the inner cadre on the progress of the invasion.

Lark's fear of the cold, brutal Hedra Kaga was very strong, but he was far more afraid of the inner-circle priests, especially the inner-cadre Nine. Delving deeper into his fears, I discovered that the boy was terrified that the Nine would punish his beloved father for daring to oppose his will. According to Lark, inner-cadre members were proud and vengeful; if his father was arrested and taken into the Herder Compound on Herder Isle, it was unlikely that he would ever return.

I shivered at the potency of the boy's fears, and again I had to force myself to remember my own needs. I was lucky to have found him, and he would have access to his father, who was the shipmaster. Not that I had any illusion about who was master here. The Nine was the ultimate authority, but he and the other priests must rely upon the sea skills of the shipmaster, who would have some power until they returned to Herder Isle.

I had always assumed that the Norselanders willingly served the Hedra, but from what I saw in the boy's mind, they were an occupied people forced to serve and obey the Faction. This news would greatly interest the Council of Chieftains, but I had much to do before I could share what I had learned.

The first step was obvious. I needed the boy to convince his father to remove his demon band, and then I would coerce the shipmaster to secretly order his men to remove *their* bands. Once I had coerced them, they could overcome Kaga, and as soon as they removed his band, I could use him to deal with the other five Hedra aboard. Then I would have the ship signal the *Orizon* and have the Nine command the ship to remain anchored. No seaman would be a match for a trained warrior, I reminded myself, so I must be careful not to incite any open confrontation. Now that I understood that the Norselanders were little more than slaves, I could not in good conscience put them in danger to further my own plans.

Lark moved toward the foredeck, deciding he would go below into the hold to check the repair and see if the leak was worse. Delicately, I changed his mind and directed his attention to Ari-roth. He noted that she was still leaping spectacularly from the waves, glittering with phosphorescence, but she was moving steadily away. Lark observed that the leaping ship fish would make a fine image to render as an offering to the goddesses to ease his passage into the longsleep. I was startled at his use of the term that beasts used for death, and my curiosity again led me further into his mind. At a deeper, half-repressed level that connected with memory, he was thinking that ship fish were supposed to be the willing servants of the three goddesses of forbidden Norse myths, which his mother whispered to him at night. The myths were banned by the Faction. Once he had asked his mother why they must be kept secret, and she had answered that until the Norse Isles were free, the stories must remain secret, for anyone repeating them would be burned.

Lark's mind told me that his father and mother had

265

been born on Norseland, and I delved deeper, seeking to understand how his parents had come to dwell upon Herder Isle. I was very surprised to learn that Herder Isle was actually an island divided in two by a channel, where once there had been an isthmus. A vast, walled Herder Compound occupied most of the larger island, which lay closer to the Land, while the Norselanders dwelt in villages on the lesser island, arrayed about the edge of a great swampy expanse of land surrounding a single low hill at the center of the island. The smaller island was called Fallo after a Norse city that had once stood on that side of the isthmus. This bridge of land, called the Girdle of the Goddess, had been destroyed by the Faction, along with the cities of Fallo and Hevon. Hevon had stood on the larger island, facing the bay and the Land, and had been surpassing fair. I tried to find out how the Faction had destroyed two cities and an isthmus, but the boy did not know. Indeed, much of his knowledge came from tales his mother told him and, occasionally, by what he had overheard from his father's shipfolk.

Lark, his parents, and all the shipfolk lived in the village nearest the channel. His mother and father had been brought from Norseland to dwell upon Herder Isle so they would be better placed to serve their masters as shipfolk and shipwrights. The *Orizon* was one of several smaller greatships built at the Herders' behest, Lark's mind told me with faint disparagement. Many of these had foundered at sea, Lark believed, because they had not been dedicated to the goddesses who protected the Norseland shipfolk. But the *Stormdancer*, which was the ship his father mastered, had been built by one of his own ancestors and had been sailed in the days of freedom, before the Faction came. Now the Herders owned all the ships, and the Norselanders served them as they required, for anyone who defied them was taken to the Herder Compound for questioning, where they faced death by burning, or worse.

I wanted to know what "worse" entailed, but this part of Lark's mind was darker and more sensitive, because it connected to his fears of what might happen to his father upon their return to Herder Isle, so I dared not venture there.

I turned instead to Lark's childhood. He had no memory of Norseland, for his mother had given birth to him on Fallo, but he had many glowing visions, fashioned in his imagination through his mother's stories of the island. These were peopled with noble men and women akin in strength and courage to the Norse kings who had made the high rocky island their ancestral home, who farmed and tilled and wrested a living from the barren island, yet who never forgot to keep their blades sharp. His favorite fantasy was that those upon Norseland were planning an uprising and would someday come to free Fallo and Herder Isle from the Faction. But I saw from his memories that the Norselanders who served aboard ships traveling regularly to Norseland spoke of only a few scattered villages of farmers and two sizeable towns, the entire population of these being less than the number of Hedra in the training camp there.

Brydda, too, had spoken of the training camp for warrior priests on Norseland. I remembered that, according to the priests in the cavern, Ariel had a residence on Norseland, too.

The boy looked up at the moon. I saw it clearly in

his mind's eye, a shining sphere across whose face now unraveled skeins of purplish cloud. I sent him to the other side of the ship to survey the Land, and the sight of the high dark cliffs evoked in him uneasy apprehensions about Landfolk whom the Herders described as little better than savages, preyed upon by dreadful fanged mutants.

I could not resist constructing and implanting a question as to why the Faction would invade the Land if it was full of savages and bestial mutants. The boy's mind immediately seized on the question but could come up with no answer. This troubled him, and he decided he would ask his father. Then he began to think about the training exercises the warrior priests had practiced on the decks. He wondered if those techniques would aid them against the mutant hordes. Seeing the exercises in his memory, I noticed they truly were very like coercer training exercises. Gevan had devised these with the help of Beforetime books unearthed by the Teknoguild, so perhaps the warrior priests were also using Oldtime books, despite their being forbidden by the Faction.

The boy's mind registered the shipmaster's summons, and he hurried to meet him, love for his father filling his mind. The shipmaster's cabin was not the best chamber aboard, as was traditional, for that had been taken by the Herders. Through Lark's mind, I saw his father close the cabin door firmly after them and turn up the wick on a lantern. The boy sat on the edge of the bed, anxiously waiting to see what his father would tell him. I prompted him to ask the question I had placed in his mind, interested to discover that it had already formed strong connecting threads to other doubts and questions. If I had not encouraged the boy to ask why the Herders were invading a land inhabited by monsters, it was clear that Lark would soon enough have come up with it for himself.

The boy watched several expressions chase one another across his father's face: astonishment, anger, concern, and, finally, wariness. But last of all, he smiled, and Lark knew this meant that his father would tell him something true, something dangerous.

"Perhaps the Landfolk are not the bloodthirsty monsters the priests preach about but are only folk who do not wish to be ruled by the Faction," the shipmaster said quietly. "But you must never speak of that possibility with anyone but me or your mother."

Lark nodded seriously, pride swelling in his mind at the trust his father placed in him. Then, prompted by me but not yet controlled, he asked, "Why do you wear a demon band if you think the people of this Land are not mutants with dreadful nullish powers?"

His father frowned. "Because it is what the priests command."

"Can I look at it?" I made the boy ask, holding out his hand.

His father hesitated, then sighed, and the boy watched him unfasten it. "Just for a moment, then." As the lock opened, I abandoned the boy for his father's mind.

His name was Helvar, and his mind showed that he was, incredibly, all that his son believed him to be: noble, strong-minded, compassionate, and generous. He was also troubled by Lark's sudden interest in the demon band and his questions about the Land's inhabitants, and he was aware that his answers, repeated, would see them both burned. He had answered Lark truthfully, because he knew the boy would appreciate his trust. He believed the questions his son had asked were a manifestation of the lad's fear of the Nine. Helvar knew very well that Lark was afraid the Herders would punish him for protecting his son, and he feared that, too. But his fear was not that he would vanish into the Herder Compound, for his skills as a shipmaster and shipwright were too valuable to be wasted. Besides, the priests' punishments were always cruel and subtle. They would be far more likely to do what both Helvar and his wife feared, which was to claim the boy as a novice.

Ever since Lark had been born, this possibility had haunted Helvar, for most Norse boys were taken from their families to become Herder novices. Helvar had done what he could to protect his son; he had taught the boy all he knew, hoping that, by the time he was old enough to be considered as a novice, he would have too many valuable ship skills to waste. And it might have been so, save that by stowing away, the boy had drawn himself dangerously to their masters' attention.

I threw up a thin coercive shield, realizing I was becoming dangerously absorbed in the compelling thoughts of a man I could not help but like and admire. My control loosened, and Helvar immediately reached out to pick up the demon band, remembering that it was death to be caught without it and wondering at his carelessness in failing to put it back on immediately.

I coerced him to set it aside again and cast about to find a thought I could use before making him ask Lark to fetch their nightmeals on a tray from the galley. As the boy closed the door behind him, his father reached again for the band, and again I had to turn his mind away. Helvar knew that the bands were dangerous, and he had told his son the truth when he had said he wore it only because he must. I made him button his shirt to the neck so the demon band's absence would not be noticed if someone entered the cabin.

Leaving his conscious thoughts, I delved deeper into the shipmaster's mind, searching out his knowledge of Herder plans for the Land. Unfortunately, he knew no more than the boy's mind had already yielded, the Norselanders being little more than a source of bonded labor and novices for the Faction. Helvar's memories showed me that he and the other shipmaster had been informed only two days before the journey that the *Stormdancer* and the *Orizon*, led by the *Black Ship*, were to carry a Hedra invasion force that would reclaim the Land from the mutants who had driven out the Faction and enslaved the Landfolk.

The shipmaster of the *Orizon* had asked where the force would land and had been told there was no need for him to know. He need only follow the slavemaster Salamander and obey the Herders' commands.

Helvar had been as amazed as the rest when Salamander had led them up the narrow inlet, with its towering stone walls, and through the impossibly tight space between the stone teeth that lined the vast sea cavern. He loathed the slavemaster but acknowledged that he guided a ship as if touched by the goddesses. For all his skill and experience, Helvar would not like to have led two ships into such a rough and narrow passage, and he had wondered if they were all sailing to their doom, for the way was too narrow and rough to turn a ship.

Half the Hedra on the three ships had disembarked immediately and vanished through an opening in the cavern. The ships had remained anchored through several tides, until Salamander had fetched the two inner-cadre priests, whereupon he had bade them sail back down the inlet.

Anger flowed briefly though the shipmaster's mind at the memory of the arrogant Hedra captain who insisted on judging the timing and angle of their departure from the sea cavern. His error of judgment had resulted in substantial damage to the ship, and I felt Helvar's anger turn to apprehension at the thought of the roughly patched hull. He was aware, as Lark had not been, that the damage would make crossing the strait a perilous enterprise. But Helvar told himself that once the Land was taken, the Nine would surely agree to the ship being properly repaired. Priests might preach about the meaninglessness of flesh compared to spirit, but they were as devoted to protecting their own skins as any man. Not the fanatical Hedra, of course, who believed that their spirits were so pure that Lud guided and blessed their every action.

Anxiety about the ship gave way to renewed anxiety about Lark and the realization that Kaga often eyed the boy with grim purpose. Helvar regretted that the captain had not gone ashore with the rest of the force because then at least the brute might have been slain. Though who would be brave or foolish enough to attack Kaga, whose bulk and strength alone would intimidate anyone, without their even seeing his deadly ability with a knife and pole?

There was a tap at the door, and Helvar rose to open it for his laden son. I waited impatiently while they ate, constantly fending off Helvar's desire to put on the demon band in case one of the priests entered. Love for his son now slightly distorted the older man's mind. He told himself that he ought to prepare the boy for the possibility of being taken as a novice, yet he could not bear the thought himself, so how should he comfort his son? And what if he was chosen to be turned into a null? He had shown no nullish abilities, but they sometimes came on when a lad's voice changed. It would kill Gutred if the boy was taken by that demon-spawn Ariel. She must already be frantic at her son's disappearance. Lark swore he had left a note with his friend Alek, explaining his intention to stow away on the *Stormdancer*. The note would say nothing of an invasion, because Lark had not known of it. But Gutred knew because Helvar had whispered the truth to her in the night. She would be mad with fear for them both.

At last the meal was done, and I immediately coerced Helvar to have Lark return the tray to the galley. Then I moved deeper into the shipmaster's mind, seeking to learn more about nulls. His conjectures had given me the horrible suspicion that nullish powers were Misfit powers.

I had to proceed more carefully, because the information I sought was contained within the area of Helvar's mind made sensitive by fear for his son. I learned that the boys who would become nulls were chosen from among the new intake of Herder novices. Ariel inspected them as soon as they entered the Herder Compound, and he tested them with a machine. Helvar had never seen the machine, but he had heard the Herders speak of it as something that fitted over a boy's skull and caused intense pain, which somehow caused them to reveal any nullish powers they possessed, even those unbeknownst to the lad being tested. Salamander then transported those whose nullish powers had been revealed to Ariel's residence on Norseland, to be purified to receive messages from Lud.

Helvar did not know what *purification* meant, save that those who survived it, and many did not, returned to Herder Isle many sevendays later, transformed into shambling idiots whose babble and wild nightmares were interpreted by Ariel as visions sent by Lud. Helvar wanted to dismiss their transformation as a cruel and insane charade, save that the nulls were known to predict the truth.

I gritted my teeth, sure that the visions seen by the nulls were coerced into their minds by Ariel to conceal the fact that they arose from his own Misfit powers.

When I had climbed into the ship boat, I had intended to take over the mind of the shipmaster so he would summon and unband his crew. But having entered into his mind and learned the sort of man he was and that the Norselanders were being forced to serve the Faction, I found myself deeply reluctant to use him as a puppet. Helvar was a good, courageous man with no evil in him, and in other circumstances, I had no doubt that I would be glad to regard him as an ally and even a friend.

I made my decision.

"Do you wish to save your son?" I farsent, using coercion to reach his untalented mind.

✦ 16 ✦

I FELT ASTONISHMENT shudder through the ship-master's mind. But Helvar was a strong man with a cool head, and he mastered himself to ask aloud, "Who speaks?"

"For your own safety, Shipmaster, do not speak aloud. Think what words you wish to say, and I will hear them, for I am one of those your masters name *monster* and *mutant*. They name me so not because I am deformed physically, but because I can speak to your mind. When I was no more than Lark's age, the Herders occupied the Land, as they did yours, genera-tions ago. They dragged my mother and father to the fire and burned them in front of me. My parents were guilty of nothing more than opposing the Council's op-pressive rule."

There was pity in Helvar's mind, but he thought a hesitant question. "You are able to reach my mind be-cause I removed the demon band?"

"It was I who made your son ask you to remove it. I was able to reach his mind because he does not wear a band."

"Then it is true that you have the ability to control minds?"

"I could have simply made you help me. Indeed, it

was what I meant to do, until I saw from your mind that you and your people are not in league with the Herders, nor do you serve them willingly. So instead I ask your help. Indeed, I think we can help one another. Your son is in danger, and I have seen what you fear for him. Knowing the Herders, I think your fear is reasonable. You believe that you have no alternative other than to accept the situation, but I will show you a way to save Lark and yourself and maybe even to bring about the peace and freedom that your wife desires."

"I cannot stop the invasion," Helvar said.

I could only admire the firm calmness of his response, for I could feel that his senses were reeling at how effortlessly I had plucked from his mind knowledge of him and his family. "I do not ask you to stop the invasion," I said. "The people of the Land, who are people like me as well as ordinary folk like you, know of the Herders' plan to invade, and they have made their own preparations."

"I hope they have many warriors, for the Hedra have made themselves the weapons of Lud, and their sole purpose is to kill anyone who opposes the Faction," Helvar said.

His words chilled me, but I did not let doubt enter my mindvoice as I replied, "I believe that the Hedra will be defeated and driven back to their ships. But it is my hope that their ships will not receive them."

"You want the ships," Helvar guessed.

The swiftness of his mind did not surprise me. I sent, "The Herders burned our ships when they fled the Land a year ago, and recently, they had their agents burn replacement ships we had begun to build. It will be many months before new ships are ready, but with these two ships, we could carry a force to the west coast immediately and free the people there. Once this is done, we will unite to deal with the priests upon Herder Isle and Norseland."

"I understand what you are saying, but what if you are wrong about your friends triumphing? You have never seen the Hedra fight. . . ."

"And you have never seen my people fight," I sent. "But I swear to you that if matters go ill for my friends, and the Hedra do win this battle, I will coerce the Herders aboard this ship not to recall that you helped me overpower them. They will think only that they were bewitched by mutants who crept aboard. I can even make them remember both you and Lark defending the Nine, and you and your shipfolk driving off the horde of invading monsters so heroically that any plan to punish Lark for stowing away will be forgotten. Then I will swim ashore."

"You could do this?"

"I could, but only if the Nine and the other priests are not wearing demon bands."

"But once they restore them . . ."

"The coercion will hold even after the bands are put back on. I promise. If you agree to help me, summon your seafolk one at a time and have them remove their demon bands so that I can be assured they are trustworthy."

"My crew will not betray me," he said, and his mind projected an image of his first shipman, a tall, scarfaced man called Oma, with dark hair rather than the usual Norse blond, who was his best friend. "Indeed, it may be *you* who has to prove that you have the power to undo what you begin, for the sake of their families."

277

"I will convince them," I promised. "But I must first be sure for myself that they can be trusted. We have been betrayed more than once by those who pretended to be allies."

"Very well. Then what?"

"You and your men must overcome one of the Hedra. Preferably the Nine."

"Impossible. The captain of the Hedra, Kaga, watches him constantly, and there are not enough of us to overcome him," Helvar answered. Then he frowned. "But I can ensure that a potion is put into his night-meal."

"If he is dead, I cannot use him to command the other Hedra to unband."

"I speak only of a sleep potion. We have plenty aboard, because many of the Hedra suffer wave-sickness. Without Kaga to deal with, I think we could overcome his immediate underling, Ruge. But it might be simpler to drug all the Herders aboard, for then there will be no need to guard them."

"We will require at least one of them with sufficient rank to deal with the other shipmaster and any Herder aboard his ship. My suggestion is to drug Kaga, if he is as formidable as you say, and overcome the Nine to remove his demon band, for once that is gone, I can use him to control the rest."

"That can be done," Helvar said. "Where are you?"

"It is best that you do not know until we have control of the ship," I told him. This produced a surge of suspicion, as I had anticipated.

"If I refuse to help you, will you not simply use your powers to force me, despite what you have said about our not being your enemies?" Helvar asked.

"I would not force any man or woman or child to obey me, nor enter their mind and thoughts without their leave, save in direst emergency. Would you judge it so, sirrah, when your land is invaded by fanatics who will kill anyone who resists them and enslave the rest? The answer is yes, I will force you to help me, although there are many of you and I might fail, for I am alone. But before you judge me evil, remember it is not I who threatens your son. Our enemies are your enemies."

Abruptly, the connection between us dissolved as rain began to patter down on the canvas. My heart sank. Within minutes, I heard the sound of boots ringing on metal and a thud as someone jumped into the boat. The canvas covering me was wrenched away, and I found myself looking into the face of a Norselander with his unmistakable blond side plaits. He carried a lantern, and his expression in its light was so completely astonished that I wondered if I had been mistaken in thinking that Helvar had sent him to find me. I could not probe him, of course, because a demon band glinted at his throat.

He gestured brusquely for me to get up, and I obeyed, stifling a groan as my stiff, battered body protested. The Norselander immediately removed his voluminous rain cloak and draped it around my shoulders, mimicking that I should draw up the hood. I obeyed, hope burgeoning at his civility. He climbed up the ladder first, and I went after him, clenching my teeth and coercing my fingers to hold on, for I was still exhausted from my long immersion. Just as I reached the top, the hood slipped forward, blinding me. When I tried to push it back, I slipped, but before I could fall, a strong hand grasped me by the wrist. I muttered thanks and looked into the deeply scarred face of the powerfully built, dark-haired Oma, whom I had seen in Helvar's mind.

"Thank you, Oma," I said.

He looked shocked, but only muttered something to the blond Norselander, which sent him hurrying away down the deck, then he jerked his head for me to follow him. The rain that I had cursed now served us, for it had driven the Herders inside. Oma led me to a stairwell. I followed him down spiraling metal steps into a dark passage, reminding myself that Helvar trusted him like a brother. Oma had not bothered to get a lantern, but he was clearly very familiar with the ship, for he continued on swiftly, though I could see nothing. Then he stopped so suddenly that I cannoned into him, and I heard a door opening. Oma guided me through it and closed it. Only then did he light a lantern.

We were now in a tiny compact cabin with a porthole above a narrow bed fixed lengthways to the inner hull wall and a single long locker at one end. Sitting on the bed was Lark, a gaunt-faced lad a little younger than Zarak, with very long, very pale hair, partly braided as Oma's was.

I pushed the sodden hood back, and the boy gasped. "You are a woman!"

Only then did I understand the surprise of the man who had come to find me. It had not occurred to me to mention to Helvar that I was a woman, and Oma had obviously been sent to find a man. Lark was frowning. "Who did that to your face?"

"The man who betrayed the Land to the Herders," I said.

"You are not afraid?" Oma asked in his rough and

yet oddly pleasant voice. He hung the lantern neatly on a hook.

"I am not, for Shipmaster Helvar will not turn me over to the Herders."

"You have the means to prevent him betraying you?" Oma asked coldly.

"I meant only that betrayal is not in his nature," I said.

The bleakness faded from the other man's ravaged face. He said, "Shipmaster Helvar asked me to bring you here. It is safer than his cabin, where the Herders might enter at any moment. This is my cabin, and it is far from the priests' sleeping chambers." He gave me an openly appraising look. I did not know what he saw, other than a lean woman with strings of drenched black hair, sodden clothes, and black and purple bruises. His eyes fell to the floor where a puddle of water was forming about my feet, and he frowned and bade me remove the cloak.

I struggled to obey, but the cloth was heavy and clung. With a murmur of exasperation, Oma reached out, peeled it off me, and hung it on one of the hooks set into the door. His fastidiousness reminded me of Reuvan, but perhaps it was more that there was so little room, even upon a greatship, that any clutter or mess could not be tolerated. In its weariness, my mind meandered like a lost sheep, and I tried to think what I should say that might convince Helvar to agree to help me, if he was yet undecided, but a grayness bled across my vision. I swayed, and Lark leapt to his feet. Catching my arm, he steadied me as Oma laid a towel on the bed so I could sit.

Oma said, "Val—that is the man who found you—

will have let Helvar know that you are here, and he will come to speak with you when he is able. In the meantime, Lark, see if you can't go and beg some food from the cook."

"Can I have some water?" I croaked, speaking aloud for the first time.

Lark hurried away and Oma poured water from a silver jug into a beaten metal cup. "How did you get aboard?" Oma asked as I drained the cup.

"I . . . swam," I said, too tired to explain what would not be believed.

"Helvar says your people are waiting for the Hedra."

"We knew of the invasion, but there were some aspects of it we did not expect. I got caught up in one of them, so I don't know how things are going."

"The Hedra all wear demon bands." He touched his own.

"We expected it," I said. I met his gaze and found it watchful. "What I did not expect to find was a man like Helvar Shipmaster serving the Faction."

Oma gave a snorting laugh. "Hel's greatest enemy is his nobility of mind. It has always got him into trouble."

"You believe he should not help me," I guessed.

He shrugged. "If the Herders have successfully invaded the Land, and they learn that we helped you, we will be doomed along with our bondmates and children and family. The fact that we were dead would not prevent their slaughtering our children down to the last babe."

I nodded. "I know that there is risk in your helping me. But I assure you I can do as I told Helvar and erase from the Herders' minds anything that will cause you harm, if things go ill for my people."

He frowned. "You disconcert me, woman. I expected to hear you argue that yours is the right cause and we ought to help out of the goodness of our hearts."

Before I could answer, there was a loud clanging of bells and the sound of raised voices from above. Oma stiffened at the sound of boots running back and forth on deck and in the passages on the underdeck. Suddenly the door opened and Lark burst in. "The Hedra are retreating! Your people have driven them back!"

He sounded elated, but Oma's face was somber. Like me, he realized the consequences of what Lark was saying. The Hedra were retreating before I had begun to coerce the priests aboard, and now there would be no time to do so. I had lost the chance to win us the ships!

Lark's delight faded as he saw our faces and understood, too. "I am sorry," he told me. He looked at Oma and said, "Kaga has ordered our shipfolk to go and get them. All the ship boats are going out now."

"I must get off the ship," I said. "I will swim to shore."

"I am sorry," Oma said. "There is no possibility of your leaving the ship unseen now. All the priests, including Kaga, will be on deck, and we will have to go up as well. You must stay here and be silent."

"Here is what the cook gave me," Lark said, thrusting a bread roll and a mug of milk into my hands. Oma snuffed the lantern, and they both left, closing the door firmly behind them. I groped for the shelf I had seen set into the wall by the bed and then got up to unfasten the porthole. Rain flew into my face, driven before a rising wind, and I could hear distant shouts, but I could see nothing because the porthole faced away from the Land.

I sank to my knees and buried my head in my hands. *Fool!* I cursed myself. If only I had not come aboard the ship. How conceited I had been to believe I could single-handedly stop the Herder ships from leaving.

Hours seemed to pass as the Hedra were gradually ferried aboard, and I sat helpless, listening to their boots hammering on deck, wondering if they had merely been driven down the steps or if there had been fighting on the beach. I could not imagine what had happened ashore, and a thousand possibilities crowded through my mind as I vacillated between joy at the fact that we had forced a retreat and despair at the realization that I had trapped myself. Then I heard the unmistakable sound of an anchor being hauled in, and a chilly terror flowed through me at the thought that I was being taken to Herder Isle.

I knelt up at the porthole again and watched as the ship turned, until I saw the long wet cliffs of the Land as they hove into view, silver-sheened wherever the moonlight had found a rent in the clouds. I saw specks of orange light moving rapidly down the cliff where the steps would be and knew that must be people descending, carrying lanterns; Landfolk, for the ships were moving away from the Land on the tide. Watching the lights cluster along the beach, I wondered with a wrench if Rushton carried one of them. Certainly he would have ridden in with Dardelan and the rebel force, for they must have arrived, otherwise, how else would the Hedra have been defeated? Then it struck me that even if Rushton was standing on the shore, neither he nor anyone else could have any idea that *I* was aboard one of the fleeing Herder ships.

I watched helplessly until I lost sight of land, and then I sank back on my heels, appalled at the mess in which I found myself. I was trembling, and I told myself sternly that it was because I was cold. Glad to have some activity to distract me momentarily, I climbed off the bed, peeled off my sodden outer clothes, and hung them and the towel under the cloak on the back of the door. Last of all, I dragged one of the blankets from the bed and wrapped it around me, grateful for the prickly warmth. I sat back on the bed and sternly told myself not to panic. Helvar and his crew would hide me, for if I was found aboard, they would be suspected of helping me. I was going to Herder Isle, but not as a prisoner.

Not *quite*, said a voice drily in the back of my mind.

I ignored it, telling myself that the Norselanders could smuggle me into their village on Fallo, and I would simply hide there until Dardelan and the others built their ships and came to deal with the Faction. I had no doubt they would come, though I dared not guess how long it might take, for lacking the ships we had hoped to capture, they would have to build them first. In the meantime, everyone I loved would think I was dead or taken captive. Unless Maryon foresaw what had happened to me.

I gritted my teeth in anger at the thought that the futureteller might have foreseen it already and chosen to remain silent. Then I chided myself that she would only have done so if she truly believed that it was necessary. But what good could possibly come of my being carried against my will to Herder Isle? And how long could I hope to remain hidden on Fallo before the Faction learned of it? A village was not like a city where a lone person could live unnoticed. And if I was discovered, it would not just be the seamen aboard the *Stormdancer* who would die, but all those in the village.

I ought to have been too frightened to sleep, but I was weary to the bone, and as I sat there growing warmer, my eyelids began to close. I fought sleep for a little while; then I lay down, simply too tired and wretched to worry about someone finding me.

I dreamed the old dream of walking through a dark tunnel filled with the slow drip of water into water. The dream seemed colorless and remote, as if it were the memory of a dream. I slipped from it into another dream in which I was flying. It was vivid and thrilling. *I'm free*, I thought. Then, without any sense of the dream changing or any feeling of disruption, I was somewhere dark, and Matthew turned to me, smiling reassurance.

"I need to gan close enow to hear," he whispered.

"What do ye think ye'll learn?" asked another voice.

"Listen, these slavemasters of ours came here; they murdered th' queen an' enslaved her people. No one kens where they came from or why," Matthew said. "An' now this ship has come with its strange white-faced lord, who wants to negotiate the purchase of a great many slaves. Thousands! That is what I heard one of the masters say yesterday. He said someone suggested breedin' us to meet the demand. But the white-faced lord said that breeding slaves would take too long. Th' masters mun provide full-grown slaves in a year. The white-faced lord says he will return with ships enow to carry them and with payment. Why do they want so many slaves all at once?"

"An' ye think ye'll find answers to yer questions pokin' in th' heads of a few ragtag seamen?" The speaker sounded older than Matthew, and weary. But I could not make myself see him. The vision was fixed on Matthew.

"Seamen ken more than anyone else about other lands," Matthew said. "I want to find out where this white-faced lord comes from."

"What difference does it make? It's all th' same to us."

Matthew shook his head impatiently and leaned forward to peer around the corner of the building in whose moon shadow they stood.

I opened my eyes to see Lark's face illuminated in a spill of sunlight from the porthole, and the events of the night flooded back into my mind with devastating clarity.

"What is happening?" I asked, pushing the dream of Matthew to the back of my mind.

"It's morning. Let's speak inside my mind as you did with my father," Lark whispered. "It will be safer than talking aloud."

I nodded and evoked a picture of us in his mind.

He flinched.

"This will make it easier for you to speak to me with your thoughts," I farsent the explanation to him.

"Is it true as Oma said that you made me get my father to take off his demon band?" Lark asked, his image laboriously articulating the words loudly and slowly.

"Yes," I told him, resisting the impatient desire to

simply sift the information I needed from his mind. "What has been happening?"

"Kaga is furious. He demanded to know why the Hedra who went ashore here retreated without even engaging in battle. The captain who had led the force up from the sea caverns said he had commanded the retreat, because almost all of his Hedra had been killed or taken prisoner by a host of mutants and beasts as well as ordinary men and women whose minds were controlled by the mutants, he said no human force could oppose them, however brave. Kaga killed him. He wanted to lead another attack, but the Nine has forbidden it. We are going back to Herder Isle."

I had known where we must be bound, yet it was still a blow to hear the words. "How many Hedra are aboard the *Stormdancer*?"

"Over half. It is a pity more were not killed, for both ships are overloaded, since they must bear all those who came here on the *Black Ship,* and the *Stormdancer* is taking on a lot of water. We are lagging behind the *Orizon*, because we dare not go any faster."

"What will happen when we reach Herder Isle?"

"We will anchor in Hevon Bay, which is very close to the entrance to the Herder Compound. Usually, the ships are anchored out from the shore in deeper water, but my father will ground the *Stormdancer* so we can repair her damaged hull. My father thinks that the Hedra and the priests aboard the *Orizon* will have gone inside the compound by the time we drop anchor, but the crew of the *Black Ship* are not Norselanders. They always remain on board, save for Salamander, who will go inside for a time. My father says you must remain hidden on board until it is safe to move. We will cross to the channel in Fallo in small ship boats as soon as we land. I am to go with Oma because my father may have to go into the compound to make a report."

I did not need to be an empath to read the boy's fear for his father. "Lark, I am sure that the Herders will be too concerned about the failure of the invasion to worry about your stowing away. What happens after Helvar makes his report?"

"If they allow it, he will come home, too, in our ship boat."

"Perhaps I can come to Fallo with him?"

"You must wait until the next day," Lark said. "The Hedra always set a watch on the ships, but they change them every few hours. Oma says you must slip into the water when the watch goes ashore and remain in the shadow of the ship until the new watch comes aboard. They will inspect the ship as the old watch marches back to the compound, and that is when you will be able to swim to the boulders at the end of the beach. Wait until the third watch to move, for the Hedra will be less alert. Oma says to hide in the rocks and wait until my father and the others return to clean the ships and begin repairs on the *Stormdancer*. We will tether our ship boats by the rocks, and while we are working, you can get aboard and hide under the canvas that will be there. The boat is called *Gutred*, after my mother. At the end of the day, we will bring you home with us."

My heart sank at the thought of hiding in the rocks for a night and day. "Can't I just swim across to the village? The channel cannot be very wide."

"Nor is it. But there is a watch-hut atop each corner of the wall surrounding the Herder Compound; one overlooks the channel. You would be seen if you tried to swim across," the boy answered. "I must go back out now. I will try to come again later in the day." He rose to his feet, but I forestalled him to ask how long it would be before we reached Herder Isle. "It is not long past dawn now, but because of the currents and the shoals, we will not arrive at Hevon Bay before tomorrow night."

After Lark had gone, I got up and stood indecisively in the darkened cabin. I would have paced except that I feared making any noise. Eventually, I ate the stale roll Lark had brought, drank the milk, and then lay on the bed. But there were shouts and thuds and footsteps in the hall outside the cabin, and I leapt up a dozen times in fright before I decided to make a seat for myself in the locker. I left the door open and stretched out my legs, knowing that I need only pull them in and close the locker door if anyone entered.

For a time, I cheered myself by imagining the shock the warrior priests must have got at finding themselves opposed by beasts as well as humans in Saithwold. I wondered what would be made of my disappearance. Linnet, Khuria, Gahltha, and Wenda all knew where I had gone, and eventually the tunnel in the cloister would be discovered and followed to the sea cavern where the debris left by the priests would tell its own tale. Then what? They would assume I had been caught. I doubted anyone would judge me fool enough to willingly board one of the ships, though that was exactly what I had intended to do.

Weary of thinking, I drew the locker door closed and made myself as comfortable as I could. Sleep claimed me then, and I was glad. After a good night's sleep, I would be physically ready to face what the morrow brought, if not mentally.

A thunderous crash brought me out of the locker, my heart hammering. It sounded as if a great cliff of ice had fallen on the ship, but there had been no impact. I scrambled up onto the bed, opened the porthole, and peered out. It was night still, and I could see the lanterns that marked two ships in the distance. One was likely the *Orizon*, though it was impossible to tell at that distance in the darkness. It looked as if the larger ship was approaching it. There was another great clap of sound, and I saw something bright red fly in a swift high arc from the larger ship to the smaller. Then there was a violent explosion, and a flower of orange and white bloomed against the velvet-dark night as the smaller ship burst into flame. I cried out in shock and then, realizing in horror what I had done, pressed my hand to my mouth, but no one came to investigate my cry. Probably everyone had rushed up on deck, hearing the first crash, and so there had been no one to hear a woman scream on a ship of only men.

I looked out the porthole again and saw that there was now a wedge of drowning flame and a single ship visible. I had no doubt it was the *Black Ship*, for no other ship had such deadly power. But why would the *Black Ship* strike its ally?

I remembered suddenly that I could reach Lark's mind. I sent out a probe that located swiftly, but rather than communicating with him, I merely listened to the information his senses were bringing to his mind. Incredibly, it seemed that the *Black Ship* had fired on the

Orizon, and from the furor among the Hedra, no one had any idea why. Then Lark registered with frightened excitement that the *Black Ship* was signaling them. I waited within Lark's mind, sharing his anxiety as the shipman reading the flags spelled out the message: *The other ship was sunk because it had been boarded by mutants.*

My ears roared, but I forced myself to remain within Lark's mind in case there was more.

"How could Salamander know there were mutants aboard?" he heard one of the warrior priests ask another.

"He has one of Ariel's nulls aboard," the other answered impatiently.

"But everyone knows their visions can only be interpreted by Ariel," another spoke.

My blood turned to ice in my veins at the thought that Ariel had been aboard the *Black Ship* all this time. And how long before he knew that I was aboard the *Stormdancer*?

Lark did not come until dawn lightened the sky, staining the clouds rose-gold. He brought a tray heaped with food and a privy pot that he handed over with a blush, explaining that his father had pretended to be angry and had sent him to Oma's cabin. Most of the crew were on deck, and the Hedra were practicing their martial arts, so it was unlikely anyone would come along the passage, but, he warned, we must be careful to keep our voices very low.

I nodded and asked where Oma had been sleeping. He answered that the big shipmate had slept on the deck like others of the crew. Fortunately, this was a common practice, so no one thought it odd.

Lark began to tell me what had happened to the *Orizon*, but I told him that I had seen its destruction. I told him what I had overheard and asked if it was true that Ariel was aboard. To my intense relief, the boy shook his head. He said, "Salamander always keeps at least two of Ariel's nulls aboard his ship, and it is said he can read their visions almost as well as Ariel himself. The flagman told me that the *Black Ship* had been on its way back to Herder Isle so the Herder could make a report to the Three when Ariel's nulls began screaming that mutants had taken over the *Orizon*. I have known those shipmen all my life, and now they are dead. But I think you must grieve, too, for your people were also aboard."

I nodded, my mind still groping to take in the news that nulls were capable of seeing the future even when Ariel was not with them. Which had to mean that they were real futuretellers! Then I thought of those who had perished aboard the *Orizon* and felt like weeping. "I do not know which of my friends were aboard or how they managed it. But Ariel has been responsible for too many deaths of people I loved," I said, feeling the weight of my grief.

"Ariel is responsible for many deaths on Herder Isle, too," Lark said. "But you need not fear that you will be exposed by the null as your friends were, for the flagman sent that both nulls died confirming the vision. Nulls are fragile and rarely last more than a few visions."

"It is strange that the nulls did not see the failure of the invasion," I said.

Lark shrugged. "They do not see many things, but what they do see is almost always true."

293

I did not want to think about which of my friends might have died, so I forced myself to change the subject. "Tell me what you know about Ariel's residence on Norseland."

He answered that he knew little, save that the residence stood on a rocky knoll at the high island's less populous end. The closest settlement to it was Cloistertown, which had grown up around what had once been a Herder cloister. It had been abandoned, and now all the priests on Norseland dwelt in the island's only other cloister. This was walled, Lark added, and its watch-huts overlooked Main Cove where all ships anchored to unload those who would climb the narrow road up to the top of the island. Covetown had grown up around the top of the trail from the Main Cove and was the largest settlement on the island.

"I heard there was a training camp on Norseland," I prompted.

He nodded. "That is on a plateau that rises up from the flatland behind Covetown and the cloister."

"How did the Herders take control of the Norselands in the first place?" I asked curiously.

"Partly by treachery," Lark said. He went on to explain that some generations past, when the Norse king was making his annual journey from Norseland to Herder Isle for the sevenday summer festival, a great storm had blown up. After the storm, a broken ship carrying thirty-nine Herders was found cast up on the beach at Hevon Bay. They were brought to Hevon City to be cared for, and when the king asked where they had come from, they said only that their homeland was no more. Pitying the stranded priests, the old king had offered them land on which to build homes. He also gave them permission to woo and bond with the Norse women that they might settle more truly. But these men wanted no women, and it was not homes they built upon the rocky land behind Hevon City but a small compound where they lived communally and worshiped their punitive Lud.

Next summer festival, when the king came to Herder Isle, the priests bade him forsake the three goddesses worshipped by the Norselanders. The old king laughed and said the priests might worship a male god if they chose, but he preferred the softness of the three goddesses. Being a generous and good-humored man, he granted the priests' request for more land to extend their cloister, for they had persuaded a shipwright to rebuild their ship and had begun to make trips across the strait, bringing back young boys they claimed were converts to the Faction.

No one thought to question the boys, who had been immediately taken inside the compound for the cleansing period of isolation and silence the priests claimed was needed to prepare them for the Faction. Indeed, the king was often heard to comment that life in the Land across the strait must be harsher than it had been when Norselanders had gone there to trade, for why else would any lad agree to join this loveless order?

"Eventually," Lark continued, "by dint of wheedling and begging and demanding, the Faction took over an entire section of Herder Isle. The Norselanders gave little protest because the area included a patch of deadly Blacklands. But there were some rumblings of discontent when the Faction began to build a high wall around the land they had been given. The Herders claimed this was merely to protect the compound and its farmlands from bitter sea winds."

I guessed that this must have happened about the time the Council had formed an alliance with the Faction, bestowing upon them land to build their cloisters in each province. No doubt they had recognized that an alliance with a terrifying religious order could only strengthen their hold upon the Land. I had not realized that the Herders had first established themselves upon the Norselands, but I had no doubt that the boys who had supposedly wanted to become novices were given no choice. "But you still have not said how they took control," I prompted.

Lark nodded and went on to explain that the old king had been interested in the order's apparent vigorous growth and the stern discipline it imposed on its converts. They worked very hard and did not speak, and their silent dedication seemed to him admirable. He thought his own son an overindulged weakling, too much under the sway of his mother, grandmother, and aunts, so when the One of the Faction offered to educate the boy in the austere ways of the cloister, he agreed. By the time the king died, his son was a devout believer in the Herders' Lud.

Lark went to get some water from a wooden barrel behind a wall panel and to listen awhile at the door. Then he came back to sit on the bed and continued his tale. "By the time the old king died," he went on, "there were many more priests, and the Faction all but ruled the Norselands through the old king's son. He came to be known as the Last King, for when he died, the Herders claimed that he had abdicated in their favor.

296

There was no proof of it, and there was an uprising to oppose it. That was when the cities of Hevon and Fallo were destroyed and Herder Isle divided."

"But how . . . ?"

"The Faction used Beforetime weapons. My father believes they brought them when they came to Herder Isle, though then it was all named Fallo Isle. In any case, once they had taken over, they sailed to Norseland. Instead of fighting, they released several people who had witnessed the destruction of the cities on Fallo and the Girdle of the Goddess. The Pers—they are our leaders—refused to surrender, for how could the invaders manage to get their dread weapons up onto the land?

"Again the Herders struck, using some terrible weapon that flew like a bird, and the great city of Kingshome and the cliff upon which it stood, broke away and plummeted into the cove. Not one person survived. What else could those who remained on the island do but lay down their arms? The Herders have ruled the Norselands ever since. To begin with, they ruled from Norseland, but after the compound was complete, that became the center of power," Lark concluded solemnly.

A picture rose in his mind of great black metal gates, set in an impossibly high stone wall, opening slowly to reveal a big black square surrounded by stone buildings similar to cloisters, save that they were formed of black rock instead of the gray of the Land. The compound buildings had the same high narrow windows and sloping roofs as Land cloisters, but they were roofed in some dark stiff thatch instead of being tiled, as was the custom in the Land. Herders passed back and forth in gray robes, and there were smaller figures in white or black robes. All moved like objects underwater, as if driven not by their own will but by a slow inexorable current. The vision was very dark and loomed oddly and unnaturally, which told me that the memory was distorted by Lark's emotions. Even so, it was clear that it was not just a large cloister behind the wall but a city. A city of Herders.

I slept on and off through the long slow day that followed. The moon had risen before I was roused by the sound of the horn, which Lark had told me would signal our approach to Hevon Bay. I could see nothing from the porthole in Oma's cabin but open sea; however, I was able to catch glimpses of the island in Lark's mind. At my request, he made a careful point of visualizing whatever he thought might interest me. In this way I saw that unlike the Land, there were no high dark cliffs to be surmounted. Like the west coast, the moonlit island was very flat, yet it was impossible to see the channel that now divided the island, or the villages on Fallo, or even the hill that was said to rise from its swampy heart, for an immense stone wall rose up all along the island's coastline, so high that it obscured everything behind it. It had been built so close to the edge of the island that it looked like a wall rising straight from the sea. Indeed, when the tide rose high or was storm driven, it must crash against the base of the wall. From Lark's description, I knew that the wall surrounded all the land that had once been Hevon City and that it ran right along the channel that separated it from Fallo Island. The only bit left unwalled was a wide flat spit of land that curved around the beach that formed Hevon Bay. As we passed along the wall, which surely could not be as high as Lark's mind showed it, I noted the watch-house overlooking Hevon Bay and remembered that Lark had spoken of another surmounting the corner of the wall facing the channel. No wonder he had said I could not swim it without being seen.

"Why build a wall?" I asked when Lark came down a little later.

"No one knows, but it is said that they were matching a bit of Beforetime wall at the end of the island near the patch of Blacklands," Lark said. We heard a shout, and the boy stiffened and listened a moment before saying, "We are about to anchor. I had better go up on deck. Remember, stay hidden until the third watch is sounded, and find a place in the rocks to hide as close as possible to where the ship boats will be tethered. You will see the places where pegs have been driven into the stones," he told me earnestly. Then he muttered a curse and added, "I am a fool. I forgot to tell you that the *Black Ship* is not here."

"Not here? But it was coming here to report to the Herders."

"It was here not two hours past, the flagman on the walls signaled. But now it has gone to Norseland. The route passes on the other side of Fallo, which is why we did not see it leaving. You will be pleased to know that Ariel has gone with him."

I was more than pleased; I was relieved. After Lark had gone, I climbed into the locker and locked the door. I could undo it from inside the cupboard, but we had agreed that it would be safer for me to be locked in since each new watch would make a cursory inspection of the ship when they came aboard. I was trying to find a comfortable position that I could maintain for some hours, when the ship lurched hard and gave a loud creak. It was coming about, I guessed, and then I heard the rattle of a chain as the anchor was lowered. The noise of disembarking that followed seemed to go on forever, but I distracted myself from the cramped locker by watching it in flashes in Lark's mind. In the end, I left him because his fear for his father now filled his thoughts and had begun to rouse my own fears. When I tried to reach Lark a little later, I could not contact him, which meant that the Norseland crew had gone ashore, and the boots I could hear now all belonged to Hedra.

It was hot and stuffy in the locker, but I resisted the temptation to unlock the door and get out. Better to be uncomfortable and alive, I told myself. Suddenly, I heard footsteps coming down from the deck. From the sound of the boots, several people were coming along the passage toward the cabin where I was hidden.

". . . that is what he told us . . . ," a man said.

I heard the next cabin door open and then close. Then Oma's door opened, and I held my breath.

"This is it," said a man's voice.

Footsteps and then the locker door rattled. "It's locked," said another man's voice.

"Break it open," said the first speaker. "She must be there."

◆ 17 ◆

THERE WAS A great crash, and wood splintered under the force of a hard heel. I had a brief glimpse of a group of Herder priests, bald, robed, and demon-banded, peering at me, and then the sundered remnants of the locker door were torn aside and a rough hand reached in to haul me out by the hair. A Hedra captain stared into my face with eyes that burned with a fanatical icy fire above a thin nose and a lipless slash of a mouth.

"A woman!" he said in disgust.

"Not a woman, Bedig," said the slow quavering voice of an old man.

The Hedra dragged me around to face a tiny wizened priest with coal-black eyes set in a face collapsed into a nest of wrinkles. The thick gold band about his upper arm denoted him a Three and one of the most powerful men in the Faction, save for the mysterious One. Ignoring the younger priest's half-incoherent bleating, he drew closer to me and peered into my face.

"A female mutant," he said with a soft, hissing emphasis that brought gooseflesh to my arms.

Another younger priest appeared at the cabin door, panting, "Master, the Norseland shipfolk have already gone across to Fallo, including their master. He was dismissed by the Nine."

The Three turned to look at the younger priest. "I bade you inform me the moment the *Stormdancer* anchored."

"Master, the null said the ship was damaged and that it would be near morning before—"

"It is a fool who relies upon the visioning of a single null. Did you confirm the vision, Daska?"

The other seemed to shudder under the old man's glaring disapproval. "Master, there was only the one null left," he whispered. "They die so easily. . . ."

"I know that, you fool. Why do you think I bade you organize a watch?"

"I spoke to the watch—"

"I told you to organize a separate and specific watch for the ships."

"The *Orizon* . . . ," Daska began.

"Ariel told us what happened to the *Orizon* at the same time he informed us of the null's prediction that another mutant was hidden aboard the *Stormdancer*. But none of that is your concern. Why did you not do as I commanded?"

The other priest cringed. "Master, forgive me. . . ."

The Three turned to the Hedra holding me. "Bedig, see that Daska is whipped and then confined to a tidal cell for a fourday," he said indifferently. "Let the crabs teach him obedience."

"Master," the Hedra captain intoned.

"Also, I want this ship's master and his crew brought back for questioning immediately."

"Their families, Master?" Bedig asked.

The Herder considered it, then shook his head. "Not yet. Let the Norsemen hope that they can prevent us from punishing their families by offering us information.

Then when we bring the families in, the pain of learning that they have been taken will be much greater because it will contain true despair." He spoke blandly as if he was telling someone how to arrange a vase of flowers or lay a table. "Now let us get this mutant into the compound and see what we can learn about why it boarded this ship, rather than the *Orizon*."

"Master, is not the interrogation of the mutant to wait until Ariel returns from Norseland with his interrogation machine and the special null?" asked Bedig.

"Ariel left instructions that the creature not be damaged, for the interrogation will be vigorous and requires a subject in good condition. However, despite his undeniable usefulness, Ariel is not one of the inner cadre. Now band the mutant," snapped the Three.

The demon band was heavier than the one Malik's armsman had put on me and the taint so strong that it made me feel sick. But it turned my stomach less than the knowledge that Ariel had known I was aboard the *Stormdancer*. Bile rose in my throat, and I leaned forward and vomited.

The Three uttered a disgusted sound and went out, leaving Bedig to drag me after him. Strangely, after that first overwhelming moment of sick terror, I felt no fear as they marched me through the ship and up onto the deck. It was as if I had vomited it out. It was dark enough that lanterns had been lit, for the tide of black clouds I had seen from Oma's cabin now covered the face of the moon, and even as I was hurried down the ladder and into the ship boat, I heard the rumble of thunder, and it began to rain.

I ought to have felt guilt, knowing that the shipfolk would be taken into the compound because of me, but

303

my emotions seemed to be locked in a distant room. Once the boat had run aground, Bedig pulled me out and marched me up the shore. A flash of lightning revealed a monstrous wall, which was easily as high as Lark's mind had shown, and giant metal gates opened to receive us like a great black maw. As I was ushered through them, there was a long, low growl of thunder, and it came to me that I would never leave this fearsome place alive. As if to underline this truth, the gates swung closed behind me with a dull clang that rang in the air with deadly finality.

It was so dark now that I could see no more than patches of the wall's great hewn stones where lanterns hung. Lightning flashed, and I saw that we had entered the wide yard surrounded on three sides by the black buildings I had glimpsed in Lark's mind. The façade of buildings was broken here and there by narrow streets. From one of these, a number of bald, white-robed novices came hastening with lanterns. No doubt the gate watch had seen us approach and had summoned them. One carried a fresh cloak for the Three, and the old man allowed himself to be ministered to without acknowledging the novice. For his part, the boy replacing his wet cloak was so self-effacing that I had the feeling he strove to be invisible. Thunder rumbled again as another novice held out the basket he carried, and the Three and the other priests removed their demon bands and placed them in it. Then Bedig barked a command, and the other Hedra departed, the terrified-looking Daska in their midst. The novices left, too, save one with a lantern, and at an impatient signal from Bedig, he set off and we followed, the Hedra once again grasping my arm.

I tried to control my mind's skittering by mentally building a map as we passed along one narrow street after another. I had invented the technique and taught it to farseekers as a way of controlling and calming the mind as well as gaining useful information. Its effectiveness was weakened by my knowing that I was unlikely to have the chance to use that knowledge.

As we passed along yet another black, rain-swept street, lightning flared on the long blank face of the buildings on either side of us, and it struck me that I had not seen a single door in any of the buildings, which meant that all the buildings must be connected. Indeed, there were even elevated stone walkways passing overhead from one side of the street to the other, linking the buildings. This was not a city filled with Herders working and living individual lives; it was a nest such as ants or bees construct, with the whole community living for one single idea and purpose.

At last we came to a deep-set black door atop a short flight of steps. There were Hedra standing before it, but seeing the Three, they pressed their hands to their throats as if in salute and stepped smartly aside. The novice with the lantern ran up the steps to open the door, and as we followed the Three inside, I thought, *I will never leave this place alive.*

This time, strangely, the cold weight of the thought calmed me.

Two boys clad in hooded black robes awaited us in the shadowy foyer, each bearing a lantern that swung from a stick. There was no sign of the white-clad novice, and I realized that he had probably departed when we entered the building. I had no idea what the black attire signified, but if the novices had seemed to wish themselves invisible, these boys were invisible, for neither Bedig nor the Three even looked at them. I could not make out their expressions, for they kept their heads tilted forward.

The Three had taken two steps across the foyer when a young Herder priest, accompanied by yet another black-clad lantern bearer, emerged from the door farthest to the left and bowed to the Three. His armband revealed him to be an inner-cadre Nine, which surprised me, for Farseeker research had shown that seniority ruled all matters in the Faction, yet he was no more than Rushton's age. He commiserated with the Three about the rain, and there seemed something in his voice less obsequious than there ought to have been, given that he was speaking to a Three. Perhaps the Three thought so, too, because the old man made an impatient silencing gesture and asked sharply what he wanted.

The young Herder bowed and said, "Master Mendi, the One bids you come to him at once. He wishes to see the mutant whose presence upon the *Stormdancer* was foreseen by Ariel's null."

The Three frowned. "The One cannot wish to trouble himself with this creature, Falc."

"I do not presume to know what the master wishes. I tell you only what he told me to say, Master Mendi." The delicate malice in his words was unmistakable.

The Three hesitated a moment, then snapped, "I will come as the One commands, of course. I am only concerned for his comfort and health."

"The comfort and health of the One have been much disturbed by the failure of the invasion," the young priest said, going back through the door by which he had entered.

"That has disturbed all of us," Mendi responded coldly, keeping pace with him and ignoring the hooded lantern-bearer who had slipped ahead to light the dark passage. "It is only a pity that Ariel's nulls did not foresee it or the loss of the *Orizon* in time to avert it," the Three added.

"Perhaps you will convey your displeasure with Ariel's nulls to the One, Master Mendi," Falc said with an arch smile. "Or maybe you would prefer to wait until Ariel returns so you can make your complaints directly to him."

Mendi's lips tightened. "Shall we make haste? I am sure the One will not be pleased that I was slow to answer his summons, because you felt the need to air your thoughts on the way."

Falc stopped before a door and curtly bade us enter. We obeyed and found ourselves in a very narrow passage of rough stone with a roof high enough to defeat the weak light shed by the lanterns. The passage ran straight for so long that its end was lost in shadow. We had been walking along it for some time before I realized that its stone floor sloped slightly upward. Despite the absence of doors or windows, the air was fresh, which suggested vents leading directly to the outside. I wondered why anyone would bother building a roof and walls over such a long walk.

We must have gone on for ten minutes before I saw a light ahead. It was coming from an open doorway. Two Hedra bearing metal-capped staffs stood before it, but they moved aside at once when Falc commanded it. The younger priest hurried through, leaving the rest of us to follow, and I glanced back to see the black-clad lantern bearers withdraw. The chamber we entered was long and narrow and was empty except for a large carved chair drawn up to a fireplace in which flames crackled brightly. It was not wood burning in the fireplace but some queer red-brown rock that gave out great heat but almost no smoke. The floor was carpeted from wall to wall in thick overlapping animal pelts, and one wall was entirely curtained in heavy gray cloth, making the room almost stiflingly hot.

Falc went through a door on the fire's other side, and I heard the low, deferential hum of his voice, then he reentered, followed by two more black-robed boys. One carried a small enamel table and a goblet of water, and the other had two soft gray cushions, which he arranged carefully on the carved chair, then he crossed the room to draw the curtain. It must have been heavy, for he struggled with its weight. The curtain parted to reveal an enormous window with a wide, spectacular view of the dark, rain-swept sea, lit momentarily by a flash of lightning. I forgot about the mystery of the black-clad boys, for how should a building have such a view inside a monstrously walled city?

Then I understood. I thought of the long narrow tunnel we had followed and realized the passage and this chamber must be embedded *within* the wall surrounding the compound!

Bedig's grip tightened painfully on my arm, and he sank into a low bow along with everyone else in the room, dragging me with him, as an enormously fat old man wearing a gold-edged robe and a thin golden circlet about his brow was helped into the chamber by a solicitous Falc and two slender, black-robed boys. Because I was on my knees, I caught sight of the thin face of the nearest black-robed boy, who could be no older than Dragon, and for a fleeting second, his shadowed gray eyes looked into mine. He turned away, and I was left to study the huge, querulous-looking bald man being settled into his chair. It was hard to believe that this old man with his obese helplessness was the supreme priest of the Herder Faction: the terrifying One in whose name my parents and hundreds of others had died.

More than anything else, he reminded me of a great fat baby, for although his body was corpulent, the hands protruding from the gold-edged sleeves of his robe and the feet in their soft woven slippers were tiny, and his mouth was a very small, wet red bow. Only his eyes betrayed his age and power: small and as black as obsidian, they glittered with malevolent purpose.

Belatedly, I realized that fierce gaze was now fixed on me.

"The creature dares to look at me. Put out its eyes," the One said in a queerly feminine voice.

"Of course they must be put out, Master," said another voice, and I turned with everyone else in the room to see another Three enter the chamber. Unlike Mendi, this was a man in his prime, with a barrel chest and well-muscled arms. If not for his gold band, I would have taken him for a Hedra. The robust newcomer crossed the room, dropped to his knee before the One's carved chair, and lifted the tiny plump fingers to his forehead.

I glanced at Mendi, who regarded this obeisance sourly. The newcomer lifted his head and said in his smooth, creamy voice, "You should not trouble yourself to command what is as obvious as the sun rising, Master. For how should a mutant be permitted to gaze upon the glorious face of the first-chosen of Lud and then look upon anything hereafter? Its eyes and its life will be extinguished as soon as it has been questioned."

The One glared at the newcomer. "Where have you been, Grisyl?"

"It has pained me to take so long to answer your summons, Master," the Three answered, rising gracefully to his feet. His eyes flickered toward me. "I presume this is the mutant revealed to us through Ariel's null and by Lud's grace?" His voice might shame honey with its warm, sliding sweetness.

"Ariel," crooned the One, his expression an odd mixture of frustration and irritated indulgence. "Yes, our faithful and clever Ariel; what did he recommend before he left, Falc?"

"To leave unharmed the mutant we would find hidden in the shipman's locker until he returns. He will bring special devices to force it to speak the truth and a special null with the power to prevent its foul powers hindering us during its interrogation, and such an interrogation will require a strong, healthy body," Falc answered eagerly.

"So Ariel said to me also," Grisyl agreed smoothly. "Of course, once the mutant has been drained of information, it will die, and that death must be slow and painful, for such a mockery of Lud's highest creation cannot go unpunished."

The One made a sound like the greedy mewling of a baby spying its mother's uncovered breast.

Mendi spoke then, his voice dry and harsh after Grisyl's mellifluous tones. "It is puzzling that Ariel's nulls did not foresee the failure of the invasion."

The One turned his black gaze onto the Three, but

before he could speak; Grisyl said, "Ariel has told us many times that the nulls are unstable tools."

"Where is the Nine who commanded the invasion force?" Grisyl asked Mendi. "He was one of yours, was he not?"

Mendi gave him an impassive look. "I have ordered a period of penance and fasting, after which I will question him."

"Where is Zuria?" the One demanded.

"He is interrogating Kaga and the other Hedra who survived the abortive invasion," Grisyl said. "Naturally, he is especially anxious to learn why it failed." There was a lick of malice in his words.

Mendi opened his mouth and then closed it, as if thinking better of whatever he would have said. From what had been said, I guessed Zuria had been most strongly in favor of the invasion. But given the structure of the Faction, the invasion would never have been undertaken without the One's approval. Not that anyone would remind him of that now.

I thought of Ariel and wondered about his intentions. He had told the Herders that he would return to interrogate me, and I had no doubt that he would do so, but I doubted he would want to question me in front of the Herders about the signs and keys Kasanda had left for me. Most likely, he would contrive to get me alone. A terrible weariness assailed me at the knowledge that I would have nothing but my own will to shield me from his questions, for I had little faith in that. Long ago at Obernewtyn, Ariel, Alexi, and Madam Vega had tried to torture information from me using a machine. It had not been courage that had kept me from speaking, but a tenuous physical contact with

311

Rushton that had allowed him to absorb part of the pain.

But there would be no rescue this time. Ariel would force me to tell him all I knew of Kasanda's instructions and the signs that would have led me to the Beforetime weaponmachines. My only comfort was that I did not know all I needed to know, nor had I all I needed to have in order to complete my quest. Perhaps Ariel intended to use me to find the remaining clues. The only way to prevent that would be to wipe my own mind clean. *Memory-death*, we called it.

I clenched my fists and felt my nails dig into my palms. Why hadn't a premonition stopped me from climbing aboard the ship boat? Why hadn't Atthis warned me not to do it? I groaned softly, realizing that even if the bird had tried to warn me, she would have been unable to reach me, for Maruman was her conduit, and he and I had been separated almost the whole time I had been in Saithwold.

Maruman, I thought, and grief stabbed at me with the knowledge that I would never again hold him or feel his dear heavy presence in my mind.

"Of course, Master," Mendi was saying. "I am only pointing out that it might have been useful to discuss what happened before Ariel hastened off. But I suppose the delay will not be so great if he returns immediately."

"Ariel must go first from Norseland to the west coast to accomplish Lud's will," said the One, giving Mendi a glare of malevolence that made the older Three step back. "You have never served Lud as well as he, Mendi, for while you seek a scapegoat for the failed invasion, Ariel is already thinking of another way to strike a blow for Lud." A fit of coughing shook the old man's enormous body. He looked at me, and his expression suddenly registered exaggerated disgust. "Who dared to bring a woman into my presence?" The words were almost a shriek.

"She is a woman only in appearance, Lord," Grisyl said swiftly, and began to stroke the One's hand as if he were a fractious child.

"Get her out of my sight." His face filled with sudden rage. "All of you get out of my sight." Grisyl offered a goblet, but the old man smashed it from his hands. "Get out, I say. Get out! Falc! Summon my shadows!" The last glimpse I had was of several black-robed boys converging silently on the One while Falc wrung his hands.

"Do not imagine that your manipulations go unnoticed, Grisyl," Mendi said as we again traversed the long wall corridor. The two Threes walked ahead, illuminated by the lanterns, and I came behind with the cold-faced Bedig, his fingers locked about my arm.

"What do you mean?" Grisyl asked coolly.

Mendi gave a sneering laugh. "You seek to ingratiate yourself with the One. But as you see, Lud has his own means of shielding our beloved One from those who wish to pursue their own desires."

Grisyl gave him an ironic look. "Of course, Lud knows the selflessness of his two faithful servants, Zuria and Mendi."

The older Herder made a scornful sound. "I do not say that we have no ambitions of our own. But this is not the time to be divided. You seek to ally yourself with Ariel, because he is favored by the One, but Ariel is as unreliable as his precious nulls."

"I will not be held accountable for this disastrous invasion, Mendi," Grisyl said with sudden anger. "I was not with him when Ariel broke the news, thank Lud, but Zuria was, and he said the One ordered the shadow serving him to be flayed alive, because a drop of fement spilled on his robe."

"Better a hundred shadows than one of us," Mendi said dryly. "The One will calm down when we can offer him an explanation for the invasion's failure, or at least a scapegoat. I suspect we were betrayed by Malik. I said all along that it was ludicrous to trust an ex-rebel. Personally, I am more interested in learning how the mutants on the *Orizon* took control when all aboard should have been wearing demon bands until the anchor was raised. Unfortunately, we have no one from the *Orizon* to interrogate, since Salamander sank the ship and all aboard. We have only his word and the testimony of a null, now dead, that the *Orizon* was boarded at all."

"What could it serve Salamander to sink one of our greatships?" Grisyl asked. "Zuria is furious about it, of course."

Mendi grunted. "What about Ariel being sent to the west coast after going to Norseland? What is he to do there?"

Grisyl shrugged. "Lud's will, apparently. But perhaps the One simply confuses Ariel's present journey to Norseland with the longer journey he has been planning to make to the Red Land."

"I had the feeling from the One's words that Ariel is to undertake some specific task on the west coast," Mendi persisted. "Did he not specifically say that Ariel will strike a blow in Lud's name?"

"Something like that," Grisyl agreed, frowning. "And now that you mention it, I *have* heard that Ariel has been working on something special. Something to do with two nulls he has kept locked in his chamber. He has taken them with him, you know."

Mendi said, "My concern is less what Ariel has gone to do than that he chose to go or was sent without our being consulted. I dislike this policy of secrecy that excludes us but includes one who is not of the Faction."

"You speak as if Ariel desires it to be so, but you know as well as I that our master has grown more and more . . . *particular* in these last few years," Grisyl said. The two men exchanged a look as if Grisyl meant another word that Mendi knew.

"All I am saying is that Ariel should not undertake some important activity about which we have not been informed," Mendi said.

"I agree, but I doubt either of us is likely to express our indignation to the One," Grisyl said dryly. "Or have you forgotten the last Herder foolish enough to criticize Ariel to our master? Whatever Ariel will do in the west, the One has approved it, and therefore it has Lud's blessing."

Mendi scowled. "That is so. But tell me, why did the null aboard the *Black Ship* warn Salamander about the boarding of the *Orizon* yet fail to reveal the mutant aboard the *Stormdancer*?"

"Perhaps the null did reveal it and Salamander failed to understand," Grisyl said indifferently. "In any case, it is fortunate, since Ariel says that this one ranks high among the mutants and is a friend of the Black Dog and the boy chieftain. I will be most interested to hear what she can tell us."

"I, also, yet it is strange that someone so important would board a Herder vessel alone," Mendi continued. "It makes me uneasy, and I do not like that we are bidden not to interrogate her until Ariel returns. Especially if he has not merely gone to Norseland as I was led to believe. It could be a sevenday before he returns."

Grisyl nodded. "Longer, depending on what he is to do there. And you know how much more *particular* the One becomes when he is frustrated or impatient." He turned and gave me a cold, appraising look. "No doubt this mutant had some specific part to play in whatever scheme the mutants aboard the *Orizon* had in mind, for Ariel said she is extremely powerful and warned that she must not on any account be unbanded. Apparently, the null spoke her name, and Ariel knew it. He said she is the woman of the Master of Obernewtyn."

Mendi's brows rose high. "That *is* interesting. I suppose Ariel learned of the woman when the Master of Obernewtyn was our guest. But remind me, did not Ariel have some grand scheme for him?"

"Ariel has many schemes," Grisyl said dismissively. "In any case, whatever it was clearly failed. Rushton Seraphim is returned to the mutants and leads them as if nothing ever happened. Indeed, given the results of the invasion, it would seem he is more effective than ever as a leader, even if he is broken as a man. It may have been a great mistake to leave him behind in the cloister." He stopped abruptly and gave me a speculative look. "I wonder . . ."

"What?" Mendi asked impatiently.

"Well, it just occurred to me that this woman may know Ariel. After all, he did originally come from Obernewtyn, before the mutants took control."

"What of it?"

Grisyl frowned. "Perhaps this talk of special implements is merely a way to control how much the mutant
tells us. I always thought there were too many gaps in
his tales of what occurred in those days."

Both men glanced back at me speculatively, and
Mendi said slowly, "You know as well as I do that
someone will have to pay for the failed invasion. And a
dozen shadows, a few Hedra, and even a Nine will not
satisfy the One. But I see no reason why we should be
blamed for a plan that was not of our choosing. Zuria
proposed it, and Ariel supported him. Instead of trying
to ally yourself with Ariel, you might see this as a perfect opportunity to drive a wedge between him and the
One. None of our desires will be harmed if Ariel has
less power."

"Zuria may not agree. . . ."

Mendi laughed scornfully. "Oh, I think Zuria's infatuation with Ariel will be well and truly extinct since the
Orizon sank. Some of his best people were aboard.
Besides, I doubt he will object to seeing this failure laid
squarely at Ariel's door, for otherwise he must bear the
brunt of the One's anger." A pause, then, "My intention
is not to dispose of Ariel or harm him in any lasting
way. He has been useful to us over the years, and he will
no doubt continue to be so, especially when it comes to
dealing with the heathens from the Red Land. I merely
feel that it would be wiser to curtail his power."

"What are you suggesting?" Grisyl asked. We had
now reached the entrance hall, and he turned to face
the older Three. The two men acted as if Bedig, the hovering black-clad shadows, and I were trees growing
about them.

"I think that we might question this woman ourselves," Mendi answered. "As a Nine, I believe you showed a rare talent for interrogation that left no marks."

"What of Zuria?" Grisyl asked. "Should he not be present?"

"Let us leave him to his interrogations for the time being." The two men exchanged guarded smiles of complicity.

"You would have us believe that Ariel is a mutant?"

I gasped for breath. "He was at Obernewtyn. Why . . . why else would he have been there?"

"He was the son of Alexi, who was in the employ of Stephen Seraphim," Grisyl snapped. I must have looked as stunned as I felt, for no one had ever whispered that Alexi was Ariel's father—unless it was all a fabrication.

"He is a Misfit," I said. "He sees into the future."

"His *nulls* see into the future," snapped Mendi.

"How would he locate Misfits among your novices if he was not one himself?" I asked.

"Do you dare to mock us by claiming that he is like you?" snapped Grisyl. "Why would a mutant work against its own kind? I will cut the mouth from your face if you lie to me again."

"But not yet," Mendi drawled, sounding bored and irritated.

"I must cut her to make her speak. If I hold her under the water any longer, she will drown," Grisyl snapped.

"Perhaps you have not the skill needed for this task after all," Mendi said.

"I have the skill but am hampered by your prohibitions."

"Ariel's prohibitions," Mendi corrected.

I was lying in a puddle of water I had vomited up, marveling bitterly at the irony that I had told them the truth about Ariel, yet for all their suspicions and doubts about him, they did not believe me. They were now arguing about whether to go on asking about Ariel or to try finding out how I had come aboard the *Stormdancer*. They were convinced that I had been in alliance with the mutants aboard the sunken *Orizon*, but they could not see why a group of mutants would come to Herder Isle at all, when there were thousands of Hedra to oppose them even if they managed the impossible and breached the wall and the black gates.

I felt a renewed ache of sorrow for the coercers who had drowned when the *Orizon* was sunk. My thoughts shifted to Ariel, and I wondered what plans he could have had that would involve allowing us to find Rushton.

I stifled the urge to cough, knowing it would draw the deadly attention of the Threes. *If only I could faint,* I thought. They would not be able to do anything to me until I woke. But for all Mendi's sneering, Grisyl was a skilled torturer. Darkness had fluttered at the edge of my vision many times since we had entered the cell, yet Grisyl had never once allowed me to lose consciousness. And he had known when I had tried to pretend. Time and time again, I swallowed the foul water into which I was dipped, but the moment I could hold my breath no more and sucked it into my lungs, I would be hauled out, thrown on the floor, and the water pushed out of me by Bedig.

And all this was a prelude to what Ariel would do when he returned. Fear slipped through me like a cold blade, but I thought of the scribed words of a Beforetimer that Pavo had once quoted to me: *A brave person dies but once; a coward many times.* I thought of Lark and wondered wearily whether he and his father and the crew of the *Stormdancer* were even now in the compound being interrogated, too. *Save them,* I prayed to the three goddesses worshipped by the Norselanders.

"Try again," Mendi said, dragging my head up by the hair. "Make her tell you how she got aboard the ship."

"Why don't you try?" snarled Grisyl.

"Defeated already?" Mendi asked scornfully. "You have no stamina. I will show you how to have her begging to speak the truth. Bedig, remove her clothes."

Before the Hedra captain could obey, boots approached the cell door. Mendi dropped me to the floor as the door swung open with a rusty whine. I forced my eyes open, wanting to see who entered, but the barrel into which I had been repeatedly dipped blocked my view.

"Zuria," Mendi said warily.

"You are to come at once, both of you. The One summons us," announced a cold, haughty voice.

"We have spoken to our master already, Zuria. You will have to make your report yourself," Mendi said slyly.

Zuria replied sharply, "It was the One who sent for all of us to attend him. Shall I go and tell him you two are otherwise occupied?"

"We will come, naturally," Grisyl said.

"Of course we will, but I do not understand this

summons when we were with the One not two hours past," Mendi grumbled. "Are we to bring the mutant with us?"

"Mutant?" Zuria asked.

"The mutant found hiding aboard the *Stormdancer*. The one Ariel's null foresaw," Mendi said irritably, pointing down at me.

Footsteps came toward me. Someone knelt beside me, and I clenched my teeth to steel myself against the pain of being lifted by my hair. But instead I was turned gently onto my back and the sodden curtain of my hair lifted away from my face.

If I had possessed any breath for it, I would have cried out in astonishment, because staring down at me, clad in a split Herder robe, his head shaven, was the Misfit coercer Harwood.

✦ 18 ✦

"Guildmistress!" Harwood cried, shock draining his face of color.

"Har, what are you . . . ?" The face that appeared above his shoulder was that of another coercer, Veril. He, too, wore a Hedra robe and was shaved bald. Seeing me, concern became incredulity. "Guildmistress!" he gasped. "But how . . . ?"

"Quiet," Harwood told him urgently, keeping his voice low. His eyes sought mine. "Guildmistress, can you speak? Are you badly injured?"

I managed to shake my head and relief flashed in his eyes, but it was nothing to what I felt—astonishment so great that it was as if a hot river surged through me, warming my overwrought flesh and numb spirit. Harwood bent closer to examine the demon band and then shook his head. "It needs a key." He turned his head and looked at someone out of my sight. After a moment, he sighed in frustration. "None of these bastard Threes or the Hedra have one! Help me get her up, Veril."

They lifted me to my feet, but I was so dizzy and nauseated that it took me some seconds to notice that Zuria, Mendi, Grisyl, and Bedig were standing docilely in a row against the wall, staring at the floor. My knees buckled and I retched, but I had already voided the contents of my stomach. Harwood helped me to a stool against the wall, looking worried.

"How . . . how did you both get here?" I rasped.

"Aboard the *Stormdancer.* Eleven of us came as part of the so-called retreating Hedra force. But you?"

"I was aboard the *Stormdancer,* too. . . . I didn't sense any of you."

"We wore demon bands. We had to or we would have been recognized as impostors, and there was no time to have false ones made. But how did *you* get aboard the *Stormdancer*?"

"Later," I said. "What happened in the Land?"

Harwood shrugged. "I don't know a lot of it. After you left for the cloister, Linnet sent the eleven of us down to the sea caves with supplies and instructions to wait for the invading ships. She told us to board if we had the chance. We shaved our heads and planned to steal robes from Malik's men and coerce them to ease us on board. We had plenty of demon bands that we had taken from Vos's armsmen. But Linnet and Reuvan came to tell us that the Land was swarming with Hedra who had been hiding within the old cloister.

"Reuvan said that Aben died trying to probe Malik when they reached Sutrium. Dardelan had immediately begun assembling a force to ride back to Saithwold. Reuvan had been sent to warn us and rode into the middle of the fighting." The coercer took a steadying breath and said, "Linnet said the knights, Vos's armsmen, and all the fighters Noviny had been able to muster were concentrating on keeping the invaders away from the beach, because they had learned from a captured Hedra that three ships were to drop hundreds of Hedra on the beach where we were hiding. Reuvan said that Dardelan had specifically charged him with making sure that the ships didn't leave."

"Why were they keeping the invaders away from the beach?" I interrupted.

"Because Linnet had coerced a Hedra captain and his men into believing they had been defeated. The plan was to send them rushing to meet the arriving Hedra with such dreadful tales of massacre and mayhem as would turn them back, convinced that the force from the sea cavern were all dead except these few. The whole idea was for the retreat to give us cover to board the ships. As soon as they had retreated, one of the coerced men was supposed to break down and admit that he had been forced to say what he had said, and then he would tell them that the battle was still raging. The Nine would immediately command the Hedra ashore again, and that would leave the way clear for us to take control of the ships. And hopefully by the time the Hedra did get ashore again, Dardelan and his people would have arrived to reinforce Linnet's band of fighters."

"So what happened?" I asked.

He shrugged. "Everything went according to plan to begin with. The Hedra went ashore, and after a time, they began to retreat. Then things started going wrong. We had intended to get aboard the *Orizon*. We talked it over and decided to focus on one ship rather than spread ourselves over three, and the *Orizon* was anchored closest to the caves. But when the retreat started, the *Orizon* got under way much faster than we expected, so by the time we had caught our eleven men, stripped them, and donned their clothes, we had no choice but to board the *Stormdancer*."

"You know that the *Orizon* . . ."

He nodded soberly. "We saw it from the deck of the *Stormdancer*. I guess Ariel's null envisioned us talking about the *Orizon* in the caves and missed the last-minute change of plan."

"Maybe," I said. "So what happened when you got aboard?"

Harwood sighed. "None of us had reckoned on the ship's actually leaving, because the coerced captain was supposed to break down and admit he had been made to lie, whereupon everyone would rush ashore again. Unfortunately, Kaga was so furious about the retreat that he killed the captain who had ordered it, so no one could reveal that the Hedra were not truly defeated. We dared not call attention to ourselves by suggesting the dead captain might have been coerced, so before we knew it, we were on our way to Herder Isle. We were not too worried, because Linnet had told us the bands were always taken off once the ships lifted anchor. We figured that once that happened, we would take control and coerce the shipmaster of the *Stormdancer* to put in at Sutrium. But the Nine was so frantic about the Hedra captain's description of our force that he commanded everyone to keep their bands on. We might still have managed to get control, but then the *Black Ship* turned back and sank the *Orizon*, and we knew that if the *Stormdancer* did turn toward Sutrium, Salamander would destroy it. So we had no choice but to let the ship come here. Before we knew it, we were marching with the rest of the Hedra through the black gates. I have to tell you that when they closed behind us, I thought we were all doomed." He shook his head. "Then up comes a boy in black with a basket, and we all take off our demon bands! By the time

Kaga had marched us to our barracks, we had control of him and a good many of the other Hedra.

"Our initial plan was to escape from the compound, but when Zuria marched in demanding to know what had been happening, I realized that we could take him with us to ease our way, for who would dare to oppose a Three? Taking him with us would also give us a unique chance to learn more about the Herder Faction and its long-term plans. I was just beginning to coerce him when a message came from the One summoning all the Threes. Veril suggested we take all of them with us as prisoners. In one stroke, we would deprive the Faction of its head and have the means to learn everything about its inner workings! It was a brilliant idea, so I coerced Zuria to take Veril and me with him to find the other Threes. That is when we found you!"

I looked at the Threes, still standing in a row, their faces bland. "You have coerced them all now?"

"And the Hedra captain, Bedig, but Zuria is the only one deeply enough coerced that I can send him out to act alone. How do you feel now? Could you walk?"

I nodded absently. "Harwood, you said you thought it would be a good idea to take all three of the Threes with you. But take them where?"

"Why, to the *Stormdancer*, of course," Veril said eagerly. "Once we get out of here, we will have Zuria dismiss the men guarding it, hoist the anchor, and be gone before anyone realizes. The beauty of it is that no one can follow us, because all other ships are anchored in Main Cove in Norseland."

"You can't sail the *Stormdancer* back across the strait," I said. "The hull is damaged. Surely you heard the shipfolk speak of it when you were on board? That

326

is why the *Stormdancer* was lagging behind the *Orizon*. The shipmaster has grounded her so she can be repaired, but I do not know when that will happen, because Mendi ordered the entire crew to be brought in for interrogation."

Harwood and Veril exchanged a look of consternation. "I'd better let the others know," Harwood muttered. "We will have to hide on the other part of the island. I heard one of the Hedra speak of it as a wilderness."

"Wait," I said, realizing that he was about to send out a probe. I told him what I had learned from Lark and his father about Fallo. "From what I could see in Lark's mind, the swamp is full of quicksand and sinkholes, as well as poisonous plants and swift, deadly vipers. No one lives there for good reason, and we would not survive it without a Norselander to aid us. But how can we ask for their help when I am already responsible for bringing disaster to the shipfolk from the *Stormdancer*? Even if they were willing to fight, they have no arms and would be outnumbered by Hedra. There is only one thing we can do. We have to take over the compound."

Both men stared at me as if I had lost my wits. "You can't be serious, Guildmistress," Harwood said. "This place is the size of a city, and there must be thousands of Herders living here. We can't coerce or kill them all."

"We don't have to control all of them, just the ones who control the rest," I said. "The way the Faction is set up, those with real power are few. We have three of them right here in this room—and an invitation to see their master. We can use them, and the One, and their power and knowledge to get the ship repaired and to keep anyone from realizing we are here. When we are

327

ready to leave, we will take the Threes with us as you suggested, plus all the Hedra captains that can be fitted in the brig cells in the hold, as well as the crew, the shipmaster, and their families, so that they will suffer no retribution."

Harwood had begun to nod. "We will need a safe location to operate from within the compound."

"And we need to find out if the shipfolk are here yet. Where are the others coercers?" I asked.

"In the barracks with Kaga," Harwood said. "We could go there. . . ."

I shook my head. "We need a place where fewer people will come but where the Threes can logically be seen coming and going." Inspiration struck and I smiled. I was amused to see that this caused Veril to adopt the same apprehensive look Ceirwan sometimes had when I proposed a difficult rescue plan.

"Guildmistress—" the coercer began, but I cut him off.

"The One's chambers lie within the wall surrounding this compound. You can only reach them through a very long passage that runs inside the walls. The One is very old and obese and uses his assistant, Falc, to summon anyone he wants to talk with. If we go there now and coerce the One and Falc, and we have the Threes, we will virtually control the entire compound, so long as no one guesses they are not acting under their own volition. We can send Falc straightaway to demand that the shipfolk be brought to the One."

"You did not tell us how you got aboard. Or how the Herders discovered you," Veril said.

"For now I will tell you only that my getting aboard was an accident. I was discovered because Ariel foresaw it and told the One before he left for Norseland with Salamander. He forbade anyone to interrogate me until he came back to do it himself. He has some machine he would use upon me, which he keeps in his residence on Norseland."

Harwood interrupted. "We will have to leave Herder Isle before Ariel returns from Norseland on the *Black Ship*, else the *Stormdancer* will suffer the same fate as the unlucky *Orizon*."

"We have a little time," I said. "The *Black Ship* has only just left, and Ariel has an errand to perform on the west coast before returning to Herder Isle to deal with me."

"What errand?" Harwood asked.

I shrugged. "The Threes don't know, but we can find out from the One, for it was he who sent Ariel. All I know is that it has something to do with a couple of special nulls. Have you heard aught of nulls?"

Both men nodded, grim-faced. Veril said, "We guess that they are weak futuretellers whose minds Ariel has damaged to make them passive and biddable."

Harwood frowned. "Have you considered that one of these nulls may discern our activities here and that Salamander might return immediately, cut us off in the strait, and sink us as he did the *Orizon*? Or that he will come here with a ship full of demon-banded Hedra? Even if we stay here and coerce the gate guards to lock them out, Salamander could simply bring the *Black Ship* close to shore and use the same weapon he used on the *Orizon* to break open the wall."

I nodded soberly, remembering what Lark had said about the destruction of cities using Beforetime weapons. But I only said, "You may be right, but I don't see

329

what we can do other than trying to get the ship repaired as soon as possible." I explained how to reach the wall passage that led to the One's chamber and bade Harwood ask the other coercers to meet us there. It was unwieldy having to explain in words instead of being able to farsend directions, but I had no alternative until I could remove the demon band. Harwood suggested that one of the knights remain in the barracks with Kaga and the other coerced Hedra so we could summon an obedient force if something went wrong. While he contacted the others, I bade Veril find out if the shipfolk from the *Stormdancer* were in any of the cells. He hurried off, taking Bedig with him to use as a source of knowledge.

Harwood asked, "Are there any guards with the One?"

I nodded. "A couple of Hedra guard the door and, as I told you, the younger priest who serves the One, Falc, but he is no fighter. In any case, all are unbanded, so you can easily coerce them. Oh, there are also several boys dressed in hooded black robes. I don't know how they fit in, but they will have to be coerced, too."

"Maybe not," Harwood said unexpectedly. "From what I can make out, they are mute slaves. The priests call them *shadows,* and they seem to have no more will than a shadow. I don't think we will have any trouble with them. It is the Herder warriors—the Hedra—that we need to be careful about. So far as I can see, they are vigilant and stern watchdogs who don't hesitate to speak against a Herder priest of any level if they believe he is infringing Herder lore."

"Maybe you can gradually put their captains under sleepseals in their rooms," I suggested.

"There are too many to put sleepseals on, because they would all need to be watered, fed, and kept clean," Harwood said. "I would rather deeply coerce them and use them. But that will take time, too."

"We can't do anything until we knew more about how this place works," I said. "We must coerce the One, and then Mendi and Grisyl must be deeply coerced so we don't have to keep a constant watch on them, and during that process, we will gain the knowledge we need. Then we will begin to coerce the inner-cadre Nines and the highest ranked Hedra."

Veril returned with Bedig to report that the Norselanders were not in any of the interrogation cells, but he added that there were several other places within the compound where they might have been taken.

"You'd best investigate," Harwood said. "Take one of the Threes to smooth the way. Take Zuria, since he is deeply coerced. The guildmistress and I go to meet the others in the passage to the One's chamber. Follow us if you do not find the shipfolk, and send a probe if you do. If you cannot reach us, send Bedig." He paused, obviously offering Veril the directions I had given him. Veril nodded.

"See if you can find keys to unlock this demon band as well," I said.

"And some shoes," Harwood said, pointing to my bare feet.

Veril looked at Zuria, who suddenly barked an order for the young man to follow him. The Three stalked out followed by Veril, who winked at us over his shoulder.

Ironically, while we had been in the cell, I had felt safe. Saved. But as Harwood took my arm and we followed Mendi through the labyrinthine interrogation buildings, I thought of the hundreds and hundreds of fanatical Herders within the compound, and my hasty plans began to feel childishly, dangerously foolish. Yet what else could we do? We were on an island controlled utterly by the Faction, with no immediate means of escape and the possibility that Ariel and Salamander would eventually arrive with a shipload of Hedra.

We came through a door into bright daylight, and I stopped in astonishment, hardly able to believe that the whole stormy night had passed while I was in the cell. Unlike the night before, when the rain-swept streets had been all but deserted, now many acolytes, novices, and ranking priests passed back and forth, most accompanied by several of the black-clad shadows.

We set off toward the front of the compound, and I found myself leaning heavily on Harwood, for the hours of watery torment had taken their toll. I was almost trembling with relief when at last we reached the entrance hall where Falc had appeared to command Mendi to bring me to the One. As before, two of the shadows appeared with lanterns. I would have liked to dismiss them, but I knew the long passage was dark enough that we would need light, and it would look odd if we took the lanterns ourselves.

Soon we were following a lantern-bearing shadow along the passage inside the wall, the second shadow following close behind. After some moments, Harwood murmured very softly, "Am I imagining it or does the floor of this passage slant up?"

I was uneasy about speaking aloud, but I was still demon-banded. So I said softly, "The One's chamber is probably halfway up the wall. He has no need to be easily accessible. Indeed, he has probably found it effective to be mysterious and elusive. And he can use the Threes to do anything beyond his rooms."

"It is a wonder the Threes don't overthrow him," Harwood replied. I saw the hooded head of one of the shadows tilt slightly and guessed he had heard the coercer's voice. I nodded pointedly at him, but Harwood shrugged and said softly, "Don't worry about the boy. If he looks like giving us any trouble, I will coerce him, but until then I might as well conserve my energy. When we stop to wait for the others, I want to coerce Mendi and Zuria more deeply so that I need not probe them continually."

Despite my anxiety about the shadows overhearing us, I answered his earlier comment. "The One is not just the head of their order. The priests believe he is the Chosen of Lud and beloved for that reason."

"Feared more than loved, I would say," Harwood said. "But tell me how you got aboard the *Stormdancer*."

Keeping my voice low, I told him what had happened.

"A ship fish," the coercer marveled at the end of my tale. "I had no idea they could be beastspoken."

"How should we know it?" I asked. "We Misfits have never had that much access to the ocean, and we avoid water because it inhibits our Talents."

"I have always thought it odd that water produces such a strong barrier," Harwood mused. "It has less substance than the earth, after all." He frowned. "There is light ahead." Again I saw the shadow's head lift slightly. He might be mute, but he was certainly not deaf.

"It is coming from the One's audience room," I said softly. "We had better stop here and dim the lanterns or the sentries outside it will see their light."

Harwood made Mendi bid the shadows halt and lower the wick of their lanterns. As they obeyed, I caught a fleeting glimpse of a shadow's face, and though it was unknown, it struck me that there was something odd about it. Before I could discern what it was, Mendi commanded both shadows to sit. I sat down, too, and massaged my cold feet, noting that the shadows sat with their heads lowered. Harwood was now staring fixedly into Mendi's face.

After a time I glanced in the other direction and noticed a light approaching. I stood hastily and touched Harwood's shoulder to get his attention.

"It's all right," he said after a moment of concentration. "It is Sover and the others. Give me another ten minutes, and I will have finished here." He turned back to Mendi.

It was not Sover but Yarrow whom I saw first. He grinned in delight, mugging his incredulity, and then I was surrounded by Hilder, Colwyn, Sover, Geratty, and Ode, all of whom had come to my guild at one time or another to learn to hone and control their coercive probes so they could use them to farseek. Each greeted me with a dozen questions, and then I saw Reuvan, who had hung back slightly.

"It is good to see you," I said. The seaman laughed and embraced me with some of Brydda's painful force.

"It is astonishing to see you here," he countered, releasing me.

I remembered the shadows then and turned to look at them to see how they regarded our greetings. Two had accompanied the coercers, and now there were four, all standing, for the other two had risen. Rather than gazing steadfastly at the ground, they looked at me. All had thin, pale, delicate faces and unfathomable expressions.

"I forgot," Yarrow said suddenly, drawing my attention back to him. "Veril said you might find a use for one of these." He withdrew a small gray key from his pocket with a triumphant flourish, and in a moment, the demon band lay on the passage floor. I prayed I would never feel one of the foul things about my throat again.

"I have done as much as I can do now," Harwood announced, looking weary as he turned away from Mendi. He cast his eye over us and asked, "Where are the others?"

"I left Asra with Kaga in the barracks, and I sent Tomrick to the watch-hut atop the walls to keep an eye on Hevon Bay and report on any approaching ships," Yarrow said. "Veril said to tell you he cannot farseek you, but he has gone to the black gates to find out if the *Stormdancer*'s shipfolk were brought into the compound."

"The stone in this wall must be too thick or tainted," Harwood muttered.

When we reached the Hedra standing before the door to the One's audience chamber, Mendi barked at them to stand aside. Instead of obeying, one of them said sternly that no one was permitted to enter the One's apartment unless summoned, and no one had been summoned. Then the eyes of both Hedra glazed, and they turned and went into the firelit audience room. We followed, and I had a brief glimpse of a startled Falc leaping up from the One's carved chair before the expression was wiped from his face and he moved to join Mendi, Zuria, the two Hedra guards, and the shadows, all of whom had gone to stand against the wall.

"According to this Falc, the One is asleep through there," Harwood said after a moment, nodding toward the door through which Falc had gone the previous day. "There are also six shadows in there."

We looked at the four who had accompanied us, and they looked back, but their faces revealed nothing. Harwood gently bade them sit down, and they obeyed at once. Then he turned back to me and said in a low voice, "I think the ones inside are like to be as docile as these four, but you'd best be careful just the same."

I nodded and bade Ode, Sover, and Colwyn to come with me. We entered a large dressing chamber hung with gray robes, their gold edging glittering in the light of the lantern held up by a slender shadow who had risen at our entrance. Immediately, he dropped his gaze to the floor.

I wasted no time on him and passed into the next chamber. This was a small but lavishly appointed bathing room, complete with a gold-tiled bath sunk into the floor. There were two shadows here, and both rose to their feet, one holding a lantern, but these also kept their heads meekly bowed and made no attempt to hinder us.

At last we came to the One's bedchamber. The One lay snoring softly on an enormous carved bed piled with white quilts and silken pillows. Three more black-robed shadows sat on the floor in front of a curtained wall, but I ignored them. The overlapping fleeces on the floor swallowed the sound of my footsteps as I approached the bed, but as if he felt my movement in the air, the One opened his eyes and stared up at me in dim confusion.

"You are not Falc. Where is Falc?" he said in a high,

quavering voice. Then he came properly awake, and his expression was one of affronted disgust and malice. "You are a woman! How dare you! Who allowed this? Falc!"

"He cannot come at this moment," I said softly, and reached out to probe his mind. The old man gave a thin scream, clutched at his head, and cringed back against the pillows. I withdrew in astonishment and said to the others, "A block has been constructed to cause him excruciating pain if there is any intrusion. If I press deeper, his mind will collapse. Indeed, it seems the block is intrusive enough that it has already eroded his sanity."

"But who could have done this to him?" Sover asked in a low voice. "Such a block would require great coercive skill."

"Ariel," I said bitterly. "This certainly explains how he got the Herders to take him in and why the One favors him so strongly. Go and get Falc." Sover went out and returned with the priest and Harwood. I directed Falc to approach his master, who lay whimpering and clutching his head.

"What is it, Master?" Falc asked in a crooning voice. "Did you have another nightmare?"

"Night . . . nightmare?" the One echoed, peering up at the Nine as if through a mist. "Yes. It was a terrible nightmare! I saw that female mutant that Mendi brought in. The one Ariel wants to question. She was leaning over my bed seeking to possess my mind. I want her killed. Bring her here and do it before me."

"It was only a nightmare, Master," Falc assured him. "The mutant is even now in a cell, awaiting the return of our good Ariel from Norseland."

"Norseland?" The One sounded confused and

337

distressed. "But he will not come from Norseland. He must go to the west coast first." He gave a groan. "Why must he go there? I told him that I need him here. But he said it was Lud's will. . . . My head aches so."

"Master, *you* sent him to the west coast, because he has a vital mission to perform," I made Falc say in his smooth, oily voice. "Don't you remember?"

"Of course I remember, fool," snapped the One. "I ordered him to take the null and unleash the wrath of Lud on the Ludless." He groaned. "My head aches. Where is Ariel? He is the only one who can take away the pain. Lud bestowed upon him the power to heal me."

"I am sure that he will return quickly," Falc soothed.

"Of course he will return swiftly, dolt, else he would be doomed," snarled the One.

"What does he mean?" Harwood farsent urgently.

I shrugged and prompted Falc to speak again. "Master, Ariel will not die. No one would dare to harm him. Lud would protect him from—"

"Shut up!" screamed the One. "No one will harm Ariel. He knows well enough not to linger after he sets the null ashore, lest he perish with all the rest on the west coast." The priest ground his teeth together and rocked in agony, clutching his head.

"The null must have some sort of weapon, and we need to find out what it is," Harwood said softly. "Can't you ease him?"

I shook my head. "Aside from the block, Ariel has constructed a pain mechanism that will worsen each day until he releases it," I said softly. "I can't get into his mind to stop it without breaking open the block. If Ariel does not return within a day or two, the old man's mind will crumble under the pain."

"But Ariel will only just have reached Norseland," Colwyn said. "And a journey from there to here via the west coast will take at least a fiveday."

" 'Perish with all on the west coast.' " Ode echoed the One's earlier words bleakly, and I remembered that Ode's sister was among those assigned to the west coast during the rebellion and trapped there still.

"Nothing but a Beforetime weapon could kill everyone on the west coast," Sover said.

"The Herders used Beforetime weapons to gain control of the Norselands," I said. "Whatever they used was capable of destroying cities. Maybe the null is supposed to go from city to city destroying each."

"That was my thinking, too," Harwood admitted. "I will see if I can dig up any scraps of information from the two Threes about a store of Beforetime weapons. Meanwhile, Sover, perhaps you can ease the One somewhat."

As he departed with Zuria in tow, I looked at Sover, who said, "I have a secondary empathic ability. I can empathise acceptance and serenity in the One so you can question him further." He bent over the Herder, who squinted up at him through streaming eyes. "Who are you! How dare you come in here? I don't want you. I need Ariel!"

"Ariel is serving Lud on the west coast," Sover said soothingly from the other side of the bed. "But he knew you would suffer in his absence, Master. He sent me."

"You are a healer?" the One quavered, his eyes flickering fearfully to Sover.

"I am not gifted, as Ariel is, but I can help you, Master," the coercer said gently. "If you will permit me to touch your head?"

"No! No!" The One cringed back; then he screamed, a horrible thin sound that made the hair on my neck rise. "Yes . . . ," he gasped. "Help me."

Sover placed a gentle hand on the old man's brow, and as the One sank back with an exhausted exhalation, the coercer's face contorted with empathised pain. His expression gradually became one of intense concentration.

"It is working," Colwyn murmured. I forced myself to relax as we waited. Then Sover turned to nod.

"Master," Falc said. I had made him sound too eager and modified his tone before continuing. "Master, I fear that our good Ariel places himself in danger. Surely Lud cannot have intended that."

The One stirred and mumbled, "No man can presume to know Lud's intention."

I decided to risk a direct question. "Can the gain of this dangerous mission be worth the risk?"

The One stirred irritably under his quilts. "I have told you, fool. There is no danger as long as Ariel does not linger after leaving the null ashore. The sickness will not become infectious for some days."

Sover gave me a horrified look, and the One groaned. Immediately, the coercer returned his attention to the older man.

"A plague," Ode hissed into my ear. "It can be nowt else. It were always rumored that the Herders were responsible for the first plague."

I nodded. "But one in three were affected, and only a third of those became seriously ill. Fewer still died."

"Then it is a different plague," Colwyn said. "One that kills three in three if all are to die."

"Why?" Ode asked. "What possible use can it be to

th' Faction to kill everyone on the west coast?" His voice had risen in his agitation, and the One heard him but appeared not to realize that someone other than Falc had spoken.

"Lud's will is not to be questioned," he answered dreamily in his strange girlish voice. "He used pestilence in the Beforetime to signal his divine wrath, and he showed Ariel where the plague seeds were hid upon Norseland. All who look upon the desolation that will result from this plague shall know the power of Lud's wrath. And the west coast will be purified so it can be populated with the pure of heart who worship Lud and obey his servants."

"This doesn't make sense," Colwyn hissed. "Why invade one part of the Land if you intend to unleash the ultimate lesson on the rest?"

I could not think past the horror of a sickness deadly enough to kill everyone on the west coast. *Everyone.* "He must be stopped!" I said. "Ask him where the null is to be taken on the west coast."

Sover obeyed, but the One spoke only of a city where sickness would spread like wildfire.

"He means one of the cities," Ode said.

"Even if we could sail the *Stormdancer* within the hour, it would take days to visit and search every city on the west coast," Colwyn said. "And we have no idea what this null even looks like!"

"We need not search every city. We need only put into every port and ask if the *Black Ship* has been there. And Ariel can only just have got to Norseland. He has yet to travel to the west coast before he can think of coming back here. That will give us a couple days' grace. Send someone to find out if Veril has news of the shipfolk yet." I stopped, horrified to realize that I was on the verge of tears, for aside from the thousands of innocent people who would die if Ariel succeeded, among them would be Merret, Jak, Dell, and Ode's sister Desda, all of whom I had sent to the west coast. Mastering my emotions, I turned to Sover. "Keep trying to find out where the null will be taken."

Sover nodded, his expression blank with dismay.

I left the bedchamber and found Harwood focused on Mendi, but Yarrow, Geratty, and the others turned to look at me as I entered the firelit audience chamber, followed by Colwyn.

"What is happening?" Yarrow asked.

I gathered my wits and told them, seeing their faces reflect the shattered dismay I felt. Harwood had ceased probing Mendi, and he asked in disbelief, "Did you say *everyone* will die?"

"Everyone," I said, and I seemed to hear the high mocking sound of Ariel's laughter.

PART III

✦

THE SONG
OF THE WEST

◆ 19 ◆

"Someone must go to Fallo to speak with the shipfolk," I said when Veril arrived to say that the shipfolk had not been brought into the compound, even though a number of Hedra had been sent to summon them. None of us could imagine why they had not yet returned, unless the Norselanders had fled rather than be brought in. The more I thought about it, the more likely this seemed, for what had the Norselanders to lose by fighting?

"I will go," Yarrow volunteered.

"It will take an hour to reach the gate from here." I fumed. "We need somewhere more central as a base."

Harwood touched my arm, and I turned to see that one of the shadows had risen. The boy beckoned and went on silent feet to the dressing room. I followed, intrigued. He went through into the bathing chamber and crossed to the wall behind the bath. Then, to my amazement, he slid open a panel to reveal a dark stairwell. As I went to the opening, he stepped onto the first step and pointed down. Seeing the thin wrists, delicate hands, and slender neck, I realized suddenly what I ought to have seen sooner: the shadow was a *girl*. She began to descend the steps, indicating that I should follow.

"Be careful," Colwyn called down after me uneasily. Stopping, I glanced back and saw that he and the other coercers had followed us into the bathing room, along with the other shadows, and now I saw clearly that all were starveling girls. I turned to the shadow who had led me to the stairs. "You know that I am a Misfit, don't you?" I asked her aloud. "That which the Herders call a cursed mutant."

She nodded, and I was surprised to see no fear in her eyes. Perhaps she had not understood me clearly. I said, "I am called mutant by the Herders, because I have the power to speak inside another person's thoughts and to hear their thoughts as well. I know that you cannot speak, but if you will permit me, I can enter your mind and speak with your thoughts."

The girl seemed to consider this carefully and nodded, coming back up the steps.

"My name is Elspeth Gordie," I sent, and some impulse made me coerce an image of us both in her mind. She gasped in astonishment as my image smiled reassuringly at her image.

"What is your name?" I asked.

"I . . . I can't . . . oh, I am *speaking*!" Her image lifted its hands to its mouth, and she wept.

"Your name?" I prompted gently when she had recovered herself. Shyly, enunciating very carefully, she told me.

"Cinda," I repeated aloud.

An incredulous smile broke over her pale little face, and she pressed her hands to her cheeks and nodded. From the corner of my eye, I saw the other shadows clutch at one another in evident excitement. Concentrating, I forespoke her image for some time, then she led me down the stairs, where, as she had explained to me, a discreet door opened into an obscure corner of a vast laundry built up against the wall surrounding the compound. Through a door and windows on the opposite side of the laundry chamber, I could see into a walled yard with washing lines strung from one side of the wall to the other. Cinda explained that a gate in this lesser wall led directly to the main body of the compound. From here, it was only a short walk to the black gates.

When we returned to the others, I explained what she had told me, adding that if it were true, we could remain in the One's quarters. Then I charged Yarrow and Veril to go to Fallo, find the Norseland crew of the *Stormdancer*, and bring back Lark's father at all speed. They took Grisyl and were to collect Asra and the coerced Hedra from the barracks on the way, in case they needed a fighting force. After they had gone, using the bathing-room steps, I sent Hilder to the watch-hut atop the wall that overlooked the channel, bidding him let me know the moment he saw a ship boat coming back across. I also told him to let Tomrick in the other watch-hut know what had been happening.

Harwood then ordered Geratty, Colwyn, Reuvan, and Ode to sleep, for we had all been up for many hours and must begin sleeping in shifts if we were to have our wits about us. Sover he bade sleep in the One's chamber in case the One woke and might be questioned further.

"I daresay it is tasteless of me, but I am too hungry to sleep," grumbled Geratty.

"We all need to eat," Harwood agreed, and he asked Cinda, who hovered close by, how the One got his meals. She looked at me, and I entered her mind to learn there was a kitchen that served all in this sector of the compound. Ode went with Cinda and four other shadows to coerce a proper meal out of the kitchen workers. They soon returned with pease pudding, bread, and some queer sour vegetables, and we ate hungrily. We had just finished when Hilder brought news from Veril. Two of those sent out by Mendi to fetch the Norselanders had returned to the compound.

"Veril coerced them," Hilder said. "We were right about the Norselanders guessing what the Hedra intended. The village where they lived was deserted when they arrived. The villagers have taken refuge in the swamp, and the Hedra have been searching for them, to no avail."

"Have Veril and the others left?" I asked.

"They have, but I can reach them from the watch-hut before they cross the channel," Hilder said.

"Do it," I said at once. "Tell them that they probably cannot reach the Norselanders because according to the shipmaster's boy, the swamp is full of tainted patches. Tell Veril to go to one of the other villages. Have them ask for the Per and tell him everything. He may even know how to find Helvar."

Hilder nodded and departed at once. As I turned to speak to Harwood, Cinda came to me shyly with a battered pair of shoes such as shadows wore. I accepted them gratefully, and as I sat to pull them on, I noticed the other shadows watching with sorrowful expressions. I set aside my apprehensions for a moment to enter Cinda's mind and ask why they were so sad; they need not fear they would be left behind when we sailed away to the Land.

"They do not fear being left," Cinda's image explained. "Many of us were taken from the west coast, and although none of us had any hope of returning to our families, we grieve at the thought of their being harmed."

Full of pity for them as I was, it suddenly occurred to me that the ubiquitous shadows might have heard something said that would help us find the null more swiftly. With this in mind, I bade them come and sit with me by the fire. As they obeyed, Sover entered to say that the One had awakened briefly, but in his opinion, the old man did not know where the null was to be left ashore.

"I think the whole idea of a plagued null was Ariel's notion," he added. "The One said that he found plague seeds in some Beforetime storage place, and from what I can make out, he presented to the One the idea of sending a null infected with plague as if it had come to him from Lud. The fact that it would involve a lot of death seems to have made it especially pleasing to the One."

"With Ariel, there might be no intention, save the desire to use what he has created," I said grimly.

Sover ran his fingers through his thick, red-brown hair. "I have soothed the One to sleep again. He needs to rest if we are to get anything more from him." He looked curiously at the cluster of shadows seated by the fire.

"We were just about to talk," I said, and Harwood bade Sover return to the One's chamber and rest while he had the chance. I turned to Cinda and asked her to tell me her companions' names. I was aware of Harwood entering my mind discreetly to listen, but I ignored him and repeated aloud the name of each woman once Cinda's image had conveyed it. As she heard her name spoken aloud, each shadow reacted strongly.

"Most of us do not ever hear our names spoken aloud," Cinda explained.

I asked aloud if any of them knew what Ariel was doing on the west coast. At the mention of his name, several of the girls started in alarm, and one looked sick.

"It was Ariel who chose us and supervised the . . . the cutting. . . ." Cinda gestured to her mouth. "Also, he . . . he uses us as he wishes, and he is very . . . cruel." Then she told me that they knew nothing of Ariel's conversation with the One, for he always made them leave.

Another shadow made several slight gestures with her hand, and Cinda raised her own hand and made several evocative gestures in return. I realized that the women had invented their own language of signals, just as Brydda had done to enable unTalents to communicate with beasts.

Harwood asked aloud how Cinda had come to Herder Isle, for she was not a Norselander. Cinda and the other shadows gave him a wary look. To her eyes, I realized, he was another Hedra with his split robe and shaven head. I explained to her and the others aloud that Harwood and all of us, save for Reuvan, were mutants in Hedra guise. Harwood added that his Talent was coercion: the use of deep-probe abilities to control the minds of others. Cinda glanced in sudden comprehension at the blank-faced Threes, the Herder Falc, and the two Hedra guards seated in a row against the wall, blank faced and docile, and Harwood admitted that he had manipulated their minds. He added that the shadows need not fear he would use his abilities on them, for Misfits did not tamper with the minds of allies. He smiled as he said this, and although he had a kind face, none of the shadows responded to his smile.

Cinda returned her serious gaze to my face and tapped her head. I took this as a request to raise an image in her mind and obliged, but I told her that the image was not really necessary. As long as I was within her mind, she need only imagine speaking, and I would hear her words. Her image nodded, and she began to tell her story.

She had been taken from the west coast by the Herders, along with her brother, who had been destined to become a novice. He had killed himself before he could be made an acolyte, and she had only learned of it some time after because Ariel had selected her to serve the One, and she had been in the healing hall while her severed tongue healed.

Harwood interrupted to ask if all shadows had their tongues severed, and she shook her head. It had been Ariel's idea that girls be used as body servants for the One, she explained, for although the old man hated clumsiness and roughness, he hated women even more. Ariel had suggested that his body servants ought to be slender girls whose hair was shorn and whose tongues were cut so he need not consider them females. They would serve until they began to develop breasts and were starved to put puberty off as long as possible, for the One disliked change, too. Once the chosen shadows became too old or shapely, they were put to work as invisible drudges in the compound's kitchens and washhouses with the other women, many of whom could speak but did not for fear of having their *own* tongues cut out.

"Are all shadows women?" Colwyn asked, for he, too, had been monitoring the tale.

"There are male shadows, but they work in the

351

mine or at the demon-band works. Their tongues are not cut," her image explained. There was pity in her face, which astonished me, because how could one whose existence sounded so awful find it in herself to feel pity for another?

One of the other shadows, whose name had been given as Lure, made some gestures, and Cinda told me she had said that the Lud of the Herders must have died, else how could we have come to destroy the Faction?

Pity rose in me again, and I said aloud, "We did not come here to do battle. There are too few of us to fight. We must leave as soon as the ship we came on can be repaired. We must stop Ariel from bringing plague to the west coast. But know that in the Land, we have been preparing ourselves for a battle against the Faction, and the day is near when we will come here to fight them."

The shadows exchanged looks, and then Lure made some emphatic gestures to Cinda, who nodded and said, "Lure says that you have begun the battle here already, and you must remain to finish it. She said that we will fight with you. All of the shadows will, from child to eldest. We will fight with teeth and nails if you have no weapons for us."

"We are too few," Harwood said aloud gently.

"You are few, but there are hundreds of us," Cinda's image told me in a low, fierce mindvoice. "It is as Lure said. If you will command us, we will serve. We will kill the Herders."

I stared into her stormy eyes, amazed that such savage purpose could issue from such a waiflike figure. And when I looked at the others, their eyes held the same grim fire.

"If you rise up, many of you will be killed, especially if the Herders still have Beforetime weapons," I told her gently.

"They *would* die, if they rose up without any plan," Harwood broke in. "But with a plan, if there truly are hundreds of shadows willing to oppose their masters, it may be that we really can take control here."

I gaped at the coercer in astonishment, for I had always seen him as rather cautious. "You know that when I spoke of taking control, I meant only that we should do so to get the ship repaired," I said.

"I know it. But, Guildmistress, by pure chance we have managed to slip inside the very skin of the Faction, and we have the One and the Threes in our power. Would there ever again come a moment so ripe for the taking, even if we sailed up with ten ships to Hevon Bay? We came here, as you did, by accident, but these shadows have made me wonder if it was not mere chance that brought us here, but purposeful fate."

Cinda and the other shadows gazed at the coercer-knight as if mesmerized.

Cinda touched his arm, and because I was still within her mind, I felt him enter her mind and heard her say, "Lead us and we will fight until the last of us drops!"

"Wait!" I said. "I understand what you are saying, but we have to go after Ariel and stop the plague, or there will be more deaths on the west coast than any of us could imagine in our most terrible dreams."

Harwood rose and came to pull me to my feet. "Elspeth," he said fiercely, "we can do *both*. Once the ship is repaired, you will travel with some of the others to find the null, and I and whoever else remain will lead these shadows."

I farsent to him, "Harwood, only think! These are starveling girls and women with no fighting skills, and the shadow men are like to be the same. If they rise against the Faction, many will die."

"We are dead already," Cinda's image said, for both of our minds were still within hers, and she had heard me. "If we fight, we will fight to live."

Harwood said aloud, "Guildmistress, people died in the Land, too, during the rebellion, to achieve freedom. And we need not wage an open battle here. Look how these shadows move around within the Herder Compound, hearing everything, seeing everything, unnoticed. They cook food and serve drinks that might be drugged. They can go anywhere without anyone wondering why. They deliver messages that can be falsified or altered. Their very meekness and fragility would stop anyone seeing them as a threat. With their help and knowledge and our Talents, we could cut the heart from this place before the Herders know they are in danger."

His words made me think of what my father had cried out before the Herders burned him. If we were to strike a blow against the Herders here, we would be striking at the heart of the foul organization that had killed my parents and my brother. "The Norselanders might fight, too," I said at last, and Cinda and the other shadows nodded excitedly.

Slowly, I nodded. "All right. We will try. But nothing must hinder us from making the *Stormdancer* seaworthy."

Cinda turned to gesticulate urgently at the others, and Harwood sent to me, "I agree. Our first priority must be to stop Ariel, but until the shipfolk return, let us begin to make a map of this place."

354

His words gave me another idea. Aloud, I said, "Ariel has chambers here. Coerce the Threes to find out where they are, and I will search them for clues about which city is the destination of the plague null."

Cinda reached out to touch my wrist, and when I turned my attention to her mind, she said, "I will take you to my friend. He may know more of Ariel's doings."

Twenty minutes later, I was following the slender girl down the steps from the bathing room again, Falc's hood drawn forward to conceal my hair.

Cinda opened the door to the laundry, and I froze, seeing that it was no longer empty. The coppers were now full, and there were shadows flitting about, their thin dark-clad forms half obscured by dense steam clouds. I hesitated, but Cinda assured me that no shadow would trouble me. Sure enough, the black-clad women paid so little heed to us as we passed that we might just as well have been invisible. But then Cinda stopped and gave me a reassuring look before she clapped her hands loudly. All the shadows turned to look at us, their faces bland. Cinda lifted her fingers and flicked them for a long time. Gradually, the blankness in the women's faces gave way to wariness and then to amazement, hope, disbelief. Some of the women lifted their hands, but Cinda shook her head, fingers still fluttering, and in a moment, all the women had returned to their work, leaving me to feel I might have imagined the brief transformation I had witnessed.

"I told them to rejoice, for we are about to rise up against our masters," Cinda said, leading me out of the overheated washing chamber into the yard, where the numerous lines I had seen earlier now sagged under the weight of wet sheets, towels, and hundreds of white, gray, and black robes. "I told them that you and your friends are powerful mutant spies who have already overpowered the One and the Threes and that you will lead us in the fight to come." She saw my unguarded reaction and read it accurately, saying, "Do not fear that any of us will give you away. All who work in this laundry once served the One and so cannot speak, and the priests know nothing of our hand-speaking."

"I do not believe you would betray us even if you could speak," I said, shamed by my momentary doubts.

We reached the gate Cinda had mentioned earlier, and it brought us to a narrow lane that passed along the rear of two long rows of buildings. As we hastened along it, Cinda explained that this way was safer because such back lanes were used only by shadows, novices, and the occasional acolyte. They were called shadow paths because the Hedra rarely used them.

"Are there other paths in the compound?" I asked, and she nodded. We came to a small area outside a door where a Herder novice of about fifteen chopped kindling. Before I could think what to do, he turned and saw us. Cinda stepped forward, moving her fingers rapidly. The youth flicked an incredulous glance at me, but Cinda caught his arm and continued speaking with her hands. I realized this must be the friend she would have me meet, but I had not imagined he would be a novice. He was as tall and strongly built as she was thin and small, but when they turned to me, they wore the same look of yearning. The youth said in an uneven voice, "Is it true what Cinda says? You are the mutant who hid aboard the *Stormdancer*? I heard that you had been taken to the cells."

"I am a Misfit," I corrected him. "And I was rescued by friends who are also Misfits."

"Cinda says you can speak inside her head and hear her thoughts."

"I can listen to what she wants to tell me," I said. "I can show you, if you like."

He shook his head hastily, and Cinda flicked her fingers at the novice and laughed quietly. He scowled at her, red-cheeked. "I am not afraid!" Her expression became contrite, and she moved her fingers until he seemed mollified.

"Cinda asks me to tell you how I ended up here," he said. He glanced warily both ways along the lane and then said, "I never wanted to be a Herder. Hardly any of us do, but those who fail the training are sold as slaves or become mine shadows. Those considered difficult are sent to the demon-band works, and after a few moons there, all of your hair and teeth fall out, and your bones start crumbling inside your skin. So I do my studies and I am obedient. But I am not a Herder, and I never will be," he added almost savagely. "Is it true that you and your friends mean to overthrow the Faction?"

"All that she told you is true," I said. "But there are few of us, and it will take time to establish real control, even with the help of the shadows. We must proceed with care, for the moment your brothers realize we are in their midst, they will put on their demon bands and we will be helpless."

"If you control the Threes and the One, you are far

357

from helpless," said the youth. He glanced at Cinda, then back to me. "She said you need information about Ariel, but you need not trouble yourself about the Pale Man, for he has gone to Norseland. It is said that he will go to the west coast before he returns."

His last words gave me pause, but realizing Cinda had told him nothing of the plague null, I did so, explaining that I needed to know where he might have taken the null. "Faugh!" the lad spat. "It does not surprise me that the Pale Man should come up with such a foul plan. All novices fear him, because when first we come, he tests us to see if we would suit being made into nulls. He smiles when we scream, as if our suffering pleasures him. I know nothing of this matter of the west coast, but I can question the other novices at midmeal. It is unlikely anyone knows more, for the Pale Man's chambers are in a sector on the other side of the compound where few of us have call to go."

"How many sectors are there?" I asked.

"Twenty-one," he answered. "The only reason novices leave their sectors is because a Herder bids them go, and you must go only where you are told and then return directly. Sometimes my master sends me to the ink house or paper press, but occasionally I accompany him to the library, which is right across the compound."

"Is movement controlled?" I asked.

He nodded gravely. "Any unaccompanied novice or acolyte outside his sector must produce his master's token to show he has been sent on an errand, and the token is marked with chalk to tell where he is meant to go. If he is in the wrong place, a whipping or time in the tide cells would be the least he would suffer." He glanced again both ways along the lane.

I nodded and thanked him. "If you can find out anything that might help us understand more about Ariel's plans on the west coast, even an overheard phrase or gossip, it may mean the difference between saving the west coast and not," I said. "But you must not let anyone guess why you are asking."

"I will be careful," he said. "But you should know that I am not the only novice who would be glad to be free of this robe and this place. There are three I know who would gladly fight if it comes to that. There are more in other sectors, but it is better for us not to know one another in case one is questioned. Yet if there is real hope of getting free of the Faction, then maybe it is time for us to know one another. Where do I find you if I learn something?" he asked.

"Seek out Cinda, and she will bring you to us," I said after the slightest hesitation. It struck me that I did not know his name. I asked him, but before he could respond, the door behind him opened, and an older Herder stepped out. "Novice, why are you taking . . . ?" He stopped, his eyes widening at the sight of Cinda and me. Before he could even begin to formulate a suspicion, I entered his mind and made him come outside and close the door behind him. I felt Cinda and the young novice watching me as I coerced the priest. The novice gaped openly when his master turned, blank-faced, and went back inside, closing the door quietly behind him.

"Right now he thinks he has just told you to hurry up. He won't remember seeing us at all, but later this afternoon he is going to become terribly sleepy and lie down until nightmeal. Before he sleeps, he will give you a token with his mark. You need only speak Cinda's name into his ear and say whatever you wish him to scribe, and he will do it. Now go back in, and be careful," I warned him.

The novice squared his shoulders, and his eyes flashed. "You asked my name, lady? It is Elkar, and you may count on me."

When we returned to the One's chamber, I was disappointed to find that there was still no word of Helvar, but the compound map was beginning to take shape, complete with shadow paths, sectors, and even details about buildings. Harwood was fascinated to hear about Elkar and as eager as I to see what the lad might unearth. He invited me to look at the map, and I knelt down to study it.

I ran my eyes along the shadow path I had taken with Cinda. From what I could tell, the building Elkar had come from was marked "Scrips." I guessed it must have something to do with scribing since he had mentioned an ink house and a paper press. I searched until I found the library he had mentioned. As he had said, it was on the other side of the compound. Harwood was now explaining that although most sectors were virtually self-sufficient, each had at least one activity that served the entire compound.

"These communal activities seem to be the key to moving safely around the compound," Harwood said. "For instance, here is the food store for the entire compound. Shadows and novices from here make deliveries to kitchens all over the compound, including to the Hedra and the inner-cadre walled garden."

Cinda touched my arm and said that we ought to poison the food meant for the Hedra sector, for we could kill all of them at one stroke. I exchanged a startled look with Harwood, who told her gently that we intended to take control with as little killing as possible.

"Why?" she asked, looking confounded. "Better to kill as many priests as possible, so they can never harm anyone again."

I hid my shock and said mildly that poisoning them would have all sorts of repercussions we could not possibly cope with, such as hundreds of dead bodies that would need disposing of before they rotted. I had thought to bring home to her the grisly reality of her suggestion, but she merely shrugged and said the bodies could be piled up in the exercise yards and burned.

Harwood began asking Cinda about the routines within the compound, but I was puzzled. If Cinda and the other shadows were so willing to see their masters die, why had they not rebelled already?

I turned my attention back to the map, noting the repetition of sleeping halls, meal chambers, and cloister in each sector. I also spotted an unmarked area at the compound's end, farthest from the gate. Before I could ask what it was, Cinda rose and touched my arm, explaining that she and one of the others must go to fetch the One's nightmeal, for it was always made ready at this time.

"Ye gods," Harwood muttered after she had gone. "I thought when she said the shadows would be willing to fight tooth and nail it was romantic rhetoric, but if the rest think as Cinda does . . ."

"They can't, or they would have rebelled before now," I said. I drew his attention back to the map and asked if he knew yet of Ariel's chambers.

He pointed to a small section alongside the library,

explaining that they were contained within the wall surrounding the library. Then he tapped another largish section. "That is what interests me. It is the healing center, and it serves the whole compound, according to the shadows who go there to collect medications for the One. I have not scribed it yet, but the whole sector is one immense labyrinthine building with three levels above the ground and two below. Instead of having meal halls kept separate from the healing facility, the acolytes, novices, and shadows live in chambers on one of the subterranean levels while the ranked priests live on the topmost level. I suppose this is because healers have to be available constantly. They are trained within the building and rarely leave it save to go to daily prayer meetings in a nearby sector, because the healing center lacks a cloister."

I touched the place on the map where the Hedra sector ran up against the healing center. "Do priests from the healing center attend the Hedra cloister?"

"No, but the healing center is one level higher than any other building in the compound and two levels higher than most. And it overlooks the Hedra training grounds. One watcher up there—"

"But we already have Hilder and Tomrick on the outer wall."

"They are too far away, and they would have to divide their attention," Harwood said. "If we put even one watcher on top of the healing center, they could watch the whole central area of the compound, including the Hedra sector, and could serve as a conduit for farsought information."

I nodded. "Then do it."

"I was also thinking that the healing building

would make the perfect command center," added Harwood. I have just sent Sover there with some of the shadows, supposedly to get something to ease the One. Sover will remain there and begin coercing healers at once. I have sent Colwyn over to take a look at this sector." He pointed to a small area that ran up against the outer wall of the compound behind the Hedra sector. "This is the compound armory. It is walled, and the only way to enter it is from the Hedra training ground. Apparently, it is guarded constantly, but we need to get control of it, given that it may contain the Beforetime weapon you mentioned."

I shuddered; then something struck me. "If you sent Sover to the healing center, who is watching over the One?"

Harwood said dismissively, "Some of the shadows. Geratty is sleeping in the dressing room, and they will wake him if the One stirs." He pointed to the large area I had noticed at the end of the compound, naming it tainted ground.

"Tainted ground?" I echoed.

"Strictly speaking, it sounds as if it is more a patch of blacklands centered on a tainted pool," Harwood said. "The whole area is walled and encompasses the mine where the male shadows work. There are sleeping quarters and an eating hall for the shadows who work there. They never come out, apparently. Lure told me that some of her sisters take in food once a day. I think we need control of it, because aside from the armory, it is the only other place where the priests will be able to get demon bands."

"What of the bands taken from us at the gate?"

"They are returned to the armory," Harwood said.

I pointed to Ariel's chambers again and asked Harwood what he had learned of them.

"Not much," Harwood said, frowning at the map. "The shadows do not go there, any more than novices or acolytes. Apparently, Ariel uses nulls to attend him. I probed Mendi and Grisyl to see what they knew and found they have never been in Ariel's chambers. Moreover, they were remarkably incurious about what goes on there, despite their doubts about Ariel. That lack of curiosity made me dig into Mendi's mind until I found the coercive structures Ariel had set up to ensure that no one interferes with him. It is the same with Grisyl."

"I wonder what is of such importance there that Ariel would keep everyone away," I said.

"Maybe plague seeds," said Harwood. "I would like to do a little more nosing around before you try searching there."

"All right," I said reluctantly. "I will wait until the shipfolk begin work on the *Stormdancer*. But no longer, for there may be information there that will help us find the null quickly."

Cinda returned, accompanied by a beaming Ode who carried a great black cauldron of stew and a basket of bread and boasted of having coerced every person in the sector seven kitchen. Harwood bade Cinda give the One's tray to Falc and sent him to see if he could wake his master to eat. Then he woke Reuvan and Geratty, and we all ate sitting cross-legged on the floor, the shadows among us, as Harwood outlined his plan to take over the healing center and capture the armory. We had barely begun when Elkar appeared at the dressing-room door.

"I did not realize you would be here," he said. "You said to seek out Cinda if I had something to tell."

"You know of the secret stairs to the One's chamber?" I asked.

He glanced at Cinda. "I usually wait for Cinda or one of the shadows on the stairs, but I heard your voice." He was looking about at the others with open curiosity, and I explained who he was and let them offer their own names. Then I said, "Have you learned anything about Ariel?"

"One of the novices in the dining hall told me of another novice who had talked of seeing the Pale Man and his special nulls, but he could not recall who it was. He has promised to try to remember."

"The Pale Man?" Harwood echoed.

"Ariel," I said, and nodded for Elkar to continue.

"Mainly I came to tell you that the other novices are willing to help." He gave a sudden laugh. "Willing! Say rather they are demanding to help. You cannot imagine how the idea of freedom fired them. Even I could not have predicted the strength of their reaction. In truth, none of us *guessed* there was anything to escape to, for it seemed that the Herders were the masters of the world. But then the invasion failed and you came."

I bit back the urge to remind the novice that I had asked him to disclose nothing to anyone yet and said, "Harwood, you should meet with these partisan novices as soon as may be." I added privately that he had better coerce them to make sure there were none among them like to betray us.

But Elkar said eagerly, "That is why I came. There is a prayer meeting tonight that will be attended by all the novices from this sector and by a Herder who will rant at us about serving Lud with a pure heart. I was thinking you could make him stop and then talk in his stead."

"You would have us address all the novices?" I asked in disbelief. "Surely not all of them are ready to rise against the Faction!"

"Of course not," Elkar said. "But you can force the others to obey."

"This is getting out of hand," Harwood sent to me forcefully enough to let me know he blamed me. Then he asked Elkar to describe a prayer meeting. As the novice obliged, Cinda made some signals to the other shadows, which Elkar noticed and translated as a suggestion that all the dissenters had better be killed. The other shadows nodded with such ferocious expressions that I found myself wondering if, after all, they *did* think as Cinda did. Then Elkar said calmly that it might be the best idea.

I farsent uneasily to Harwood that we had best be careful we did not light a taper of rage that would set the whole compound ablaze. The coercer nodded slightly and bade me leave it to him. Then he told Elkar he hoped that the novice had done or said nothing to make his masters guess something was afoot. Elkar laughed, saying that his own master was so excited over a new kind of ink that had been delivered that he would not have noticed if the novice was walking about naked. Then he frowned and added that the Herder who had brought the ink had told his master that Salamander had sunk the *Orizon* not because mutants had boarded it, as had been reported that morning, but because the Hedra aboard had contracted a deadly plague in the Land.

"A plague?" I echoed aloud, unable to see how such

a rumor could have arisen unless something had leaked about the null that Ariel was taking to the west coast. I turned to Harwood, but his eyes had the distant look that meant one of the others was farseeking him. After a long moment, he said, "That was Tomrick. He says he walked around the top of the wall until he calculated he was above us, and as he had hoped, he was able to farseek me. He is going to stay in that position now so the others can farseek any news to him to be relayed to us. But he says there is a mist rolling in, and from what he has seen, it won't be long before it comes into the compound. Apparently, Hilder says it is already creeping along the channel."

I stood up decisively. "I am going to Fallo. I need to know what is happening with the shipfolk."

"I will come with you," Reuvan said. "I have slept enough and feel useless here."

Elkar broke in to ask if he and Cinda could come with me. I was about to refuse when Harwood farsent that I ought to let them accompany me to the gates since we would make a reasonable entourage; I could wear Falc's robe again and go as a ranked Herder, accompanied by a lantern-bearing shadow, a novice, and a Hedra escort, for of course Reuvan was bald and clad in a Hedra robe like the coercers.

I told the novice that he and Cinda could come as far as the black gates but that it would look suspicious if they came farther, since Cinda had told me that neither novices nor shadows ever left the compound. And besides that, Elkar ought to be at the prayer meeting. He looked disappointed but acquiesced willingly enough. We were soon descending the hidden stairs and passing through the once more deserted laundry. It was dusk, and the laundry yard was veiled in mist, but Elkar shrugged, saying that the mist would grow much thicker before it abated. I asked if he would not be missed, and he answered that his master would merely assume that Elkar was still in the dining hall.

"Do the Herders keep such casual control of you?" I asked, surprised.

He shrugged. "They keep a tight hold on new novices, but with novices my age, it depends on the master. Mine is old and less strict than many," he added.

Two priests appeared before us in the mist, followed by a lantern-bearing shadow. The Herders nodded to me without breaking off their conversation, but I noticed the shadow flick her fingers at Cinda.

"She asked if it was true that mutants had secretly invaded the compound," Cinda told me when I asked what had been signaled.

As we walked, the mist thickened as Elkar had predicted, and I noticed how empty the streets and lanes now were. Was it a curfew or the mist? I wondered.

Soon a group of Hedra came marching along the street toward us. I prayed they would march past without bothering us. But the leader stopped and commanded us to do the same. I obeyed and was relieved to find that there was no barrier as I entered his mind. A relentless fanaticism snaked through his thoughts like a river of poison, sickening me, but there was no time to be squeamish. I took complete and rough control of him, but before I could make him dismiss us, one of the other Hedra asked me suspiciously, "Where are you going, Master?"

"Our master is ill and wishes a potion from the healers," I said in as low a voice as I could manage.

"Who is your captain?" asked the same Hedra of Reuvan.

I jabbed coercively at the Hedra in my control. He gave a loud bray of pain and clutched at his stomach, and the other Hedra looked at him in astonishment.

"It seems my master is not the only one who is ill," I said with pretended alarm. An inspired thought came to me, and I added, "I pray it is not the plague that was aboard the *Orizon*."

A look of deep unease passed between the Hedra, and I made the priest clutching his stomach give another good long bellow of pain, then offered to take him to the healing center, since we were bound there.

"You had better go, too, Gelt," said the Hedra who had questioned Reuvan to one of the others.

I saw from the expression on the other warrior priest's face that he would protest, and I coerced him to nod obediently, then I went back to the mind of the groaning Hedra and jabbed at him again, causing him to utter another groan and double over. The Hedra Gelt stepped forward to take his arm.

"Help them," I ordered Elkar, who had been watching with openmouthed astonishment. He obeyed as the other Hedra marched away.

"It's all right," I assured all of them when we were alone but for the two Hedra, both now silent and blank-faced. "I am controlling them."

"You did that to him?" Elkar whispered, looking at the Hedra who had been shouting and groaning.

"He is not truly ill," I assured him. "I just found a

deep memory of a terrible stomachache he once had and grafted it into his conscious mind. Then I gave his muscles a jab to set him off. But let's go on. We can't stay out in the open like this."

"What are we going to do with them?" Reuvan asked softly.

"We will take them into the healing center, just as I said, in case their comrades come back to see what became of this one. This is it, isn't it?" I asked, nodding to the building beside us.

Elkar agreed, adding that the entrance was on the other side, facing sector three. Soon we were approaching the entrance. Mercifully, it was not guarded. I would have liked to leave the others to wait outside, but the door opened before we could reach it, and several low-ranking outer-cadre priests came hurrying out, so immersed in conversation that they did not even see us.

We entered a windowless hall lit by lanterns hanging from hooks set into the walls. Two outer-cadre Nines standing outside a door a little distance along the passage broke off their conversation to look toward us inquiringly, so I made the Hedra begin bellowing and groaning again.

"What is wrong with him?" asked one of them.

"I do not know," I said, keeping my voice and my head low, for I feared they would see that I was a woman. "I was on an errand for my master when we came upon a group of Hedra. He was in their midst, and I was ordered to bring him here."

Fortunately, the healer was more concerned with the bellowing Hedra than with me, but his companion eyed me suspiciously. Before I could shape a coercive probe to deal with him, an older Herder wearing the

370

gold armband of an inner-cadre priest arrived and demanded to know what was going on. He had the harried air of a real healer, and though his face was much lined, it lacked the coldness I had seen in most Herder faces. Perhaps it was hard to be cold and remote when trying to heal sickness.

I gave the groaning Hedra's mind a hard tweak, and when the Herder bent to examine him, I said anxiously that I would have to go because my own master would wonder where I was. One final jab and the Hedra collapsed. As the three healers tended to him, I withdrew, ushering the others ahead of me. Not until we were outside did I realize the Hedra Gelt had followed us, because I had forgotten to command him to stay.

"He will have to come with us," I decided, and we turned back toward the compound gates. I farsought Sover as we walked, explaining briefly what had happened, and he promised to take care of it.

"What will the healers do when they realize that there is nothing wrong with that Hedra?" Elkar asked softly.

Before I could respond, Geratty's voice scythed into my mind with a force that would have dropped me to my knees had Reuvan not caught me.

"Geratty! What is it?" I demanded, clutching at my head.

"Elspeth, the One . . . Ye gods, it is the shadows. They've killed him!"

Suddenly, bells began ringing loudly.

✦ 20 ✦

I FROZE, BUT Elkar assured me that the bells rang only to announce the beginning of the evening acolyte prayer meetings. "The novice prayers will be in an hour, and then will come the bell for the rest of the outer-cadre priests. . . ." He glanced at my face, and his own grew tense. "What is it, lady?"

"Wait," I said, and stopped. I had to farseek Geratty to find out what on earth he had meant by saying the One had been killed. And by *shadows*! But I could not locate the coercer. I realized he would have had to come outside to reach me, and no doubt he had now gone back inside.

Opening my eyes, I announced that we had to go back to the One's chamber immediately. We retraced our steps along the misty path. When we drew near the laundry, Elkar suddenly announced that perhaps he ought to make an appearance in his master's chamber. He would come after us as soon as possible.

"What's wrong?" Reuvan asked me softly when he had gone.

I told him what Geratty had sent.

He grimaced. "Why?"

"Geratty didn't say, and now I can't reach him," I said worriedly.

Cinda touched my hand. "It does not matter if the One is dead, lady. You can make any Hedra or priests believe he is alive. And you still have the Threes."

I did not know what to say to her, for she seemed to have no sense of the wrongness of murder. She was considering only the consequences of the death, yet this was the death of the most powerful man in all the Faction—at the hands of shadows like her. How could she not be shocked?

Minutes later, we were mounting the stairs leading up from the laundry. A shattered-looking Geratty was waiting for me.

"What on earth has happened?" I demanded.

"Harwood woke me to say he and Ode were gannin' out to deal with some problem with shadows and a Herder priest. He took Grisyl. He said the shadows were feeding the One because he had been asleep earlier when they tried. I was just gannin' a bite to eat myself when I heard a cry. I went to th' One's chamber. The two of them were . . . bending over him. Emaciated lasses more like children than women; they looked so innocent, but their hands were covered in blood." He shuddered. "They had the knives from the meals they had brought. Poor blunt things, but . . . Guildmistress, they . . . they had blinded him and were trying to cut out his tongue!" He looked at me. "They seemed . . . surprised that I was so upset. Apparently, the One woke an' saw one of them without their headdress. He started screamin' for the Hedra to chop their hands off and put out their eyes . . . ye gods." He faltered to a halt, suddenly seeing Cinda gazing at him in bewilderment.

"Is he dead?" Reuvan asked quietly.

The coercer drew a deep breath and shook his head. "I thought he was at first, but no. He lives yet, but he's in a bad way. I tried to reach Harwood or Sover, but my probe wouldn't locate. So I sent one of th' shadows to the healing center. Not one of the two who . . ."

"Where are the shadows who did it?" I asked.

"In the other room. I . . . I sent them in there while I was cleaning him up." He looked into my eyes. "Guildmistress, I've seen killing before, but nowt like this. Those pretty mild-faced girls with their bloody hands . . ."

The sound of boots coming up the steps behind us brought us to our feet. To my amazement, it was Yarrow, accompanied by Asra and a rather bedraggled Zuria.

"You found the shipfolk!" I said.

"No. We found the Per of Gelan; that is the village on Fallo where your shipmaster dwelt," Yarrow said. "Or at least, the Hedra Mendi sent out had found him and were torturing him when we arrived. He had fled with the rest of the villagers after one of them saw the Hedra take a prisoner off the ship. Apparently, your Helvar realized it was you and guessed that it was only a matter of time before the Hedra came for him, his shipfolk, and their families, so he warned the Per, who ordered the evacuation of the village. They did not want to bring strife to the other villages, so they fled into the swamp. But the Per is old, and when he could not continue, they hid him. Unfortunately, the Hedra found him, and they were so engrossed in their foul labor that we had only to creep up on them and knock them on the heads."

He went on to explain that their rescue of the Per

had been fortuitous, because it convinced the old man that they were no friends of the Faction. He had told them that his village had been abandoned, because Helvar had given aid to a young mutant from the Land. "I let him rattle on, because I wanted to see whether he or maybe this Helvar had any resentment toward you over what happened. They don't, by the way."

"Where did the Per think you came from?" I asked.

He grinned. "He was so relieved to have his head on his shoulders that it took him a good bit of time to wonder that. When he did get to it, I said we were friends of yours who had come aboard the ship disguised as Hedra. I explained you hadn't known we were aboard any more than we had known you were aboard."

"I'm glad they're not full of ire," I said, for I could not truly have blamed the Norseland shipfolk for resenting me.

Yarrow went on to say that although the Per did not know where the shipfolk and their families were hiding, he had only to tie a swatch of cloth to the topmost branch of a certain tree to communicate with them. A red swatch warned that the person flying the flag was summoning them under duress. A yellow flag, on the other hand, denoted that it was safe to return.

"He said he was glad we had come along to save him the mortification of flying the red flag," Asra added.

"So you hung out the yellow cloth?" I asked.

"A blue one," Yarrow said. "That means that it is safe and to come in haste. But the Per said that how much time it took Helvar and the others to respond would depend upon where in the swamps they had taken refuge. He promised that as soon as they came out, he would send them across with tools to repair the *Stormdancer*."

"Did you tell the Per what is happening here?"

"I told him that we had rescued you and that we had control of the gate guards and the wall watch, so the Norselanders need not fear an attack. I showed him how we could make Zuria dance a jig and a Hedra stand on his head, which was enough to convince him I was not exaggerating. I also told him we had control of the other two inner-cadre Threes and the One . . . What is it?" He was looking at Geratty, who had flinched at his words.

My elation faded. I said tiredly, "Reuvan will explain what has been happening here. In the meantime, Geratty, you had better go down to the laundry and wait for the healer."

"The shadow said he would come along the wall passage, so I will wait there," the older coercer said. He went through to the firelit audience room, and I followed him. It was easy to see which of the shadows had attacked the One, for they sat huddled against the wall near a blank-faced Mendi, watching us with huge, lost eyes. I went over to them. I saw with revulsion the blood on their hands and asked Cinda to fetch warm water so they could wash. I knelt down before them, seeing that both were little more than Dragon's age when I had found her in the Beforetime ruins. If not for the blood on their hands, I would have found it impossible to believe that they had done what Geratty had described. I reached into the mind of one, meaning to reassure her that she would not be punished, and I recoiled from a vivid, bloody vision of myself torturing her. I realized with horror that even though they knew we were allies, they imagined I would resort to torture to seek information or punish them.

The words I had intended to say died on my lips, for I saw that I could say nothing about what they had done that would make any sense to them. They had spoken to the One in the language he and his foul brethren had taught them—the language of cruelty and pain—and it was the only language they knew.

"Come over to the fire. No one will hurt you or punish you," I told them.

They obeyed, and as Cinda came with water and began to wash their hands, I tried to think of something that would allow us to bridge this moment. Nothing came to mind, and when Cinda sat back on her heels, I asked her rather desperately to tell me Elkar's story, adding the inward request that she tell the story with her fingers as well as her mind. She looked puzzled, but she obeyed, and as I had hoped, the blank devastation ebbed in the eyes of the two younger shadows as her tale unfolded.

Elkar had been born on Herder Isle, Cinda explained. Like so many other Norse boys, he was taken from his family to become a novice. He had resisted the training until he and the other novices had been taken to see the mine and demon-band works, and he had understood that this would be their fate if they did not succeed in becoming novices. Elkar had given up his rebellious refusal to cooperate and had tried to forget his family and believe the words of Lud, as expressed by his masters. He had worked hard, and when it was found that he had an aptitude for scribing, he was sent to the Herder scribes. Eventually, he had been assigned to his present master who, although devout, was one of the few Herders with a passion for something other than worshipping Lud. Although friendship was impossible, Elkar had come to respect his master's ability to read and scribe.

The boy had proven so quick and willing to learn that almost before he had realized what he was doing, the old man was teaching him to read and scribe. This was forbidden, but his master had known that Elkar would work more swiftly and efficiently if he could read and scribe, and his own eyesight was beginning to fail. Elkar was careful never to reveal his abilities, realizing that he would be killed if anyone learned that he knew how to read. In time, his master trusted him so well that he had given over the scribing of older scrips to Elkar.

"Why rescribe older scrips?" I interrupted.

"The reason given was that they were old and falling to bits," Cinda explained. "But more often it was because a bit of the scrip had become unacceptable and needed to be altered. This was supposed to be done by Elkar's master and merely copied by the scrip novices."

That scrips said to have come to the One in visions sent by Lud were altered and sometimes even reversed made it impossible for Elkar to believe in the Herders' Lud. But he was older now and wise enough in the ways of the Faction to make sure he never revealed his disbelief.

Cinda ceased her story as Geratty reentered and passed through the chamber with a blank-faced Herder priest carrying a healer's bag. Instead of referring to the interruption, I asked her how she and Elkar had become friends. She smiled shyly and said that he had

378

noticed the shadows' finger movements. Elkar had studied the movements of the shadows, and one day, when Cinda had been serving food to him, he had made the signal that he believed was a greeting between shadows. She had started so violently that she had spilled hot soup on him, but the novice had said nothing. Frightened and confused, she had managed to stay away from the meal hall for some time, and when she had to go there, she had been careful to avoid him. Yet she had not been able to forget the movement of his fingers, which had expressed the word *friend.* Then one day as she was taking a tray to the One, Elkar had been outside the scrip cutting kindling. He had approached Cinda, again using the finger signal for "friend," then told her aloud that he wanted her to teach him the signal language.

"I was afraid at first," Cinda said. "I knew that many of us would be killed if our masters knew how well we could communicate. Yet I feared to refuse him. I decided I would pretend to be very dull-witted and show him only the simplest language so he would believe we used it to communicate only what was necessary for our work. I hoped he would grow bored, but he was so clever and quick. He would make this or that signal and ask what it meant. My sisters told me that we must poison him, but I did not know whom he had told about me, and I wanted to know before I killed him. As time passed, I understood that Elkar had told no one what he had guessed. I asked why he wanted to know how to speak to a shadow, and he answered that he was curious and that he envied our freedom of speech."

The words Cinda used in her upper mind were less

eloquent than the picture in her undermind, which was loud and radiant. Cinda had at first feared the white-clad novice, but she had soon learned that his regard was not unfriendly. Indeed, to her astonishment, it had dawned on her that it was the opposite: He was lonely and wished them to be friends. She resisted until, one day, he said that he would repay her for her lessons by teaching her to scribe and to read. Knowing that he could be killed for being able to read, she had taken it as an offering of friendship. But by now, her own feelings for him ran deeper than that, though she never dared let Elkar see how she felt.

Then came the day that she had scribed her name for the first time with a thrill of pure terror, and Elkar had read it aloud. She had looked up at him in wonder and sorrow, for she had not heard her name spoken aloud since her brother had been dragged from her arms, screaming it. She wept, and Elkar had taken her in his arms and kissed her tears away. This gentle tenderness had shown Cinda that his feelings ran as deep as hers.

When Cinda's image spoke again, it was to say that Elkar's feelings for her made him sympathetic to the plight of all shadows, whose lives he realized were much harder than any novice's. He had become determined to find a way to help the shadows, but save for being as kind and considerate as he dared, he could not think how.

Then one day, Cinda asked if he could scribe a note that would transfer a young shadow from one sector to another, where the girl's sister labored. Since shadows were used as messengers, it was no difficulty for one to deliver the note Elkar had scribed, and soon the sisters were reunited. With this note, Elkar had proven himself to all the shadows, and thereafter he had become their secret champion.

More requests followed, and Elkar came to recruit others among the novices and acolytes, and even one ranked priest, who felt as he did. The little secret group passed among themselves messages of hope, warnings, and occasionally books Elkar had stolen from the library. Some were from the Beforetime and told of a world that was nothing like the Beforetime of the Faction's preachings, which passionately interested all of them. But their main task was to ease the lot of the shadows. And the shadows found ways of helping them, too. A novice being punished would be starved, but the shadows would bring him food; a note sent to command the punishment of a novice would be brought to Elkar, who would rescribe it and simply send the boy to another sector. Cinda assured me that there was little danger, because no priest could ever imagine anyone disobeying him, so he did not check that his orders had been carried out.

I wondered why Ariel had not foreseen what was going on, unless, like the Herders, he simply never focused his attention on the shadows.

Yarrow was hovering, and when I rose, apologizing to Cinda for interrupting her story, he drew me into the dressing room where Geratty waited. The older man told me that the healing Herder had given the One medicines to soothe his pain but that his mind, already teetering under the weight of Ariel's block, was broken altogether now. Certainly it would be some time before they could even attempt to enter it.

I nearly shuddered at the thought.

"Has Harwood been in contact yet?" I asked them.

Geratty shook his head. "Asra has been outside trying, but neither he nor Tomrick has heard a peep from him since he summoned Hilder down from the wall, and now they can't reach him either. They will keep trying."

Yarrow said suddenly, "You know, I don't think Ariel ever meant to come back here."

I stared at him. "We know he is going to the west coast before he returns to Herder Isle," I said.

"No, I mean I don't believe he meant to come back here at all."

"What makes you think that?" I asked.

"Because he must have known that he would not return from the west coast in time to save the old man's mind, and yet he set no safeguards against its being destroyed. Why on earth let him die or go mad when he had been so useful? Unless Ariel had no further use for him."

"Maybe he plans to let one of the Threes take his place. After all, the One's mind is disintegrating."

"True enough, but it is more than that," Yarrow said. "Ariel has always contrived never to be there when something he is involved in falls apart. And now, when we are making a good start at bringing this place down, Ariel is elsewhere. Maybe he foresaw that Herder Isle would fall."

"If he did, then why didn't he take steps to stop it?" I asked.

"Maybe he foresaw that it can't be stopped," Yarrow suggested.

"He has access to an army of Hedra on Norseland,"

I said. "He could have had Salamander blast the wall down."

"He *could* if he wanted to protect the Faction, but why would he? He has just been using them to further his own interests, hasn't he? The way he used Henry Druid and the Councilmen. He has never hesitated to betray people in the past."

"You are saying you think he has left this place for good? Left it to us?"

"That is what it seems like to me."

"Where would he go after he has poisoned the west coast?" I asked. Even as I spoke, my mind flew to the Red Land.

But Yarrow said, "He has a stronghold on Norseland. It seems to me that he will return there after he has left the null on the west coast. I was speaking to the Per about Norseland, and it sounds as if it is virtually unassailable, being all high cliffs, save for Main Cove, where there is a single narrow road leading up to Covetown, overlooked by the cloister. Not far from there the Hedra have their own permanent encampment, inhabited by an army in waiting. I do not doubt that Ariel can coerce its captains into accepting his authority, but maybe he would not need them to defend himself. I was also poking around in Zuria's mind on our way back here, and it seems that Ariel found other weapons from the Beforetime when he found the plague seeds, and the Threes believe he keeps them in his residence."

My blood ran cold at the thought of Ariel in possession of Beforetime weapons.

"But if Ariel knew he would not return to Herder

Isle, why leave instructions that the guildmistress be left unhurt until he came to interrogate her?" Geratty asked.

Yarrow frowned. "Hmm. I had forgotten that." He fell silent, mulling it over, but I knew why Ariel would have ordered me not to be harmed. He needed the Seeker alive. He may even have foreseen that I was the Misfit aboard the *Stormdancer* and acted to make sure I would not be tortured before the coercer-knights took control of the compound. That he had not stayed to take me captive himself meant he knew that I had not yet gathered all I needed to find and disable the weaponmachines that had caused the Great White. Perhaps Yarrow was exactly right, and Ariel would return to Norseland once he had done with the west coast, to wait until he futuretold that I was ready for the final stage of my quest. Then what? Did he plan to capture me then or simply follow me to the weaponmachines so he could snatch victory from my hands?

What did not fit was that at least one of the remaining clues was on the west coast, and though Ariel need not know it, he must know it might be possible. Yet he was willing to spread a deadly plague. Did he know that my body's capacity to heal itself could survive even exposure to a deadly sickness, or had he reasoned that once the last plague victim died on the west coast, the plague itself would die?

Suddenly Yarrow stiffened, and seeing his absorbed expression, I waited impatiently for his eyes to clear, my heart sinking at the grim expression on his face.

"That was Tomrick. He says that Harwood farsent him," he said at last. "Colwyn and Hilder are trapped with the Hedra. Harwood wants all of us to come now, and we are to bring Zuria and Mendi."

❖ ❖ ❖

Less than half an hour passed before Geratty, Reuvan, Yarrow, and I approached the dye works where Harwood had bidden us meet him, having left Asra to watch over the shadows, the Hedra guards, Falc, and the One. Cinda and two other shadows had accompanied us, bearing lanterns for pretense more than need.

Harwood looked pale and grim as he ushered us through the door of the dye works and closed it behind us. A row of Herders tied up along the wall glared at us, watched by a composed Ode and a little cluster of frightened-looking shadows hovering in the back of the large room. Cinda went to greet them as Harwood explained that he had taken over the place, because we would draw attention if we were all standing out in the open.

"You did not coerce them?" I nodded to the bound priests.

"I did not want to waste my energy, for we may need it," Harwood said.

"How were Colwyn and Hilder caught?" I asked.

Harwood shook his head. "I did not say they were caught. They are *trapped*. About two hours ago, one of the shadows came to us to say that a group of shadows had locked a Herder in a cellar. He had been beating one of them, and instead of standing back and watching as they would normally, the shadows attacked him. Fortunately, they had the sense to send to us for help. Ode and I came to sort it out. I coerced the Hedra to believe he had fallen down some stairs and sent Ode to take him and Grisyl to Sover while I calmed the shadows. I was growing concerned about Colwyn, because I had not been able to reach him since I had sent him to

385

investigate the armory. So when Hilder farsought me to say he might as well come down from the watch-hut because the mist made it impossible to see anything, I sent him to look for Colwyn. As I discovered later, Hilder found him still awaiting an opportunity to sneak across the Hedra yards to the armory. I had not been able to reach his mind, because he was too close to the tainted wall." Harwood sighed and said that before the two coercers could retreat, one of the Hedra captains spotted them and commanded them to take their places in the ranks for the evening exercises. They had no choice but to obey, for every Hedra in sight was streaming down to the exercise yard.

"I knew none of this yet, of course, because now I could not reach Hilder either," Harwood continued. Worried, he had gone close enough to the armory to discover that the wall was tainted, but there was no sign of either coercer. "Finally, I spotted Hilder going through an exercise movement with a vast troop of Hedra. I tried to reach his mind, but it was locked to me. It was the same with Colwyn."

"The Hedra must have been wearing demon bands," Yarrow said. "If there were enough—"

"No," Harwood interrupted. "In exercising together with such precision, concentrating their whole minds upon the synchronized movements of the rest, the Hedra create a group mind that is impenetrable save to one who would mesh with it. Colwyn and Hilder would have had no choice but to mesh."

Yarrow and Geratty looked horrified.

Harwood said heavily, "That is why I summoned all of you here. I want to get control of the armory tonight, and it might take all of us to break the group mind."

386

"But surely Colwyn and Hilder will be free as soon as the exercise ends?" Yarrow said.

"That is what I believe. If not, I will send Zuria in. I did not send for the rest of you to rescue them. I want to go ahead and penetrate the armory, but if something goes wrong, it may be that the Hedra will form a group mind when they fight. If that is so, I will need your help to break it."

"What is your plan?" Yarrow asked.

"We will wait until this exercise ends, in the hope that Hilder and Colwyn will be released. I should be able to reach them then, and I will send them to the armory to tell whoever is in charge that Zuria and Mendi are on their way to make an inspection at the One's behest. Soon after, we will march in with the Threes, and during our so-called inspection, we will coerce every Hedra we encounter until we have control. If at any point the Hedra form a group mind, we merge to crack it open."

"Who controls the Hedra group mind?" Yarrow asked.

"I have been thinking about that," Harwood said. "In an ordinary unconscious group mind, the group itself has a natural leader, but in the case of the Hedra, there is no central mind. That is what makes it impossible to probe. I think the group mind is actually centered on some sort of shared illusion of the Herder Lud, and the group does what it believes this Lud desires. Our one advantage is that the Hedra form this group mind unconsciously, so they are unaware of the advantage it gives them over us."

"What if you can't crack it?" Reuvan asked.

"Then we had better discover that sooner rather than later," Harwood said grimly.

I drew a deep breath and bade Geratty explain what had happened to the One. Harwood grimaced as Geratty told his story, and once it was concluded, he remarked almost sadly, "I thought we could take over this place as stealthily as beetles burrowing into wood and with as little bloodshed as when we took the Land from the Council. But it is the Herders we are dealing with, and the Faction traffics in death and brutality so readily that it is no wonder even the shadows have learned it." He glanced at a time candle he had set on the table. "According to the shadows, each set of exercises goes on for two hours, which means we have less than an hour to wait."

Harwood turned his attention to Yarrow, asking what had been happening on Fallo. The coercer explained all that he had told me and concluded, "Veril will farseek Tomrick as soon as he gets across the channel with the Norselanders, but given what the Per said, I doubt that will happen much before morning. Maybe it's just as well given what we are about to do."

Harwood nodded.

The others began to discuss the need to find somewhere to put prisoners, for we could not be forever rearranging the priests' memories, and unless deeply coerced, they had to be coerced again frequently. I left this to the others and wrapped myself in my cloak to sleep while I had the chance.

It seemed but a moment before Harwood was shaking me gently awake.

"I just spoke to Sover. He says the rumor you began is spreading like wildfire. Several Hedra have come to the healing center to ask if there is plague in the compound. Hard to believe a rumor could spread so swiftly from such a small event. It seems that the failure of any of the Threes to return to their cottages these last two nights is being seen as proof that something is wrong. I have told Sover he might as well put Grisyl into a bed and let it be known that he is ill, for it occurs to me that the rumor of sickness could serve us very well."

"The rumor of sickness was already established," I said. "Remember, Elkar told us he had heard talk that the Hedra aboard the *Orizon* had caught plague in the Land and that this was the real reason Salamander had sunk the ship."

Harwood opened his mouth to speak and then stiffened. A moment later he nodded and looked relieved, saying aloud, "That was Colwyn. He and Hilder are both fine, but they are being marched to a meal with the other Hedra. They will have to wait until after the meal to go to the armory." He fell silent again, and as I waited for him to finish communicating with Colwyn, I farsent Tomrick and bade him check how the One was. After farsending Asra, Tomrick reported that the One was still alive and that several shadows had come looking for Cinda, as had Elkar. "Asra said the lad insisted on knowing where Cinda was, so I told him you were in the dye works. He is like to be there any minute."

I withdrew and told Harwood what I had learned. He nodded, but I could see that he was preoccupied. When I asked what troubled him, he said that he thought we should use the enforced wait to search Ariel's chambers, given that they were so near the dye works. We quickly decided that he and I would go alone. Yarrow was left in charge and, in case anything went wrong, was bidden to take the armory as planned.

"Do you expect anything to go wrong?" I asked as we left the dye house.

Before he could answer, a figure emerged from the thick misty darkness, but it was only Elkar. Once he heard what we intended, he insisted that he lead the way, for Ariel's chambers were *through* the labyrinthine library. He also insisted that Harwood wear the cloak of an ordinary priest, for Hedra never went to the library. Once the dye-works master had been divested of his cloak, we set off again.

The lanes and streets we passed along were thick with mist and very dark, but Elkar now carried the lantern I had been carrying, having pointed out that no Herder priest of rank would do such a thing. Glancing at the stark black stone buildings on either side of us, I marveled aloud that anyone would deliberately create such a dreary place to live. The mist was so thick, muffling even the noise of our steps, that I had no fear of speaking aloud. "Do these priests think their Lud dislikes beauty as well as women?"

Elkar gave me a quizzical look and answered softly, "My master would say that a woman's beauty is an illusion."

"Is the beauty of a tree also an illusion, then?"

"I do not think that Lud objects to trees," Elkar said. "It is only that trees will not grow here, nor any flower or plant or lichen."

"But what of the walled garden if the land is so barren?" I asked.

"It is barren, save for the earth behind that wall," Elkar insisted. "It was many years before I was born, but the One commanded a garden to be created to honor Lud, so earth was brought from Norseland to allow things to grow."

I gaped at him, unable to imagine how much earth would need to have been shipped to Herder Isle from Norseland to allow *trees* to grow.

"Here," said Elkar, gesturing to an open gateway in a wall. Beyond was a cobbled yard swathed in mist. "The library is on the other side of that yard," whispered the novice. "There are no guards outside."

We went through the gate with some trepidation, but as Elkar had said, there were no guards at the entrance to the large library building. But after we had entered the doors, two young Hedra stepped forward. Elkar nodded to them familiarly, introducing Harwood and myself as his master's new assistants, and they moved aside to let us enter. In a moment, we had passed out of their sight. Almost at once we came to shelves full of books separated by narrow aisles. Interspersed between them were tables where priests sat poring over tomes and making crabbed notes, lanterns pulled close to their elbows. I tried to look studious, though Elkar had promised they would pay no heed to us, as long as we did nothing to draw their attention.

We passed through two more chambers and then came through a door to a small courtyard. From the smell of it, there were privies here, but Elkar indicated a door set into a wall on the opposite side of the yard, saying this was the entrance to Ariel's chambers.

The door was locked and a taint emanated from it, strong enough to make it hard to focus my mind as I laid my hands over the lock and closed my eyes. The mechanism was so astonishingly complex that it could only have come from the Beforetime. I took a deep breath and concentrated all of my will on it. Then I stepped back, the cold chill of premonition touching my heart. My mind had shown me that anyone opening the lock without a key would set off a small explosive device. It was so small that I doubted it would have force enough to break the door down, yet the premonition of danger had been so strong that nothing would bring me to try disarming the lock.

"What is it?" Harwood asked.

My mouth was so dry that I had trouble speaking. "No one must touch this door," I said. "There is . . . some terrible danger here."

"You had a premonition?" Harwood guessed.

I nodded, and shivered. "No one must enter this chamber."

"Very well. Let us return to the others, then."

We had been gone scarcely a half hour, but by the time we got back to the dye works, Yarrow and the coercers had gone, taking Zuria and Mendi and leaving Cinda and the shadows to watch over the trussed and rather red-faced Herders. She explained that Yarrow had tried to reach us, and when he had failed, he had elected to go on with the plan, for Hilder and Colwyn had got away sooner than expected and had gone at once to the armory.

I bade the shadows loosen the Herders' gags slightly so the priests could breathe but to have a rock handy in case they tried anything. I spoke more as a warning to the Herders than as a direction to the shadows, until it occurred to me the women were all too likely to batter the priests' heads in, given what had happened to the One. I bade Elkar wait with them.

Outside, it was now raining, which dismayed me, because it would be impossible to farseek the others. It would also prevent Veril from farseeking Tomrick. He would have to come into the compound, and of course he would go first to the One's chamber. I regretted that I had not sent Elkar back there to wait, but it was too late to do so now. Harwood cursed the ill timing of the rain, but I said that although it was inconvenient, at least rain would ensure that no one would be outside, save those commanded to be there, so we likely would have an easier job ahead of us.

We spotted the end of the narrow path that ran between the walls surrounding the library yard and the inner-cadre garden; beyond lay the Hedra buildings. Someone reached out from a darkened doorway and caught my hand. I stifled a cry, for it was Yarrow, and pressed into the doorway behind him were Reuvan, Ode, Geratty, and Zuria, their faces slicked with rain.

"What is happening?" Harwood asked, wasting no time. He spoke aloud because the taint from the armory wall was strong enough to make farseeking impossible, even if it had not been raining.

"Hilder and Colwyn presented themselves at the armory gate and were taken to the Hedra master," Yarrow said.

"Did you say Hedra master?" I repeated.

He nodded. "It seems that he is one of seven Hedra generals who run the Hedra force, and from Zuria's memories, he is the most powerful, for he reports each new moon directly to the One. That means he will likely take this inspection by Zuria as interference at best and an insult at worst. We will need to be very careful how we proceed, especially if even a lesser number of Hedra can form this group mind outside of an exercise."

Harwood said, "It is a great pity we cannot reach Hilder or Colwyn to find out how they have been received by this general."

"Colwyn did send a mental picture of the yard," Yarrow said, and both Harwood and I reached out to make physical contact so we could take it from his mind. I saw a dark rain-swept yard paved in black cobbles and a single blocklike building set against the outer wall of the compound. Before its two huge metal doors stood ten armed Hedra.

"It seems small for an armory," Harwood muttered.

"A lot of protection for seemingly little," I said.

"Therefore, there must be more than there seems," Harwood added.

"There might be levels underground," Reuvan suggested.

"Let's find out," Harwood said.

"Who goes there?" demanded the Hedra at the armory gate, his bald head gleaming wetly in the light of the lantern he carried.

Zuria stepped forward as he had been coerced to do and asked sharply if the two Hedra sent ahead had not arrived to announce him. "If they have not delivered my message, I will have them confined in the tidal cells," he snapped.

The other Hedra made the throat-tapping gesture that we now understood denoted obedience and said that two Hedra had arrived a short time ago and had been taken to the Hedra master.

"And are two Threes to wait in the rain while two Hedra are questioned?" Zuria snarled.

"I am sorry, Master," said the first Hedra. "If you will accompany me, I will bring you to the Hedra master."

We followed him along the path, which ran to the right of the gates and along the inside of the armory wall to a barracks built against it. I bit my lip, aware that being so near the tainted wall would prevent us from coercing anyone, including Zuria or Mendi. I moved close enough to make contact with Harwood and pointed this out. He said calmly that he had anticipated it and had already given both Threes their instructions. Moreover, he would stay close enough to both to be able to make contact.

I nodded and, falling behind again, glanced across the wet cobbles at the lantern-lit face of the armory with its phalanx of guards. It looked bigger than it had in Yarrow's memory vision, but even so, it was smaller than I would have expected, given the number of Hedra warriors. Reuvan might be right about levels underground, but how many could there be in such a flat island?

The two Hedra on duty at the barracks door snapped to attention as we approached and stepped aside. The guard pushed open the door, and we followed him into a long, low room that was bare save for a battered-looking desk. Behind it sat a muscular man whose stiff bearing and frigid gray gaze reminded me chillingly of Malik. I had no doubt he was the Hedra master, for he emanated authority and his eyes were calculatingly intelligent.

The Hedra master's eyes turned to Zuria and

395

Mendi. "Masters Zuria and Mendi, as foretold," he said. He did not rise, and this calculated discourtesy seemed to confirm Yarrow's feeling that there was bad blood between the Hedra master and the Threes.

"As you have been informed, we have been sent by the One to inspect the armory, Master Hedra," Zuria said in his hard, clear voice. "Will you accompany us?"

The Hedra remained seated. Indeed, he sat back as if to make himself more comfortable and asked why the One had sent them to inspect the armory at such short notice.

"The One has experienced a vision that troubled him," Zuria said haughtily.

"What was the nature of this vision?" the Hedra asked.

"The One did not confide that to us, nor did we think it meet to question him about it," Mendi said reprovingly. "Shall we proceed? The One is impatient for an immediate report."

"Very well," the Hedra master said smoothly, at last rising to his feet. "When you return, I will accompany you in order to offer any additional information our illustrious One may need about the armory." It was not a question, and rather than waiting for a response, he led us into the rainy night.

"Where are the two men sent to inform you of our imminent arrival?" Zuria asked as we crossed the yard.

"The men you sent lacked proper discipline," the Hedra master said. "They need reminding of the standard expected of them. You may take Volent and Davil here in their place."

"I do not like the sound of that," Yarrow farsent,

having maneuverd himself close enough to touch my arm.

"Nor I," I sent. "See if you can make contact with any of the Hedra as we go out, to learn where Colwyn and Hilder are."

Within moments, we stood before the great metal doors, and the Hedra master commanded them to be opened. They were heavy enough that it took all ten men standing guard to open them—five to lift the great metal-shod bar and the rest to open one of the heavy doors.

We entered the cavernous darkness beyond and stood a moment in a slice of dim light that flowed through the open door. But even as the door was heaved closed, the Hedra master snapped his fingers, and the Hedra Davil opened the flaps on his lantern. The glow that flowed out seemed to move slowly, as if the darkness resisted or had some heavier form than ordinary air. Gradually, I saw that we were in a big square room rimmed with doors; here and there, instead of a door, a narrow set of steps rose sideways to a second tier and then to a third tier of doors that ran just under the ceiling. They were all low doors and the tiers narrow, but it was an ingenious design that made much of little.

"What do you wish to see?" the Hedra master asked. There was a thread of mockery in his tone.

"Everything," Zuria said.

The first several doors led to long narrow cells lined with shelves piled high with the metal-shod poles favored by the warrior priests. The next contained short swords and another daggers. There were enough for five hundred men but not more. Of course, double that many had been taken for the invasion. There were also metal shields, though I had seldom seen those used. The Hedra master said in the same amused tone that the poles were conveniently placed on the lowest tier, because they were used constantly in training exercises. Zuria observed that the swords and daggers had a shine that made them look fresh-honed, and the Herder master said they were indeed, for each man was responsible for the weapon he used, and all were inspected before their return to the armory. Anyone whose weapon was not spotless and well sharpened was like to find himself in the tidal cells.

"We believe that all activities are a preparation for Lud's holy war to come; therefore, every activity must be undertaken with discipline and resolution." His voice had taken on a lecturing tone as he led us to another door and snapped his fingers for another of the Hedra with us to open it.

This one and the rest along the left wall contained demon bands, but there were a good many empty shelves here.

"The store is much depleted," Zuria observed.

The Hedra master gave him a narrow look, which reminded me that I could probe him now that we were out of the rain and shielded from the wall's taint. I shaped a probe, but before I could assay it, Yarrow plowed into my mind to stop me, for both the Hedra master and Davil were mind-sensitives. Unless great care was taken, they would know if anyone probed them and would command the other Hedra to capture or kill us. Relieved to have been stopped in time, I thanked Yarrow for the warning and bade him, Geratty, and Asra coerce two apiece of the Hedra who were escorting us. I would do the same to another two so we would have them on our side when we returned.

The Hedra master gestured at the doors along the rear of the room and Davil and the other men opened them to reveal hundreds of barrels like those I had seen in the minds of Vos's armsmen in Saithwold. It was no surprise when the Hedra master announced that they were filled with black powder. What did surprise me was the Hedra master's casual mention that after Salamander's next trip to the Red Queen's land, they would have even more barrels and a supply of fist-sized compacted powder balls that, when dipped in liquid whitestick, would explode on impact. Davil added enthusiastically that the balls could be fired by catapult or slingshot or even hurled by hand.

The chambers all along the right side of the room contained amphoras of something the Hedra master called *honey fire*. The mind of the Hedra I had entered told me that it was a liquid that stuck like honey to skin and would burn the flesh like acid. I was sickened to catch a fleeting memory vision of the honey fire being tested on two hapless Norselanders.

"It is only a pity this is too volatile to be shipped by sea," said the Hedra master. "Next time we must ensure that we have the makings of it sent to the Land to be concocted."

On the next level, we were shown a room full of small black metal objects that were made to fit comfortably in the hand and which had a protruding metal tube. I had no idea what the devices were, but they had a Beforetime look. The Hedra master lifted one and explained that they had been a recent gift to the armory from Ariel. Realizing we were not expected to know what the devices did, I prompted Zuria to ask. The Hedra master readily explained that each device possessed the capacity to spit out small darts of metal at great and killing speed. I was not much impressed by them, for what harm could a dart small enough to pass through the tiny hole in the tube of the device do? Especially given that, from what was said, Ariel had not been able to explain how the devices could be made to work. But Davil put in with an enthusiasm almost equal to his master's that even now scholars in the library were researching Beforetime texts to learn the device's secret. It was hoped that these, too, would be ready for the next invasion.

"Where were they found?" Zuria asked, this time at Harwood's behest.

"You will have to ask Master Ariel when he returns," the Hedra master answered, moving to the next cell.

"We have to take control now," I sent urgently to Harwood. "We may never get another chance like this."

"I know it," Harwood sent determinedly. "Get ready. I will deal with the Hedra master; Yarrow, you, and Geratty must overpower Davil. Reuvan, you and Ode will hang back and use the coerced Hedra to give help as it is needed." He stepped backward and turned smoothly, lifting his elbow and driving it into the Hedra master's gut—or he would have driven it in if the blow had connected. Instead, the Hedra master stepped back as if he had read Harwood's intention in his mind, lifting his hands to ward off the attack. But

Harwood had made his move so that the Hedra was very close to the edge, and he overbalanced and fell. Yarrow and several of the Hedra had leapt on Davil and were bearing him to the ground under their weight as Geratty drew out a dagger. Another Hedra was sprinting toward the door, and I realized that none of us had coerced him. I flung out a probe after him but was horrified to find he had been chewing spiceweed, so his mind was impenetrable.

"Reuvan! Ode!" I called. "Stop him! The door!"

They whirled and raced after the fleeing Hedra, who turned and drew twin swords, his eyes glittering in the guttering light of a lantern that had been dropped and smashed. Its oil was now spreading, and where it spread ran fire. Reuvan and the Hedra began to fight, and Ode stood by, ready to strike if they gave him the chance. They were right against the door, and I prayed it was too thick to allow anyone outside to hear the battle inside or to allow them to catch the smell of burning, for the flames were now licking up the open wooden door to one of the sword cells. Beams ran along the top of all the cell doors, and if these battles were not quickly concluded, we were like to have the place burning about us. A chill ran through me at the thought of those barrels of black powder, and who knew how the vile honey fire would act in heat.

Harwood and the Hedra master were fighting savagely, bare-handed. As I watched, the coercer executed a perfect turn, which ended in a savage gut-level kick that ought to have dropped the Hedra master. But again he swayed back from the strike, agile as a snake, and suddenly he stepped forward and struck a blow that took Harwood full in the face and sent him staggering sideways, blood gushing from his nose. In the hiatus, the Hedra master cast a devouring look around the armory, seeing Davil held by his own men while Yarrow bent over him, Geratty and the Hedra by the door, circling one another, and the other Hedra standing about, their faces blank. His face darkened with enraged comprehension and loathing.

"Mutants!" he bellowed.

Afraid that he would be heard through the door despite its thickness and the rain, I hurled a probe at his mind, only to find that, as sometimes happened with sensitive unTalents, his mind also possessed a natural shield.

"You see, filth," he snarled, turning to look at me. "Not all Hedra are weak and impure enough to allow your maggot minds to devour their will." Without warning, he turned and ran into one of the cells, slamming the door so hard after him that the outer bar fell into place.

"He locked himself in," Harwood said incredulously, mopping blood from his face.

"Your nose is broken," I said.

"Just bloodied," he answered impatiently. I was moving to the door, but the coercer caught my arm. "Let him stay there while we coerce the others. Reuvan and Ode, smother that fire."

It took us twenty minutes to issue instructions about what would happen when we left the armory; the air was acrid with the stench of the smothered fire. I was more than relieved to see it quenched, though the flames had gone nowhere near the black powder barrels.

Yarrow learned that Colwyn and Hilder were in a

402

shallow punishment cell under the barracks where we had met with the Hedra master, and I suggested we coerce Davil to go with him to release them when he left the armory. The Hedra master would come with us. His men had already heard him speak of accompanying Zuria to see the One.

"The only problem is that his mind is both sensitive and has a natural block, so we cannot make him behave normally," I said.

Harwood scowled, still wiping blood from his nose. "Then we will coerce these men into believing that a weapon he was demonstrating misfired and knocked him out. That will explain my nose. We will render him unconscious, and he will be taken to the healing center."

"What about just sayin' he took a fit an' collapsed?" Geratty suggested. "We can have one of his own men say he caught you in the face with a flailin' fist, and another one can say that their master was just yesterday speakin' to another Hedra who was taken to th' healing center suffering some sort of an attack."

"It would explain the smashed lantern and the fire," Reuvan said.

"It is a brilliant idea," I agreed, remembering how the notion of sickness had rattled the Hedra who had stopped me alongside the healing center.

"Very well," Harwood said. "Yarrow, you will take the coerced Hedra and their master to the healing center. Command some of the Hedra guarding the door to help you. Take him to Sover and explain what has happened. We need him to spread the rumor that the Hedra master is suffering from plague and must be isolated. Coerce the men who carry him to return to their barracks with reports of a fevered delirium and . . .

Well, ask Sover what other symptoms he might show if he had some sort of plague."

"The guildmistress and I will leave, ostensibly to report to the One with Zuria and Geratty. We will have Davil demand to come with us in his master's stead. Before he goes, he will command one of the other Hedra to take you, Geratty, to Colwyn and Hilder. Ode, you remain here. I will send in the Hedra who wait outside to close up the cells. Coerce as many as you can and deepen the coercion when possible. Prepare one to send as a messenger if there is any trouble you cannot handle. Station yourself outside the door and let no one enter. Say it is the One's command. I will send relief when I can. Yarrow, when you have done with the healing center, come to the One's chamber. I want to plan how we will take the sector where the demon bands are made, for this night has shown me that, although it is my desire to proceed carefully, events might force our hand, and the Hedra must not have the chance to don demon bands. Any questions before we face the wolf in his den?" Harwood concluded.

There were none, and we set about opening the door to the chamber where the Hedra master was hiding. The falling bar had bent one of the hooks, so it was hard to raise, but once it was done, Harwood grasped the handle and flung open the cell door. To our astonishment, the cell was empty.

❖ 21 ❖

"HE HAS CONCEALED himself, the snake," Yarrow cried, but Geratty was already entering the chamber with another lantern. The cell was deep, and the shelves were piled with demon bands. I called out to Geratty to be careful, though in truth the natural block on the Hedra master's mind would make him as difficult to locate as if he had been demon-banded.

"He's nowt here," Geratty said.

"There must be a bolt-hole," Ode said.

"Or a tunnel out," Reuvan added. "Seems to me the Faction make tunnels wherever they go."

My heart began to hammer. "If you are right, the minute he gets out, he will alert the other Hedra to our presence, and they will go straight for the demon-band works."

"Here!" Geratty shouted suddenly, and we crowded in behind him to see the tunnel opening concealed in a fold in the wall. I looked into it and sent a probe after the Hedra master, but even if the stone had not blocked my way, I would have had little hope of touching his mind.

Geratty took a lantern and went into it. I swiftly probed the Threes, only to discover that they knew nothing of this tunnel. Gerraty returned and said to

Reuvan, "Seaman, ye've th' right of it. 'Tis a tunnel running inside the outer wall like that leadin' to the One's chamber, an' it may be just as lengthy."

"He must not warn the rest," I said. "Yarrow, you and Geratty go after him. He has a start on you, and we must not lengthen it."

They nodded, and Yarrow snatched up a fallen sword and hastened after Geratty, who had already gone into the tunnel.

I watched until their light vanished, and then I turned to Harwood. "We have to secure this place so the Hedra cannot get at the weapons, in case he does manage to set off an alarm."

"We are too few to secure it, given that we cannot reach past the armory wall to farseek help," Harwood said grimly. "We must destroy this place and as many weapons as we can. I had hoped to take this compound slowly and carefully, but it seems that events have decided the matter for themselves."

"All right," I said. As always in moments of high danger, my mind seemed to grow clearer and to work more swiftly. "We will use the black powder. If it is true that fire will run along it, we can lay a trail of it throughout this place, going into every weapon chamber at the front of the building. It will go to a pile of barrels set up near the front wall of the armory. That ought to be enough to prevent anyone being able to get into it. The powder trail must meander far enough that, once lit, it will be many minutes before it reaches its target. I suggest that once the trail is laid, you go back out into the yard with everyone save Zuria, Grisyl, and me. Have Davil explain that their master sent you all out so that he could show the Threes some new secret weapon. If anyone notices that Gerraty, Hilder, and I are missing, then you can say that we were needed.

"Harwood, let us say that you irritated the Hedra master, and he struck you. Have Davil confirm it and command you to go to the healing center. Then he can send Ode to find Colwyn and Hilder straightaway. They might be safe enough in a cellar chamber, but best if we can get them out of here, too. Reuvan must be dismissed and sent to his barracks, and he can slip away when he is outside the armory yard."

"What of you and the Threes?" Reuvan asked.

"I will remain to light the trail of black powder and take them with me into the tunnel. When the explosion happens, if Yarrow and Geratty manage to stop the Hedra master in time, we can spread the word that he, the Threes, and three Hedra were killed when he was showing them his new weapon."

There was no discussion, for there was no time. At any minute, one of the Hedra might enter with a message for his master. We piled three barrels of the black powder behind the door. Reuvan punched a hole in another with a dagger and rolled it hither and thither, leaving a thin trail that looked like black yarn. None of us knew how swiftly the flame would move or how much of an explosion would result. The others shut the cell doors save the one leading to the secret tunnel, for we did not want to risk a spark setting off the other barrels or the honey fire.

The moment we had finished, Harwood departed with Reuvan, Ode, and the coerced Hedra. I sent Grisyl and Zuria into the tunnel with a lantern, snatched up a short sword left on the ground and a second lantern,

407

and followed them. I turned back and took a deep breath before hurling the lantern at the end of the black-powder trail. It flared and hissed like an angry viper, and then a thread of flame sped away.

I turned and bade the Threes run, and I ran after them. On and on we ran, and still there was no explosion. I began to worry that something had gone wrong. Perhaps there had been a small break in the trail of black powder that we had not noticed. Or maybe the Hedra had decided to enter before the thread of flame had reached the barrels and had managed to avert the armory's destruction.

All at once there was a deafening thump, and moments later, a wave of heat rushed after us. But we had come far enough that it did not singe us. We had barely slowed to a panting trot when there was another explosion. The ground shook so violently that all three of us were thrown to our knees, and the tunnel was filled with choking, blinding dust. Zuria's lantern was smashed and the flame snuffed out by the dust, so we groped along the tunnel in darkness. I wondered what had caused the second explosion. Then there came a third, which was the worst of all, and it made the heavy stone wall above us creak and shudder so alarmingly that I was terrified it would come down on us.

Knowing that the few barrels of black powder could not possibly have caused three separate explosions, I realized that the flames must have penetrated the thick cell doors, igniting the other barrels or maybe the honey fire. I could only pray that the others had got away in time. The delay had been long enough that I was sure Harwood and Reuvan had escaped, but what of Colwyn and Hilder, and Ode who had gone to find them?

I mastered my apprehension and farsought Geratty and Yarrow, but the passage curved to match the uneven edge of the island, putting too much stone between us. Or maybe they had already reached the end of the tunnel. I wondered uneasily where it came out, given that it was a secret known only to the Hedra master and his brothers. One thought that gave me pause was that it might end in Ariel's chamber, but by my calculation, we had long since passed that point. Indeed, it seemed we had walked the full length of the compound, but distances were always distorted when traveled in the dark and in panic.

The tunnel began slanting down very steeply, and soon it became steps. Then I saw the orange glow of firelight ahead. I coerced the Threes to wait and crept toward the door at the bottom of the steps.

What I saw when I looked out was like a nightmare. There was a vast cave of black stone with many openings going off in different directions. The tunnel had brought me inside the mine in the walled area at the end of the compound. The whole place was lit by a multitude of small greenish fires flickering on the surface of glimmering black puddles of liquid caught in depressions and cracks. I shuddered, for such witchfire burned on lakes and pools in the Blacklands. It seemed the mine suffered seepage from the black pool.

Then I saw the Hedra master not far away, talking to a group of Hedra. My heart plummeted at the sight of Geratty and Yarrow lying at his feet. At that distance, I could not tell if they were unconscious or dead, and when I tried probing one of the Hedra, the vibrating rejection told me he wore a demon band. It did not take long to learn that all wore demon bands. There must be a store kept in the mines or somewhere nearby. That meant the Hedra master had been outside already. But why come back here? Unless he intended to lead them along the wall tunnel to the armory, but no doubt he had heard the explosions. Indeed, there could be no one in the entire compound who had not heard.

I wished I could hear his plans, but the Hedra master suddenly turned to head up one of the winding tracks on the mine's far side. All the Hedra followed, and the last two heaved up Yarrow and slung him between them. This must mean he lived, but Geratty they left lying there, and tears blurred my eyes at the knowledge that he was dead.

You sent him to his death, a cold voice told me.

I gritted my teeth and forced back guilt, knowing that I must get out into the open air to farseek Harwood and let him know that the Hedra master was at large in the compound with a group of demon-banded Hedra. I must also warn Asra of what had happened, for it was likely that the Hedra master would go to the One's chamber. My only hope was that Cinda had been right in thinking that none, save the shadows, Falc, and the Threes, knew of the stair leading from the laundry to the One's chambers, for that would mean they would have to take the long wall passage.

The instant the Hedra vanished, I burst out of the tunnel and ran to Geratty. He was not dead, but his face was a mask of blood, and there was a terrible wound in his chest. His eyes opened when I touched his face.

". . . uildmistress," he gurgled, and blood bubbled crimson at his lips.

"I will get help," I said.

"No . . . use," he rasped. "Bastard ran me through . . .

Help . . . Yarrow." His eyes widened, and I realized he was looking at something behind and above me!

I rolled to one side and rose, lifting the point of my short sword and blinking tears from my eyes. But the man facing me was no Hedra, despite him being bald. He was unarmed. Indeed, he was near unclothed, such was the state of the rags hanging from his filthy, emaciated limbs. His eyes were a startling blue in his pallid, withered face, and there was astonishment in them.

"You can talk," he rasped. "I have not heard the voice of a woman in twenty years."

I forced myself to relax, though my heart was still thudding wildly, for he must be one of the mine shadows Cinda had spoken about. No wonder there had been pity in her eyes.

"I must see to my friend," I told him somewhat breathlessly, but when I knelt again beside Geratty, I saw that the life had gone from his eyes. Swallowing sorrow, I reached out to gently close his lids.

"He is dead. He is lucky," creaked the shadow almost reverently. He muttered something else, but I scarcely heard him, for now I saw that other mine shadows were emerging from dozens of crevices and openings in the mine's walls, creeping and hobbling over the rough floor, edging round the fiery pools, their faces gaunt and filthy. All were bald and most had weeping sores over their bodies, crusted with black filth. Their collective stench as they gathered about me turned my stomach, but I suppressed revulsion and fear. I could see that they had neither the strength nor the will to harm me.

The first man who had come reached out to touch my hair, but when I turned to scowl at him, he cringed back so pitifully that my brief anger faded.

"My friends and I are enemies of the priests," I told them. "We have invaded the compound, and we are trying to take control here. If we succeed, you will be free to leave this place and go where you will."

I saw only incomprehension in their faces and knew I was wasting precious time. I pushed through them, but even as I looked for the path taken by the Hedra, I realized there were numerous twisting paths leading to many openings in the mine's sloping side, and I had no way of knowing which one was a tunnel that would lead outside. I turned back to the growing crowd of skeletal men gazing up at me.

"Please, show me the way out," I urged them.

This seemed to penetrate their fogged minds, but they only goggled and muttered at one another.

"They won't," said the clear piping voice of a child. I looked down and all but gaped to see a small boy of about five gazing up at me from beside the blue-eyed man. He was very thin and bald like the shadow men, but his eyes were bright with intelligence.

"Why won't they help me?" I asked him gently.

"They are afraid of going out lest they be chosen for the black pool," said the boy.

The men crooned and rocked and tried to draw the boy into their midst, but I knelt and looked into his eyes. "How does a child come to be here?"

"My mother was a shadow. My father brought me here when she died bearing me. He is an acolyte. The shadows say he wept. They have looked after me and hidden me from the Hedra since I was a baby. When I am old enough, I am to become a novice so I can change things, but I do not want to be a priest."

"You must," croaked one of the shadows. "There is only that or this."

"I would rather stay here with you and Colyn, Terka."

"You will die if you stay here," said the shadow he had spoken to. "The mine is poisoned by the black pool. . . ."

"Look," I interrupted. "I am sorry, but those Hedra who left are going to kill my friends, and I need to get out of the mine to warn them. Come with me!"

The shadows recoiled.

"I will show you the way out," offered the boy solemnly.

The shadows moaned and fretted, hissing and rustling, and the boy turned to assure them that he would soon return, but they shook their heads and wrung their hands, and I saw that Terka was weeping. I realized that their concern for the boy had roused their wits, though his will was clearly more robust than theirs.

"I will make sure he comes to no harm for helping me," I promised them, grimly aware that I might not be able to keep my vow beyond the next half hour. I asked if they would sit vigil over my companion. Then I pointed to the opening to the wall tunnel and asked if they would bind up the two men they would find waiting there. This request seemed to cause the mine shadows some consternation, but I could waste no more time, and I urged the boy to lead me out.

He set off up one of the paths and I followed. The boy climbed more slowly than I liked, but for all his eagerness to help, he was not strong or in good health. My heart twisted with pity at the thought of his life, but

413

I resisted the urge to question him further, because it would slow him.

At last we approached an opening. As we entered, fresh air brushed my cheeks. The boy felt it, too, and would have spoken, but I shook my head and mimed that we must be silent. But the boy whispered with certainty that warrior priests never stayed long within the wall surrounding the mine and the black pool. They came only to administer punishments or to usher in the female shadows, who brought food and carried away brown rock from the mine, or to collect crates of demon bands. Then they departed, locking the gate behind them and leaving a guard outside. The boy added that the Hedra had been in the middle of choosing those to be punished when the Hedra master had burst from the forbidden tunnel.

"What happens to those who are punished?" I asked, wondering what could be punishment to the poor wretches condemned to work the tainted mine. More than half of my attention strained toward the end of the tunnel, in case the boy was wrong about the Hedra leaving the sector.

"They are sent into the black pool to get stuff for the demon bands we make here," the boy said. "No one who does that lives long."

I shivered.

At last we reached the opening. It was night and there were no lanterns. To my dismay, I saw that it was still raining, which meant I could farseek no one. I crouched down in the tunnel opening, squinting through the slanting rain, but it was too dark to see more than a stretch of broken ground dotted with muddy pools of water.

The boy pointed to the right and said the wall of the compound ran there, and along it was a room for the shadows to eat in and a long hall of beds. Then he pointed to the darkness in front of us, saying that the black pool was that way, and on the other side of it were the demon-band works. Last of all, he pointed to the left, explaining that the inner wall that surrounded the sector lay there, and if I felt my way along it, I would find the door to the rest of the compound.

"But it is locked," he said, adding that even if it were not, there was always a guard stationed outside. Still alert for any movement, I asked the boy his name.

"Terka and Colyn call me Mouse," he answered. "What is your name?"

"I am Elspeth," I said. "Tell me, when do the shadows bring food?" I prayed he would not say morning.

"I hope they bring it soon, for I am hungry," he answered wistfully. All at once, he seemed to grow uneasy. "I do not usually come outside until after the food has been brought, in case I am seen."

"You had better go back to the shadows, then, for they will be worried about you," I told him gently. "But I promise that all I told them was true. My friends and I are enemies of the Hedra, and if we can overcome them, all of you will be free."

The boy looked searchingly into my face. Then he said, "Will my father come for me?"

Before I could answer, another explosion rocked the ground, and a shower of small stones rained down on us. As I lifted my hands to shelter my head, Mouse leapt up and fled back down the mine. I did not try to stop him, knowing that, for now, he would be safer with his shadow protectors.

I made my way to the inner wall and felt along it, seeking the door. Just as I reached it, another explosion rocked the ground under my feet. My senses told me the explosions were coming from the direction of the armory, but I was terrified that it had not been destroyed and the Hedra were using the weapons there against Harwood and the others.

I heard the sound of voices raised in alarm. People were moving along the path on the other side of the wall. If only the rain would stop, I might have coerced their help. As it was, I pressed myself against the wall and listened to find out what was happening, but the noise of the rain defeated me. When the voices had gone, I examined the door. It was a great heavy slab of wood encased in metal and locked as the boy had warned. I laid my hands over the lock and concentrated hard to form a probe strong and delicate enough to manipulate the lock despite the rain. It was a simple enough mechanism but heavy, which meant it was likely to make a noise. I hesitated, picturing the Hedra outside, standing with his back to the door, his hand resting on the hilt of his sword. His attention would be focused on the explosions, and the rain noise was loud enough that he was unlikely to hear the tumblers turn in the lock, but the moment I opened the door, he would turn, and I had no doubt that he would be armed and demon-banded.

I licked my lips, telling myself that it would be sensible to wait until food was brought and deal with the guard when he was distracted. Except that while I waited, the Hedra master would be getting nearer the One's chamber, where Asra and the shadows waited, unaware of their danger.

I laid my hands over the lock. Moving the tumblers took a great deal of effort, and despite my care, there was a clicking sound. I flattened myself to the wall on the blind side of the door, in case the Hedra had heard it, but there was no mutter of puzzlement, and the door in the wall remained shut.

I drew my short sword, forcing myself to be calm. I did not often fight physically, but Gevan himself had taught me to do so, pronouncing me swift and strong. I reminded myself that, for all my dislike of it, I could fight. I took a deep breath and held it for a long moment to steady myself. Very slowly, I opened the door in the wall.

There was no one outside.

My mouth went dry with fear at the thought of the guard pressed to the wall, waiting for me with his sword drawn. It took all my courage to step out, only to find that the lane was truly empty. I took a long, shuddering breath, realizing that the Hedra master had probably taken the Hedra guard with him.

I set off at a splashing run along the path, visualizing the map as I wound my way back to the laundry in sector seven and blinking rain from my eyes. I heard another small explosion and then a great rumbling and cracking sound just as I reached the laundry yard. Suddenly Elkar stepped out in front of me, holding up a lantern he was half sheltering under a rain cloak. His face and neck were streaked with blood and his eyes were wild.

"We thought you were dead, lady!" he said in a shocked voice.

"What is happening?" I demanded.

"The armory blew up, along with most of the buildings in the Hedra sector and then the whole library.

417

Cinda and I were still in the dye works when it started but decided to come and see what was happening. Then the ground heaved, and the roof of the dye works fell in. The Herders we had tied up and the shadows inside were crushed under the rubble, as well as the Hedra."

"Ye gods," I said, horrified. "But where is Cinda?"

"She was hit by some falling stone. I wanted to bring her to the One's chamber, for I knew there was a healer tending the One, but then we saw the Hedra go in, so I had to take her away. I came back to see if I could find out what was happening."

My heart sank. "You saw the Hedra? They went this way?"

He nodded. I was aware of movement in the rainy darkness behind Elkar, just outside the range of his lantern. I lifted my sword.

"It is only some shadows," Elkar said. "But what happened?"

"There is no time to explain properly," I told him. "We set off the explosions, because the Hedra master escaped, and we dared not leave the way open to the armory. I came to warn Asra and the shadows that the Hedra master is like to come to the One's chamber." I thought for a moment and made up my mind. "I'll go up and see if I can hear what is happening. Send the shadows away and wait for me." I left him without waiting for an answer and crept across the laundry yard to weave through the sodden robes hanging on the lines. Inside the laundry, there were only empty boilers, and I realized the Hedra master would have seen no need to leave anyone to keep watch. After all, who would they expect to be following them? He might think the rest of us had been killed in the explosions. I cracked the door open to make sure there was no guard within the stairwell, and then I ghosted up and laid my hand on the door to the bathing room. It gave way with a slight creak that set my pulse racing, but the bathing chamber lay in darkness. I opened the door wider and saw light slanting through from the dressing room.

". . . forget the Threes." It was the voice of the Hedra master. "They are in the power of the mutants, as are some of our own men," he went on in his cold hard voice. "We cannot rely upon anyone until they have been demon-banded. That is why we must have more bands."

"But the armory has been destroyed, you said, and we took all they had in the demon-band works."

"Yes, but there are three crates of demon bands in sector three waiting to be taken to the west coast. I sent Gorlot and Neel to get a crate each as we were coming here. Once we have them, we will distribute them through the compound. Any Hedra who even hesitates to put one on is to be run through. . . ."

"If only we had the fire-throwers," said another voice.

"The mutants must have come across on the *Stormdancer*, so there cannot be many of them," the Hedra master said. "They will pay for the damage they have done here. I will peel the flesh from their bones as they live and then cook it and feed it to them for what they have done to the One. A pity the shadows who aided them had no tongues to talk. See if you can rouse the mutant. I wish to question him to see if he has any idea where his herd has gone to ground."

I clenched my teeth, realizing he might mean Yarrow or Asra. I tried to reach either of their minds, but to no avail. Either they had both been demon-banded, or they were unconscious. I closed the door carefully and went down the stairs. Elkar was waiting in the laundry, and I stifled an angry reminder that I had bidden him to wait outside and told him what I had overheard. "I want you to go in all haste to the healing center. If Harwood lives, he will be there. If not, then speak to Sover. Tell him all that has happened and bid him gather those who can fight and come here to aid me. The Hedra master must not leave this place and alert the rest of the Hedra. Bid Sover also send a force of coerced Hedra to blockade the tunnel in the wall, in case he and his men flee that way. But he must hurry. Tell him also that the Hedra captain has sent two men to sector three, where there is a small supply of demon bands. I will remain here and keep watch, but if they leave, there will be nothing I can do save follow them. Can you remember all that?"

He nodded. "But I can get help—"

"There is no time for talk," I snapped. "Go now and do as I have told you."

He turned and hurried away, and I went back up the stairs.

Asra screamed.

I clenched my jaw so hard that my teeth ached, but I could do nothing to help him. If I ran in wielding my sword, I would be killed or taken prisoner. I was about to enter the coercer's mind to see if he had noted any weakness I could exploit among the Hedra, when I heard a movement behind me. I turned, half expecting to see Elkar, but it was one of the shadows.

"What are you doing?" I whispered, going into the stairwell and closing the door behind me. "Don't you know that the Hedra might come down at any moment and you will be killed?"

"They cannot kill all of us," she said quietly. Then she looked behind her, and I saw more shadows crowding into the stairwell. I gestured urgently for them to go back to the laundry and followed them to make sure they went.

Once in the laundry, I was astonished by how many shadows stood pressed between the boilers, and by the look of it, more were arriving every moment. "Who sent you?" I demanded.

"We are done with being sent," said the shadow who had come up the stairs. "When we heard the explosions, we knew it was time to fight."

I stared at them helplessly, for though there were at least a hundred of them, they were all thin and undernourished; not one of them carried a weapon. I opened my mouth to tell them not to be fools when it hit me with the force of a blow that I was the fool, an arrogant fool. Here were grown women who had been brutally enslaved from childhood. Now they had the chance to fight for their freedom, and they wished to do so. Who was I to forbid it?

I drew a deep breath. "All right. If you would fight, then listen to me." I told them what had happened at the armory and about the Hedra master, and I told them of Sover in the healing center, and of the crippled ship that must be repaired and sent to the west coast. Some of them knew some of it, but I kept my explanation terse, my neck prickling the whole time with the feeling that the Hedra master was descending the stairs. Last of all, I spoke of the shadows I thought had been murdered by the Hedra and of Geratty and

Yarrow, who were their prisoners. Finally, I told them what I had asked Elkar to do.

"And what are we to do?" asked the woman from the stairs. She had gray eyes and a determined look and tone.

"The Hedra master is waiting for some crates of demon bands, which will not come if Elkar has done what I asked. But sooner or later, he will grow impatient of waiting and come down here. There are thirty of them at least, and you know they are deadly and remorseless fighters. Therefore, if you would stand with me, you must find weapons. Go now as quickly as you can, and bring any other shadows who would fight for their freedom. Tell all who come to bring such weapons as they can find. Axes, stones, kitchen knives, pieces of wood, brooms, and pokers. If there are enough, it might turn the Hedra back the other way. They will not know it is closed to them, and with luck, before they return, there will be others to aid us."

I thought there might be questions, but the shadows were accustomed to obedience. With a shudder of movement, all the black-clad girls and women turned and melted away into the rainy dark of the yard with as little noise as leaves blown before the wind. The woman from the stairs remained, and I asked her name.

"I am Ursa, and we are sisters henceforth," she answered.

"I am Elspeth Gordie," I told her. "And it seems we are to play the waiting game together." But then I froze, for *I could hear the sound of boots on the steps.*

"What would you have me do?" asked Ursa. Fear shone in her eyes, but she did not run.

"We ought to hide, but if we do, they will escape.

422

We must try to delay them, but this will be a deadly game."

I turned and backed away from the door until I stood beside Ursa, then I drew the sword I had sheathed. A moment later, the door to the secret stair flew open, and the Hedra master and his men came out. They did not see us at once, for it was dark and we carried no lanterns, unlike the Hedra. But when one spotted us, the silence spread swiftly until all stopped and stared. I was horrified to see that there were closer to forty than thirty. All were demon-banded, and there might as well have been a thousand for all the chance we stood against them.

Yet I spoke in a voice that rang with false confidence. "Give up your weapons, Hedra, for your corrupt Faction breathes its last breath. My people have control of your companions and your masters, and the shadows and many of your novices stand with us willingly. Now is the time to surrender this compound while you can." The insanity of two women demanding surrender clearly unnerved some of the Hedra, and I could almost hear some thinking that no one would make such a threat unless she could back it up.

"Foul mutant!" said the Hedra master. "Cursed of Lud."

"Curse your Lud and his bloodlust," I said savagely. "I am a Misfit, and I do not heed your god. And I wonder if he heeds you. For where was your Lud when we destroyed the armory? Did your Lud protect the One and the Threes from us? Now, your answer. Surrender at once and you will not die, though you will be judged and punished for all the evil you have done in the name of your Lud. Refuse, and you will fall."

"You will die in great pain and very slowly, mutant," said the Hedra master.

"If your Lud is so powerful, why does he need you?" I demanded, letting mockery tinge my words. "Why does he not strike me down himself?" I looked up. "Come, Lud of the Faction, strike me down for my insolence."

Some of the Hedra looked up, and others glared at me and muttered uneasily.

"He does not answer," I said mockingly. "Could it be that he does not exist? Or maybe he exists but is bored with your bloody prayers."

Several of the Hedra snarled curses and drew their swords. But the Hedra master turned his cold gaze on me. "You will die quite soon, mutant, and Lud will hurl you into the fiery pit of hell for your heresy. Before he does, you may dare to ask him why he chose the Hedra to do his will." He glanced at the big Hedra beside him. "Take them, Aleppo, but do not kill the mutant. I would teach her a long, complex song of pain to sing to Lud."

"What of the shadow?" asked the Hedra.

"Kill it," the Hedra master said indifferently.

"Run," I farsent to Ursa, but instead of obeying, she took up a boiler prod and stepped very deliberately in front of me. Oh, it was so gallant and foolish a gesture that it brought tears to my eyes. The Hedra master and his men gaped at the shadow in disbelief.

"Look well at her, brave strong warriors of Lud," I snarled. "Look at the face of courage, for you have never seen it when you look into the mirror."

One of the Hedra laughed, but his laughter dwindled and his face fell. He and the others were now staring beyond us. Wary of a trick, I flashed a look over my shoulder, only to see that the laundry and the yard beyond were filling with shadows. But they were not the shadows that I expected to see. They were the male shadows from the mine, and as they drew close, the light from the lanterns some of them carried revealed how pitifully thin and filthy their limbs were and made their hideous sores glisten horribly. They must have come through the door in the wall that I had not bothered to close. But how had they come here?

"Lady Elspeth, get out of the way!" Elkar called. The urgency in his voice made me obey, and I pulled Ursa back with me, but I lifted my sword in case any of the Hedra tried to seize us.

"Fools!" spat the Hedra master. "You are many, but you will fall before our swords like sheaves of wheat!"

"It is the Faction that will fall," rang out a new voice.

To my astonishment, the speaker was a tall, frail-looking Herder priest of middle years standing in the midst of the shadows. Elkar stood beside him, and between them was the little shadow boy, Mouse.

"Herder Sabatien, you are possessed by the mutants!" roared the Hedra master.

"No," said Sabatien in a measured voice. "I am no longer a priest. I am a Norselander again, and I am possessed by courage for the first time in my life. I stand with these men by choice, and I command you to lay down your weapons in surrender."

"You will die with this filth, traitor," hissed the Hedra master, and he took a step in the direction of the priest. But one of the shadows hurled something. I reared back, as did the Hedra, but instead of an explosion, there was a wet splat as it fell to the floor. Hedra and shadow alike stared, bemused, at the blackened rag lying on the ground, dribbling moisture.

"Mud will not save you," jeered one of the Hedra at last.

"No, but it will kill you if you do not surrender," rasped the man who had thrown it. I saw that it was Mouse's friend Terka, and now he held up his hand, revealing another sodden rag. The other shadows did the same, and I suddenly understood. I moved farther back, pulling Ursa with me. The movement caught the Hedra master's gray gaze. His eyes widened as he, too, understood.

"The cloths have all been dipped into the black pool!" Elkar shouted. "If you do not lay down your weapons at once, the shadows will throw the rags at you instead of the floor. You may then kill them, but look well as you do, for soon you will bear their same ghastly sores and disfigurements."

There was a long silence as the faces of the Hedra sagged with fear and indecision. They would have rushed us in a second if we had threatened them with swords, but faced with disfigurement, crippled limbs, and bleeding sores, they quailed. Perhaps it was merely that the ravaged shadows were the threat made real. One sword clattered to the ground, and though I could not see whose it was, it was the signal for more to fall until the Hedra master snarled at his men to hold.

"Do not be fools! They will kill us if we lay down our weapons," he bellowed.

"No," I said, stepping forward and keeping my voice calm. "That is the way of the Hedra. It is not our way. I told you. You will be judged and punished for what you have done, and in time, you will be given the chance to atone for the horrors you have committed. There may even come a day when you will bless this moment, for the life you have lived within these walls is bleak and loveless, though you cannot see it. Now choose. Throw aside your weapons and kneel if you would surrender."

Another silence, and then another sword fell and another. I felt a great welling of relief, but when the Hedra Aleppo dropped his sword, the Hedra master turned and clove open his chest in a swift flowing movement. Even as the Hedra toppled forward, life gushing darkly from him, his master spun and leapt back into the stairwell, barking orders for his men to follow. Many obeyed, perhaps as much from instinct as loyalty, and more might have followed, except another of the sodden rags was thrown. It flew high and landed against the side of the door, splattering the face of the Hedra about to pass through it. He gave a high-pitched, horrified scream and reeled back, throwing down his sword and clutching at his eyes.

That was the end of it. The rest threw down their swords and knelt.

The shadows surged forward to gather up the swords, and when I turned to Ursa to thank her for defending me, she threw her arms around me, weeping and laughing. I hugged her back and found myself weeping, too, wondering what had happened to cool, untouchable Elspeth Gordie.

"I wish I had been there," Harwood said later when I went to see him in his bed in the healing center. He had been injured badly in the second of the armory explosions, which had killed most of the Hedra. Fortunately, Reuvan had been behind the wall, which had shielded him, so he was untouched. He had managed to staunch Harwood's wounds and bring him to the healing center.

"I am only glad you are not dead!" I told him.

"I might as well be for all the use I am, lying here like a fool," Harwood fretted. "We have a long way to go before this place is secured. Sover said there are still Hedra who have some idea of what is happening, and they have demon bands."

"They are the pair sent by the Hedra master to get crates of demon bands. Unfortunately, they were not taken prisoner, and they have demon bands enough to hand out to at least a hundred men. But you can't do any fighting when you can't even sit up without feeling faint," I said. "Sover told me you had lost a lot of blood."

"I would worry less if your Hedra master would surrender," Harwood responded. "If only he did not have Yarrow and Asra as hostages."

"If wishes were fishes," I said more sharply than I had meant to, because I worried about the coercers, too, despite Sabatien's certainty that it was only a matter of time before everyone surrendered.

Harwood gave me a faint smile. "Gevan would be gratified to know that you have taken his pet sayings to heart."

"Gevan will be gratified if you would cease demanding to get up and relax and heal. Tomrick and Ode have coerced a veritable army of Hedra now, and Ode is ordering them hither and thither, warning the Herders of the plague-crazed Hedra who is setting off explosions within the compound and bidding them lock themselves up tight until he is caught. Tomrick, meanwhile, has coerced and chivvied the inner-cadre priests into agreeing to hide in the cells of the correction house where you found me, if you can believe that. And we have all the other Hedra generals well coerced. They are busy either hunting down their own men or cleaning up the rubble from the explosion under the supervision of a handful of novices and shadows."

Harwood sighed and lay back against his pillows, visibly relaxing. "I must say, I can't believe Elkar did not mention that one of his friends was a renegade Herder."

Elkar had told Sabatien about us, of course, and the Herder had counseled patience and watchfulness, feeling we were too few to truly take over the compound. He had instructed the novices to aid us as much as possible without endangering themselves, but neither Sabatien nor the novices had realized how strongly the shadows would react to the vision of freedom.

Sover entered with a Herder healer, and I shifted out of the way as Harwood's bandage was changed. Sover had told me that Reuvan had found Hilder carrying an unconscious and badly hurt Colwyn from a mess of rubble. Hilder had been in the midst of describing the collapse of the underground cell in which they had been confined for interrogation when another explosion sent a piece of stonework flying, killing him instantly.

Shocked at the suddenness of Hilder's death, Reuvan had shouldered Colwyn and carried him back to the healing center, where he now lay, still unconscious. Reuvan had gone out again to bring in Hilder's body and then again to look for me, Geratty, and Yarrow. I had met him on the way to the healing center after the defeat of the Herders in the laundry.

Looking back, I realized it had been madness to set fire to the armory, for we might have guessed one explosion would set off the rest of the black powder. It was only luck that we had not set off some truly dreadful Beforetime weapon, such as those with which the Herders had destroyed the city of Hevon.

Harwood was convinced that the many subsequent explosions were the result of the black-powder fire reaching hidden weapon caches within the wall tunnel I had taken to the mine. A small explosion in the wall tunnel near the library had set off the much larger explosion that destroyed the library and Ariel's chambers, and given my earlier premonition, neither of us had any doubt that Ariel's chambers lay at the heart of the explosion. Harwood thought that a cache of black powder or something more potent had been set to explode as soon as the chamber's door was forced; he had pointed out grimly that it was proof enough that Yarrow had been right in guessing Ariel had never intended to return to Herder Isle.

The earlier explosions had weakened the wall surrounding the compound, so when the library went up, a great wedge of the wall broke away and fell into the channel, forming a stone ford that had effectively reconnected the islands. When he had brought Cinda to the healing center, Elkar had told me that this fulfilled a legend that claimed the Norselanders would be free when the Girdle of the Goddess had been restored.

"I meant to ask, is the One dead?" Harwood inquired after Sover and the healer had gone.

"Sabatien thinks he is," I said. "He says that as far as he can make out, the One died after the Hedra master killed the healer tending him. But we will not know for sure until the Hedra master surrenders. Sabatien told him if he kills Asra or Yarrow, he and all of his men will be killed, but if he surrenders them, he and his men will be taken prisoner."

Harwood ran a hand through his hair. "What of those poor wretches from the mine?"

"The female shadows are moving those not too badly injured into the inner-cadre cottages in the walled garden. It is a good deal closer than the healing center. The rest are gradually being brought here on stretchers. Indeed, between the mine shadows and those hurt by the explosions, there is not an empty bed in the place."

We were silent a moment, and then Harwood said, "What news of the shipmaster?"

"Veril came in half an hour past to say that Helvar and the Norselanders had come across from Fallo. It seems they actually witnessed the fall of the compound's outer wall."

"That must have been a splendid sight," Harwood said. "What of the *Stormdancer*? How long will the repairs take?"

"Veril left the shipfolk as soon as they had crossed the channel," I said. "I sent Reuvan to assure the shipfolk that we have control here."

"So we do," Harwood said soberly. "Still, Geratty and Ode are dead, and Yarrow and Asra prisoners." He looked at me. "You ought to go down to the ship and talk to the shipmaster yourself."

"I mean to," I said. "I just wanted to see how you were first."

"What happened to Zuria and Grisyl?" Harwood asked as I rose.

"They were killed in the wall passage when it collapsed," I said.

Cinda followed me out into the passage, and I was about to bid her go and lie down when I noticed the fragile-looking Sabatien talking with Sover. Mouse was sound asleep on the older man's shoulder. I approached and asked for news of the Hedra master, but there was none.

Sover took the sleeping child from Sabatien, who said, "I will return soon. I just wanted to bring the boy to have his sores tended." He kissed the child's head tenderly and added, "His friend Terka is here. Put the child with him."

Sover carried the boy away, and I asked Sabatien, "He is your son?" He nodded. "He told me his father was an acolyte."

The older man sighed. "I was when he was born. You know, I have spent a lifetime creeping up the ranks of the Faction, hoping I would one day manage to change it, but you and your friends come here like a storm and scour the place out in mere days. I can hardly believe you have managed it, but I am more grateful than there are words to tell."

"It is not finished, and it was not only us," I said. "We could not have done it without Elkar and the other novices, and the shadows." I smiled at Cinda.

Sabatien's thin face grew sad. "The shadows," he murmured. "Some can never regain all that the Faction has taken from them, and yet who would have guessed there would be such ferocious courage in them? Yet was not my beloved Matty brave and strong? How she would have rejoiced to see her sisters rise up as they did." He sighed again and said he must go and try again to convince the Hedra master to surrender sooner rather than later.

"You think he will surrender?" I asked.

"What else? He knows it is only a matter of time before we send his own men against him. That we have not done so already is only because of his hostages, and your Asra is badly hurt."

"I wish to come with you," Cinda told me when I had taken my leave of Sabatien and Sover. I was going down to see to the *Stormdancer* and was about to suggest she wait until daylight, but then it struck me that this would be the first time she had been out of the compound in years. How should I tell her that she had better wait until the sun shone?

It was close to dawn, but still pitch black and raining hard as we stepped out of the healing center. Cinda volunteered to run back and get lanterns, but then we heard boots on the cobbles. My heart sped up as I turned, but it was only Elkar and several novices bearing lanterns and leading a hobbling line of mine shadows.

Seeing me, Elkar sent off the other novices. He spied Cinda. For a moment, he froze. Then he laughed aloud, took two steps toward her, and enclosed the startled shadow in an exuberant embrace. Cinda's face above his shoulder was suffused by delight as she hugged him back. It was all at once borne home to me how very much had been accomplished.

"Where are you going?" Elkar half shouted to be heard over the rain. She lifted her hands and her fingers flicked. Releasing the shadow but keeping his arm about her shoulders, he looked at me, and I said resignedly that he had better come with us since he had a lantern.

It was raining harder than ever by the time we reached the black gates, but there was no difficulty passing through, for the Hedra guards had been thoroughly coerced by now. The gates swung open, and as we passed out through them, it was hard for me to believe that only a few days had passed since I had been marched inside, and harder still to believe that we had accomplished so much, so quickly. But our victory was already eclipsed by my knowledge that, even now, the *Black Ship* might be sailing toward the west coast.

The Futuretell guildmistress, Maryon, had told me that I must travel to Sutrium to prevent trouble on the west coast, and I had wondered, leaving Obernewtyn, what she could mean. Now I understood that I must find Ariel's plague null in time to prevent the west coast's destruction. I did not know how we were to find a single null, but I told myself that Maryon would not have sent me if there was no possibility of succeeding. I knew too well that even though the chance might be terribly small, still it must be taken. Time was of the essence now, and though the repair of the ship lay in the Norselanders' hands, its course would be of my choosing. I felt that Ariel would take the null to Morganna, Aborium, or Murmroth, because they were the largest and most populous of the west coast settlements. But we dared not neglect the smaller towns, because it would take twice as long to backtrack.

I fell twice in the dark and turned to ask Elkar to walk ahead with the lantern. At the sound of footsteps, I swung round and saw Reuvan coming toward me with a lantern. Beyond him, farther along the shore, I saw a dim shifting cluster of lights near the hull of the *Stormdancer.*

"Are you all right?" Reuvan said, clasping my arm.

"I am," I said. "Do the shipfolk know yet how long it will take to complete the repairs?" I asked.

"They are still assessing the damage." Reuvan's gaze slipped past me, and I glanced back to see Elkar smiling at Cinda over the glowing lantern, which she now held. But even as I watched, her smile faded as her gaze shifted beyond him to the dark, heaving waves now illuminated by the lantern light. She walked down the sand until a wave ran over her sandaled feet; then she stopped and gazed out. As we walked back to where Elkar stood watching her, I noticed that the rain was beginning to abate.

"She was six when she was brought to Herder Isle with her brother, and she remembers nothing of the journey but sickness and fear," Elkar murmured. "It is different for me. I was ten when the Herders came to the village on Fallo and took me. They said it was an honor, but I knew I would never see my mother or father again. I can hardly believe that we are free. I pray it is not a dream."

"If it is, then we are all dreaming it," Reuvan said gently, laying his hand on the boy's shoulder. "Come. Let us find out what Shipmaster Helvar has to say about the *Stormdancer,* for the tide is almost out."

Elkar went to take Cinda's hand and draw her away from the sea, and as we moved on, she lifted her fingers and moved them gracefully. He said, "She says it is hard to believe that so few could bring down the Herder Faction."

"We would never have managed it if we had been

attacking the compound from the outside," Reuvan said. "The Faction sets itself up to appear impregnable. That is a defense in itself, for if something appears impossible to break, then no one even tries. But that same appearance of invulnerability is a weakness if those maintaining it believe it, too. The Herders believed their compound was so fearsome that no one would dare enter it save those who had no choice, so they did not defend themselves within its embrace. In a way, taking over the compound has been like taking over the Land in the rebellion. The Councilmen had run things for so long, they could not imagine truly being challenged, yet most of the Council's power rested on our accepting that it could not be challenged."

"When you speak of it in that way, it seems that power is like some strange agreement between the oppressed and the oppressor," Elkar said.

Cinda lifted her hand, and as it flickered, Elkar translated. "She says that power is not a real thing, like a ship, but an idea. And only by accepting the idea do we make it real. She says that freedom is the same sort of thing—an idea that is nothing, until people believe in it enough to make it real."

I turned to look at the slight girl with faint wonder, aware that Reuvan was doing the same. Then I heard my name called and turned to see Lark running along the beach toward me, his face near split in two by his smile. "We saw the compound wall fall! I can hardly believe that you did it!"

I laughed. "I did not do it alone, and we have not completely won the day. But I don't think you need to fear being turned into a novice any longer. Now let me introduce you to my friends and fellow fighters. You have met Reuvan, I think, but here is Elkar, who has been a novice and is no longer, and Cinda who was once a shadow."

Lark looked with open curiosity at the older youth and then at Cinda beside him, her black hood slipped from her head to reveal the dark fuzz of hair above her thin, sweet face. Then his eyes returned to Elkar, and he asked, "You are a Norselander?"

"I am," Elkar answered with pride. They began to talk, and I left them to it and continued along the beach toward the cluster of lanterns. I recognized Oma among the men standing in a huddle talking, and when he caught sight of me, the scarred seaman strode over, grinning, and swiftly clasped my hand.

"I did not imagine we would see you again," he said, suddenly solemn.

"I did not imagine it either," I admitted. "I am glad we were both wrong."

Oma hailed Helvar, who was coming up the beach with a preoccupied look, and the shipmaster came to join us, smiling his welcome and laying a warm hand on my shoulder. "When I first heard your voice inside my head, I little thought how much of a change you would bring to us," he said. "We owe you much, for it seems as if you and your companions have freed us from the Faction's long tyranny."

"I am afraid there is still a good bit to do, for there are Hedra to be captured, and the Hedra master and some few of his men are barricaded inside the One's chambers with two of our people as hostages. But I think he will surrender in the end. I only hope it will be soon enough for my friends. But now comes a hard task, for you and your people must decide what to do with the Hedra and

Herders. Indeed, the sooner you can send some of your Pers up to the compound to take charge, the better. I suppose Reuvan spoke to you of Sabatien?"

The Norselander nodded.

"You must meet him and those novices who worked against their masters in secret so that together you may decide what will come next for Herder Isle."

"I would not usurp your place for the world, lady."

I laughed. "I am no more than a friend, Helvar. Indeed, with your help, I will soon depart."

He took my meaning at once and glanced toward the ghostly bulk of the *Stormdancer*. "Veril has told us of your need of our *Stormdancer* to seek this plague-bearing null, which the *Black Ship* will transport to the Westland. Of course, it will be at your disposal as soon as it is repaired."

"Do you know yet how long it will take?"

He sighed heavily, and my heart sank at his expression. "If the damage were no more than when we sailed into Hevon Bay, we could have patched the ship more easily. But we were not able to haul the ship onto the beach, so the damaged portion of the hull has been gnawed at by the currents, and the sea has filled its hold."

"How long?" I repeated.

"A sevenday at the least," Helvar said. "I am sorry."

◆ 22 ◆

THE RAIN CEASED, and the shipfolk began to make preparations to haul the *Stormdancer* higher up the beach once the tide rose, but I was shattered by the realization that nothing I could do would help the thousands on the west coast that would perish of plague. There was no question that Ariel would have left his null ashore to spread plague long before a sevenday passed. Despair extinguished all the joy I had felt upon overthrowing the Faction.

Leaving the others, I walked along the beach toward the mounded boulders where Lark had once bidden me hide. I sat on a smaller stone rising from the wet sand, trying to accept that it was no fault of mine or Maryon's that something had occurred to disrupt the future she had seen, in which I had the chance to stop the spread of the plague. Perhaps it was no more than the accidental damaging of the hull that had ended that possibility, and there was nothing I could have done to avert that.

So why did I feel as if I had failed?

I buried my head in my hands, unable to bear the thought of what was to come, and yet unable *not* to think of it either. There would be death on a scale unequaled since the Beforetimers had lived, for the last plague had killed only some of those who had contracted it. It had caused hundreds of deaths, and many more had been left scarred or permanently weakened, but the One had said this plague would be caught by everyone who came in contact with it, and all who caught it would die. *All.* And among the thousands of innocent people I did not know who would die were the few I did, those whose presence on the west coast was my doing: Merret, Blyss, Seely, Ode's sister, and all the others from Obernewtyn whom I had sent to the west coast. All of them would die because of me.

"It is not your fault," Reuvan said softly, kneeling beside the rock where I sat. He pressed a mug of something hot into my hands and wrapped a warm cloak around my shoulders, bidding me come back to the compound, for nothing could be done until the tide was right. Helvar wanted to meet Sabatien and speak of the future. "Come back with us, Guildmistress."

"I cannot feast and plan, knowing what is coming to the west coast," I said blackly.

"Drink something at least," Reuvan insisted, pushing the mug gently toward my mouth. I sipped a mouthful of the hot, spiced fement, because the effort of refusing was too great, but my teeth chattered against the rim. The fiery brew warmed the chill in my bones and gut, but it did not touch the ice that had formed about my heart. I could think of no words to say, so I drank until the mug was empty and handed it back to the seaman. I saw pity in his eyes and wondered why he would pity me. It was not I who faced death.

As if he had heard the thought, he said, "It is hardest when you can do nothing."

"Go with them," I said. "I need to be alone now, but I will return after a while."

"Very well," he sighed, and departed.

I sat for a long time staring blankly out to sea. My head was spinning slightly because of the fement, but I was only dimly aware of the others leaving. I was glad none of them came to talk to me, for I had no desire for conversation. It was not until my chin hit my chest that I woke up enough to realize I had fallen into a near stupor sitting there. I told myself that I ought to return to the compound and sleep rather than indulging in an orgy of pointless grief and guilt. But the effort of rising was beyond me.

If there had been a bed laid out beside me, I would have fallen gratefully into it. As it was, I was sitting upon a rock on a pale beach running down to a gray ruffled sea, with no idea how I was going to get myself anywhere. A delicate rosy light bloomed along the horizon, limning the crippled *Stormdancer*. A seam of dazzling silver opened along the horizon to allow the day to be born, and as the sun rose at last, streams of pale gold light pierced the thinning clouds to give a shimmering edge to the waves rolling in, and the mist wove a gauzy rainbow.

And quite suddenly, *I knew what I must do.*

I got to my feet, shrugging off both the cloak Reuvan had laid about my shoulders and the Herder robe I had worn, and I walked the few steps to the sea's edge. I slipped off my shoes and stepped into the waves. The water was very cold, but I went deeper until I felt it seeping through my clothes to touch my warm skin with icy fingers. I had to brace myself against the strong incoming tide to prevent being pushed back toward the shore. When at last my mouth was level with the water, I shouted aloud and inside my mind.

"Maruman!" I called as I had done before.

Nothing happened, and as I stood there waiting, all the fatigue I had shed seeped back into me, bringing with it leaden despair.

"Fool," I muttered.

A movement at the edge of my vision made me turn, and I was startled to see Cinda racing down the beach toward me, her black hood flung back, her eyes wide with alarm. She waved her arms wildly, and knowing she could not call out to me, I waded wearily back to shore.

"What is the matter?" I asked, and entered her mind so she could answer me.

"I kept thinking of you, alone here," she told me. "When my brother died, I blamed myself for surviving, but what could I have done to stop his death?" She looked out across the strait. "You must not blame yourself for what you cannot change." Her voice was kind but stern.

"I sent many of my friends to the west coast, and now they will die because they did what I asked. How should I not blame myself?"

The shadow did not answer, but after a long minute, she said, "I saw you go into the water. You went so purposefully that I . . . I thought . . ." She stopped, her face darkening in a blush.

"You thought I meant to drown myself?" I asked gently.

"There were times over the years when I wished I would die. After they cut out my tongue and when I learned of my brother's death. But if I died, I never would have met Elkar." She glanced toward the compound.

"He loves you," I said aloud.

She smiled.

"I was not trying to die. I sought to call a ship fish to me," I told her aloud. Because I had not withdrawn my probe, my emotions and thoughts were laid bare, and Cinda gasped at what she saw fleetingly in my mind.

"You can speak with the minds of ship fish?" she marveled.

"One saved me once, but I must have been mad to imagine I could call it to me here."

Cinda nodded, but all at once, her eyes widened, and she pointed back over my shoulder to the sea.

I turned to see a fin cleaving through the waves, and hope flowed through me like hot fement. Without hesitation, I ran back into the water. The fin vanished, and I stopped, confused. Then a silvery shining head emerged from the water in front of me. Trembling, I stretched out my hand, but the ship fish neither approached nor retreated. It waited, its liquid eyes fixed on me. I was but a finger length away when it surged forward, pressing its head to my palm. It was not Ari-roth.

"This one is Vlar-rei. Name of Ari-noor, podsister to Ari-roth. Come now and this one will bear she where she must go, Morred-a," the ship fish belled.

I turned back to where Cinda stood shivering at the water's edge and shouted, "She will bear me across the strait. It is the only chance we have of saving the west coast, and there is no time to waste. Tell the others. Bid them repair the *Stormdancer* and sail to Sutrium. Dardelan and the rebels must be warned not to cross the

Suggredoon until the next full moon, just in case I cannot stop the plague. Whatever happens will be over then."

Cinda wrung her hands and shook her head helplessly, but I threw my hand over the ship fish, taking care to avoid her blowhole. As she turned and began to swim strongly straight out to sea, I looked back and caught a glimpse of Cinda lifting a hand slowly. By the time I managed to get a better grip and lift my own hand, the girl was no more than a shadow on the sand.

Soon the cold I had experienced upon entering the water faded, along with my mind-numbing exhaustion. This told me that Ari-noor was feeding me spirit energy as her podsister had done.

"Morred-a is smaller than this one expected," she sang. Her tone and manner were more formal than Ari-roth's, but I had the same soothing sense of her gliding presence in my mind.

"Ari-roth spoke of me to you?" I asked.

"The waves know the name of Morred-a. It will be a long journey for she," Ari-noor sang enigmatically with several gloomy subnotes. "Longer than the journey with Ari-roth and longer than the journey made by the calf of Mornir-ma. Morred-a must not take shortsleep lest longsleep come. Must not let ohrana flow into dreamwaves. Morred-a must never, ever, let go of Ari-noor."

I tightened my grip and thought about what she had said.

By the "calf of Mornir-ma," she must mean Dragon, confirming once and for all that the red-haired waif had been brought to the Land by sea creatures after she and her mother had been stolen from the Red Land. And so

Mornir-ma must be a title given by the Vlar-rei to the Red Queens, or maybe to beastspeakers who could commune with them. But what had she meant by warning me against letting my ohrana flow into the dreamwaves? *Ohrana* was the name Ari-roth had used to describe her aura or spirit form, so dreamwaves might be the spirit form cast by the sea; after all, mountains, fire, and all manner of inanimate things cast spirit forms. If I was right, the ship fish had warned me not to let my spirit merge with the spirit of the waves. But that made no sense, for I would have to *assume* my spirit form even to see or be aware of the dreamwaves. Unless dreamwaves were more closely connected to the real sea than the dreamtrails were connected to real places on land.

A different thought occurred to me. If the dreamwaves were connected to the dreamtrails, it might be that Atthis was using the ship fish, just as she used land beasts, to protect and aid me. Yet it was hard to imagine a bird, even one as ancient and powerful as the Elder of the eldar, manipulating these strange fish.

A wave slapped me hard in the face, almost dislodging me, and I tightened my grip. Ari-noor had warned me sternly not to let go of her. I would certainly be left behind swiftly if I did so, for we were cleaving through the water at a far greater speed than Ari-roth had traveled. In truth, I did not see how the ship fish could maintain such a pace. But even if she slowed, I was sure that I would reach the west coast before Ariel's null had time to spread the plague. I had asked Ari-noor to take me to Murmroth landing, because it was closest to Herder Isle. I would have to travel by foot to the city, if the *Black Ship* had docked there. If not, I would acquire a horse and immediately ride toward Aborium. As soon as I was close enough, I would farseek the Beforetime ruins where Jak and Dell had intended to set up a refuge. Then I would have all the help I needed in locating the null.

Something in the waves ahead caught my eye, and I squinted until I was able to make out a fin cutting through the water toward us. At first I thought it another ship fish, but then a chill ran down my spine, for this was the squat black fin of a shark!

"Yes," Ari-noor sent calmly. "Many azahk are here. They will not harm she while our ohrana are connected. But if Morred-a lost hold of this one, even for a moment, the azahk would catch she in its teeth."

I tightened my grip convulsively. It was fortunate that I did, for suddenly we went from high swells to a great heaving and pulling and churning of white water that told me we had entered the strait's tempestuous central current. I knew that ships preferred to take a gradual diagonal bearing across the strait, partly to avoid the stress of the contrary currents on their ship and partly to avoid a series of long, wickedly sharp, mostly submerged shoals called *The Teeth*. I had supposed that Ari-noor would cut directly across the strait, weaving through the shoals as effortlessly as she had done through the waves, but to my disappointment, she turned into the current. Our passage became immediately smoother, and if anything, our speed increased, yet this new course would take longer, for by the time we left the central current, we would be well down the coast. The ship fish would have to turn and swim back up the coast to deliver me to Murmroth.

In addition, the shark was following us.

Gritting my teeth, I told myself resolutely that the

shark was the least of my worries, for Ari-noor was feeding me her energy, and as long as I held her, it would not attack. But my arms and back were already aching, and I had not even been in the water as long as I had when Ari-roth took me from the narrow inlet to the beach at Saithwold.

As the hours wore on, it was not the buffeting of the waves nor physical weariness that troubled me so much as the constant ominous presence of the sharks, for now there were three fins. Sometimes they circled us, as if to mock our slower progress; at other times, one would come near enough that I would see its blunt, pitted snout and blank, black eyes.

"Azahk ohrana is hungry," Ari-noor observed, but her mindvoice was serene. I took this as an indication that I was in no danger, though I could not help wondering how a hungry spirit could be fed by eating flesh.

"What ohrana desires, flesh does echo," Ari-noor sent imperturbably.

As if to underline her warning, a shark fin rose from the water so close to me that I could have stretched out my hand to touch it. I told myself that I was safe, but I also drew in my legs. After a long, anxious period, the fin turned and vanished beneath the waves' churning surface. In relief, I relaxed, and my grip loosened slightly. Ari-noor immediately belled a warning, so I locked my muscles, ignoring their aching protest.

Time passed, and I tried to converse with Ari-noor to distract myself from the thirst and monotony of the journey, but my attempts to engage her won only reluctant and monosyllabic responses. Despite looking similar to her podsister, she was more reserved than Ari-roth and held herself aloof in my mind.

447

There was no sight of the land on any side now, and I began to fancy the light had changed subtly. Surely it was afternoon. I prayed so, for although I had no more to do than hold tight to the ship fish and be carried to my destination, there was something in the relentless movement of the waves and my being saturated to the bone that made me feel as if the water was sloughing away layers of my spirit. I imagined dreamily that when the last shred of it was gone, I would let go of the ship fish and drift helplessly into the blue void until the waiting sharks bit into my sodden flesh and spongy bones.

"Do not sleep!" Ari-noor sent with surprising sharpness.

I jerked awake, horrified to realize that I had begun to drowse—doubly horrified, for close by, a fin cut through the water like a dark knife. The shark circled away and vanished, as before, and I wondered with an internal shiver if it had come closer because it had sensed that I was falling asleep. Despite the fright I had given myself, my eyes still felt heavy and my mind sluggish. I cursed my stupidity for sitting awake on the beach the previous night instead of sleeping. Yet how could I have known what awaited me?

I told myself that it mattered not if ignorance as much as courage had brought me into the strait, so long as I reached the west coast.

All I had to do was stay awake.

There was a low rumble of thunder, and I looked up, noting the dark, congested clouds overhead, and wondered what sort of storm was brewing. Aside from the danger of being struck by lightning, I welcomed the possibility of a storm, for surely there would be rain,

448

and the thirst of hours before had become a torment. The temptation to drink a mouthful of seawater was so compelling that I was frightened I might succumb.

"Do not drink," Ari-noor warned.

Desperately, I cast about for something to occupy my thoughts. Strangely, I found myself remembering the day I had ridden away from Obernewtyn. In retrospect, there had been a brightness to that day, although I had been in no mood to appreciate it. I had been so full of grief over my estrangement from Rushton and worry about Khuria's letters and Malik's trial that I had not properly appreciated the feel of Gahltha's warm faithful flesh moving under me and Maruman's softness about my neck and curving into my mind.

Then it occurred to me that I was guilty of doing exactly the same thing again. Only a few days past, I had believed that I would never see Maruman or Gahltha or Rushton again, for I had thought myself doomed to a horrible death at the hands of the Herders. Yet now that I knew that I *would* see them again, instead of rejoicing, I was full of self-pity. I felt a surge of disgust for myself and deliberately turned my thoughts to wondering if they had any idea of what had been happening to me. Atthis might have let Maruman know where I was, and the old cat would have let the others know through the beastspeakers. Or maybe not. Maruman was contrary and uninformative at the best of times, and he had been angry with me even before I abandoned him in Saithwold.

Maryon might also have dreamed of me and sent a messenger to Sutrium to let the others know what had happened. But how much could she have seen? Had she known that I would find myself trapped aboard a

Herder ship and taken to Herder Isle? I wondered what I would have done if Maryon had brought me into her high chamber in Obernewtyn's Futuretell wing to tell me all that would happen to me after I left the mountains. Would I have gone to Saithwold, knowing that Malik awaited me, even if I had known that his attempt to kill me would fail? And what of the tunnel under the cloister? Would I have taken that, knowing it would lead me to Herder Isle and into the hands of the Herders? And what lay at the end of this journey across the strait, which I had begun so impulsively?

"She mind swims in circles," Ari-noor sent soothingly. "Will the waves change because someone swims through them? What has happened has happened, and what will happen will happen."

Night fell subtly, for the storm that threatened all afternoon had not broken despite the sullen mutter of thunder. The clouds that had masked the sun now hid dusk and then the rising of moon and stars. Night gradually darkened from steel gray to black, and I scanned the sea in the distance, seeking the dull blurs of orange light that would denote land, though in my heart I knew it was too soon. By my reckoning, we were still moving along the strait and had yet to angle toward the shore and enter the coastal currents.

I turned my mind to what Elkar had told me when we had first arrived at the healing center after the confrontation with the Hedra master. He had managed to track down the novice who had seen Ariel's special nulls when he had been sent to deliver a message to the One's favorite. Ariel had just locked the door of his chambers, and he had two nulls with him. According to

450

the novice, one had been very small—a midget, he had supposed—until it looked at him, and he had seen that it was a child. It had been impossible to tell if it was a boy or a girl, because its head had been shaven like all nulls' heads, and its face had been horribly scarred. I doubted Ariel would give a child the responsibility of spreading his plague, because a child would be vulnerable and might come to harm before it had done his bidding. But the other null had been described as a grown man, sickly pale as one long imprisoned in a cell without fresh air or sunlight. I was certain he was the null I must seek. But when I learned where the null had gone ashore, I would concentrate my search not on him but on Ariel. Of course, he might not have accompanied the null ashore, but if it were safe to do so, he would be unable to resist the vicious pleasure of walking through a crowd and gloating over what awaited them. All I needed to do was to ask around until I found someone who had seen a fair, astonishingly handsome young man accompanied by a very pale, dark-haired man.

"Just as long as he is not in a cloister," I muttered.

A wave cuffed me hard, knocking the breath out of me. "Anything else?" I gasped wrathfully at the heavens. Another wave broke against me, and by the time I had finished coughing and choking out swallowed seawater, I had ceased thinking of Ariel and the null. The wind had been growing steadily, and it now howled overhead, whipping the waves into high peaks that broke over me until I feared I would drown clinging to the back of the ship fish. Ari-noor seemed unaffected, yet I was buffeted mercilessly by the sea, and every breath was a struggle. When I remembered my surrender to the waves in the narrow inlet, I relaxed, and at once I

451

became aware that a song throbbed in the air, made up of the sea's roar and hiss and the wind's howling. The strange, wild music had a rhythm, and Ari-noor's movements synchronized with it and were part of it. I thought of Powyrs, the shipmaster of *The Cutter*, telling me that the sea was too strong and vast to be fought. One must surrender to it. I thought I had surrendered to it in the narrow inlet, but I had only given up struggling against it. In order to hear the song of the waves, I began to understand that I had to give up singing my own song of fear first. Powyrs had called it *surrender*, but in truth he meant that one needed to cease one's own competing song. Only then could I listen to the song of the waves and become part of it as the ship fish did.

The sensation of being in tune with the vast, mysterious ocean was profoundly soothing, and the wild waves and the roar of the storm overhead and the dreadful thirst I felt were no less a part of it than Ari-noor. I thought of the mindstream that lay at the bottom of all minds, connecting us to one another and to the past and the future. Perhaps the sea and the creatures in it were closer than creatures of the land and air to that final merging of all life that was the end of individuality, which we humans called *death*.

I shivered, noting dimly that I was growing cold. Ari-noor had long since ceased to feed me from her ohrana. Indeed, she no longer scolded me or reminded me to keep hold or stay awake, and I could feel her fatigue. I had the feeling that if I let go of her, she would swim lightly on, hardly noticing that she had lost me. The thought no longer frightened me. Death, too, was part of the song of the waves. A serene fatalism possessed me.

I drifted, and while I did not sleep, sleep was no

longer separate from waking. Both states flowed through me, and my spirit become loose and free in my body, as if I need only lean over for it to pour out into the waves. Liquid into liquid. I felt no urge to pour myself into the sea but no fear of it either, and in that utterly passive state, I heard something. It was not music, yet it was; and it was not exactly sound, yet my spirit floating in my flesh heard it. It flowed through the water, wave after wave of exquisite sound. Swells and eddies and currents of sound that, incredibly, moved through me as if I were part of the sea, as if my flesh did not separate us. This was the wavesong that Ari-noor and Ari-roth had spoken of, I realized in wonderment. This was what sea beasts heard and what had carried the song of my need across time and space.

I floated for a long time, listening and feeling the wavesong before I understood that there was meaning in it. Not one single meaning but a thousand meanings flowing side by side. Not meaning that could be understood as words are, but meaning as music carries meaning. Even a musician without empathy can evoke anger or sorrow or fear with music, and this was like that, only a thousand times more complex. Eddies and rills and coils of meaning merged and flowed and seemed to change and develop, as if meaning communicated with meaning.

As I lost myself in the wavesong, I began to feel a warning or a foreboding of something immense and dark and utterly strange. I struggled to understand what it could be, but its meaning was too fluid. There was death in it.

Frightened, I asked Ari-noor what it was.

She made no response. I called again and realized

that I could not feel her in my mind. Unease flowed through me, thickening the fluid softness of my spirit, and as I became aware of my body—how cold and stiff it was—the wavesong faded.

Again I tried to farseek Ari-noor, and to my dismay, I discovered that she was *no longer with me*!

Panicking, I tread water and turned, seeking the sleek gray form of the ship fish, but if she was near I could not see her, for a thick, soft, blinding mist swirled above the waves. I called out her name again, mentally and aloud, but there was no response. Either she had been too weary to register my departure, or she had felt that my letting go severed the commitment she had made to bring me across the strait. Or perhaps in allowing the wavesong to enter me, she felt I had no more need of her.

Abruptly, I stopped splashing and shouting, aware that I was alone in the rain-swept sea and that sharks were probably scything through the waves, drawn by the discordant song of fear I had been emanating.

Something banged against my feet, and I would have screamed in fright if I had had any strength. A wave crashed over me, thrusting me downward with such force that it felt as if I had hit something solid. I thrashed my arms, desperate to reach the surface, and grazed my elbow. I imagined sharks seething in the water, snapping at my flailing limbs. I managed one breath of air before another wave pummeled me, this time sending me tumbling head over heels. Dizzy and confused, I was no longer sure which way was up or down. Again my elbow and then my knee struck something hard, and I realized I must have been washed into a shoal! I could be battered to pieces on the rocks just below the surface. Another wave lifted me and threw me down. My head struck something, and I dropped into blackness. I sank like a stone to the depths of my mind. The descent was so swift that I knew I would not be able to prevent myself from entering the mind-stream. Instead of feeling fear or desperation, my will dissolved and I ceased trying to slow my descent.

But I came to a sudden violent stop above the mind-stream. Stunned at how abruptly my fall had ended, it took me a moment to understand that some other will had stopped me. Only one will was powerful enough for such a thing.

"Atthis."

"Even *I* could not stop your fall alone," sent the Agyllian. "It took all of the eldar, and even we would have failed without your friends."

"My friends?" I echoed.

"The cat and the horse who are your protectors," Atthis said. "The dog Rasial and the funaga Gavryn, Swallow, and Maryon. They have agreed to let us draw on them."

My mind reeled at the names. "But . . . how?"

"I entered their dreams and summoned their aid. When they opened themselves to me, I drew on their spirits to strengthen our merge, just as the ship fish fed you their ohrana," Atthis answered.

"Then my friends know what has been happening to me?"

"No," Atthis answered. "They know only that ElspethInnle was in great danger of death and must be saved. I asked their aid, and they gave it. Now you must exert your own will and rise, for it drains all of us to hold you."

455

I tried to do as she bid me, but my mind was sodden and responded sluggishly. "I can't," I sent.

"You are hurt badly," Atthis said. "We have taught your body to heal itself, and it will begin to do so when you withdraw from the mindstream. This close, your body cannot heal. Draw back, and we will send help."

I strove again to focus my mind and rise. This time, I managed to withdraw from the mindstream a little, but I felt the strange, wrenching regret of leaving behind that inevitable final merging with all that had been and would be. I tried to throw off my regret by thinking of Maruman and Gahltha, strange Gavryn and the others, who had somehow allowed themselves to be used to save me. And I thought of Cinda and the little boy Mouse, who had endured such horrors, and their will and courage to go on living. Most of all, though, I thought of the west coast, that I alone had the chance to save. If I died, thousands would die of plague.

"If you perish, a world will die," Atthis sent. "All beasts and funaga and plants. All."

"If I live, I will save them?" I asked.

"You will try, and you may succeed," the Agyllian elder answered. "Now rise, for even augmented, our merge weakens."

I tried again to rise, but the mindstream sang to me, its song as great and alluring as the wavesong, and I was weak. There was only one way to save myself. I delved into myself and tapped the dark killing force that slumbered deep in my mind. I was careful not to rouse it, but its dark hot strength flowed through me, and I heard Atthis gasp as I began to rise swiftly. As I felt Atthis slip away from me, I faltered in my will to rise. A bubble of matter rose lazily and inexorably from the mindstream to engulf me.

". . . I am Cassy," said Cassy. She was smiling at a middle-aged woman.

"I am Hannah Seraphim," the older woman said in a warm, soft voice.

I stared at her in wonder, for this was the first time I had ever seen Hannah Seraphim, leader of the Beforetime Misfits and the first woman to dream of me and my quest. She was shorter and smaller and more ordinary-looking than I had imagined her, but her mouth was full and smiling, and her eyes were extraordinary. They were brown. Not the opaque brown of stone and earth, but the clear transparent brown of a forest stream, a warm, dappled brown with moving glints of green and gold in their depths. Beautiful eyes, watchful and intelligent.

"I only got in this morning," Cassy was saying. "I . . . I couldn't wait until tomorrow."

Hannah answered in her deep slow voice. "I'm glad you are here and gladder still that you've wasted no time in visiting us." Hannah held out a small strong hand to Cassy, and after a slight hesitation, the tall younger woman laid her own in it and smiled nervously.

"Welcome to the Reichler Clinic, Cassandra," Hannah said formally. "I am afraid this is a very grand building of which we have only a small part. Our patron, although he would laugh to hear himself described so, would happily give us the whole building, and indeed he has the means for it." She smiled a private, rather lovely smile. "But what we have here is

457

sufficient and safer." There was a slight grimness to her mouth now, and her eyes were stern.

"Please, call me Cassy," said the younger woman as they began to climb a flight of steps. She looked around, prompting me to do the same, and at once I recognized their surroundings. They were in the entrance foyer of the building that contained the Reichler Clinic Reception Center, in the city of Newrome, under Tor. But I could hardly reconcile the dim, water-stained foyer within the crushed building in a submerged and ruined city into which I had dived, with this shining hall of marble and glass. Through the windows, I saw huge trees and shrubs growing where now there grew a dark submarine forest of waving fronds sunk in an endless emerald twilight.

Hannah and Cassy had reached the top of the steps, to the foyer's main section, and I noticed the absence of the enormous glass statue of a woman surrounded by beasts. It was missing because it had yet to be created. Cassy gazed around, her eyes narrowing speculatively, and I wondered if this was the moment when the seed of the idea for that statue had been planted. "It seems so impossible and so wonderful to be here," she said. "All those years ago when I was tested in one of your mobile units, I was so desolate to be told that I had no paranormal abilities."

Hannah sighed in vexation, and after one swift assessing glance around, she said in a soft voice, "Those mobile units! Who knows how many like you were turned away because the equipment was useless. At the time, I thought William was just technically incompetent because, after all, he had written *Powers of the*

Mind. Of course, he had not written the book at all, but it was not until later that I discovered it."

"When will I meet the others?" Cassy asked shyly.

Hannah looked at her and, after another glance around, said very softly, "Cassy, listen to me carefully, because I won't be able to speak like this once we enter the elevator. There are listening devices in it and also in our reception center. The other paranormal students are not here, because despite its name, this is not the Reichler Clinic. The government and the general public believe it is, because that is what we want them to believe. Our real work with paranormals is undertaken elsewhere so we can be sure there will be no repeat of what happened at the first Reichler Clinic facility. I have been unable to speak of this in our e-mails. I have often warned you to say little in our communications, citing competing factions and cyber pirates as the reason. The truth is that we must protect ourselves from the government."

"But where . . . ?"

"The true Reichler Clinic is not so far away, but we will not go there today. Now you are going to meet those who come here to maintain our facade. Some are paranormals and others are not. You and I are about to enact a performance for the spy eyes and listening devices planted throughout our rooms."

"But why bring me here if we cannot speak freely?" Cassy said in confusion. They were approaching a bank of gleaming metal doors, and Hannah laid her hand lightly on Cassy's shoulder as she reached out to press her palm against a glowing square on the wall beside the doors. Cassy's eyes showed a fleeting look of astonishment, but she managed to turn a cry of surprise into a sneeze. Sensing what was happening, I entered her mind.

". . . how we will communicate," Hannah was far-sending. "But it was necessary for you to come here because of our communications so far. You are, after all, the daughter of the director of the institute at which kidnapped paranormals are being secretly held, and you have been communicating with and have come to visit the Reichler Clinic from whose destroyed compound they were taken. No matter what you sent me, I have been lukewarm in my enthusiasm. No doubt it frustrated you that I have many times suggested that you are likely to test normal, despite the fact that your e-mails made it clear that you were definitely paranormal."

"My e-mails." Cassy gasped aloud.

"Exactly," Hannah farsent. "But don't worry. After you communicated with us the first time, we knew there would be official consternation. We set up programs to alter all of your communications before they were logged, and we hacked into your computer to erase all traces of the original messages. What the officials monitoring our incoming e-mails read were the rather fatuous and romantic ideals of a girl who believes herself to be special. Not an uncommon feeling among young women, and one that might be expected of a neglected young woman who is the product of a broken relationship between two busy, rather cold parents with careers, who are less than attentive to their only daughter. Forgive me if this pains you."

"It . . . it is only the truth," Cassy said.

"I am sorry, but the truth is always the best shield for a greater truth. The e-mails I sent you were responses to those false e-mails. Of course, you were careful because the captive paranormals would have warned you to be careful. Nevertheless, we removed even your veiled references to the kidnapped paranormals and your communications with them, because although much time has passed, we do not want the government to guess that we know they destroyed the original Reichler Clinic."

"It was not the paranormals who warned me to be careful, and it was not because of them that I contacted you . . . ," Cassy began, her mindvoice clearer as she forgot her self-consciousness in her urgent desire to communicate. "I did not know how to explain without sounding mad, but it was the flamebird—"

"I have some inkling of what you will tell me. But the elevator is coming now, and we must concentrate on our performance for this meeting. The output of the spy eyes and listening devices will be very closely scrutinized because of who you are, and we must give the government nothing upon which to hang their suspicions. You will take various tests that will reveal very slight latent paranormal ability—that you are basically normal. You, of course, will be terribly disappointed. And tomorrow you will console yourself by hiking in the mountains near the entrance to Newrome with a handsome young student of Newrome University who will come this evening to your hotel bar and offer to buy you a drink. But we will speak more of that later. Remember, guard your expression and play your part convincingly, lest you put all of us in danger."

"Your voice is so . . . so clear," Cassy sent.

"In part because I am touching you," Hannah sent. She released Cassy and stepped forward to press at the panel with apparent impatience. Then her mindvoice came again, but with less strength and clarity. "The closer you are, the easier it is. But rest assured, although my mindvoice may seem strong and clear, with very little training, you will surpass us all."

"How can you be so sure?" Cassy asked.

"I have seen it," Hannah said aloud, but softly. Her face was suddenly ineffably sad, and her sadness lapped at me.

I became aware that I was floating. Somewhere in me was a terrible thirst, but before it could surface, I saw that there was a red-haired woman floating in the water beside me. The water about her was red with blood, and I recognized her from Dragon's comatose dream as the betrayed queen of the Red Land—she whom sea creatures called *Mornir-ma*. In the coma dream, the dying Red Queen had summoned whales to smash the slave ship that had carried her and her little daughter from their land. Then she had called a ship fish to bear Dragon to the nearest land, the west coast. There was no sign of Dragon, though, and as the woman's blood flowered into the sea about her, I understood that the ohrana of the sea was drinking her spirit.

"Is this the dreamsea?" I asked.

The red-haired woman opened her eyes and looked at me. Then she answered in the bell tones of Ari-noor. "The sea is without end. It ebbs and flows between. It is the place where all things meet and change. It is infinite."

I am dreaming, I thought. I began to rise again toward consciousness, but I had too little strength to maintain a shield against the drifting tendrils of dream stuff.

Suddenly I was kneeling in rustling brown and

yellow leaves, cupping my hands under a rill of water that bubbled from a cleft in an outcrop of stone. The water was so cold that my palms grew numb as I scooped some to my mouth.

"Do not drink," commanded a somber voice in my mind.

I spat out the salty water and turned to see the white dog Rasial, who had once been called Smoke. Her white coat glowed in a dappling of light falling through bare branches interlaced overhead, but even as I watched, the sunlight dimmed, mist rose and coiled about the trees, and Rasial changed. Her coat darkened and roughened until she became dear shaggy Sharna, who had died so many years before, saving my life from Ariel's maddened wolves at Obernewtyn. Almost before I registered his identity, Sharna's fur and muzzle shortened, his color deepened, and his ears sharpened until I recognized Jik's companion, the Herder-bred Darga, whose coming was to mark the beginning of the final phase of my quest as the Seeker.

"Where are you?" I asked, but he only blinked his dark eyes at me.

"Elspeth?"

I turned to find Matthew standing in the thickening mist. His gaze swept over me, partly in wonder and partly in disbelief. "This dinna feel like any dream," he muttered.

My heart leapt as I understood that he was right. This was not a dream I was experiencing. "I think it is real," I sent. "I am farseeking you."

Matthew looked elated, stunned, then confused. "But how can your mind reach me when I am so far away an' over the sea?"

"I am dreaming, but I think I have drifted onto the dreamtrails. Matthew, listen to me. I, and others at Obernewtyn, have true-dreamed of you, as you have of us. I know where you are and what you are trying to do. I know that Dragon is the Red Queen's missing daughter, and we will bring her to you as soon as it is possible."

"Dragon is in a coma," Matthew said sorrowfully.

"No! She has wakened, though as yet she has no memory of her life before or after the ruins. She has no memory of me or . . . or you."

"Perhaps that is best," he said, and there was pain in his eyes before he vanished.

"Elspeth?"

I turned again in hope, but it was not Matthew this time. It was Rushton, smiling at me from the center of a hot spring veiled in thick white steam. Snow lay deep on the ground, and my boots crunched through it as I walked to the rim of the pool. *This is a memory dream*, I realized. I could have wrenched myself out of it, but how my heart yearned for him as he floated back in the water and bade me join him. For this was a memory of the last time we had been alone together before Rushton had been taken captive by the Herders. I had ridden from a meeting at the Teknoguild caves to meet him at the spring in the foothills of the highest mountains, and we had swum together. I allowed myself to merge with my dream self to more fully experience the memory. Stripping off my clothes, I entered the water, and Rushton's arms closed possessively about me. But when he kissed me, I did as I had always done when we were so close, drawing back from final surrender, shutting up the core of myself, for how could I surrender my body without surrendering my mind? To lay that bare would mean opening up all that I was, to reveal the quest that lay at the heart of me like a black pearl that none must ever see.

There was hurt in his eyes at my withdrawal, but no reproach. And I saw in the memory, as I had not seen in the moment, that Rushton encompassed my resistance with a grace that I had never noticed, because I had been too busy protecting my secrets. He released me and drew away from me so the misty steam veiled him. Then there was only the mist, caressing my cheeks.

"Rushton!" I croaked.

Tears blurred my eyes, and I knew with sudden, utter clarity that I had been a fool to refuse him then and all the other times. Was not the song of love like the song of the sea? One must surrender to it to understand it. What would it have mattered if I held my deepest mind apart and allowed him to make love to me? I could have taken comfort from his body, giving him the comfort of mine. What did it matter if that black pearl was kept in a hidden chamber? And the cruel final thought came to me that if I *had* loved him, the memory of that loving might have given him the strength to endure when the Herder priests delved so cruelly inside him.

I wept, and as the water about me grew cold, I drifted from memory of dream to reality.

I was lying on my side with rain falling on my face. Rain!

Thirst roared to life, and I rolled onto my back and opened my mouth to drink.

Upon quenching my thirst, I realized that I was not in the water. I was lying on the sand some way above the waterline, my clothes stiff with dried salt, though the rain

465

was now softening them. I gave a choking laugh as I understood that *this* was what the wavesong had been trying to tell me: land was ahead, a great dark bulk where no sea creature could venture. A vast and deadly mystery for one who could not walk on dry land and live.

I must be on the west coast! I had made it! I looked around, and through the veils of falling rain, I saw, the hazy dark outline of a city. It was not more than an hour's walk away, but I could not tell which city it was, certainly not Murmroth. I wanted to walk there at once. I needed to find out if the *Black Ship* had been there.

But when I tried to move, I was devastated to discover that I was so weak, I could not even sit up. Lying there, I remembered Atthis telling me that I must rise so my body could heal itself. I had been badly injured, she had said, which was why I felt so monstrously weak. My body had drained itself of strength to heal me.

Gritting my teeth, I gathered all of my will and sat up. My head swam with the effort, and I knew that I would not be walking anywhere, at least for a few days. Fortunately, it was not cold, and the rain had enabled me to drink. I was not hungry, but I soon would be, and I would need food to regain my strength.

And gain my strength I would. I thought fiercely. For I had a plague to stop. And when I had done that, I would return to Obernewtyn and I would find Rushton and I would say to him everything I had been too cowardly to say. I would lay myself bare to him in all ways, and perhaps that would be enough to heal the breach between us.

"I am coming, my love," I thought, and hurled the thought forward with all the will that remained in me.

✦ ACKNOWLEDGMENTS ✦

This book was written in La Creperie in Janovského, Prague, and in The Bay Leaf, Seagrape, and Cafe 153 in Apollo Bay, Australia. Thanks to Cathy Larsen for her persistence and generosity in her quest for a new look for the Obernewtyn Chronicles and for the new map, and to Nan for being all that she is, editor and friend. And a special heartfelt thank-you to the faithful readers of this series for waiting, patiently and impatiently, for what turned out to be, after all, not quite the last book.

The story Continues

Look out for:

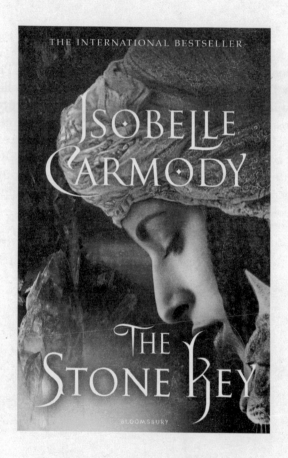

THE INTERNATIONAL BESTSELLER

ISOBELLE CARMODY

THE STONE KEY

BLOOMSBURY

Coming soon from Bloomsbury